BETWEEN
YOU and ME

Books by Jennifer Gracen

Between You and Me

'Tis the Season

Someone Like You

More Than You Know

and novella

Happily Ever After

BETWEEN YOU and ME

Jennifer Gracen

ZEBRA BOOKS
KENSINGTON PUBLISHING CORP.
http://www.kensingtonbooks.com

ZEBRA BOOKS are published by

Kensington Publishing Corp.
119 West 40th Street
New York, NY 10018

All Kensington titles, imprints, and distributed lines are available at special quantity discounts for bulk purchases for sales promotion, premiums, fund-raising, educational, or institutional use.

Special book excerpts or customized printings can also be created to fit specific needs. For details, write or phone the office of the Kensington Sales Manager: Attn.: Sales Department. Kensington Publishing Corp., 119 West 40th Street, New York, NY 10018. Phone: 1-800-221-2647.

Zebra and the Z logo Reg. U.S. Pat. & TM Off.

First Printing: December 2017
ISBN-13: 978-1-4201-4528-1
ISBN-10: 1-4201-4528-2

eISBN-13: 978-1-4201-4529-8
eISBN-10: 1-4201-4529-0

10 9 8 7 6 5 4 3 2 1

Printed in the United States of America

This book is dedicated to my sons,
Josh and Danny.

You two are the best, most important part of my life, the best things I've ever created, and you own the most important piece of my heart. You are kind, smart, loving, funny, vibrant . . . like any proud mom, I could gush over you both for the length of a novel and still not run out of things to say. But for once, I'll keep it short and sweet.

I thank the stars every day that you're mine. You are the greatest gifts I've ever received. I'm beyond proud of you and love you more than I could ever possibly express.

And no, you're not allowed to read any of my work until you're older.

ACKNOWLEDGMENTS

As always, I am grateful beyond words to the village of magnificent people that got me to this point. But I'll try to find adequate words.

Never-ending thanks to my editor, the wonderful Esi Sogah. I don't know how many writers look forward to their editor's feedback, but I always look forward to yours—like, with glee—knowing you're going to polish my rough gem into a shining diamond. Working with you is always a pleasure.

Thank you to my agent, Stephany Evans of Ayesha Pande Literary. Your support and level-headed calm always anchor me and make me feel better about all things writing-related. Glad to have you in my corner.

Thank you to everyone at Kensington who has been involved with me and my books—my copy editor, the art department, publicity, marketing—with specific shout-outs to Jane Nutter, Lauren Jernigan, Norma Perez-Hernandez, and Ross Plotkin. I really appreciate what you do.

Thanks to my immediate family: my mom, Linda; my dad, Rob; my brother, Jamie; Natasha, Kyle, Teri, Stevie, and of course my kids. Thank you so much for everything. That you guys are proud of my writing career is pretty cool. I love you all very much.

I'm so lucky to have a network of amazing friends. To all of you, both in person and online, your support, enthusiasm, and kindness helps get me through the days more than you realize. A million thank yous from the bottom of my goopy heart.

Thank you hugs to Nika Rhone, my beta reader extraordinaire. Your insightful feedback combined with your obvious enthusiasm for the story helped me more than you know.

Special hugs and shout-outs to: my online writing group-slash-pseudo family: the FB group The Quillies. To have writing friends who get it, who support and cheer you on, who you can truly trust and be vulnerable with, is a gift. Plus you're all naughty and make me laugh every day—you are my people, and I love you. Thank you Jeannie Moon and Patty Blount; we have each other. Thank you to the FB group Team Gracen!

Most importantly, boundless thanks to my readers. That you take some time out of your busy lives to read my work means the world to me, and I am deeply grateful. Thank you for your support and for taking this amazing ride with me.

Chapter One

Tess Harrison surveyed the festive scene around her. It was Christmas Day, and over sixty relatives were celebrating at her father's enormous estate. The mansion, set atop a hill on hundreds of acres beside the Long Island Sound, was filled with the sights and sounds of a picturesque holiday gathering. The grand main living room was decorated elegantly, beautifully, as the staff did every year. No lights—that would be gauche—but red ribbons, garland, holly, and faux white candles made the whole ground floor look like something straight out of a Christmas movie. Bright flames crackled and popped in the enormous stone fireplace, and the eight-foot-tall tree stood majestically in the corner. That *did* have white lights, and decorative ornaments that went back four generations. Tess suppressed a yawn. She was officially over the holidays.

She cradled her china cup of eggnog and watched her eldest brother, Charles, and his wife, Lisette, sit together on one of the longer sofas as they played with their infant daughter, Charlotte. Tess adored her newest niece, and had spent a lot of time with her. Bonding with that baby had wakened things in Tess she hadn't known existed. Now five months old, the dark-haired cherub squealed as Charles's strong arms raised Charlotte up, then back down to kiss her sweet face, over and over, as Lisette smiled brightly at his side. They'd married in May, and the love they shared was tangible. Tess was so glad for them. But oh, how she adored that little girl. Every time Charlotte squeaked, she felt it in her core. Such pure love, such pure joy.

Across from them, Tess's middle brother, Dane, and his wife, Julia, sat together leisurely and smiled along as they watched too. The baby's giggles were infectious, and everyone around Charlotte was under her spell. Tess relaxed against the lush cushions of the armchair and sipped her drink. She loved all four of Charles's kids deeply; they'd brought the kind of light to her life that only children could.

She longed for that kind of light in her life, the kind that children brought.

Charles's three older children from his first marriage sat huddled in the far corner of the room, playing hand-held video games with some other cousins close to their age. The youngest Harrison, Pierce, and his wife, Abby, were absent, and Tess felt it keenly. But Pierce would rather die than spend a family holiday with their father, and gladly went to Abby's family for every major holiday. Tess couldn't fault him for that, given the tumultuous history, but she still missed her baby brother.

At least Pierce and Abby had been at Charles's house the night before. Charles always hosted Christmas Eve, and it had been a lovely gathering. Only twenty people, only closest family, with the exception of the Harrison patriarch . . . which was why it was a lovely gathering. No vitriol, no stress, no walking on eggshells waiting to see who'd fire the first verbal shot that would kick off a horrible fight. Last night had been even more special, though, as Pierce and Abby—who'd just been married in a lavish ceremony in August—shared their surprise news: Abby was pregnant. They'd only found out a few days before and were bursting with it. It was a lot sooner than they'd planned, but they were excited and their joy was palpable. Tess was thrilled for them.

She sipped her eggnog again and gazed at the Christmas tree. The lights blurred as she zoned out and slipped deeper into her thoughts. More than anything, she wanted a baby of her own. There was no reason that she couldn't make it happen. She was thirty-seven, healthy, wealthy . . . but she lacked a candidate for the father. She had always believed in love, and been deeply in love twice in her life. The second time, she'd come close . . . and then had to break her engagement after being betrayed. In the years since then, she'd hoped to find someone else, but she knew the truth of it: she didn't trust enough to open her heart that completely again. She dated perfectly nice men, and some not so nice . . . none were a father-to-her-future-children candidate.

And over the last few months, spending time with Charlotte had driven it home more than ever: she wanted children of her own, and time was ticking away.

By Thanksgiving, she'd decided to take matters into her own hands. She had the means, so why not? This was one of the times that being born into a ridiculously wealthy family, along with making her own strong and vital career, gave her benefits and options that other single mothers didn't have. And while a part of her wanted to talk about it with her brothers . . . most of her wanted to keep it to herself until she was actually pregnant. They'd all have something to say, and for once, she didn't want to hear it if it was negative. Not from any of them.

"Hey, Tesstastic." Dane's jovial voice interrupted her thoughts. "You sure Julia and I can't convince you to spend a few days with us in Cancun?"

Tess smiled but shook her head. "You're both sweet to ask, but I don't need to be a third wheel during your three-week jaunt in paradise."

"Don't be ridiculous," Dane scoffed. "You're no such thing."

"Colin is coming for the whole second week," Julia pointed out. Her grown son from her first marriage was a quiet, kind young man. "We won't be alone. He's not worried about being a third wheel."

"He's twenty-four," Tess reminded them. "He's not worried because he'll be at the bars and clubs every night trying to pick up women, I'm sure."

"God, I hope so," Julia said. "But it's not a good reason for you not to come too. Come on, who wants to be in New York in January? It's miserable. Come down for a week."

"Again, I thank you both," Tess said. "But I . . . have plans of my own. They would overlap."

"You do?" Dane arched a brow. "Why didn't you just say so?"

"I tried, brother dear." A grin tugged at the corners of Tess's lips. "You keep asking anyway. Which is sweet, but . . ."

"I think I smell a deflection tactic," Dane said.

"I think you should leave her be," Charles piped in. Lisette bit down on her lip.

"It's so wrong that I want my sister to have some fun?" Dane asked him.

"Of course not," Tess said.

"You just finished months of hard work, pulling off another massively successful Harrison Foundation Holiday

Ball," Dane said to her. "You need a real vacation. To go somewhere and be pampered. I offered to make that happen, since you don't do it enough for yourself. Sue me."

Tess rolled her eyes at her big brother. "I love you too, you big nag."

"I'm a nag now?" Dane put his hand to his chest. "You wound me!"

They all snorted out laughter.

Tess had had enough of this conversation. She rose to her feet and swept her long curtain of curls back over her shoulders. "I'm getting more eggnog," she said. "Anyone want some?"

The four of them murmured various forms of "no thanks," and she crossed the room to the cavernous crystal bowl that held enough lightly spiked eggnog for a small village.

Tess couldn't help but smile to herself as she refilled her mug. Charles, Dane, and Pierce weren't just her brothers, they were some of her closest friends. They were incredibly devoted to and protective of her, and she counted on them as much as they all counted on her. After all, she'd spent years watching over the three of them. When their parents split up and their mother left home over two decades before, as the only female left in the family, Tess had slowly but surely slipped into the role of mother hen. Some of it was a conscious decision, some of it wasn't. She never minded—her brothers needed her, even when they didn't realize it, and she was all too happy to provide crucial emotional support. She was a caring person, with so much love to give—who better to lavish it on than her own siblings, who needed it so desperately?

But they were all fine now. Grown men, they'd eventually found their place in the world, especially now that they had the help of good women who loved them and believed in them. Tess was grateful beyond words that she genuinely liked her three sisters-in-law. Charles, Dane, and Pierce were strong men, but pairing with women like Lisette, Julia, and Abby had truly completed them. They had all built, or were building, their own families, and didn't need Tess's pseudo-mothering like they had before.

And Tess found herself feeling like something was missing. Despite that she had adoring siblings and family, good friends, a fulfilling career running the Harrison Foundation, the family's massive nonprofit organization . . . maybe it was the holidays and the slight melancholy that could sometimes accompany the season, but for months she hadn't been able to deny the basic facts: She was creeping up on forty, she wanted a baby, and she'd somehow have to get that done on her own.

She considered herself to be a positive, upbeat person. A woman who accomplished things, took the lead, and knew how to get things done—she didn't wait around and let life happen to her. Why should having a baby be any different than her other goals and successes? That thought had churned in her head for too long. It was time to take her future into her own hands. She was ready.

"How's my best girl?" Her father's confident baritone sounded behind her.

She turned to him with a fake smile. "Great, Dad. Hope you're having a nice Christmas?"

"I am," he said. "Thank you again for the painting. What a special gift."

"I'm glad you like it," she said as he kissed her cheek. She'd been able to find a small Picasso piece that she knew he'd love to add to his impressive collection, and called in a favor from an acquaintance in Paris to make it happen.

"You're very thoughtful, as always." There was the tiniest

shift in his gaze, but Tess knew him so well, she steeled herself. "So. Charles tells me that Pierce got Abby pregnant already. I guess expecting my youngest son to call me himself with that kind of news is too much to hope for, eh?"

"Dad." Tess touched his arm with her free hand. "He only told us last night. They only found out last week."

"So? He told you all last night. He could've called to tell me, or to say 'Merry Christmas,' anytime since then. He hasn't. Yet another intentional snub."

"Did you call him to say 'Merry Christmas'?" Tess asked.

Caught, Charles II scowled and sipped his drink.

"I thought not." She gentled her voice to soften the blow, but looked her father right in the eye as she said, "You blew that relationship sky-high two years ago. You attacked him and Abby both. You did that."

"There were *two* of us in that fight," Charles II reminded her, an angry edge to his voice. "But everyone always holds only *me* responsible."

"Dad—"

"And they had their big, elaborate wedding," Charles II barreled on, "and I was shunned! Not even invited to my own son's wedding, purposely kept away, unwelcome. That was disgraceful."

She was tired of this argument that always remained unresolved. "I'm not going to get into all this with you now," Tess said. Her tone was mild, but her words were firm. "I refuse. It's Christmas."

He nodded curtly, lips pursed, but grunted, "Fine."

Tess knew he wouldn't push it with her then, not with the room filled with extended family on such a major holiday. Since the heart attack last year, at least he'd softened that much. "I'm sorry you're upset. Just be happy for them. Send a nice gift when the baby's born. Who, by the way, will be your fifth grandchild."

Charles scowled. "Pierce will likely keep me away from that child, you know."

Tess sighed. He was right, of course. But she said, "Maybe by then, if you try and are truly invested, you can attempt to make things better with Pierce somehow."

Her father snorted derisively. "That stubborn ass will never have it. He holds grudges; it's one of the few things we have in common. And now he's going to be a father?" Charles II huffed out a laugh. "Good luck to that baby."

A split second of ire made her stomach twist. Her younger brother was a good man, in spite of what her father had said, done, or still thought. "Merry Christmas," she said, and turned her back on her father to cross the room, back to the safe haven of her older brothers.

She shook off the irritation as she walked. Starting his usual crap on Christmas? His problem, not hers. Pierce had completely shunned him, as he'd said. Charles and Dane still talked to him, showed up at family occasions and the like, but both had withdrawn considerably. She was the only one of the four siblings who still tried to maintain a good relationship with their difficult father. Times like this, she wondered why. Why was she still being the dutiful daughter after all these years? She did love her father, but she didn't like him. It'd been a habit she hadn't been able to break, borne from a sense of duty, even though it led to frustration more often than satisfaction.

As she retook her seat with her brothers and sisters-in-law, someone turned on Christmas music, likely a member of her father's household staff. A classical arrangement of "Silent Night" played softly, Charlotte let out a high-pitched peal of delight as her father lifted her over his head once again, the adults around them smiled and laughed, voices of others rose in a low but merry cacophony. Charles smiled broadly and dropped tiny kisses all over his baby's face, and she squealed and wiggled in delight. A pang hit Tess's heart, and she suddenly felt tears sting the backs of her eyes. She looked around at the heartwarming scene . . . she thought of her own dreams for a family . . . God, she wanted that. She didn't want to spend another Christmas aching and wishing for a child of her own.

Something clicked inside her, soft but sure. *Now. Do it now. Go for it. What are you waiting for?*

Adrenaline and excitement and a deep sense of knowing all whooshed through her, almost leaving her breathless.

"I'm leaving," she blurted out.

Charles and Lisette hadn't heard her, but Dane and Julia's heads swiveled to look at her. "What?" Dane asked, as if he hadn't heard her correctly.

"Why?" Julia asked, her hazel eyes narrowing to study Tess. "Are you feeling okay?"

"I'm fine. But I'm leaving. As in, leaving New York," Tess said, only formulating the plan as the words poured from her mouth. She'd been thinking of it for weeks, but something now prodded at her, pushed up from inside, and flooded out. "I'm going away for a while. I need to go. So I am."

All eyes were on her now, rounded with shock. Dane gaped, his mouth an O of surprise. Charles stared hard at his sister as Lisette gently took their baby from his hands. "What's going on, Tess?" he asked softly, as if talking to a wounded animal.

Tess set her cup on the nearby end table before turning back to them. Again she swept the heavy mass of her long curls over her shoulders. Her heart rate was climbing, but now that she'd said the words, they made more sense than anything had in a long time. "I need to be by myself for a little while. To change things up. So I'm going to go to Aspen, and stay at the house there. You'll be in Cancun for most of January," she said to Dane, "and you'll be at the Palm Beach house for two weeks," she said to Charles. "So neither of you will be using the ski house. I am. I'm just letting you all know."

Dane made a sound that sounded like sputtering.

"Why is this the first we're hearing of it?" Charles asked.

"Umm, because I don't have to report to anyone," Tess replied evenly.

"I didn't mean to insinuate that, and you know it," Charles said, shifting forward in his seat. His eyes, the bright marine blue they'd all inherited from their mother, were now focused like lasers on Tess. "If you need to take a break, of course you should. I'm just surprised."

"Ten minutes ago, we were talking about Cancun, and you didn't even mention it." Dane was equally focused on her, studying her as if sensing something was off. "So yeah, this seems like it's coming out of nowhere."

"And if it is?" Tess inquired sharply. "So what?"

"You guys are acting like her parents," Julia remarked. "Might want to take it down a notch."

"She's right," Lisette said, bouncing Charlotte on her knees.

"We are not," Charles said, but it came out weak with recognition.

Dane kept staring at his sister. "How long will you be gone?"

"I'm not sure," Tess admitted. But she knew what she really wanted to do, so why not do it? Throw herself into researching sperm donors, in vitro, whatever it would take to help her have the baby she so desperately wanted. Be away from stress and prying eyes, cleanse her body and mind . . . "At least two months, I think. Until the end of February, probably? Maybe more. I'll see."

The wave of shock was palpable as her brothers and their wives all exchanged brief glances of astonishment. Charles got to his feet. "Come on, Tess. Let's find a quiet place to talk."

"There's nothing to talk about," Tess said, looking up at him. It was so strange how she felt utterly calm and pulsing with exhilaration at the same time. The adrenaline rush was invigorating. "I'm merely telling you all that I'm going away for a while. It's not up for discussion. End of story."

"Bullshit," Charles said tersely. He crouched in front of his sister, took her hands in his, and stared into her face, searching. "What the hell's going on?"

"I'm with him," Dane said, scooting to the edge of his chair and leaning toward her. "Did something happen? This just seems so sudden, and—"

"I've been thinking about it for a while, actually," Tess said. "New Year's is just around the corner. I need something new. I need a change. So . . . I'm going to just go somewhere else for a while."

"Please give us something more here," Charles implored quietly. "I'm worried about you now."

"Me too," Dane said. "What he said. Tess, honey . . ."

She smiled at both of them, squeezing Charles's hands before pulling them free. "There's nothing wrong. I'm fine."

"I don't believe you," Charles said.

"Okay." She rose to stand, and he mirrored her.

"Talk to me," he whispered fiercely.

Dane stood too, reaching out to grasp her elbow. "When are you leaving?"

"Day after tomorrow," Tess said, deciding as she said the words.

"What?" Charles hissed at the same time that Dane asked, "Why so soon?"

"You both act like I'm heading off to parts unknown without a note," Tess said. She was touched by their concern, but at the same time, so excited to move forward with her new plan, she couldn't get away from them and out of the mansion fast enough. "I'm not going to Tibet, I'm going to Colorado. To the ski house the three of us own together, so I believe you have the address."

"Don't be cute. This isn't like you and you know it!" Charles bit out, eyes flashing. "You can't be surprised that we're so surprised, much less that we're concerned. You don't make spontaneous plans, you don't go away for *months* at a time, and definitely not without talking about it with one of us first."

Tess nodded, a smile spreading slowly on her face. "You're right. That's why it feels so good, I guess."

Charles and Dane both stared at her, speechless.

"Let her go, guys," Julia said from her seat.

"Stop mothering her," Lisette added softly.

Charles jolted as if he'd been hit, looking to his wife, who only nodded.

"Tess," Dane said. "You can't just leave without telling us a little more than *I'm outta here, see ya in a few months*. Come on. If it was one of us pulling this, you'd be flipping out. So just talk to us."

"All right. I will. Tomorrow. But now, I have things to do. Be with your loved ones." She leaned in to kiss Charles on the cheek, then Dane. She moved away to give quick hugs to her sisters-in-law, and an adoring snuggle to her baby niece. Then she turned to them all and said, "Merry Christmas. Talk to you tomorrow. I have to get packing." And before any of them could utter another word, she walked across the long room to say a few more goodbyes so she could get out of there.

Even as she hugged her older niece and nephews, Tess felt invigorated. Brimming with excitement, she couldn't wait to get going. She had a lot to take care of if she was going to leave in less than forty-eight hours, and she absolutely intended to make good on her words. She was a woman of action, dammit, and now that she'd decided to take action, nothing would stop her from seeing her whole plan through.

Chapter Two

Logan Carter checked the thermostat once more before turning to sweep his eyes across the long, wide living room. He'd been the house manager for the Harrison family's ski house for the past five years, so he knew well what needed to be done before one of them arrived.

He'd already done his weekly house check for the place on Tuesday, as he always did when none of the Harrisons had visited in a while. So he knew the heat, water, all of that, were already in working order. He'd turned the lights on so Tess wouldn't walk into a dark house. Well, he amended mentally, Tess, and likely her tiny white dog that often came with her. The wood was all stacked, both out in the back and some in the iron stand by the fireplace. He double-checked that the wood, paper, and fire starter were in place in the large stone hearth. Then he straightened the area rugs.

Scrubbing a hand over his full beard as his eyes canvassed the spacious room one last time, he mentally ticked off the checklist in his head. He'd made sure to put some potted poinsettia plants on the mantel above the fireplace, on the long dining room table and living room coffee table, and on tables by the front door and up in the master bedroom to add splashes of color for her. He didn't do that personal touch for many of his clients, but he did leave cut flowers for some, the ones he knew appreciated it. The Harrisons were good people that he respected, and he knew she'd appreciate the gesture.

Ah, who was he kidding? He did it for Tess because he liked her. She was plain nice, and goddamned gorgeous. Not many women caught his eye anymore, but she always had. He could admit a . . . tiny crush, if he had to label it, to himself. Hell, he couldn't imagine *any* normal straight man could resist a tiny crush on a woman like Tess Harrison.

Even if she'd stung him with an insult last year that he still hadn't shaken off.

One day, he'd been over there to take out the trash as he always did twice a week. Tess had struck up a conversation with him, and mentioned she'd gone hiking up the mountain by herself the evening before, making it home just before dusk.

"By yourself? Close to dark?" His eyes narrowed.

"Um, yeah." She cocked her head at him and put her hands on her hips. "Jeez, I know I'm a city girl and all, but sometimes I think that you seem to think I can't take care of myself."

He actually blushed. "No, no, I didn't mean to—that is, I'm sorry if it seems that way. I just . . ." He huffed out a laugh, a mixture of frustration and self-deprecation. "Look, my master certificate was in disaster mental health and trauma studies. Crisis counseling, dealing with disasters . . . so my mind has a tendency to go to a worst-case scenario." His shoulders lifted as he shifted his stance and admitted, "What I'm trying to say is, it means I worry about people. I never meant to imply you're not a capable woman. If it seemed that way, I sincerely apologize."

"No apologies necessary. That you worry about people is . . . nice." She stared at him with a look of amazement. "Um . . . that's an interesting thing. The certificate. You have a master's degree?"

"Yeah. In social work. Why?"

"No reason. I was merely curious. I . . ." She cocked her head to the side, studying him as if she'd found a rare specimen or something. "I'm just surprised. I mean, you work here, doing this for a living, so . . ."

Something in his gut churned. He'd always thought her to not be one of the mega-rich mega-snobs. He'd pegged her as not entitled, and kinder, an exception to the rule. Man, did he hate being wrong on this one. It stung more than he thought it should. But he schooled his features into neutrality. "Ahhh. I see. You didn't think a big lumberjack type like me would be so highly educated, huh?"

"I didn't mean it like that," she said, but her face started to bloom hot pink.

"Uh-huh." His temper flared, but he kept his voice cool. "Well. Hate to burst your bubble, but I actually graduated summa cum laude."

He watched her marine-blue eyes widen a bit as the color bloomed in her face, betraying her.

"Logan, I didn't mean to imply you were—" She visibly cringed, and he took some comfort in that. "God, that must have sounded . . . It's obvious you're a smart man, but I didn't think you'd have a master's, that's all."

"Because I'm a house manager for a living? Careful, Miss Harrison," he said slowly. He grinned, a hollow one, and couldn't help himself from adding, "Your blue blood's showing."

That blood flooded her face, but she didn't look away. "Again, I really didn't mean it like it sounded. But if that's how you perceived it, I apologize. That came across as horribly judgmental, and I'm very sorry."

He shook his head, his grin leisurely, belying the burn he felt in his chest. "Don't sweat it."

"No, I am sweating it. You were right, I made an unfair assumption. I'm sorry." She peered up at him more closely. "But I admit it, now I'm curious. How'd a guy with a master's in social work end up being a house manager for a living? Must be an interesting journey there. I'd love to hear it."

"No, you wouldn't." He hadn't meant to sound churlish, but it came out as something of a growl. "Trust me."

"Um . . . okay." She looked sheepish, wide-eyed. His sharp words had been a reprimand, clearly not what she'd expected, and she blinked before clearing her throat. "I'll let you get back to work."

That was last March, almost a year ago, and it still burned his ass when he thought of it. He'd always thought she wasn't uppity and haughty like most of the super-wealthy clients he had. Between that incorrect assessment and the tiny crush he'd always harbored, her disparaging words had stung, left a bad taste in his mouth. She'd gone back home two days after that, so they hadn't discussed it again—he hadn't even seen her, only talked to her briefly on the phone about how he'd close the house up. And when he'd gotten there, the house feeling empty without her presence, he'd found a cream-colored envelope on the granite kitchen counter with his name on it. She'd left two crisp hundred-dollar bills for him, a generous and unnec- essary tip that was likely more about assuaging her guilt than his skills, which had only served to leave him even more agitated.

Plain and simple, he'd been disappointed—both that he'd thought her to be different, and that he'd been wrong about her. Hell, she'd apologized immediately, and seemed truly mortified that she'd insulted him, and he believed her when she said she hadn't meant to insult him at all. But the damage was done; it'd changed how he thought of her.

Now, as if on cue, he heard activity outside. Running a hand through his hair and over his beard, Logan went to meet his formerly favorite client.

Opening the front door, he waved as he made his way down the steps to the driveway to meet the sleek black Escalade parked there. The driver was already at the back, pulling suitcases out, and Logan heard the familiar yippy bark of Bubbles, Tess's Maltese, from inside the truck. A grin curved his lips. He couldn't help it, he liked that dog. She was spunky and cute as could be.

"How's it goin', Clay?" Logan said to the chauffeur with a quick handshake.

"Hey, Carter! Goin' fine, thanks. You?" Clay asked as he grabbed another suitcase.

"Fine. Here, let me help you with those."

"Nah, I've got 'em." Clay hauled out the last bag. "I'll take these straight into the foyer."

"If you insist. Door's open. Good to see you."

"You too. Take care."

Logan turned to see Tess emerge from the truck, and his breath caught. *Damn.* Seeing her never failed to stir something inside him. She was still the most beautiful woman he'd ever seen with his own eyes, anywhere, ever. Her dark corkscrew curls tumbled down the back of her red parka, almost to her very fine ass. Standing tall at five-foot-ten, her height may have intimidated other men, but since Logan was six-four, he liked that he didn't have to look too far down to talk to her. Her willowy body was made to glide and strut down a catwalk, but she'd likely dismiss the notion. Those long, long legs were encased in black leggings and knee-high black leather boots, and he admired them as discreetly as possible. He'd always been a leg man, and her shapely, graceful ones were out of this world.

Finally he met her eyes. Those brilliant blues were sparkling, and she was smiling as she approached him. She always looked happy, or at least content—he didn't think he'd ever seen her in a bad mood. To him, her friendly personality made her as beautiful as her physical appearance; women like that were rare.

He took a deep breath and shook himself mentally. This woman sometimes put him under a spell. Apparently, even though he hadn't seen her in almost a year, and he didn't think of her as sweetly as he once had, her magic over him hadn't changed.

He cleared his throat and grinned. "Hi, Tess. Good to see you."

"It's good to see you too!" She went right to him, stopping only a few steps away. Her dog wiggled in the cradle of her arms, yipping and wagging her tiny tail. "Hope you had a good Christmas."

"It was nice, thank you," Logan said. "Quiet." Just him and his mom, at her house. He'd made them dinner since she was too weak from radiation, and they'd watched *It's a Wonderful Life* and *White Christmas*, as was their tradition. "You had a good Christmas too, I hope?"

"I did, thanks." She turned at the sound of Clay slamming the trunk closed.

"All set, Miss Harrison," he said, moving around the truck to climb back in.

"Wait . . ." she said.

Logan watched her walk to Clay, heard her thank

him and discreetly slip him what Logan was sure was a generous tip. Clay smiled and laughed at something she said, raised a hand in parting to Logan, and drove down the long, winding driveway.

She went back to Logan and said, "I'm glad to see you here, but a bit surprised. Were you waiting for me?"

"I was," he said. "Just to make sure you got settled in all right. You said it was a spur-of-the-moment trip when you called, so . . ." He lifted a hand to rub the head of the eight-pound dog squirming in her arms. "Hey, Bubbles. Hello, you tiny princess."

The dog barked and licked his hand, squirming even harder.

"Thank you for waiting," Tess said. "You didn't have to. I'm sure you're busy, I know it's the busy season here." Her breath escaped in white puffs.

"No problem at all." Logan waved a dismissive hand. "More bags than usual, I noticed. How long are you staying?"

"Actually, I'm not sure." She shifted the dog in her arms for a better hold. "Definitely until the end of February, possibly longer. I'll see. For once in my life, I'm playing it by ear."

"Really." Logan's eyes widened a bit and his brows lifted. The longest any of the Harrisons had stayed for a visit had been for two weeks. Curiosity pricked him.

"Mm-hmm." She grinned and added, "So you'll be seeing more of me, I suppose."

"I have no problem with that," Logan said. "C'mon, let's get you both inside, it's cold out." Shoving his hands into the pockets of his ski jacket, he stepped aside to let her walk before him. He couldn't help but admire the sway of her hips and her long, long hair as she moved. His eyes ran up and down those long, gorgeous legs. She'd be in Aspen for two months, maybe longer? That bit of interesting news had brightened his day. Maybe his whole week. In spite of how he had his guard up around her, there were few women he enjoyed looking at more than Tess Harrison.

Chapter Three

Tess set Bubbles down as soon as they stepped through the door. The dog took off, skittering across the polished hardwood floor and barking happily. The warmth of the house was a wonderful contrast to the cold outdoors; Tess pulled off her leather gloves and opened her coat. She hadn't been there since last March, and she looked around with a smile as she took it in, the familiar space a comfort. The door closed behind her and she turned to gaze at her house manager, who flashed an amiable grin as he stepped toward her.

From the first time she'd met him, she'd thought Logan Carter was a seriously striking man. Incredibly big and tall—tall enough for *her* to think him tall—broad and muscled, with shaggy blond hair and pale green eyes, he was ruggedly handsome, a quietly powerful presence. He reminded her of a Viking; picturing him in that garb with a heavy sword in his hand wasn't too far a stretch.

But his beard, a shade darker than his hair, was neatly kept. His gorgeous eyes twinkled with geniality, not bloodlust. His large hands were calloused from hard work, and his cheeks were often ruddy from working outdoors. Standing in her elegant foyer in his worn jeans and work boots, navy hoodie under a royal-blue ski jacket, he looked a little out of place, but his presence was both commanding and reassuring. She'd always liked him, and yes, liked looking at him too.

But his powerful stance and chiseled good looks weren't the only reason she found him striking. It was the way he carried himself. This strong, very physical man was quiet, somber, and intelligent, which to her made him only more potent. He was attentive to details, clever, and was a born leader—he radiated natural command. Quick to grin, but not to talk; unlike most handsome men she'd met, this guy wasn't in love with himself or the sound of his own voice. He thought before he spoke; she loved those pauses because they held weight. She loved to coax big smiles from him, because she sensed he didn't do it often enough. A gentle giant. She'd wondered more than once how a man like him had gotten into the house-managing business. There was a story there, she was sure of it.

"The place looks great," she said brightly. "Didn't realize how much I'd missed it until just now. Thank you so much for being willing to get it ready for me on such short notice."

"Like I said before, not a problem." His deep voice was resonant, utterly masculine. "I'm glad I was able to do it."

She'd called him early the day before, the morning after Christmas, to ask him to have the house ready for her arrival in twenty-four hours. He hadn't given her an ounce of attitude. "Well, I really appreciate it." She pulled off her parka and set it on one of the three rust-colored couches in the living room. "Today, you're my knight in shining armor."

He snorted out a dismissive laugh and stuffed his hands

in his coat pockets. "Nah. A woman like you doesn't need a knight." But his green eyes sparkled as he smiled.

His pleased smile made her feel like she'd earned a gold star. "Can I get you something to drink?" she asked.

"No, thanks, I'm fine." He glanced toward the back of the house when the dog barked, then looked back to Tess. "I'm going to my mom's place for lunch when I leave here, so don't you worry, I'll be overfed."

Remembering, Tess's smile faded some. "How is your mother doing? Hopefully better?"

His grin faded too. "Uh . . . no, actually. Last rounds of chemo and radiation have made her weaker, but haven't beaten the cancer. So, well . . ." He shrugged. "It is what it is. But she had a nice Christmas, so that's something. It's, uh . . . well. Yeah."

"I'm so sorry," Tess murmured. She didn't know much about Logan's personal life. He was a private man, and she had never pried for details that weren't her business. But she remembered their chat last year when she'd made him a travel mug of tea on a particularly cold day, and he'd revealed a few personal details. How he'd grown up about half an hour outside Aspen, and when he'd moved back to start work in his cousin's house-managing business, his mom had sold his childhood home and bought a condo in Aspen to be closer to him.

He'd told Tess that a few years ago things had changed, and he was also helping her—she was a widow battling breast cancer on her own. After a double mastectomy, she'd gone into remission for a year or so, but apparently . . . damn.

Tess sighed and said gently, "I hate to hear that. I really do wish her well. If there's ever anything I can do, for you or for her, please ask."

His pale eyes fixed on her, rounded a bit. "That's very kind of you. Thank you."

Bubbles barked and came running in, sliding a bit on the polished floor. Tess crouched down to scoop her up into her arms. "Silly girl, you're going to slide right into a wall if you don't slow down!"

Logan chuckled. "I put the poinsettias high so she couldn't eat them," he said, his voice stronger now, not husky as it'd been a minute before. "I know they're not poisonous to dogs—that's a myth—but it *can* make 'em sick if they eat 'em. So I just figured better safe than sorry."

"You did that?" Tess glanced at him in surprise, then her eyes darted around to the bright red plants, then back to him. "How thoughtful of you. Thank you! The color is so fabulous. Red's my favorite color, you know."

"I didn't know that." He eyed the parka she'd removed. "But come to think of it, I guess you do wear a lot of it."

"Yes, I do. Because I love it." She grinned and walked across the living room to the glass wall. One of her favorite features of the house, the entire back wall was made of glass, from the foundation to the roof. The views it afforded of the mountains and the landscape beyond were absolutely breathtaking. Pristine snow covered the peaks, both close and in the distance, and the clear blue sky seemed endless. "Have to hit that mountain soon," she said. "I haven't been skiing in a long time; I'm likely rusty."

"If you want me to set up a time on the mountain for you," Logan volunteered, "I can do that."

She turned back to him with a smile, stroking her dog's soft fur as she walked back to him. "Oh, I can do that, but thanks. I don't know when I'll go just yet." She paused. "Is the Lotus Yoga Center on Blake Street still open?"

"Oh sure. Business is booming, actually—they expanded the studio over the summer. Added another three rooms." Logan ran a hand over his dark blond beard, an absentminded gesture that made something in Tess's belly ping low. His beard looked like it was soft. She was suddenly seized with an urge to touch it and find out. "Their spa expanded too. My cousin Rick's wife, Sami-Jo, is the manager now. Anytime you wanna set something up, ask for her. Tell her I sent you."

"I will. Good to have connections in town," Tess said with a conspiratorial air.

"Ah, I just know folks, that's all." He reached out to pet Bubbles's head, then said, "You have any questions, need anything, don't hesitate to call me, okay?"

"Thank you, Logan. I absolutely will." She grinned as Bubbles licked his hand.

"I'll be by the day after tomorrow to take out the trash for you, restock the wood if you need, the usual." He zipped up his jacket all the way. "So, uh . . . staying by yourself for two or so months, huh? Charles and Dane, not coming at all?"

"I needed some time to myself," she said, lowering Bubbles to the floor again. When she straightened, she looked him in the eye as she said, "I've got some things I need to do. On my own. But . . . I'll admit, I feel better knowing you're around. Someone to call if I need to."

"Of course you can," he said. "For anything, anytime. Promise me."

She nodded and said, "I promise."

He glanced around the living room, a distracted sweep of his eyes. "I don't mean to sound like this'll sound," he said with a bit of hesitation. "But knowing you're up here by yourself . . . I'll be checking on you sometimes. Just to make sure you're all right." His eyes glittered with a hint of protectiveness. "If that's okay with you, of course. I don't mean to insinuate you're not a grown woman who can take care of herself. I'm just . . ." He ran a hand through his golden hair, tousling it. It was long enough that the ends settled past his square jawline. "You're up here by yourself . . . I'm kind of old-fashioned that way."

Her stomach did a slow flip, surprising her. "Your mother raised you right," Tess said softly. "There aren't many gentlemen left in the world these days. It's okay with me to be checked on occasionally." She smiled and added, "Thank you in advance."

His chin bobbed in something like a tiny bow, and the chivalrous gesture made her stomach wobble again. "All right then. Good. Well, I'd better get going." He looked at her for a moment longer, then headed for the door. "Your SUV's in the garage. I took it out yesterday for a quick spin to gas it up; it's running fine."

"Oh. I hadn't even thought of it. Thank you for doing that."

"Of course." He turned to look at her as he opened the heavy front door. "Hope you enjoy your stay."

"I will." She followed him, holding the doorknob as she looked up into his handsome face. "Thanks again, for everything. Have a great rest of your day."

"Thanks. You too." He flashed her one last grin, then stepped outside.

She watched his long, strong legs carry him as he strode to his truck, a silver Ford F-150 with a long flatbed. The truck, like its owner, was big and powerfully built. She closed the door and turned back to look at the wide, high-ceilinged rooms, the burnished wood and glass, the rusts, tans, browns, and olive of the décor . . . and let out a long exhale of contentment. She'd done it. She was far from home, on her own, free to do what she wanted.

And what she wanted was to make herself a temple to peace and serenity. So her body would get ready to become pregnant, and then hopefully conceive without too many attempts once she picked a sperm donor. She'd already started her research on the plane, and narrowed the clinics down to a top-notch facility, just outside Aspen city limits. She intended to interview the staff there right after the new year.

This trip would be her personal retreat. Without being watched over by her family or friends, free to have wobbly days if they happened, free to do whatever she liked before committing herself one hundred percent to life as a single mother.

A feeling of calm washed over her as she sank down onto one of the plush rust-colored sofas. She stared out at the magnificent view of the mountains and the spread of forest before them. She'd done the right thing, coming here. Something told her it was going to be exactly what she needed to venture into this new part of her life.

By the end of her second day, Tess felt more settled. She'd gone grocery shopping; stopped into the yoga center to sign up for classes twice a week and a one-on-one session every Wednesday; stocked up on paints, brushes, and two new canvasses; and taken a morning hike along the winding path up the mountain. While in town, she'd run into a few acquaintances who were also in Aspen for the holidays, which was a pleasant surprise. She'd even made a lunch date with Allie Connors, an old friend from grad school who'd married well, had three kids, and had a house on Red Mountain not far from hers. Allie had always been able to get Tess to open up and enjoy herself; she'd be good company for the few weeks she'd be around.

Initially, Tess had thought she'd live like a monk while in Aspen, but seeing Allie had excited her. She was a social butterfly, she couldn't deny it. Seeing people here and there would be better for her than living in complete isolation.

Tess took her tall glass of ice water into the living room and sank down onto the longest couch, opposite the fireplace. A yawn escaped her as Bubbles hopped up to snuggle her, and Tess checked the clock on her cell phone. Just past four, it seemed like an ideal time to catch a catnap. She stretched out on the soft cushions, propped a throw pillow behind her head, cradled Bubbles, and let her eyes slip closed.

Her phone rang, and she groaned. She had personal ringtones for all the men of her family: Frank Sinatra's "My Way" for Pierce, Justin Timberlake's "Can't Stop the Feeling" for Dane, David Bowie's "Heroes" for Charles, and Coldplay's "Viva la Vida" for her father. Now, as Bowie sang at her for the fourth time in two days, she knew she couldn't put her eldest brother off anymore and answered the call. "Hello there."

"About time you answered," Charles half growled. "You let me go to voice mail one more time, and I was getting on a plane tomorrow to make sure you were okay."

"God, you're a bear," she teased. "I'm fine. I just want some alone time."

"You're not fine," he asserted. "You took off. You're not answering calls, not mine, or Dane's, or Pierce's. Why won't you tell any of us what's going on?" He paused. "I'm really worried about you. I *care*. I'm not trying to be a jerk, I'm just concerned. Don't you get that?"

"I do. I'm sorry." She sighed and shifted her position, rolling onto her back so she could gaze out the glass wall while they spoke. Pine trees parted just enough to reveal the majestic mountaintops beyond. She knew this would be a long talk, and opted to enjoy the view during it. "I didn't mean to worry anyone, and didn't think I would. You're all overreacting a little. I just . . . got a little selfish for the first time in a long time. Wanted to do something for myself, by myself. I'm sorry you're concerned, and I assure you there's no reason to be."

"Two months, Tess?" Charles's voice had softened some, but still held firm. "You want to be away from everyone—your family, your huge circle of friends, your career—for two whole months, maybe more. Yes, we're all concerned. And you're still not really telling anyone why. Why is that?"

"Because my life is my own," she said, an edge to her voice she hadn't counted on. "You all have your wives, someone to answer to. I don't have to answer to anyone."

He paused, and Tess could almost hear the gears clicking in his head. Charles was an incredibly smart, shrewd man who was renowned for how he could read people. She waited to hear what he'd come up with. "Tess . . . you're not sick, are you?"

"What?" she sputtered. That wasn't what she'd thought he'd say. "No!"

"You sure you're all right?"

"Yes. I swear. In fact, I'm in the best physical health I've been in for a long time."

"Okay . . ."

She sighed again. She wasn't being fair. If it was the other way around, and one of her brothers had done what she had, she'd be going out of her mind, wondering why and worrying. "Charles . . . there's no big mystery. I'm not sick and hiding it. I just wanted some time for myself. A drastic change of scene. Something of a retreat. It's not about anyone but me."

He grunted, signifying he appreciated that, but it wasn't enough.

So she added, "I'm painting, of course, and I'll be working from here, so no, I haven't abandoned my career. I'm also taking yoga classes, I'll see some friends who are in town . . . I promise I'm still getting out and doing things. I just need to do this right now." She wasn't sure why she didn't want to tell him she was planning to get pregnant soon, but she knew it was the right call. "I swear there's nothing to worry about. You all are just so used to having me around in the background, you're aware of my absence now."

"That's . . . Jesus, Tess. That's how you think we all think of you? As merely some background support to lean on when it suits one of us?" Charles spat a curse under his breath. "I can't believe you could even say that. Don't you know what you mean to us?"

Tess smiled gently. "Yes, Charles, I do. But—"

"But nothing. You're not some Greek chorus for the Harrison brothers, dammit."

"Aren't I, though?" she said. Only as she said it did she realize how true it was. Maybe that was why she didn't want to reveal her dreams just yet. The bit of resentment on her part astounded her. She'd never thought that consciously, but it had flown out of her mouth. And now that Charles had said it . . . "In a way, I have been. And now you're all fine, and you don't need me around like you did before, and it's time for me to do something for myself. You're all busy, you'll barely miss me."

"We all love you, Tess," Charles said. "We'll always need you. You're our only sister, and our trusted friend. Sure, we've grown to count on you, because the four of us are a team. But we *adore* you. Hell, Dane named his hotel after you, for Pete's sake. You're our best girl. Always will be."

Tess didn't say anything, but something in her warmed at his words.

Charles continued, "No one's begrudging you having something for yourself. We're just concerned because it's unusual behavior for you, and I know there's something behind it. Something specific is driving this and you're not telling me. I'd bet that ski house on it."

She bit down on her lip. He knew her too well. "I'm fine. I promise you that."

"Nice deflection. It only confirms my suspicions, Tess," he said. "But I'll respect your privacy for now." He grunted softly in frustration. She could hear him shuffling papers, likely at his desk. "I don't know what's going on now any more than when you picked up the phone, and that bothers the hell out of me. But I hope you know—I thought you did—that I'm here for you always, when you're ready to tell me whatever's going on. I am, Dane and Pierce are, even Lisette, Julia, and Abby would be. We all love you."

"I hear you," Tess said. "And I love you all too. Now stop worrying about me."

"Well, now that you're at least answering your calls, I feel a drop better," Charles said. "But only a drop."

"You'll be fine," Tess assured him. "How are the kids, big ones and baby one?"

"Everyone's fine. But I think Charlotte misses her favorite aunt."

"Aww, my little bean. I miss her too." Tess heard the slam of a heavy door outside, likely a truck, and realized it was probably Logan. Her heart gave a strange tiny flutter at the thought of him. "Look, I have to go. Logan Carter just got here."

"Ah, Logan. Good to know he's around. Tell him hello for me." Charles paused. "You *sure* you're all right?"

"Stop mothering me!" Tess said with a laugh. "That's my job, being the mother hen of the family."

"Well, with you leaving town," Charles said, "guess I'll have to pick up that title for a while. I *am* the oldest."

"Go for it. If you want to wear the tiara, it's somewhere in my basement." Tess sat up just as the doorbell rang. "Talk to you soon, sweetie. Gotta run."

"Yes, we *will* talk again soon," Charles said. "Take care."

"I will. You too." She set down the phone beside her water glass on the coffee table, then went to answer the door.

"Hey, Tess," Logan said with a twitch of a grin. "Just wanted to let you know I'm here, so when you hear noises out back you won't worry."

"Hi yourself. Okay." She did a quick once-over. The ends of his thick blond hair peeked out from beneath a navy wool cap, brushing just past his strong chin, and he wore his usual work attire of hoodie under his royal-blue jacket, jeans, and work boots. His ruddy cheeks and gloves on his hands were the only things that hinted he might be cold, though it hadn't even reached thirty degrees that day. "Long day at work?"

"Same as usual," he said. "No big shakes. How are you? You settling in okay?"

"Yes, I am, thanks." She swept her hair back from her face. "Can I get you a drink? Some water, or hot tea?"

"No, thanks, I have water in the truck," he said. "Just gonna take out the trash, then check your wood supply."

"I haven't lit a fire yet," she said. "I've been out as much as in. Maybe tonight. But hey, I went by the yoga center. You were right, what a difference! It's so much bigger!"

He nodded, his breath forming as white puffs against the cold air.

"I saw Sami-Jo, she was glad you sent me," Tess continued.

At that, he grinned. "Cool. She's a sweet lady."

"She really is." Tess leaned her hip against the door frame. "I'm going to have a one-on-one with a trainer, Susan, who'll come up here to the house for that, and I'll go there to take classes twice a week with Carrie. Do you know either of them? You seem to be like the town mayor."

For a split second, she caught a strange look in his light green eyes . . . like he'd been caught at something, maybe? But he merely said, "Yeah, I know Carrie. Susan's new, I guess. Good luck with all that."

Something about that quick, odd look intrigued Tess, and she wanted to keep him talking. "Thanks. I take yoga classes at home, but I'm upping it here with the extra personal session. I feel so good after I've done it. You ever done any yoga?"

"Me?" He laughed, making the creases by his eyes crinkle appealingly. "Hell no. But I hear people who do it love it."

"I guess you get enough of a workout just doing your job day to day," Tess said.

"Some days I do." He adjusted his hat a little, pushing strands of his long blond hair away from his eyes. "I still hit the gym a few times a week for weights and some cardio. Yoga, that's just not my thing. But kudos to you for doing it. Any physical activity is good."

"Agreed." She had a fleeting vision of him lifting weights in the gym, his biceps straining and sweat dripping down his neck . . . It was a delicious thought. "I want to hit the slopes next week, but I also love long walks. In fact, I went hiking myself this morning before I went into town. I'll do that two or three times a week, I think."

"Wait, you went up the mountain? By yourself?"

"Yessss," she said. She stepped back and held out her arms to give him a full view of her. "And as you can see, I made it back just fine. This city girl can take care of herself."

"Well. We've covered that before." He scrubbed a hand over his face and something in his eyes shuttered. The change in his demeanor surprised her. He'd gone from teasing to something dark so quickly. It made the joking smile slide off her face.

He cleared his throat and said, "I'd better get to work. Just wanted to get it done before sunset, and I've got about"—he glanced up at the sky, shades of deep blue with hints of pink in the wispy clouds—"maybe half an hour of decent light left."

She simply nodded. "I won't keep you, then. Thank you, Logan."

"Yup. Glad to hear you're settling in fine. Talk to you soon." He turned away and went down the steps. "Have a good night," he called over his shoulder before heading around the side of the house.

"You too," she called back before closing the door. He used to be friendlier to her, and it ate at her . . . She wished she knew if she'd said or done something to offend him.

Bubbles came scampering to her, yipping and wagging her tail. Tess crouched to pet her and cooed, "Are you hungry, little miss? Do I need to feed you now?"

Bubbles barked and wiggled in response.

"Okay, Bubs. C'mon, let's feed you." Tess walked through to the kitchen, her mind preoccupied with thoughts about the ruggedly gorgeous blond man out in her backyard. The more she learned about him, it seemed, the more there was to learn. She was definitely intrigued enough to find out. He interested her, it was that simple. Logan Carter was more complicated and layered than he seemed. She'd seen flashes of gruff or guarded moments, enough to suspect that his easygoing, self-assured outside was hiding something darker and more compelling inside. Somehow, over her time there, maybe she could get him to tell her his story.

Chapter Four

Logan got back to his apartment at seven, having put in a full day. He'd gotten up at six thirty to hit the gym for a workout, then gone to several houses over the course of the day. All in all, the day had flown by and he couldn't complain.

After a quick shower, he changed into a soft gray sweatshirt and navy track pants, then stretched out on his living room couch to relax for a few minutes before deciding which movie to watch that night. A few rays of moonlight shone through the far windows, slanting lines of light onto his dark brown walls. He pillowed his arms behind his head and considered his current life.

Things were fine. No drama, no angst, everything on a pretty even keel. His quiet life kept him busy, he helped people, and he was doing honest work and getting paid decently for it. His schedule was his to manage, his boss treated him well, and his clients, for the most part, were respectful and glad to have him around. It was the simple, quiet life he'd once longed for, and grateful he had now.

Being on his own was what was best for him. He almost never thought of Rachel anymore, which was how it should be. She was out there living her life, and he was living his. He dated sporadically, never letting it get too deep or complicated. Yes, women approached him, but except for an occasional night here and there, he preferred his solitude. He'd carefully crafted his post–New Orleans life that way. Fewer ties meant fewer people to hurt or disappoint.

He had friends here, a small handful which suited him fine; he'd never been comfortable as part of a big social circle anyway. His older brother had married right out of college and gone to live near his wife's family out in Portland; Shane only came to Aspen once a year now, usually in summer, when his four kids were off from school. Long ago, Logan had made peace with the fact that they led very different lives. Sometimes he thought of his dad and missed him, but that was normal, especially around the holidays.

Just the other day, on Christmas, Logan commented how he couldn't believe it'd been twenty-three years now since his dad had passed. His mom had sighed and nodded . . . She also keenly felt every one of those twenty-three Christmases she'd spent without him. She'd been so devoted to Wyatt Carter that even though a car crash had left her a widow at forty-two, she'd never married again.

Logan sighed and closed his eyes. His mom. The cancer seemed to be winning. She wasn't keeping any weight on, and her eyes were tired. The doctors tried to maintain a positive outlook, but deep down, he knew better. Would she live to see another Christmas? He had a sinking feeling the answer was no, which was why he'd tried to make it extra special for her this year. But he refused to ruminate on that. Annmarie Carter was a fighter. She'd fight to the last, whenever that would be.

Mercifully, as if to distract him from speculating on

that any further, his cell phone rang and he gladly lifted it from the wooden coffee table. A glance at the caller ID made his brows lift, curiosity sparking. "Carter," he answered, as he always did.

"Hi," came her voice, always so elegant yet friendly at the same time. *The people's princess.* "It's Tess Harrison."

"So my caller ID says," he said. "What can I do for you?"

"I hate to bother you in the evening," she said, "but I'm trying not to panic." Only then did he pick up on a note of distress in her tone. "I have a—a situation here, and I don't know what to do. You were the first person I thought to call. Unless I should just call the fire department."

"What?" Logan bolted upright into a sitting position. "What's going on?"

"I don't know what I did." She sounded embarrassed, as if admitting the words were torturous. "I don't think the house is on fire . . . but it's filled up with smoke. I—"

"Get out of the house!" he shouted. Alarm flooded him as he jumped to his feet. "Are you okay? What happened?"

"I'm fine, I'm out in front of the house," she said. "I lit a fire in the fireplace for the first time, and within five minutes, the house filled with smoke. I grabbed Bubbles and got out. I'm surprised you can't hear the smoke alarms going off."

He listened for a second. "Actually, now I can." Swearing under his breath, he headed for the bedroom. "Sure you're all right?"

"We're cold, but fine. Honestly."

"Okay." He shucked off his track pants with one hand and grabbed a pair of jeans. He wanted heavier pants, with pockets. Something occurred to him. "Tess, did you open the flue before you started the fire?"

"What?" Horror filled her voice. "No. No, I didn't. I forgot. Ah shit!"

At least he had an idea of what the problem was. "Stay outside," he told her. "I'm pretty sure your house isn't on fire, but call the fire department. I'll be there as soon as I can, under fifteen minutes." Disconnecting the call, he rushed around his small house, gathering his keys, wallet, and phone, pulling on his heaviest coat and his hat. It was under twenty degrees out right now . . . ah hell, he hoped she was okay. And the house too. It was a beautiful house, it'd be a shame if it got damaged. On his way to the door, he stopped. Eyeing the extra fleece blanket he kept in a basket by the couch, he grabbed it to bring along, just in case.

He raced through the streets, driving like a madman around the winding path up Red Mountain, and made it to her house in nine minutes flat. His headlights floated over her as he pulled into her long driveway, gliding over her red parka and a ball of white fluff in her arms before he cut them. The sensor lights over the front door gave more than enough light as he ran to her. Heart rate definitely up, he gripped her shoulders to quickly examine her. "You're okay?"

"I'm fine," she said over Bubbles's barking at him. Her nose and cheeks were pink from the frigid night air. "Just cold, and feeling incredibly stupid."

Time was ticking, every second needed. He jogged back to the truck, reached in for the blanket, and returned to her. "I'm going inside to check it out. You are staying *here*," he said as he wrapped the blanket around her shoulders. He wished it were bigger, but it was better than nothing. "This'll help for now."

Her big blue eyes locked on his face. "Thank you. That's very kind of you."

He made sure to tuck the end of the blanket around the dog, who licked his hand and yipped. "Did you call the

fire department?" As soon as he said it, as if on cue, the
sound of sirens wailed nearby. "Atta boys, they're so good."
He patted her arm and commanded, "I'm not kidding, you
stay here," before going into the house.

Billows of thick gray smoke wafted all through the
ground floor, rising to the high wood beams of the ceiling.
The fire, while small, still smoldered in the hearth. *Damn.*
He pulled his scarf up over his nose and mouth and went
right to the fireplace, peering through the smoke. It made
his eyes burn and his lungs heavy; he coughed as he
looked. Sure enough, Tess hadn't opened the flue before
setting the fire. A rookie mistake. As he worked the flue
and got it open, three firefighters burst into the room.

Half an hour later, the scene was calm. With the help of
some of Aspen's finest, they'd doused the fire, opened all
the windows to air out the house, and made sure everything was secure. Tess sat in the warm cab of the fire truck
while they worked, holding her dog tightly and looking
chagrined.

Logan went to go talk to her with Captain Bellamy
when they were done. He stood by quietly, not intervening
as the fireman went over what had happened, what to do
now, all of that. Shaking her head, Tess apologized about
half a dozen times through the short conversation; her embarrassment and remorse were palpable, and it made
Logan feel bad for her. Made him want to reassure her
beyond the fire chief's words, which were echoes of what
Logan had said and thought. Seeing the guilty look in her
sharp blue eyes made him want to pull her into his arms
and give her a hug.

It was only when the fireman said, "However, you're
going to have to let the house air out for a while," that
Logan finally spoke up.

"I'll take care of her," he said.

Tess's eyes flew to Logan's face in obvious surprise, but Captain Bellamy nodded and said, "All right, then," without a glance or a thought.

"That won't be necessary," she said.

"Really?" Logan asked. He crossed his arms over his chest. "You won't be able to go back into the house and close the windows for . . . what, Captain, two hours, at least?"

"Sounds about right," Bellamy said. "I'd give it four— or more, actually, unless you don't mind the smell of smoke in your furniture."

Logan nodded in agreement, his eyes holding his client's. "And it's seventeen degrees out right now."

He saw the understanding start to dawn in her face.

"Way I see it," he went on, "you have two choices. You can stay out here in the cold, maybe sit in your truck for a while, if that suits you. Or, you can go inside, quickly grab a few things, and let me take you into town so you and your dog can stay at a nice, warm hotel for the night. Which I'll gladly take you to, and pick you up from in the morning to bring you home."

He watched Tess as she shot a glance at the garage. Her SUV was in there, but the fire truck and captain's car were parked in front of it.

"Sounds like a good idea to me," Captain Bellamy said. "Why don't I leave you two to discuss it."

Tess stepped out of the fire truck. Still cradling Bubbles with both arms, she almost lost her balance. Logan held her arm to help her firmly onto the ground. She looked up at him, those wide marine-blue eyes locking on him, and said, "Option two sounds good to me. Thank you, Logan."

"Of course. Can't have you out here freezing to death." He rubbed Bubbles's head, bringing a short bark and licking. "You want to go in and grab what you need, or you want me to do it?"

"I'm going to need to put her down to do anything," Tess said, glancing down at the ball of white fur in her arms.

"Gimme." Logan reached out and took the dog. He laughed as she wiggled wildly. "Squirmy li'l thing, aren't ya? C'mere, missy. Let's get you in my truck for a few minutes while Tess and I get some stuff." He glanced at Tess for permission, and when she nodded and smiled, he walked back to his truck. He turned on the heated seats and blasted the heat for a minute before setting Bubbles down in the backseat. "Don't pee in here, okay, sweetie?" She barked in reply.

The captain drove away, leaving the fire truck and his men to finish up. Logan watched as the firemen set up the positive pressure fan in the front door to help force the smoke out of all the open windows. Walking back to Tess, he tried to gauge the expression on her face. Gratitude for sure, but it was mixed with something else, and he wasn't sure what. "You okay?"

"Fine," she assured him. "You're being very sweet. To me, and to Bubbles. Thank you for that."

He shrugged and said, "Just doin' my job, Tess. Here . . ." He pulled his scarf from around his neck and handed it to her. "Put that over your nose and mouth when we go inside. Still smoky as hell; you don't want to breathe that in."

She nodded, thanked him again, and turned away to go into the house. As he followed her, he noticed for the first time that though she was still wrapped up in his blanket, she was in her pj's. She wore fleece pajama bottoms, red with black dots on them. It was only as he reached her side in the living room that he realized the dots were little penguins. He couldn't help but grin. That was cute. He hadn't pegged her to own, much less wear, anything that hinted of cute. She was so aristocratic, he'd figured she probably wore expensive satin pajamas to bed.

"I'll just go upstairs and grab what I need," she said. "Could you do me a huge favor?"

"Of course," he said.

"If you could just grab"—she pointed to the corner, toward Bubbles's layout—"a few of those toys next to her bed, toss them on top, and bring the bed to your truck, that would be really great. I have a feeling a hotel might be more open to my having a dog in tow if they see she's got her own bed."

He did as she asked, and she went up the spiral wooden staircase to her room. In five minutes, he had the dog's stuff together and she was back with a small suitcase.

"That was quick," he said.

"I'm efficient, and I don't want to keep breathing in this smoke," she replied.

"I don't blame you. C'mon."

When they got outside, he locked the door behind her. "Don't worry about someone breaking in because all the windows are open. After I take you to a hotel, I'll come back here. Gonna camp out in the truck for a while, then I'll go inside to check. You know, close all the windows, take care of everything. By the time I bring you back here tomorrow morning, it'll all be just a memory, a fun story to tell your brothers."

She stammered, then shook her head. "What? No. You can't stay here in your truck all night, that's not—"

"That's me doing my job," he said firmly.

"No, it's beyond the parameters of what you should have to do. It's too cold out. Can't you stay inside?"

"It'll be just as cold in there with all the windows open," he pointed out.

She grimaced and grumbled, "Of course it would. Duh." She threw up her hands in surrender. "You're not going to budge on this?"

"No, ma'am."

"Okay, then. If you insist."

"I do." He grinned and walked to the truck. "Get in," he told her over his shoulder. "Door's unlocked." Bubbles barked like crazy while he put the doggie bed in the back, then Tess's suitcase. By the time he slid into the driver's seat, the warmth hit him like a wall. He glanced over at his beautiful passenger, who was buckling her seat belt with one arm while trying to hold her dog with the other.

"Um . . ." Logan said. "Which hotel am I taking you to? Any idea?"

"I called the Barrington Hotel while I was up in my room. They accept pets. So they're expecting me."

He blinked. "You were up there for maybe four minutes. You packed and did that at the same time?"

A spark entered her eyes as her sharp grin bloomed. "I know how to multitask."

"Well, color me impressed, then."

Her gaze narrowed as she assessed him. "Logan . . . I may have done an unbelievably stupid thing tonight, but I'm not a stupid woman. I run a company, you know. I'm usually pretty on top of my game."

Nodding, he shifted the gears and pulled out of the driveway, ignoring the barking dog and the faint burn of being put in his place. She never did miss an opportunity to condescend to him, did she. "I wasn't insulting you, Tess. I was just surprised that you did so much in under five minutes, that's all. It's respect, not pandering." He bit the inside of his cheek to keep from saying more . . . something he might regret.

"Oh." She stroked her dog's fur with her now gloved

fingers. "Look, I might be a little oversensitive right now. I'm tired, cold, and most of all, I'm really mad at myself for doing something so dumb. I could've burned the damn house down."

"Well, you didn't. No harm done, learned a lesson, all's well in the end." He kept his eyes on the road. The turns as they headed down Red Mountain were sharp and unlit; he maneuvered carefully in the dark. "I'll have you at your hotel in no time."

They drove in silence for the rest of the trip. When he pulled up in front of the grand luxury hotel, she gripped his forearm.

"You've been amazing tonight, Logan," she said earnestly. "Thank you so much, for everything. Really."

He nodded. "You're welcome. Just glad you're okay." He got out of the truck and reached into the backseat for her suitcase, then grasped the doggie bed. "I'll help you inside with this," he said as he met her outside the truck, "then I'll come back for you in the morning. Text me when you're ready to leave, and I'll be here to take you home."

"Sounds good," she said. "But can I ask you something?"

"Sure."

She hesitated, her pretty mouth twisting as she shifted the dog in her arms, then asked, "I hate that I had to call you late at night about all this. I know I'm supposed to, you told me that. I don't think I've been a pest aside from this incident. But . . . sometimes you snap at me. Like before. I feel like you don't like me very much. I was wondering if you could tell me why."

His eyes flew wide and he huffed out a shocked breath. Well, that was direct. "I don't dislike you, Tess."

"Really?" Her gaze narrowed on him, her bright blue eyes as intense as lasers. He bet that look cut lesser people to shreds. "I'm pretty good at reading people. Your whole demeanor when you're around me . . . you're curt with me sometimes. Like you're tolerating me. You didn't used to be that way when we first met. I've noticed it."

He scowled. Shit, she was right. But still. "Seriously?"

"Yes." She stared at him evenly as her long hair danced around her shoulders, the spiral curls carried by a gust of icy wind. "You just think I'm some entitled, spoiled rich bitch, don't you? Like most of the affluent people you work with here. Right?"

He shook his head no, but her words that had cut him last year echoed in his head. She was wrong that he didn't like her, but she wasn't wrong about his assessment of her after that chat, that things had shifted for him. It didn't help that, on top of his conflicting opinions of her, he was crazy attracted to her. His thoughts about her, his . . . feelings . . . were tangled. *He* didn't even totally understand them. So he was short with her sometimes. And her nailing that now made him feel like an ass.

He only said, "No." But it had no conviction, and he knew it. He just couldn't lie.

She nodded very slowly, gaze unwavering, her lips flattening into a hard line before she said, "Yeah, you do. You think I'm . . . well. Forget it. You don't know me after all. That's a shame." She cradled her dog and started to walk away from him, toward the main entrance of the hotel. Without a look back, her head held high.

In a flash, he realized he had to clear the air once and for all. She'd opened the door, he had to man up and walk through. "Tess, wait." His long legs had him at her side in just a few strides. He stepped in front of her, making her stop. "I didn't think that, what you just said. Not at first. But you . . ." He huffed out a breath, forming a quick white cloud in the frigid air. She looked prim and proper and totally pissed off. "You said something last year that insulted me, and yeah, I didn't shake it off. It . . . changed how I saw you. Even though you apologized. So I guess that's on me, not you."

Her eyes, so blue, held his gaze as she clearly tried to recall what she might have said. Then they flew wide open and she almost sputtered. "I'm here defending myself because you think I'm some spoiled, hapless woman, and why you're really pissed is because I said I didn't know you had a master's? Which, by the way, made me cringe for hours afterwards because it was one of the dumber things I've said in the last few years. I regretted it deeply." Her chin lifted in defiant irritation, making her look every inch like his mental nickname for her, a princess. "Yes? Is that what we're talking about?"

"Yes." He didn't move, just gazed down at her as he stood there holding her things. Jesus, he was an idiot. *He* was the judgmental one after all.

"I apologized for that!" she cried.

"I know you did. But it still bothered me," he admitted. "Your assumption that a man working a physical job like I do would only do it because he wasn't educated enough, or smart enough, to do something else . . . got under my skin. But yeah . . ." He shook his head again and admitted, "I've been holding that against you. I'm sorry."

"You know," she said, "it was uncharacteristically stupid of me to say something like that. I don't consider myself to be a judgmental person . . . but then I suppose most judgmental people don't, do they." She sighed and Bubbles barked in her arms. Her hand shot out to stroke her dog's head. "Regardless, that was a major gaffe on my part. I'm sorry it bothered you so much." She stared up at him, her gorgeous eyes filled with remorse. "I respect you, Logan, and I like you. I always have. Especially after all you've done tonight, more than ever. So please forgive me for insulting you so deeply."

Something washed through him . . . something like shame. He had to let this go already. "Tess . . . just forget it. All of it, okay? I'm sorry too, for being a stubborn ass."

After a pause, she nodded, her curls bouncing softly. She shifted the dog so she could extend her hand. "Let's leave it behind us. For real this time. Truce?"

Exhaling a breath he didn't even realize he'd been holding, he set down her suitcase to shake her gloved hand. "Yes, ma'am."

"All right, then." She waited for him to pick up her bag again, and they walked into the hotel together. Between the lush grandeur of the lobby and his own embarrassment burning in his chest, Logan couldn't wait to get out of there. Tess had called him out. He didn't like how it felt, but he respected the hell out of her for doing it. Now he just had to swallow his chastened pride and let his residual irritation go—and like she'd said, for real this time. He was glad he'd have a long, cold night alone to work that out.

The next morning, even from behind dark sunglasses, Logan squinted from the brightness of the sun reflecting off the snow as he drove into downtown Aspen. The sky was a crystalline blue, the mountain views behind the shops and restaurants as picturesque as always. He'd missed the mountains and the clear, crisper air when he'd lived in New Orleans, and never tired of the landscape even though he'd been back for several years now.

It'd been a long night, sitting in front of the Harrison house out in his truck, but not terrible. The heat in his truck worked, and his legs almost fit across the backseat.

It wasn't the inability to get comfortable in his backseat that kept him from sleeping, but his churning brain. All night, he'd thought about Tess Harrison. She intrigued and interested him. The resentment he felt was based on his own lingering insecurities; when she'd said her piece last night, he knew that her perceived slights weren't deliberate. He believed that now.

And he felt like he wanted to make that up to her somehow. If his damn ego would let him.

He'd finally fallen asleep sometime around midnight, and his phone's alarm woke him at six a.m. Going into the house, he found it frigid, but no traces of smoke lingered. The rooms smelled like the fresh, clear, mountaintop air. He'd taken care of the house, raised the thermostat some, got things in order. He took pride in his job, and he was sure going to do right by Tess on this easy task. By the time she texted him at nine, asking him to come get her, he'd already gone back home, showered, eaten breakfast, and watched some morning news.

Twenty minutes later, as he pulled up and around the long, winding entry to the hotel, he wondered what to say to Tess to express his remorse for how he'd been acting. Or if he even should. He scratched restlessly at his beard. Maybe he should say nothing at all. That usually worked for him too. Hell, they'd called a truce, right? No need to bring it up again, then. He'd just be nicer from now on, not such a surly bastard. Which wouldn't be hard to do at all, because the truth was he did like her.

He parked the truck and popped a mint into his mouth. Feeling calm and centered, he strode with lazy grace across the parking lot and into the hotel. But as soon as he entered the wide lobby, a loud barking set his nerves jangling. Bubbles came storming across the marble floor, skidding to a stop at his feet.

"Hey now." Logan frowned as he bent to pet the dog, who was yipping away. "Where's your mama?" He looked up to see a small group gathered in the middle of the lobby, all looking down. From his low crouch, Logan could see Tess there, apparently sprawled out on the cold, hard floor.

Chapter Five

"Tess!" Logan's heart pounded as anxious worry shot through his veins. He reached her in a few seconds. Bubbles followed, barking loudly. The circle of murmuring, staring people cleared for him as he placed a hand on her shoulder.

She looked up at him and grinned.

He stared and stammered, "What the—?"

"Hi," she said. She was totally alert, seemed okay, just . . . lying on the floor. Next to an older man in a ski sweater and jeans. "Please don't look so worried, I'm fine."

"Jesus, you scared the hell out of me." Logan looked her over quickly, then to the man beside her. Gray-haired, likely in his late sixties, he seemed a little dazed. What was going on? "Why are you on the floor, then?"

"I'm keeping Terrence here company until the medics arrive," Tess said calmly. "Which should be any minute now."

"I'm so damn embarrassed," Terrence muttered, looking from Tess to Logan and back to her again. "Friend of yours?"

"Yes," she said. "And strong as an ox. I'd let him lift

you up, but I think it's best for you to not move yet." She rolled from her side onto her stomach and pillowed her forearms under her cheek.

"Could you all please back up?" Logan asked in a sharp tone, swiveling his head around at the human canopy of nosy bystanders.

"Seriously," Terrence grumbled.

"Folks, let's give them some room, all right?" came a voice. An employee tried to make the small crowd of about a dozen leave.

"What's going on?" Logan whispered in Tess's ear as he sat up.

"I was at the front desk checking out," Tess explained, "and I heard something behind me. Terrence here tripped and hit his head on the floor. Pretty hard." Logan caught the glimmer of concern in her eyes. "He was unconscious for a minute. Pam and I"—Tess motioned to the employee trying to clear the lobby—"we rushed to help. Pam called the EMTs, and they should be here soon."

"I told her," Terrence said, "that she didn't have to lie on the floor here with me, but she insisted. Said if I'd cooperate and not move, she'd stay down here with me. She keeps talking to me to make sure I'm alert. She thinks I might have a concussion." He looked at Tess and said pointedly, "I don't, you know."

"I hope I'm wrong, believe me!" Tess grinned. "But just in case, I thought I'd keep you proper company in the meantime."

Logan glanced at Tess, admiration and respect coursing through him. He looked down at Terrence and said, "You know, I can think of worse things than having a kind, beautiful woman lying on the floor with you."

Terrence chuckled at that. "You know what, you're right."

Noise filled the lobby, echoing off the walls and marble as the EMTs rushed into the lobby, wheeling a stretcher.

Terrence reached out and grasped Tess's hand. "You were so kind to stay with me. Thank you for that, and for your concern. I'll be fine."

"Good to know." She reached for her bag, which was on the floor a few feet away. Logan grabbed it and handed it to her as one of the EMTs crouched down to survey the scene. Tess took out a business card and pressed it into Terrence's hand. "My cell phone number is on there. Call me if you need anything. And please text me later to tell me what the actual prognosis is, instead of your own. All right?"

Terrence laughed wryly. "You're a pushy young woman."

"I am. Now promise me."

"I promise, I'll let you know how I'm doing." He let the EMT shine a light in his eyes. As Tess rose from the floor, he thanked her again.

Logan watched as she scooped up her dog, then went to talk to the other two EMTs, likely to describe what had happened. He took her suitcase and moved aside to let them do their job. Within a few minutes, they'd gotten Terrence onto the stretcher and wheeled him out to the waiting ambulance.

"I'm sorry about the holdup," Tess said to Logan. "Let me just talk to Pam once more, and we'll be on our way."

"No worries," he told her. "Take your time." As he folded himself into a cushy chair, he watched her chat with the employees behind the main desk, who looked grateful and slightly in awe of her. *They should be*, he thought.

Tess Harrison wasn't the stuck-up, condescending snob

he'd convinced himself she was. How many of his other clients, much less the wealthy, powerful people of Aspen, would lie down in the middle of a hotel floor to keep someone calm and still when they were hurt? Not many, he bet.

By the time he and Tess got her things into his truck and buckled up, Logan found himself saying, "That was a damn nice thing you did in there. Let me buy you some breakfast." He started the car and put his sunglasses back on.

Tess blinked, then smiled tentatively. "Thank you, but I already ate. I get up early. I've been up since seven."

"Ah. Okay." He checked the rearview mirror, then pulled out of the spot. "I'm sure he'll be okay, by the way. Terrence."

"He scared the shit out of me," Tess confessed. She leaned back into the seat, the leather squeaking a bit. Stealing a quick look into the backseat to check on Bubbles, who was curled up happily on the warmed seat, Tess shook her head. "I was checking out, and I heard *Oh!* Then a *thwack*. That was his head, hitting the floor." She shuddered as she recalled it. "He hit it hard. I whirled around, and he was down, not moving. For a few seconds, I thought he was dead."

Logan glanced at her; her brows were furrowed and her sultry mouth was twisted tight in a frown. He said, "But he's not. Even if he has a concussion, he's okay. And your kindness made him feel a lot better about tripping over his own feet and lying in the middle of a hotel floor. That was good of you. Really."

"I was worried. I didn't know what to do for him, so I just . . ." She shrugged. Her frown loosened, and her drawn features relaxed. "You would have done the same thing, I'm sure."

"Yeah, maybe I would've," he said. He made the turn onto the main strip. "But not a lot of people around here would've. You know?"

Tess shrugged again. "I guess . . ."

An awkward silence fell over them for a minute. Even Bubbles was quiet. Logan cleared his throat. "The house is fine. Took care of everything."

"Oh God. With all of this, I forgot about it!" She laughed, a self-deprecating chuckle that charmed Logan to his toes. "Tell me you didn't stay up all night out in your truck. Please."

"Of course I was in the truck," he said, "but I slept, and I was fine. Honest."

"I can't thank you enough." She pushed a few stray curls back from her eyes. "I'm the one who should be buying *you* breakfast."

He smiled, something warm flowing through him. "I already ate too. So . . . maybe a rain check?"

Her smile was as bright as the sunlight outside. "Absolutely."

Tess stretched out in her bed, drew a deep, cleansing breath, and exhaled it slowly. Her evening yoga class had been great, and the long soak in the deep tub afterwards even better. The royal-purple cotton pajamas she wore were so soft against her skin, it was a delight. She drew another deep breath, exhaled slowly, curled up in her bed, and let herself settle into the plush king-size mattress. Serenity washed over her. Bubbles snored lightly, an adorable furry ball on top of the blanket by her feet. The fireplace in the master bedroom was a gas fireplace, so she didn't have to do anything now but stare at it from across the room and relax.

She still couldn't believe what she'd done the night before. Such a stupid mistake. But at least there was a happy ending, and now a wry grin when she thought of the whole thing. And Logan . . . rushing to her aid, staying all night to watch the house, taking care of everything . . . he'd been a godsend.

A seriously handsome, somewhat surly, somewhat complicated presence who hadn't fully left her mind since he'd brought her home early this morning.

She'd spent the day catching up on work, then had an early dinner. There were quick phone chats with all three brothers to let them know what had happened, and then she'd gone to her twice weekly evening yoga class. She liked the instructor, Carrie, the group was a good size at ten, and Tess had no problem adjusting to Carrie's instructions and ways. Between the class and then the warm bath, she felt at peace and ready to float off to sleep.

And instead lay there wondering how Logan Carter spent his evenings after a workday.

Did he have friends? A girlfriend? He seemed like the type of man who would have both of those things, but preferred his space and solitude.

Then again, what did she know? She couldn't believe he'd held a grudge against her for her thoughtless comment all this time. Yes, what she'd implied was offensive, but not enough to warrant that kind of stubborn grudge. At least, not in her eyes. But it had, and she felt bad about that. She was glad she'd brought up the problem, and glad they'd come to an understanding. Because for some reason, the thought of him upset with her made her . . . sad? Uneasy? Regretful? What the hell was her deal when it came to him?

She grunted and rolled over, plumping up her pillows and tossing her long hair back over them. She had to stop thinking about Logan Carter. There was no reason to. He just worked in her house sometimes, they were acquaintances, that was all.

There was no reason for her to be intrigued by him, dammit.

Even if he was ridiculously gorgeous, in a no-holds-barred, manly man kind of way that made her hormones race like they hadn't in some time.

The last time she'd had sex was Labor Day weekend; a casual interlude with an old acquaintance that had been merely satisfactory . . . which, in turn, left her feeling empty afterwards. It had been the last push that convinced her that having her own life, alone, was definitely how it was going to be.

She'd felt so lonely that following week that it shocked her. Yet, at the same time, she knew how it had to be now. She'd always believed in love, even after her parents' disastrous uncoupling. She'd had boyfriends and looked for love her whole life . . . but it hadn't happened for her. Only once had she fallen in deep as an adult, and Brady had been a bad choice. At least she'd found out who he really was before she'd married him.

On her own was how she'd do it. She'd tried love, been slapped by it, looked again, come up empty . . . it just wasn't in the cards for her. Not everyone was going to find their soul mate like all three of her brothers had. She was the unlucky sibling, apparently. Not that she'd ever say that to them, or let herself drown in self-pity over it . . . it just was what it was.

She'd tried to date, do the casual thing . . . it wasn't for her. Meaningless sex had proven to be just that. She could give herself an orgasm just fine and not have to deal with the hollow, awkward feelings afterwards, lying in a bed with someone she didn't care about and knowing he felt

the same. She hadn't had rock-my-world sex since Brady,
though, and that was years ago now. She'd loved him, so
it took the sex to a higher level, more satisfying both physically and emotionally . . . she'd always been that way. She
knew other people could separate good sex from love,
their body from their mind—hell, two of her brothers had
been like that before they'd met their wives. But she'd
never been able to do that. After this last attempt at a
casual fling, Tess had decided that sex was just going to
be another casualty of her lackluster love life. She'd be on
her own, have her baby, and concentrate on the new path
she'd forge for herself.

But she bet Logan Carter was good in bed. That gorgeous mountain of a man . . . oh, would she love to climb
him. Something in her belly warmed at the thought, shooting tingles straight between her legs. She imagined him
hovering over her in bed . . . his muscled, broad shoulders,
those shrewd green eyes gazing down at her . . . and shook
the image out of her mind. She had to stop thinking about
him. Yet as she lay there for the next few minutes, she
found that was easier thought than done.

Maybe that was it, why she was suddenly thinking
about Logan? Something simple like she still had needs,
and it had been long enough now that her itch needed
some scratching? And Logan was a drop-dead gorgeous,
six-foot-four, virile Viking of a man who practically em-
anated testosterone, so she was a little hot for him?

Who was she kidding? More than a little hot. He was
sexy as hell, both for his looks and just who he was. He
was smart and strong, and that drew her to him. Spending
Labor Day weekend in bed with Anton had only proved,
once and for all, that a pretty face and body on their
own just didn't cut it for her; she needed a man of real
substance to hold her interest. And Logan had it in spades.

Talk to the man for two minutes, and you could see his still waters ran deep. He enticed her, no doubt about it.

She squeezed her eyes shut. It was clear that despite their easier vibe that morning, for the most part, Logan barely tolerated her. They weren't friends. He thought she was some stuck-up princess. If he knew she was having dirty thoughts about him . . . about what his sensual mouth would feel like to kiss, or what his strong, calloused hands would feel like against her skin, or what his beard would feel like against her thighs . . . he'd probably grimace so hard at her that his ruggedly handsome face would crack.

With a heavy sigh, she took a few more deep breaths. It was only a quarter to ten, but going to sleep early seemed like a wonderful idea.

Her cell phone on the nightstand buzzed with a text message. Already sleepy, she debated whether to look at it or not. Curiosity got the best of her and she reached for it.

Hi Tess, it's Terrence, read the text. I'm okay. Still in the hospital, staying overnight for observation. Because unfortunately, you were right, I have a concussion. You missed your calling, you should have been a doctor. Haha.

She smiled and typed back quickly, Hi there! I hate that I was right. But you're a lucky man—you hit that floor hard! Very glad to hear from you, and that you're okay.

Hi! Yes, I'm okay. Just will be slow going for the next few weeks, I guess.

Do whatever they tell you and you'll be fine sooner than later.

I will, Terrence answered. Thank you again for hanging out with me on the floor. Really was nice of you. I'll admit now, when I woke up, I was dizzy as hell and that scared me. Your being there kept me calm. I won't forget that.

"Awww," she said aloud, then wrote, I'm glad I helped. Sincerely. Stay in touch, please let me know when they release you from the hospital.

Okay. Probably tomorrow. Will rest at hotel for a day or two, then head home. Hell of a Happy New Year plan, huh?

She chuckled wryly and wrote, Yeah, sounds like your New Year's Eve will be a rocking party.

Not anymore, I'm afraid, he texted. Hope you have good plans tomorrow night? Do something fun for both of us.

She sighed at that. She had no plans. Allie had invited her over to their house for a small party, but she'd declined. She'd stopped drinking at Christmas to start cleansing her body, and the noise of strangers held no appeal this time around. A quiet New Year's Eve was what I had in mind, she wrote. Sorry to disappoint you, but I'll be home alone with my dog. My choice.

Guess we'll both ring in the new year quietly, then, Terrence wrote. Okay, going to sleep now. Just wanted to let you know I am alive and okay.

Thank you for doing so, she responded. If I hadn't heard by tomorrow morning, I was going to call the hospital and try to find out how you were.

You're very thoughtful. Thank you again, Tess. Happy New Year to you.

You're very welcome. Happy New Year to you too.

She put her phone back on the nightstand and snuggled up under the covers again. As she stared serenely into the flames and drifted off to sleep, she wondered what various people in her life would be doing the next night for

New Year's Eve. Her brothers . . . her closest friends . . . even Logan Carter.

Logan helped his mother from the front seat of his truck, then carefully wrapped her arm through his as they walked across the parking lot to the hospital.

"I'm not made of glass, you know," she reminded him, but patted his arm as they walked.

"I do know," he said, but slowed his stride to match hers. She was weaker and slower, that was clear. "Why'd they have to schedule your radiation session on New Year's Eve, for Pete's sake? That's just gloomy."

"Well," she started, but shook her head and swallowed the words.

"No, what?" he nudged.

But she didn't answer. Instead, she said, "So what are we having for dinner tonight?"

"You're avoiding," he said flatly. "What were you going to say?"

"Shut up and tell me what we're having for dinner."

He chuckled wryly. When Annmarie Carter didn't want to talk about something, nothing would pry it out of her. He knew that all too well, because he was just like her. "I was thinking I'd make you a nice juicy steak. Get some iron in you."

"That sounds nice." The wind blew harder, icy and crystalline. She huddled closer to him and continued, "Any chance of some broccoli rabe sautéed in garlic and oil to go with it? You make it the best. And mashed potatoes?"

"Whatever you want," he said. The thought struck him that it could be her last New Year's meal, and a lump formed in his throat. He withdrew her arm from the crook of his elbow and slipped his arm around her waist to hold her closer as they walked against the wind. "Whatever you want, Mom, I'll be happy to make it for you."

"Thanks. You're a better cook than you own up to," she said.

"Don't tell people. They'll want me to do it for them too."

"How about finding a nice girl to cook for?"

Logan rolled his eyes. "Don't you ever get tired of that, lady?"

"What, hoping you find someone special?" Annmarie huffed out a breath. "No chance. It's what I want for you more than anything."

"I know, Mom," he murmured. He hated to disappoint her, but having been married once, brief as it'd been, was all the evidence he needed that he wasn't cut out for it.

They reached the front doors of the hospital, and the wide panes of glass parted with a swooshing sound. God, Logan hated the smell of hospitals. That piercingly antiseptic scent always brought back so many bad memories, and bringing his mom in for chemo and radiation had only added to them. He unzipped his jacket as Annmarie slowly pulled off her soft green hat. Making their way across the lobby to the elevators, his attention was so focused on her that he didn't hear the voice calling him at first.

"Logan," his mother said, "I think that man is trying to get your attention."

Logan turned to see a man in a wheelchair being pushed toward the doors. "Hey, you!" he was saying loudly. "Tess's friend! Tall blond guy!"

It took Logan a few seconds before he realized it was the man from the hotel floor the day before. "Hey, Terrence! How're you doing? You look okay to me."

"Eh, I'm fine," Terrence said. "I didn't catch your name yesterday, I'm sorry. *Tall blond guy*—how rude." He laughed at himself.

"Logan," he said, reaching out to shake the man's hand. "So they're springing you? You're okay, then?"

"Well, Tess was right, I do have a concussion," Terrence said. "They kept me overnight but they're releasing me now."

"If they're releasing you, you must be all right." Logan looked him over. Terrence had color in his cheeks, and seemed okay. "Is someone coming to get you?"

"I called a car service. I'm waiting," Terrence said. "Going back to the hotel to take it easy for a few days, then I'll go home. Why are you here? You okay?"

"I'm fine," Logan said as his mother joined them. "This is my mother, Annmarie Carter. Mom, this is Terrence. Met him yesterday."

They exchanged pleasantries, then Terrence asked, "So how do you know Tess?"

"I'm a house manager," Logan said. "Her house—or her family, rather—is one of my clients. She had a mishap the night before, so she had to stay at the hotel. I was there to give her a ride home."

"She's an extraordinary woman," Terrence declared. "And oh boy, is she nice to look at."

Logan had to chuckle as he admitted, "Yeah, she is."

"You have a girlfriend, Logan?" Terrence asked.

Logan blinked at the forward question as his mother quipped, "I wish."

Terrence laughed, then said, "I talked to her briefly last night. You know she's staying home by herself tonight? A woman that beautiful should be taken out on New Year's Eve. I'd ask her myself, but I know I'm too out of it to even make it through dinner. You should take her out."

"You don't say," Logan muttered.

"Who's Tess?" Annmarie asked her son.

Oh great, here we go. Inside, Logan stifled a groan. "One of my Red Mountain clients, Mom. Stress on the word *client*."

"Oh, don't you give me that 'I don't date clientele' malarkey," Annmarie scoffed. She looked down to Terrence. "Nice woman?"

"I fell yesterday and hit my head," he said. "She lay on the floor with me to keep my spirits up 'til the medics showed up. Perfect stranger."

Annmarie turned her assessing stare back to her son.

"Don't even," he warned.

"Does she have a boyfriend?" Annmarie asked.

"Not that it's any of your business, or mine," Logan said, "but no, as far as I know."

"Then take her out tonight!" she pressed.

"No."

"No? Why not?"

"I'm making you dinner and we're watching a movie, remember?" he said.

"After today's treatment, I'll probably be asleep by nine," she said. "So you'll be alone, and she'll be alone. Take her out!"

Logan pursed his lips, reining in the rant he wanted to let fly.

"Stop looking at me like you want to spit nails," she said. "It'd make me happy to know you're doing something fun tonight. Something besides watching me snore on the couch."

"Easy with the guilt, okay?" Logan sighed. "I'm glad to be with you tonight."

"I am too. But you can do both. Dinner with me, then going out with a beautiful young woman. Sounds like a win to me."

Logan scrubbed his hands over his beard and growled in frustration.

"Didn't mean to cause trouble," Terrence said, grimacing for Logan's sake.

"You didn't," Logan said. "My mother means well. She just forgets sometimes that I'm a thirty-eight-year-old man who's capable of making my own decisions."

She waved him off dismissively. "Excuse me for not seeing the harm in asking a nice, apparently pretty woman out for a coffee."

"Oh, more than pretty," Terrence interjected. "I thought she was maybe a model or something until I found out who she was. That long, tall, skinny look, you know, with this looooong hair . . . and that face! She's striking."

Annmarie's brows lifted. She fixed her son with a mocking glare. "You're a wimp." She turned to Terrence and said, "It was nice to meet you, but I'm afraid Radiology is waiting for me."

"Can you get up there on your own, Mom?" Logan asked. "I left my phone in the truck. I'll meet you upstairs."

He said goodbye to Terrence, watched his mother get on the elevator, then went outside. Head down against the wind, he walked a few steps away from the entrance and took his phone out of his pocket. Shaking his head at himself, he punched in a number before he thought better of it.

"Hello?" Tess answered.

"Hey, Tess. It's Logan." He paced as he talked. "I just ran into Terrence at the hospital. We were going in, he was going out. He seems fine."

"Oh, that's great," Tess said. "He texted me last night and said he hoped they'd release him today. Glad to hear he got the green light. But why are you at the hospital? Are you okay?"

"Yeah, I'm fine. Here with my mom for one of her treatments."

"Ah. I see."

"Yeah. So listen . . ." His pace picked up. "Terrence seems to be under the impression that you're going to be home alone tonight. Is that true?" Logan winced, hating the sound of his own voice just then.

Tess let out a little startled laugh, but said, "Well, yes. Why?"

"I'm making dinner for my mother," he said, "but she's here for radiation, and she's usually pretty wiped out after. She'll be asleep early, probably. So I was just thinking . . ." He looked around, seeing nothing. Was he really doing this? "Maybe you just want to be alone tonight, and I totally get that. But uh . . . if you wanted, my friend owns a coffeehouse. Quiet, very low key. We could just get some coffee, hang out . . ." He shook his head in horror at himself. He hadn't stumbled over asking a woman out like this since college. "No pressure. Just as friends, not like a date, really. If you even want to go out tonight. Some people hate going out on New Year's Eve." He grimaced hard. "Jesus, I'm rambling."

"You are. It's kind of cute."

He laughed at that. "Great. Well, I know it's short notice, but—"

"A low-key, no pressure, non-date sounds nice," Tess said. "What time should I meet you there?"

He blinked, stopping in his tracks. "Umm. I, uh . . . I'll pick you up. That way you can drink if you want. I never do, so I'm a great designated driver."

"Well, actually, I'm not drinking these days either," she said. "So, your call."

"I'll pick you up at nine thirty, if that's all right by you."

"That's fine. What am I wearing? This place is casual?"

"Extremely. Wear your yoga pants if you want."

"Gets better and better. Thanks for the invite, Logan. See you then."

"Great, you got it. See you tonight." He ended the call, shoved his phone in his pocket, and raked his hands through his hair. Holy shit, he'd really done that. And holy shit, she'd said yes, and holy shit, he'd be spending New Year's Eve with Tess Harrison of the New York Harrisons. He didn't know what had possessed him. It wasn't Terrence's hinting or his mother's interference. He never went on impulse like that anymore. Interesting. Huffing out a laugh, it flew out of him in a burst of white steam against the frigid air.

Chapter Six

"After you." Logan held the door open and Tess stepped into the small building. As she followed him farther inside, she looked around. Pale polished wood and vintage-looking chairs and love seats, all covered in rich fabrics and velvets. Dimly lit, the strings of colored lights strewn across the high beams and ceiling gave the room a soft glow, a more intimate feel. Country-rock guitar music played softly. Ford's Coffee House was a warm, cozy place. Tess liked it immediately.

"This is great," she said to Logan. "I already know I'll be back again."

He grinned. "Good, glad to hear it." He looked over toward the bar and called to one of the baristas. "Hey, Caleb. Ford held a spot for me?"

The young man behind the counter nodded as he said hi, then gestured toward a carved-back love seat in the far corner that had a "Reserved" card perched on it.

"Okay," Logan said to Tess. "That's ours."

"Oh really?" She looked up at him with a mischievous smile.

"Good to be friends with the owner." He winked and walked through the small crowd, bringing her along with a hand at the small of her back. The small touch warmed her. He leaned down to be heard over the music as he said, "It's not usually this packed, but with it being New Year's Eve and all, I wanted to make sure we'd have a good place to sit."

When they reached the love seat, covered in burgundy velvet, they took off their coats and sat, slightly turned so they were facing each other.

"Been friends with the owner a long time?" Tess asked.

"Ford? Yeah, since high school. Played football and baseball together." Logan stretched out his long legs, then leaned back a bit, easing into the plush cushions. He was such a big guy, even his most simple movements seemed powerful. "Ford's savvy as hell. He moved here after college to start up a business, and after a few different ones, started this place . . . maybe three or four years ago, now? Something like that."

"Good for him. He has great taste. This place is lovely." Tess swept her hair back over her shoulders. "So you guys grew up not far from here?" She stuck with the easy questions. Something told her even though Logan had asked her out—possibly to prove he wasn't holding his grudge anymore, that was her guess—it didn't mean he'd spill his guts. He was a private man, slow to open up, and that was fine with her. But it only made her more curious.

"We grew up in Arsdale," he said. "Maybe a half hour's drive west of Aspen. Not far at all." He leaned in, resting his elbows on his knees as he asked, "Where'd you grow up? New York, right?"

"Yes, on Long Island. On the North Shore. It's about a forty-minute drive east of the city."

"The city being New York City," he guessed.

"Yeah." She grinned and added, "To anyone who lives within a two-hour radius of it, we just call it the city."

He nodded. "I've never been there. New York City."

Her eyes widened. "Really?"

"Nope. Always wanted to, but never been."

"Oh, you really should. It's amazing. You should go." She crossed her legs and smoothed out her top. "If you ever do, you have to let me know. I'll show you around."

His brows lifted at that. "Would you, now."

"Yes, of course I would. And you'd love it." She smiled back. "That's an open, standing invitation."

His slow grin was so sexy it made her toes curl. He finally nodded and said, "I'll keep that in mind. Thanks."

She ignored the way her skin heated as he eased back into his section of the love seat. His movements were fluid, utterly masculine. And he was sitting close enough for her to know he smelled good. Not bathed in cologne, but clean and woodsy . . . She made herself talk. "I didn't grow up in New York City, by the way. Grew up on Long Island, like I said. That's the suburbs."

He scoffed at that. "You don't strike me as the suburbia-girl type. You're a city girl through and through."

Grinning slightly, she admitted, "Well . . . my suburb wasn't like most suburbs, that's true. Kingston Point is very affluent. My family goes back generations there, I went to private schools, all of that. I traveled, and I did things that most small-town suburban kids don't get to experience." She shifted, recrossing her legs, grateful for the easy comfort of her black leggings and knee-high black Uggs. "But I have a feeling you kind of knew that, didn't you?"

"I looked up the Harrisons when you became my clients, I won't lie." Logan shrugged. "But I didn't really know *where* you grew up, just *how* you likely grew up."

Tess folded her hands on her lap and leaned back. "Different than most."

"I'm sure."

"But with problems and difficulties like most everyone else, Logan. I've had hard times."

He sighed. *Yes, it must have been very hard to never worry about all that money.*

She caught it and frowned at him. "What?"

He shook his head, tamping down his thought.

"Just say it."

"I didn't take you as one to do the 'poor little rich girl' thing," he said quietly. "That's all."

Her eyes flew wide. "I wasn't."

"Kind of sounded like it." He drew another heavy breath. "Tess, you've never had to worry about money, or security, in your whole life. Your 'hard times' are likely not as hard as most people's hard times. You get that, right?"

Her cheeks flamed. "Of course I get that. I'm not that out of touch with reality. When I say I've had hard times, I've had losses. And while I've known financial security, I've never had much in the way of emotional security. My parents' ugly divorce, and my mother leaving us, were stellar examples of how wealth can make bad things a million times worse." She focused on him as the song changed from a slow, twangy groove to a more up-tempo one. She'd always liked Stevie Ray Vaughan, and his "Couldn't Stand the Weather" made her want to shimmy in her seat, even as her stomach churned. Whether or not he'd meant to slight her, she felt slighted. "Should I leave?"

"What? No! Tess . . ." Logan met her gaze and leaned her way. "I wasn't trying to smack you down. It just, at first, sounded—"

"I get how it may have sounded, but it's certainly not how I intended it to sound." She huffed out a sigh, brows drawn as she frowned hard. "Am I naïve to think you'll ever separate who I am from where I come from and what I have? I was born into a very wealthy family. I had no control over that, and I don't have to apologize for it."

"And I'm not asking you to."

"It seems to keep coming up."

"Do you think I asked you out tonight because of how rich you are?"

"No, of course not. If I thought that, I never would have accepted." She moved a stray curl back from her eyes. "But I think you do make assumptions about me because of it, and you either don't even realize it or just won't admit it."

His eyes narrowed as he considered that. She found herself holding her breath.

She didn't want to argue, but goddammit, why did their conversations seem to circle back to a theme: his assumptions about who she was? It was more than frustrating, it was starting to wear on her.

He rubbed the back of his neck as he thought, and her eyes traveled over him. His broad shoulders and strong biceps were easily visible, outlined against his snug, pale blue Henley. The jeans he wore weren't ripped or dirty, but well broken in. Brown hiking boots were obviously his idea of casual footwear. Such simple tastes in how he dressed . . . the plain clothes belied the complicated man. There was so much going on behind his eyes. She could almost feel the gears working in his mind as he gazed at her.

She opened her mouth to speak, but he said, "Look, yeah, I know about your family. I told you, I looked you guys up when you became my clients. I do that for *all* my clients. So I know how mind-bendingly rich and connected the Harrisons are. But give me enough credit to be able to separate that lifestyle from who you are." His large shoulders lifted in a lazy roll, but his gaze didn't waver. "I know you run a big company in Manhattan. That you work, you make your own way. You're not like one of those . . . what I mean is . . ." He sighed, rubbing at his beard the way he did when he was trying to figure out what to say. She'd seen that gesture more over the past few days than ever before.

"I know enough to know that while *you,* of course, are an individual, your *world* is nothing like mine," Logan said. "I've known enough people like you who come to Aspen—and worked in their homes—to know that first-hand. So yeah, you want to talk about how we grew up? Okay. But no, I can't really relate. I'm trying. I'm sorry if that came across as being judgmental, yet again. Wasn't my intention." He huffed out a breath and his pale green eyes flashed with something like remorse. "I'm not great with communication. Typical guy, I guess. I say the wrong things. I'm either too blunt, or not enough. I'm much better with actions than words."

Now she was the one who paused to formulate a proper response. His had been earnest, and illuminating. He made good points. They were from different worlds. Aspen was a playground for the rich and famous, and he worked for them. Of course he had a very different view of her social circles. That made sense. And as for him admitting he wasn't a great communicator, well, that alone made him a more decent one than he realized.

She decided to change tactics. "I appreciate your candor. It's refreshing, actually. Thank you for that." She smiled. "So. How about taking an action and getting me a hot chocolate?"

He blinked, then laughed. "You're just full of surprises, aren't you?"

Her smile widened. "I get the feeling you are too, Mr. Carter."

His heavy brows lifted as he chuckled wryly. "I don't know about that. My life is pretty tame, and these days, so am I." He rose to his feet. "You want whipped cream on that hot chocolate, Miss Harrison?"

"Oh, always."

An hour later, Logan leaned back against the soft cushions as Tess told him more about her career. He'd asked her about it, truly interested to hear about it from her instead of just reading about her online. She'd gone to NYU and majored in art history because she loved it, but minored in business administration so she'd be able to contribute somehow to her family's company, as she knew she was expected to do. For a few years, she painted and traveled and worked at Harrison Enterprises under her father's watchful eye. But when her great aunt had decided she didn't want to run the Harrison Foundation anymore, it was the perfect opening for Tess. She'd taken the reins at the company at only twenty-eight, and had improved its standing tenfold. She was proud of what she'd accomplished and didn't plan to let up anytime soon.

Logan admired that she wasn't bragging about her success—and he knew she was more than entitled to if she wanted. Because he'd read more about her online just last night. When he got home after work, he'd done a little digging, hoping to learn more about this woman who fascinated him. This time, it was all about wanting to know more about *her*.

The Harrison family was a big deal in those circles, and Tess Harrison was kind of a social darling. No one had a bad word to say about her. Every piece on her was more flattering than the one before.

As for her making her own mark beyond the family's reputation, the Harrison Foundation Holiday Ball was one of the biggest annual social events in Manhattan society, and Tess was the powerhouse behind it. This year's ball, only two weeks ago, had raised millions more for their affiliated charities than ever before. *She'd* done that. She'd both made her family's legacy continue to shine and forged her own in the process. As far as he was concerned, based on that alone, Tess Harrison was a force to be reckoned with. He absolutely respected and admired her.

Now, sitting across from him in the dimly lit coffeehouse, with Christmas lights from above casting their glow over her and her long mane of dark curls framing her heart-shaped face, she looked both devastatingly alluring and easily approachable. He could see why everyone was taken with her. Smart, driven, friendly, drop-dead gorgeous . . . How the hell was she single? It confounded him.

Was she too busy to date in New York? Could be. Or more likely, he suspected, men were intimidated by her. Hell, even if she wasn't a successful businesswoman and society sweetheart, her towering beauty alone probably made lesser men quake. Curiosity burned in him now. How was Tess not taken? As it was, he had to admit he felt a tiny swell of masculine pride tonight at not just being out with a truly admirable woman, but also being with the most beautiful woman in the place. And Jesus, she really was. He couldn't take his eyes off her.

"You're zoning out," she said, making him jolt. "I must be boring you now. I'll stop talking about work."

"No, not at all!" Logan said, sitting up straighter. "I asked about your job because I really wanted to hear it from you. But I have a confession to make."

One of her thin brows arched, making her seem regal. "Go on."

"I looked you up online last night. Wanted to know more about you."

Her gaze held. "All right."

"That's not all. The other part is . . . these pictures came up of you at that big holiday ball you hosted a few weeks back." He let a slow grin slide as he recalled the photos. He'd been knocked flat by them.

". . . and?" she coaxed with an answering playful grin, waving her hand for him to continue.

"And I saw pictures of you in that fancy designer dress. Ruby red, sparkling to your toes, all done up . . ." He gazed at her as he said earnestly, "You were stunning. Absolutely breathtaking. Really."

Her smile went soft. "Well, thank you."

He tipped his chin in a respectful nod.

A moment of silence settled over them, but it wasn't as awkward as he thought it would be. He reached for his mug and stole a sip of cocoa, which was almost cold now. "I wasn't stalking you, mind. I just . . . You blew me away with what you did with Terrence. It made me want to know more about you. So yes, I looked, and I'm just fessing up."

She cocked her head to the side, assessing him. "You're telling me flat out you looked me up, so I think we can say it was an info dig, not stalking."

"Is that how it works? Oh good."

She giggled, the light sound sparking warmth in his chest. But then she said, "So, fair's fair. If I looked you up online, what would I find?"

His grin faded. "Not much. And I'd appreciate it if you didn't. I know that's not fair, since I just confessed to looking you up, but . . ." He shook his head, stroked his beard, and looked away.

"Logan . . . ?" She moved in closer. Their knees touched; both of them had such long legs, he was shocked it hadn't happened before, but now the slight touch had his nerves tingling. She looked at him from beneath her long lashes and said, "We all have pasts, Logan. If you dug up enough on me, you'd find things I don't want to talk about too."

"Your past's not like mine," he murmured. Shit, he'd opened himself up for this without seeing it coming. Might as well just tell her some of it. "Look, Tess . . . I started out okay, like anyone else, and then messed up pretty bad. I went through some serious shit, and I didn't handle it well." He scrubbed a hand over his face, then his beard. *Just say it. Nothing to lose.* "In my midtwenties, as a result, I ended up with a serious drinking problem. That's why I don't drink now. Not to be a saint, but because I'm a recovering alcoholic, Tess." He repressed the sigh. Well, there it was. Now she knew. He steeled himself for her withdrawal.

But she didn't even blink. "Okay. You got the help you needed?"

Hey now. No withdrawal, no look of horror. He nodded. "Yes. Took me hitting rock bottom, but I checked myself into rehab and cleaned myself up. Then I left New Orleans and moved back here."

"When was that?"

"Eleven years ago."

"Have you fallen off the wagon since then?"

"Not even once."

Her mouth curved up ever so slightly, and what he saw in her beautiful eyes was . . . whoa. Only compassion and respect. Her voice was gentle when she said, "Then I'd say that's nothing to be ashamed of, Logan. I'd say that's something to be admired."

He stared into her eyes for what felt like a long time. Most people didn't have that response when he told them that dark truth. They looked at him a little differently, whether they realized it or not. Yeah, people had come a long way with understanding alcoholism, especially after they found out what drove him to it . . . but not everyone. They regarded him with trepidation, or maybe judgmental disapproval, and once in a while, pity. His own brother was a self-righteous bastard about it, one of the reasons they'd grown apart. The only ones who'd been cool, who'd been flat out positive about how he'd turned his life around, were his mother and his closest friends. For Tess to be so unfazed, so nonjudgmental . . . he appreciated it more than he could say. Something like warmth stole over him.

Which was quickly followed by a flash of self-loathing. He'd been wrong about her or sold her short so many times now, it was embarrassing. Goddamn.

"I don't know about my being admirable," he finally said, "but I am honest. You've told me a lot about yourself tonight. If you're going to find stuff out about me, I'd rather just tell you myself than have you dig up ugly old shit on the Internet." He flashed a wry grin. "Okay, that's enough of that. We're supposed to be having a good time, remember? New Year's Eve and all that?"

A warm smile spread across her face. "I have been having a good time."

"Yeah? Good. Me too."

"Then let's get the spotlight off of you so you'll relax again," she said. "I liked that you were relaxed around me. Not so gruff and aloof."

"I'm—hey, wait a minute. I'm not gruff and aloof."

"Yeah, okay. And I'm not tall and brown-haired."

He smiled and shook his head in wonder. "You don't hold back, do you?"

"Not often, no."

"Upfront city girl."

"That's right, lumberjack." Her eyes twinkled as her playful smile dazzled him. "How about this: I'll tell you one of my truths, since it's somewhat related to one of yours." She took a deep breath and fidgeted with one of her silver hoop earrings. He watched and waited for her to go on, wondering what she'd say. "Remember I told you I'm not drinking these days either?"

"Yeah."

"Well, I'm no saint. I love a good glass of wine. I'm not drinking now because I've been cleansing my body. No drinking, cleaner eating . . . because I'm planning to get pregnant soon."

Chapter Seven

Logan felt his jaw drop in surprise. *Pregnant?* He stared and stammered, "Uh . . . okay. Wow. Not what I was expecting you to say." Then another thought hit. "Wait a minute. You have a boyfriend and you're out with me tonight? I don't understand."

She smiled with obvious bemusement. "I don't have a boyfriend. I don't have a man in my life at all, actually, which is why I'm planning to . . . well . . . I'm going to do it on my own. Find a sperm donor, and all that entails. Get it now?"

He couldn't have been more shocked. She was the most desirable woman he'd ever seen, and getting to know her made her even more so. She was damned likeable, even when he was being an ass. Why would she feel she had to go that route? He was obviously missing something. But all he said was, "Okay."

"That's the real reason I came out here by myself for a few months." Tess seemed relieved to confess all this, so he stayed quiet and let her continue. "I don't want to start this process at home. My father and brothers . . . They all mean well, but they're a little . . . overbearing. We're very close, my brothers and I. I'd even say they're some of my best friends. But about this . . . Well, they'd all have something to say, and I don't need that."

Logan only nodded.

She stretched out one long leg and rolled her ankle as she continued. "This is *my* decision. They have wives, they have families . . . They'll start their whole *you haven't given it enough of a chance*, yada yada. Like I haven't given this tons of thought, done my homework. Like I just decided *hey! I'll have a baby just because.*"

He noticed her eyes made a slow canvas around the room, not meeting his, as she admitted, "Sure, I wanted to find the right man, fall in love, have a family . . . but that hasn't happened for me. I'll be thirty-eight at the end of February. My clock's ticking, and all I've ever wanted is to have children of my own. So . . . here I am, and I'm not going home until I'm pregnant." She reached over for her mug, almost empty now, but raised it to Logan in a jaunty toast, "You can be my not-drinking buddy this winter."

He grinned at that, but then shook his head in slow wonder. "Well, I . . . I wish you luck. If that's what you want to do, I hope it works out for you."

"Thanks. Just gotta find a healthy sperm sample from someone with great genes, and I'll be all set." She seemed jovial about it.

"And you want to do that *here*?"

"Why not? I own a house here, so I don't have to stay at a hotel for months. I can work remotely. And there's a clinic right here, outside Aspen, that's top-notch." She leaned in and whispered conspiratorially, "See, something like this is where having money definitely does help." She tossed him an exaggerated wink, and he burst out laughing.

He reached for his mug and clinked it to hers. "To you and your plans. I wish you success."

"Thank you very much."

"So no one knows that's why you're really here?"

Her big blue eyes locked on him. "Nope. Just my life-long best friend at home, and you."

"I'm honored you shared that, then. And, uh . . . if you need anything, let me know."

Tess giggled. "Know any sperm donors with super great sperm?"

He almost choked, but turned it into a dry laugh. "Um, no. But if I do, I'll let you know. I meant if you need anything . . . I don't know, you know what I meant."

"I do. And I appreciate it. Thank you."

They both sipped what was left of their cocoa. His was now empty. "I'll get us another round of these, if you like."

"I would, thanks."

He gazed at her as she sat back comfortably, relaxed and beautiful. The colored lights overhead shadowed her in alluring hues. Her long, long curls drifted over her shoulders, down over her arms. The expression on her face was content, but now he knew the truth: The people's princess didn't have everything after all. His heart gave a twinge for her. "For what it's worth, I bet you'll make a great mother. Because you're a really good person."

She blinked at him. "That's . . . nice of you to say. Especially since just the other day, I thought you didn't even like me."

"I was wrong," he said quickly, firmly. "I was an ass-hole. What you called me on, you were right." *I didn't want to admit to myself how much I like you, so I grabbed on to whatever I could to convince myself otherwise.* He rose and grabbed both empty mugs. "And hey, any woman who'd lie down on a hotel lobby floor to comfort a stranger?" He nodded slowly to punctuate his point. "That's a caring, compassionate person. Deep in your core, something like that shows who you are. That's what will make you a great mom."

"I hope so." Tess's voice dropped, and she looked away. "I worry sometimes. I didn't have the best role model in that department."

He sat again, suddenly curious. "Not close to your mom, huh?"

"Noooooo."

Logan caught the flash in her big blue eyes: resentment. Interesting.

"You're close to your mom, though," Tess said. "And that's lovely. How was she today? Hope her treatment was okay?"

He saw right through her attempt to change the subject, but damn, he was liking her more and more. He put the mugs back on the small table and sat down. "She's all right, thanks. Just wiped out, like usual. I cooked her one of her favorite dinners, and we watched about half a movie before she fell asleep. Which is pretty much what she predicted would happen."

"She's always right, huh?" Tess guessed with a cheeky grin.

Logan laughed. "She sure thinks she is."

"That's sweet that you cooked for her. Are you any good?"

"What, at cooking?" He put a hand on his heart as if affronted. "Of course I am!"

"Well, good. That makes one of us." She laughed, but said earnestly, "You're clearly a devoted son. Your mom is lucky to have you."

"Well, I'm all she's got." Logan briefly explained about

how his father had died years ago and his brother lived his own life in the Northwest. "So, the way I see it, she and I are lucky to have each other. Just wish she'd get off my back about getting married."

Tess gave him a look. "What?"

"Ah, hell. She means well. She just . . . She wants me to settle down. I tried that once, and it was a disaster. I'm not cut out for relationships, much less married life." He sat back. "I do better on my own. But she doesn't get that. I, uh . . ." He sighed and scrubbed a hand over his face and beard as he admitted, "I know she doesn't want me to be alone after she passes, so she worries. It's that simple. So I get it, but jeeeez, I wish she'd lay off."

Tess chuckled.

"That's funny to you?" he asked, unable to hold back his own budding grin.

"That last part? Yeah, a little," she admitted. She sat up a bit straighter to gesture over him with her hands. "Look at you! You're this tremendous, powerful guy. Strong, capable . . . and your mom's giving you a hard time about dating? That's kind of funny."

"Yeah, if you're not the one who has to hear about it all the time," Logan grumbled, but his smile gave him away. "Sounds fucking pathetic, doesn't it."

They laughed together, and Tess set her hand on his forearm. "You know what? I wish my mother gave enough of a crap about me to worry about if I'd end up alone, or if I was okay, or if I was happy. I haven't seen her in over a year. Before that, I hadn't seen her in two years, and who knows when I will again. She's too busy jet-setting around Europe to bother with her children or grandchildren. So your mom may be a little overbearing, but she sounds wonderful to me."

"She is," he said. He looked deeper into Tess's eyes. "I'm sorry your mom sounds like a real . . . piece of work."

"No worries. I'm used to it." Tess's gaze softened, turned sad. "I'm sorry your mom is so sick. So deeply sorry."

His throat tightened, and he swallowed hard. "Thank you. Me too."

They stared into each other's eyes, connecting silently. She reached over to give his hand a squeeze, and when she did, something like an electric current shot right up his arm.

Damn, he wanted to draw her in, hold her close. He didn't, though. That would blow their "no pressure, non-date" sky-high. He'd promised her a friendly evening, and he was a man of his word.

"Half an hour to midnight!" someone shouted, and people in the place cheered.

"Night's flying by," she murmured, still staring at him even as she withdrew her hand.

"I know." He cleared his throat and scrubbed his hands over his face, as if to wake up from whatever spell she'd just put him under. It'd be all too easy to drown in the depths of her marine-blue eyes. But something . . . something had just passed between them. Had she felt it too? "I have to tell you, I'm enjoying this. I'm glad I asked you out, and I'm glad we're here. Thanks for saying yes."

"Thanks for asking me. This is nice." She nestled back against the cushions. Her red V-neck top shifted, molding itself tighter to her narrow frame, and he tried not to stare. He bet her small breasts would fit perfectly in his hands, and in his greedy, wanting mouth. *Shit.* He averted his gaze, looking around the room, trying to clear the sizzling images of her naked body from his mind. "Better get those hot cocoas." He got to his feet.

* * *

At a quarter to midnight, Logan and Tess were talking about classic movies when a tall, dark-haired man came over. With an easy smile, he sat himself down on the wooden coffee table beside their mugs of cocoa. "What, you don't say hello? Some friend you are."

"I didn't think you were here!" Logan cried, and gave the man a quick clap of a hug. "Jesus, have you been here the whole night?"

"Actually, no. Bustin' your chops. I was out to dinner, just got here a few minutes ago." The attractive man turned his dark, assessing gaze to Tess. "Hello there."

"Tess," Logan said, "this is my friend Ford Rafferty. He owns the place. Ford, this is Tess Harrison."

"Pleasure to meet you," she said, shaking Ford's hand.

"The pleasure is mine." Ford's warm brown eyes drank her in. "Now I know why a hermit like Thor here would go out on New Year's Eve."

"Thor?" Tess asked on a laugh.

"He calls me that because he's a jackass," Logan said dryly.

"I call him that because *duh*, look at him," Ford shot back. "If his hair was a little longer, he'd look just like Thor. God knows he's as big as him."

"Bigger," Logan joked. "And his eyes are blue. Mine aren't."

"You're just nitpicking now," Ford said, and turned his teasing grin Tess's way. "I got him the hammer for Halloween, but he wasn't amused. I thought it was perfect."

She grinned back and said, "Have to admit, Logan . . . you do look a lot like Hemsworth. I'd have loved to see you with that hammer. The nickname fits."

"Not you too," Logan groaned.

"This woman is not only beautiful, but smart!" Ford proclaimed.

Logan rolled his eyes.

"I like this place," Tess said to Ford. "You've got a good thing going on here."

"Thanks!" His smile widened. "Glad you like it. Where are you from, Tess?"

Logan watched Ford and Tess chat. Ford was always so at ease, smooth, a natural flirt and charmer. He bet if he gave them a few minutes alone, Ford would be asking Tess out himself. And that . . . gave Logan a bit of a burn inside. Something territorial, something like jealousy. Which was ridiculous; Tess wasn't his. She wasn't anything but a friendly acquaintance.

A friendly acquaintance looking for a healthy sperm donor . . . Maybe he should encourage her and Ford to hook up. God knew Ford would never settle down with one woman, so maybe it would be a good arrangement for both of them. But the thought of it agitated him. What the hell was that about?

Ford rose to his feet. "Gotta get to work. I'm sending champagne around the room in a minute, on the house for everyone . . . sparkling cider over here?" His gaze flicked to his friend.

"Thanks," Logan said.

"That'd be perfect," Tess agreed. "Thank you." Her smile was radiant. The strings of lights sparkled around her, making her seem, for a moment, like an angel.

Logan was suddenly overwhelmed by an urge to kiss her. Hard, long, and deep.

"It was a serious pleasure meeting you, Tess. You'll

have to come back." Ford reached for her hand to shake it again and held it just a few seconds too long.

"Lovely to meet you too," she said, not seeming to notice the subtle, prolonged contact. "Happy New Year, if we don't see you on the way out," she added. "I know what it's like when you're the host, how busy it gets."

"Yeah, I better get back to it." He turned to Logan, who stood up. They clasped each other in a quick hug. "She's fucking stunning," Ford murmured. "Jesus Christ."

"Yup." Logan pulled back and said, "Happy New Year, brother."

"Same! Great to see you. We'll talk soon." Ford started to move away as he said, "Send my best to Annmarie, okay?"

"Will do."

Logan took his seat again as Tess asked, "Annmarie is your mom?"

"Yeah."

"He's known her a long time, then," Tess remarked.

"Yeah. He's a good guy," Logan said.

"He seems it. Charming, too."

"He is that." Logan slanted her a sideways glance. "You, uh . . . have any interest? Because he was practically tripping over himself over you."

"He was not."

"Hell yes, he was."

She cocked her head and stared at him. "Are you trying to set me up with him?"

"Uh . . . do you want me to?" Logan asked, even as a surge of jealous heat threatened to choke him.

"No, thank you. I can get dates on my own." Amused, she arched a thin brow at him, that regal look again. "Besides, I'm not looking to date right now. I have bigger plans, remember? I need to be alone, it's better that way. The last thing I need as I'm trying to find a sperm donor and become pregnant is someone to mess up my focus. Dating will have to come later . . . if at all. Once I'm a single mother, that'll change things too." She sighed. "Too much information?"

"Nope. I understand, it makes sense," Logan said. Relief unraveled the knot in his chest. "I just thought Ford is healthy, single . . ."

"I'll find my own sperm donor, thanks," she said on a bemused chuckle.

Heat rose in his face. "Yeah, I'll leave that to you. Sorry."

"Not at all. It was kind of sweet for you to think of that." Her eyes left his to flutter up to the girl who'd appeared before them.

"Ford asked me to bring these to you," she said, handing them two plain glass flutes filled with fizzing pale gold liquid.

"Thank him for us," Logan said as he took them. He handed one to Tess as the music overhead changed to an upbeat romp. Someone gave a hearty whoop and a holler, and the energy in the whole place went up a few notches. Logan checked his watch. "Five minutes to go."

Tess smiled in response and sat up, looking around the coffeehouse to take in the scene. Logan watched her, entranced. So beautiful. Probably the most beautiful woman in the whole damn room. He was glad to be there with her. He was glad he'd gone out at all, and that it had gone well.

"So," she said, turning back to him. She held her glass in one hand between long, manicured fingers. "Make a wish for the new year, and we'll compare notes next year and see if it came true."

"You first," he said, taken by the light in her eyes.

"Besides the obvious, I want to have a baby? Um . . ." She considered for a few moments, the sounds of the other patrons and music swirling around them. "I hope to have an unexpected adventure. Something that'll bring real joy."

"Along with being pregnant? Sounds interesting."

"Why not?"

"Why not indeed. That's a good New Year's wish."

"And you, Mr. Carter?"

He grinned, stroking his beard with his free hand as he thought. "An unexpected adventure sounds good. With what's around the bend, I'll likely need one. Something to bring me some peace."

Her gaze softened, went liquid. She gently tapped her glass to his. "That's a great New Year's wish. I hope you have that."

"To both of us having joy and peace in the New Year," he said. They sipped their sparkling cider and their gazes locked . . . then the room erupted around them. In lively shouts, the people in the room counted down the last ten seconds of the year, and all Logan could do was stare into Tess's eyes. When the clock struck midnight and everyone cheered and yelled in excitement, he leaned forward, cupped the back of her neck, and gently pulled her in. His mouth grazed hers in a soft, sweet kiss.

He lingered for a delicious moment, savoring the feel of her lips against his. But when he went to pull back, her hand flew up to cup his cheek, bringing his mouth back to hers for more. He kissed her harder this time, full and blazing. Her lips parted, an invitation, and he took it. His tongue swept inside as he deepened the kiss, tasting her sweetness. Insistent warmth flowed through him. She inched closer, meeting his heat with her own, and he lost himself in her. Sounds and colors around them disappeared . . . There was nothing but them, and the moment.

The searching kisses burned hot and slow, their mouths moving sensually together, tongues tangling, shortened breaths. His fingers sifted through her hair, the softness of her thick curls a delicious surprise. She moaned softly into his mouth, yielding to him . . . A loud cheer across the room startled him and he pulled back, breathing as hard as if he'd hiked up the side of the mountain.

Her eyes, heavy-lidded and dark with desire, locked with his. He realized she was breathing heavy too, and fire seared through his veins, leaving him stunned.

"Happy New Year," she whispered.

"Happy New Year," he whispered back. His fingertips trailed along the side of her face. Her skin was impossibly soft. He felt like he was in a trance.

Something vibrated against her leg. With a start, she realized it was her phone, which she'd left beside her on the love seat. Blushing as she laughed, she picked it up to look at the screen. "My brother," she said. "He's always the first to call on New Year's."

"Which one?" Logan asked. His voice felt thick in his throat and the room seemed a little hazy. His blood still pounded through his veins, and his jeans felt way too tight.

"Charles," she said. "Do you mind . . . ?"

"Of course not, take the call."

He sat back and gulped down the cider as he watched her briefly chat on the phone. That had been a hell of a kiss. And yes, he'd initiated it, but she'd taken it a step further. She'd been as into it as he was. Damn, she was so gorgeous. And sexy, and . . .

He downed the rest of the drink and set the empty glass

on the table. Whatever was bubbling up inside, he had to put a lid on it immediately. So what if that kiss showed the attraction was mutual. So what if it'd been steamy as hell and made him want to lay her back on the love seat and take her right there. She'd been very clear: no dating for her. She wanted to be alone.

They were friends. Kind of. And that was all they would be. If they ever kissed again, it'd have to come from her. He wouldn't push it. He was an honorable man, he'd respect her boundaries, and that was that.

Her eyes met his as she wrapped up the call, and a catlike grin spread across her beautiful face. *Damn*, he wanted her. The force of it gripped him with claws, the rock-hard evidence still straining painfully against his jeans. He schooled his features into neutrality and took some deep breaths, willing the haze of lust to dissipate. The memory of that mind-bending kiss would have to last him, and that was all there was to it. Tess Harrison was off-limits.

Tess enjoyed the warmth and quiet inside Logan's truck as he drove her home. The black sky outside was filled with stars. "It always amazes me," she said as she stared out the window, "the sky here at night. Seems bigger than in New York. And the stars! You can see so many. And they truly sparkle. It's breathtaking."

"I know what you mean." Logan's deep voice was soft. "I didn't realize how much I loved it until I moved away. The sky *is* different here, I think. Seems that way, anyway." He kept his eyes on the road as he maneuvered around the bends of Red Mountain in the dark. "When I moved from

New Orleans, I spent a lot of nights sitting outside, just staring up at the stars. It was . . . very soothing. Calming."

"Sounds very Zen," she said.

His cynical grin delighted her. "Yeah, well, that's about as Zen as I get, I suppose."

"Too pragmatic for all that?" she guessed.

"Yeah. I've just . . . seen too much, I guess." His lips flattened into a thin line. "Gave up on things like that—Zen, inspirational crap, magic, all that—a while back. I used to think everything happened for a reason. Then I came to realize it's all bullshit. Sometimes, bad things happen and there's no goddamn explanation. That's it."

His voice wasn't hard, but the words were. She wondered what he'd seen to make him feel that way. The lines around his eyes crinkled as he squinted into the darkness. He lapsed into a darkness of his own at times, and she wanted to know why. She wanted to know him better.

But he was something of a loner, a man who cherished his solitude. And things he'd told her tonight had only reinforced her suspicions: The man was an island. Which was fine, but she needed to focus all her energies on herself right now, not on this enigmatic man and what made him tick, no matter how alluring she found him. No matter how he could kiss her and make her feel like he was both devouring and revering her at the same time.

God, that kiss . . . It'd been incredible. She wondered if there was any chance of a repeat when she got home, or if that'd been a one-time, New-Year's-Eve-at-midnight kiss. Her fingertips drifted to her lips as she recalled how his warm, firm mouth felt against hers. The command in his touch, the barely restrained fire . . . Her belly did a little flip and she swallowed hard.

When he pulled up the long driveway and stopped at

her front door, he got out before she even had her coat zippered up. He opened her door for her and offered a hand to help her out of the truck, a perfect gentleman.

She murmured thanks as she stepped out. They stood there, smiling pleasantly at each other.

"Thank you for tonight," she said. "I really enjoyed our time together."

"I did too," he said. "It was great."

"So you're finally convinced I'm not an entitled rich brat?" she asked.

His eyes fell away in obvious embarrassment, then lifted to meet hers. "I was very wrong about you. Have you forgiven me for being a horse's ass about it?"

"Absolutely." Her smile broadened. He was so close that even in the frigid air, she could feel the heat coming off his large, powerful body. Warmth pooled in her limbs, searing through her more sensitive parts . . . She didn't want the night to end. She wanted to wrap herself in his strong arms. To take him inside and luxuriate in more of those hot, bone-melting kisses.

But this wasn't supposed to be a date. And it was freezing outside. She cleared her throat and said, "Good night, Logan. Thank you again for tonight." She put her hands on his broad chest, leaning against him to rise and press her lips to his cheek.

His hands came up and wrapped around her arms, holding her there. Her cheek leaned against his, his beard tickling her and sparking fresh desire. He didn't kiss her, but held her close for a lingering moment. Her heart started pounding in her chest. All she had to do was turn her face and she could kiss him . . . It seemed like maybe he wanted to? But no . . . If he wasn't kissing her, maybe he didn't want to again. Not knowing what to do, she drew back.

His pale green eyes blazed with intensity as he stared down at her. He opened his mouth as if to say something, but then stopped. A hint of a wistful smile curved his lips, and all he said was, "Good night, Tess. Happy New Year."

"Happy New Year," she said, and pulled away from him to go inside.

Chapter Eight

Logan shone the flashlight at the boiler in the dark basement of the LeFabrays' ski house, squinting as he examined it. This was the second time the pilot light had gone out in the last week. Something was definitely wrong; he just had to figure out what. It'd seemed like an easy fix when he was here on the twenty-eighth. The fact that it was out again by the second irritated him more than anything. It shouldn't have happened again. He hadn't missed anything, he was always thorough . . . He suspected it was time for a new boiler, and though his clients upstairs had more money than God, they'd grumble about that.

Half an hour later, after a slightly unpleasant conversation with Blaine and Missy LeFebray, he climbed into his truck, grateful for the whip of the cold morning air against his face. He needed a second cup of coffee, or a run on the treadmill. As he turned on the ignition and decided which to pursue first, his phone buzzed in his coat pocket. Three texts; they must have come in while he was in the basement. As it was, cell reception on Red Mountain could be spotty, but in the basement of a McMansion, he absolutely hadn't gotten those messages.

The first was from his mom, saying good morning and

asking if he'd come by for dinner. The second, from Ford, a simple *hey, what's up*. The third was from Tess, asking if he'd give her a call when he was able to, she had a question. A little thrill rolled through him. He'd had her on his mind since he'd dropped her off at her house about thirty-six hours before. New Year's Eve with her had been really nice . . . and then, more than nice. That kiss had him in lusty knots every time he recalled it, which was often. The way she felt, the way she smelled, the way her wide blue eyes sparkled with laughter or darkened with desire . . . dammit, she was in his head, and getting under his skin.

He'd decided space would probably be a good thing, no matter how much he found himself drawn to her. But one text, and here he was, answering her right away.

"Good morning, Logan. Thanks for getting back to me so soon."

He liked her voice. Warm, friendly, yet the intelligence shone through. "Sure. What can I do for you? Everything okay?"

"Yeah, everything's fine. Remember when I said I wanted to go skiing soon, and you said you could set that up for me if I wanted?"

"Yeah, sure." He reached for his sunglasses and put them on. The glare off the snow was blinding. "Which mountain were you thinking?"

"We've always gone to Ajax," Tess said. "I could easily set up a reservation myself, and I'm going to. But I was wondering if you would join me. Do you ski?"

He paused, his brain processing her request. "Uh, yeah. Of course."

"Would you like to join me, then? I haven't been skiing in two years, I'm likely rusty. And besides, it's more fun to go with someone than hit the slopes alone."

"That's true." If she skied on Ajax, she must be a decent skier; that mountain was for intermediate to expert levels. The thought of going skiing with her . . . She wanted him to go with her? He hated how he was grinning, alone in the truck like a loon. Jesus, he was like . . . smitten. Shit.

"It'd be my treat," she continued. "You took me out the other night, paid for everything on our friendly non-date . . . Now it's my turn."

"You're on. Plus, I can keep an eye on you. Wouldn't want you falling all over yourself on your own, now would we?"

"Oh good." She sounded amused. "My schedule is wide open, but you have work hours to consider. So tell me when would be good for you, and I'll set it up."

"Um . . ." He ran through his week's schedule in his head. Lighter than usual, at the moment. And Mom didn't have radiation again until the fourth . . . "I can do tomorrow afternoon. I'm free after twelve thirty. That's enough time before it gets dark, right?"

"Absolutely! So I tell you what. I'll set it all up, you just meet me there. Ajax at one o'clock, then?"

"Sounds good."

When the call ended, Logan sat for another minute in his truck, thinking over the invite. This budding friendship, or whatever this was, budding between him and Tess, gave him more of a rush than he wanted to admit. She was like a breath of fresh air, yet tangled him up in knots at the same time. Spending time with a gorgeous, smart, nice woman wasn't the worst thing that had happened to him lately, that was for sure. And just as friends, no pressure? He'd try to get out of his own way and enjoy it.

* * *

Tess yawned as she lay back against the couch. Her eyes were tired from staring at her laptop for three hours straight, and she rubbed them gently to soothe them. The house was quiet, save for the Jack Johnson music playing off her sound system. After her call with Logan in the morning, she'd gone to her yoga class, then spent the rest of the day doing more research. By the late afternoon, she'd made the all-important call: She had an appointment with a doctor at the Garrity Fertility Center for the day after tomorrow. The Garrity, located on the outskirts of Aspen, was a highly touted fertility and reproductive medicine clinic, and the doctor she'd requested was on several Best Of lists. Time to get the party started. It could take months until she conceived . . . if she did at all. She didn't think she'd have a problem, but she was almost thirty-eight already, so who knew?

No more waiting. She knew she wanted a baby. She longed for one, ached for a little boy or girl to share her life with and lavish her love upon. Maybe, if the first time went well, she'd even be able to do it a second time. She'd always wanted more than one child . . . she'd been so glad to have siblings growing up, and wanted the same for her own family.

She took a few deep breaths and kept her tired eyes closed. Peace and quiet settled over her, even as a spark of excitement hummed through her bones. This time next year, she could be pregnant. Or even, if she was extraordinarily lucky, she could be a mother already. Smiling to herself as that thought warmed her, she tried to decide what to have for dinner.

Her phone rang, shattering her serenity. Bubbles barked at the sound. Mildly annoyed by the intrusion, Tess leaned over to pick up her phone and glance at the screen. The annoyance increased tenfold. With a little huff, she answered the call. "Hello, Mother."

"Happy New Year, darling!" Laura Dunham Harrison Evans Bainsley's voice was full of overexaggerated affection.

"It's January second," Tess pointed out.

"Oh, don't be such a stick-in-the-mud," Laura said. "This is the first chance I've had to call you. I was in Saint-Tropez, on a yacht, on New Year's Eve. It was fabulous. Wish you'd been there with me!"

"Sure you do," Tess said. She rolled onto her side to gaze at the flames that burned in the fireplace. "Glad you had a nice time."

"I did, I always do. So how are you? What did you do for New Year's?"

"I'm at the house in Aspen."

"Oh! That's great. Spending a week there at the holidays is always nice."

"Actually, I'm going to be staying here for a while. Couple of months, I think. I'm playing it by ear." Tess had no desire to let her mother in on her plans . . . yet at the same time, a tiny bit of yearning snuck in, deep inside. She wished, as she planned to have a baby on her own, that she had a mother she could talk to, confide in, lean on for support.

But she and her brothers had never had that. Not since they were small kids. Tess had been ten years old when her father threw her mother out and banished her from seeing the children on a regular basis. Not that Laura tried very hard to fight him on that. She'd taken her hefty settlement and left to travel the world. She'd remarried and divorced two more times, left a trail of spurned lovers in her wake . . . and now, showed very little interest in her grown children or young grandchildren.

Charles and Dane still maintained basic contact, calling their mother on holidays and her birthday. Tess and Pierce had given up on her, the same way she'd given up on the four of them. The resentment and hurt Tess had swallowed because of her mother had made her sick in her teenage years . . . until she'd gotten to a point of no return. At nineteen, Tess had an emergency appendectomy; if she hadn't gotten to the hospital when she did, she would have died, and as it was she stayed in the hospital for an extra few days to fight off an ensuing infection. Her mother never even called, much less came to see her. Realizing, at last, how little she meant to her mother . . . something in Tess broke away then, never to rebound. Only one person on the planet really mattered to Laura: Laura.

"Are you there?" Laura asked tersely. "Tess?"

"I'm here." Tess had zoned out, lost in her thoughts. "Sorry, what'd you say? I switched ears and didn't hear you," she lied.

"I asked why you're staying in Aspen for so long. Got a hot ski instructor hidden away there or something?"

"No." Tess cringed. She'd never be a man-eater like her mother. The very thought made her vaguely sick. "Just wanted a change of scene for a while."

"For that long?" Laura paused, her tone changing. "Why? Is everything okay?"

"Yes, everything's fine."

"You sure?"

"Yes, I'm sure," Tess asserted. *Going to start playing the concerned mother now? It's a little late for that.* "So are you still in Saint-Tropez?"

"Yes, for the rest of this week. Then I'm going to Saint Bart's for the rest of January."

"Tough life you lead," Tess quipped. "Well, enjoy."

"Why don't you come join me for a few days?" Laura asked. "Three whole weeks in paradise, plenty of room in the villa. We could have a mother-daughter getaway!"

A part of Tess's heart leapt. Laura hadn't invited her along on her travels in years. The little girl in her who'd always longed for her mother's attention experienced a quick flash of happiness. But she hadn't been a little girl in a long time, and her mother hadn't been a regular part of her life for a long time either. Tess did what she'd done over and over since she was nineteen: shut her mother out. "Thanks for the offer," Tess said, "but I've got some things lined up here. I'm staying put."

"Seriously? I can understand going to ski in Aspen for a short trip, it's a gorgeous place. But why the hell would you want to spend more than a few days in the cold during wintertime?" Laura asked with a mixture of confusion and irritation.

"Just call me snow bunny," Tess wisecracked.

"Ugh. That is *so* not for me," Laura said in a haughty tone. "Well, enjoy your freezing temperatures and snow. I'll be hopping from beach to beach until May."

"I expect nothing less," Tess said flatly. "Well, I have to go feed Bubbles."

"Oh, all right. Can't believe you still have that dog. She must be old by now."

"She's only six."

"I don't know anything about dog years. Is that old or not?"

"No," Tess said, not wanting to bother with the conversation any longer. "Thanks for calling. Glad to hear you're fine. Take care, Mother."

"Oh, you too, darling. Happy New Year! And listen . . ."

Tess braced herself.

"Go find yourself a nice, strong ski instructor to keep you busy while you're in Aspen. Or a wealthy older man. Plenty of those around, I'm sure." Laura sighed. "You're not getting any younger, sweetie. Gotta get your first husband out of the way!"

Laura gave a shrill, dry laugh at her own joke. It grated on Tess's last nerve. "Goodbye, Mother."

"Bye, darling! Be good, but not too good."

Tess ended the call and tossed her phone onto the far end of the couch with a grunt of disgust. Her mother's words didn't bother her; she'd learned to ignore them long ago. It was the general worry that crept in once in a while, like now. What if Tess didn't know how to be a good mother? She'd had the worst role model possible. Her plan was basically to do the opposite of anything Laura had done . . . She hoped she'd be good enough.

All she knew was her own child would never know the heartbreak, anxiety, or disappointment of being abandoned by its mother. Growing up that way herself, she wouldn't wish those feelings on anyone, and she'd certainly never perpetuate them.

"Thank you, sweetheart." Annmarie smiled up at her son as he helped lower her onto the couch. "Dinner was delicious. The chicken was perfect, nice and juicy. You really can cook."

"Well, I learned from the best," Logan said, shooting her a little smile. "Glad you liked it." For someone who claimed to like her meal, she hadn't eaten much. He studied her as she made herself more comfortable, shifting to stretch out and lie down. Her skin looked drawn. She didn't look like she was in the final stages or anything, but she didn't look good either. He frowned, then felt his brows furrowing and schooled his features into neutrality. She wouldn't want to see him frowning over her.

"I need to talk to you about something," she said. Her gaze was direct.

"Uh-oh," he joked, but uneasiness gripped his insides as he sat beside her.

"I've been thinking all week about this," she began. "Given this a lot of thought. And . . . I've made a decision. I don't want to do the radiation anymore."

Logan's heart dropped to his stomach. "What?"

"It's not working, honey," she said quietly. "All it's doing is prolonging the inevitable. I'm tired. I'm tired of being so tired."

He shook his head vehemently, a hint of bile rising in his throat. "I'm not hearing this. No. No way."

"Logan—"

"Hell no. You can't stop, Mom. Just *no*."

"Why not?" She sat up and stared at him, a hard look on her face. "Logan. Honey. Look at me."

He did, even as his heart thudded in his chest and blood pulsed in his head.

"We've fought hard," she said quietly. "But I'm tired." She reached out and put her hand on his knee. "Sweetheart . . ."

"I can't have this conversation," he said, dropping his head into his hands.

"We have to."

"No, we don't." He looked at her again. "You keep fighting. You can't give up. That's it." He shot to his feet.

"You're not hearing me." She sighed.

"I'm picking you up at noon on Friday to take you to radiation, and that's all there is to it." He scrubbed his hands over his beard and added, "We'll talk to Dr. Cranston, discuss where we go from here, okay? See what he thinks. But giving up just isn't an option."

She looked up at him sadly. "I've never been a quitter and you know it. But sometimes . . . you need to know when to call it."

"Really?" Suddenly angry, he started to pace the small living room. His lungs felt tight, and his blood raced through his body. "When I tanked my life—drank myself into a fucking stupor, lost my job, and my wife left me— what did you do? You flew down to New Orleans. Told me to get my ass in rehab. Paid for it, if I remember correctly."

"Logan—"

"You told me to keep fighting. I'd made a wreck of everything, and you told me Carters are fighters."

"This is different," she said.

"Not much," he said. "I was fighting for my life, and I didn't even know it. You're fighting for your life now." He stood before her, stared down, and tried not to let his panic show through, only his determination. "You didn't let me give up. I'm not letting you give up. End of story."

She met his gaze, unblinking. "You didn't realize you were killing yourself," she said with quiet steel. "I know I'm dying, Logan. You know it too. Maybe I want to do it on my own terms, whatever of those I have left."

That made him stop cold. Waves of emotions crashed through him, a mixture of fear, rage, hopelessness . . . "Fuck that," he spat. "We're not calling anything yet. You hear me?"

She sighed heavily. "We'll let this go for tonight. I'm sorry you're this upset."

"What'd you think I'd be?" he cried. "How could I be anything else?"

"I haven't seen you this emotional in a long time," she admitted. "You do such a good job of swallowing things most of the time, being all stoic and sure. I forgot how fired up you can get."

He raked his hands through his hair and looked around, a bit wild. His ears were ringing, like they used to when anxiety would sweep in and take over. He steeled himself against it. "I'm picking you up for your appointment on Friday, and you better be dressed and ready to go. Got that?"

"Yes sir, bossy." She sighed and lay back down. "You want to watch some TV?"

"I want to shake you is what I wanna do," he growled.

"Go for it."

He huffed out a breath, something between a laugh and a sigh. His stomach churned and his blood still pulsed in his head, the start of a stress headache. But at least he didn't want a drink. That was a relief. He rubbed his face and rolled his head around on his neck.

"Sit down, Thor," she said. "You never did tell me about New Year's Eve with that Tess. How'd it go?"

"I didn't tell you because I don't report my activities to you." His grumble was good-natured as he sat down again in the armchair. He willfully ignored the traces of adrenaline still shooting through him, reached for the remote, and turned on the television.

"Throw me a bone here," Annmarie needled with a grin. "Did you kiss her at midnight, at least?"

The memory of their steamy kisses flashed through Logan's mind, sending a new rush through his veins. "Maybe."

"Damn, I hope so. You're cranky as hell lately. Need a good woman in your life."

"Says you."

"That's right. Now gimme." She held out her hand and he forked over the remote. "Are you going to go out with her again?"

He sighed. She was relentless. "Actually, we're going skiing tomorrow. Up on Ajax."

"Wellllll!" His mother's smile was both pleased and a bit smug. "Must've been some kiss at midnight, then!"

"She's just a friend, Mom," he cautioned. "Don't get all nutty."

"I've always been nutty," she said. "That ship sailed long ago, my sweet boy."

He laughed and sat back as she searched through the channels for the show she liked. Glancing at her, he took deep breaths . . . flexing his fingers, open and shut . . . The crisis had been avoided, but only temporarily, and he knew it. His stomach churned for the rest of the night.

Chapter Nine

Tess had forgotten how exhilarating it was to fly down the side of a mountain at top speed. She hadn't been skiing in too long, and as she pushed off yet again, the feel of the cold air rushing past her as she sailed along the slope was invigorating. As kids, her brothers were competitive with one another but doted on her, making sure she was a solid skier and could keep up with them. Some of her best childhood memories were skiing with them in Aspen, Vermont, Canada, and Switzerland. She still loved the rush of soaring across the snow, the closest thing to flying a human could experience. Few things compared.

And Logan was right beside her the whole time. He was a great skier, a natural athlete—definitely better than her. Of course, he did it more often. He told her flat out he'd all but grown up on the slopes and still went skiing two or three times a month in the winter. Knowing that, she was just glad she'd stayed upright most of the time after a two-year lapse. The one time she'd ended up on her ass, Logan had chuckled kindly and immediately shot out a hand to help her up.

The cloudy sky cut down on sun glare, but she'd still

made sure to apply sunblock and lip balm before putting on her gator. Her goggles made it easy to steal glances at her gorgeous companion. Logan was sexy even hidden under the layers of his royal-blue shell jacket and the gray ski pants that hugged his powerful legs, a delicious bonus of inviting him along. Even the way his thick hair poked out of the bottom of his wool hat, fringing haphazardly past his strong jaw, appealed to her. In between runs they chatted about the ski trips of their childhoods; she told him about the annual trips with her father and brothers, and he told her about how his family went skiing all the time, right there in Colorado.

Time flew by on the mountain. The light of the sky changed, the late afternoon bringing hints of the darkness that would soon fall. "Okay, I'm wiped," she told him. "Totally ready for some hot cocoa and to sit for a long time in front of the fire. Kind of starving too. How about you?"

"Same," Logan said. They headed back toward the main lodge. "Aww, you know what would be the capper? All that and then a soak in a hot tub. Maybe I'll pop by the gym after I drop you at your house and do that."

The thought of him soaking naked in a hot tub was too hot for her to handle. "The tub in my master bathroom doubles as a Jacuzzi," she said, "which you know, of course. When you bring me back, you're welcome to stay for a while and use it before you go home."

He shot her a sideways glance, a mixture of uncertainty and a spark of flirtation that made her knees wobble. "Really."

"Yeah, really," she said. "I'm starving, I need to eat something first, but why not? If you'd like to have some time in a tub, I have one. I'd be more than happy to let you." *And I wish I could watch*, she thought, biting her lip.

His gaze smoldered as he considered it, making a few butterflies stir in her belly. Then, his voice low, he said, "I tell you what. You paid for the lift tickets and everything so far today. Let me buy you a late lunch, and I'll feel better about taking you up on that offer. Which I just might."

Her insides went hot and wavy with pure lust. She was shocked she'd made such a suggestion, and ten times more so that he was possibly saying yes. The thought of this towering man, exuding testosterone and rugged sex appeal, being naked in her tub just beyond her bedroom . . . it sent her heart rate up a notch. But she played it cool and said, "There are three restaurants in the lodge. Get me fed, and you have a deal."

He grew quiet as they got to the ski check. They got their skis off and he grabbed the claim check before she could. But he smiled brightly at her as they approached the building, and held the door open for her as they headed into the side entrance of the magnificent lodge. Picturesque, all warm woods and glass, the Ajax Mountain Lodge was crammed with people also deciding to finish their skiing for the day. Christmas decorations were still everywhere, strings of white lights and bright red poinsettias added color and sparkle. Conversation and laughter echoed throughout, and off the high beams of the ceiling. Logan reached for her hand and led her through the crowd toward the elevator in the middle of the lobby.

"Tess!" a male voice rang out. "Tess Harrison, I'll be damned."

Logan saw how when she looked up, her features froze in shock for a few seconds. Total deer in the headlights, before she covered with cool disdain. Tess was friendly, always open and sociable; for her to react like that had

Logan's intuition blaring. Immediately on alert, he didn't let go of her hand as a tall, dark-haired man in neon-green and black ski gear approached them, a curvy, Botoxed blonde woman in hot pink at his side.

Tess mumbled, "Great."

"Right here if you need me," Logan quickly murmured, squeezing her fingers between his as the couple stopped before them.

"I can't believe this," the man said jovially, not bothering to hide the way he looked Tess up and down. "I mean, it's not every day you run into your ex-fiancée. You look great, Tess."

Ex-fiancée? Logan didn't know anything about the guy, but the look on Tess's face before she'd shuttered it was all he needed to know.

"Hello, Brady," she said coolly. "You look . . . older."

His grin hinted at a sneer. "Well, it's been a few years, hasn't it. Six or seven, right? Who keeps count." He smiled down at the blonde, then back up to Tess as he said proudly, "This is my wife, Chynna."

"Hello," Chynna said, looking both bored and haughty.

"We have twin boys," Brady went on. "Precious little things, but real handfuls, two years old. They're upstairs with the nanny. We wanted some time to ourselves today, since we head back home tomorrow."

"We've been here since the twenty-third," Chynna said. "I'm so over all of this now. *So* ready to go home."

Tess merely inclined her head, a hint of a nod.

Logan wanted to grind both of their faces into the carpet. The arrogant vibe off these people made him want to vomit.

"Brady Hillman," he said, holding a hand out to Logan. "And you are . . . ?"

"Logan Carter." He glanced at the man's hand but didn't shake it, leaving him hanging there awkwardly. Instead, he slid an arm around Tess's waist to pull her close. "That's funny, sweetheart," he said as he looked down at her. "All this time together, and you never mentioned you were engaged before."

Tess didn't miss a beat. "Not worth mentioning, honey," she said sweetly as she smiled back at him. "Besides, like he said, it was a long time ago."

Chynna huffed, offended for her husband.

"How's New York these days?" Brady asked as he crossed his arms over his chest. "Glad I left. So dirty, crowded, and noisy. Philadelphia's a much more civilized city."

"Huh, that's why you left?" Tess's voice was placid as could be. "I thought it was because the firm you worked for forced you out and turned your name to mud amongst all the top firms in Manhattan. At least, that's what I heard through the grapevine."

Brady's eyes turned cold and hard. The malice there made Logan unconsciously pull Tess closer. "And you're going to look me in the eye and tell me you had nothing to do with that?" Brady challenged, his voice dropping low.

Tess didn't even flinch. "Nothing at all. I had better things to do with my time and energy after I dumped you."

"How about your father, then?" Brady growled. His refined mask had fallen off, hinting at the rabid animal he truly was. "Maybe he had something to do with it. That was always my bet; if it wasn't you, it was him."

The corners of Tess's mouth turned up a bit. "That's . . . fascinating to contemplate." Her smile was sharp, and Logan admired the hell of out of it as she added, "My father is definitely not someone you want as an enemy. Anything's possible, I suppose. But if you're still harboring a grudge after all this time, my only suggestion for you would be therapy."

"Oh my God, you're rude," Chynna snapped.

Tess's perfect brows arched as she lifted her chin just enough to look at the other woman from down her nose. Drawn to her full height, she was easily six or seven inches taller than the blonde. Her bearing was powerful, regal, reminding Logan yet again of royalty. Tess didn't say a word; her withering stare was a challenge in itself. Chynna opened her mouth to say something, then shifted uncomfortably and looked away.

"Don't mind her, babe," Brady said to his wife, swinging an arm around her and yanking her closer. "She's probably just a little jealous because she never got married, never had kids." His dark eyes glittered cruelly as they focused on Tess. "I remember how you used to go on and on about wanting a big family. Didn't happen for you. That's a shame. Our kids, they made our life complete. You, now . . . close to forty . . . guess that ship sailed, huh?"

Logan fought back the urge to grab Brady by the front of his ski jacket and pound him into the wall. Brady was about six-foot-two, lean with a bit of a paunch. Logan had two inches of height and a hell of a lot more muscle on this worm. It took a lot to rein in his temper just then. Snide prick, rubbing Tess's past dreams in her face, especially now that Logan knew how much Tess still wanted children . . . and Chynna stood there grinning like they'd won a victory. Rage burned hot in Logan's veins and he clenched his jaw, not trusting what would come out of his mouth.

But he'd forgotten who he was with. Tess Harrison didn't need a knight in shining armor, or a bouncer, or *anyone* to do her dirty work for her. She laughed. A gorgeous, light tinkle of amusement that made Brady and Chynna blink.

"I'm very happy," Tess said. "My life is full. And the bonus is I didn't end up married to a lying, cheating, pathetic man like you. Add to that I dodged a bullet. The thought of having had kids with you, tying myself to you for life?" She let out a huff of a laugh, pure condescension. "I'd say I came out way ahead."

Logan smiled. *Atta girl.* He looked down at her and asked dryly, "Is that how this went? Just a no-good cheater?"

"Oh yeah." Tess nodded and leaned into him. "Luckily, I walked in on him and one of his many women a few months before the wedding. Saved me a lifetime of heartache. He did me a favor." She smiled a bright, sparkly smile. "And just think, honey . . . I wouldn't have met you, and we were meant to be."

"Absolutely." Logan couldn't help himself; he lowered his head to drop a quick kiss on her gorgeous mouth. He held her close, as if they were a real couple. She smiled anew, obviously enjoying herself. Then he glanced at the Hillmans. Brady looked all tight and furious, while Chynna's face was bright pink. Yup, her designer panties were in a twist now. He imagined the conversation between Mr. and Mrs. Hillman later would be very interesting indeed. He shot a wide, smug smile at Brady and said, "Guess I should thank you for being such a douchebag, eh?"

Brady scowled and Chynna gasped. Tess just snuggled into Logan's side and kept smiling as she said, "Gee, this reunion was fun! *So* glad you wanted to say hi, Brady. But we have a dinner reservation upstairs."

"We'd best get going, sweetheart," Logan added cheerfully.

Brady glared at them both with undisguised fury, then grasped his wife's elbow. He steered her away without a look back, though Chynna glanced over her shoulder at Tess once before they disappeared into the crowd.

"Thanks for the support," Tess said to Logan.

She moved to pull away, but he still held her close. He gave her a little squeeze and said, "That was more fun than either of us should admit to."

The corners of Tess's mouth lifted. "I know. Gotta say, you did seem to enjoy yourself there at the end."

"Well, calling out assholes has always been a fun pastime for me."

"Good to know." She pulled out of his arms, but said with quiet grace, "Thank you for having my back."

"Anytime." He gazed down at her. Questions rolled through his mind, but mostly, he just wanted to get her away from that whole scene. Despite her unruffled exterior, he suspected some of Brady's poison-tipped arrows had hit a mark. "Let's go get some food."

"Yes, please."

Ten minutes later, they were sitting at a table in the Sunrise Restaurant. The ceiling and outer wall were made of glass, affording spectacular views of Aspen Mountain and the scenery around it. Nearby, a fire blazed in a huge rock fireplace while acoustic guitar music played over the sound system. As the waitress left them menus and glasses of water, Tess muttered, "I need a stiffer drink than this.

Hell, maybe a whole bottle." Her eyes flew wide and shot to Logan. "Oh my God, I'm sorry."

"For what?"

"Um . . . what I just said. That was insensitive."

He grinned wryly. "Tess, there's plenty of times I think the same exact thing. I just never act on it. No worries." He leaned in a bit to hold her gaze. "Don't walk on eggshells around me, okay? It's not like if you mention beer I'm going to go running to a bar to get one. It doesn't work like that."

"Of course." She nodded. "Thanks. I didn't mean . . ."

"I know you didn't. It's fine. Hell, if I ran into an ex-fiancé who was a jackass like that guy, I'd want a drink too." He picked up his menu. "If you want a drink while you're with me, have one. Not just now, but anytime. I'm not Jekyll and Hyde, I'm not going to turn into a monster and start frothing at the mouth if a drink is near me. Honestly. Okay?"

"Okay. But no, I won't. I haven't had a drink since Christmas. Body cleanse, remember?"

They lapsed into a comfortable silence as they pored over their menus. But after a few minutes, he had to ask.

"Tell me something," Logan said. "I have to know. How'd someone as amazing as you end up engaged to a tool like that?"

"Because he's a world-class liar and manipulator," she said plainly. "And I was too trusting and blindly in love. At least I found out who he really was, and what he was really after, before I married him."

"What was he really after?" As soon as he said it, he was sure he knew the answer.

"You really have to ask? My family's money. I was the

easy in." Tess didn't skip a beat as she turned her smile up to the waitress who appeared at their table.

After the waitress took their orders and walked away, Tess leaned back in her chair and said, "Want to hear the quick story?"

"Yes, actually, I do," Logan said. He folded his forearms on the tabletop and gazed at her. "I'm all ears."

Tess swept her long curls back over her shoulders so they wouldn't rest on the table. "I met Brady at a charity benefit at the Met," she began. "He was an investment banker for one of the biggest firms in Manhattan. He approached me, we hit it off, and he swept me off my feet. I found out much later that he knew who I was; it was no chance meeting. He'd heard about me and went to the party with the specific intention of meeting me. He'd targeted me as a desirable mark."

"I already hate this story," Logan rumbled. "And him."

A flash of a grin swept across her face, but didn't reach her eyes. "We were engaged after eight months. He wanted to get married right away, but I wanted a long engagement. I'd like to say it was because deep down I knew he was a scumbag, but that wasn't it. I was so in love with him. . . ." She shook her head. "It was solely because of pressure from my father. He's the one who insisted on a longer engagement, and back then I was still easily influenced by him, so I did what he wanted. Brady wasn't going to give a man like my father grief, so he relented."

"From what I've heard today," Logan said carefully, "your father sounds like a . . . force of nature. In a typhoon kind of way."

"A very tactful way of putting it," Tess said. "Gold star for you. We'll talk about him some other time, but you're not wrong. Anyway . . ." She reached for her glass, took a long sip of water. "Brady and I got—or should I say, *I* bought—an apartment on Central Park West. God, I loved that view. Overlooked the whole park . . . I thought we were happy. He put on a great show. Had a short temper, and sometimes we argued, but nothing crazy. No relationship is without that stuff."

Logan nodded. "That's true."

"So. Two months before the wedding, I had to take a business trip to France. I was working for the Harrison Foundation by then."

"Okay."

"I left for what was supposed to be a week, but I came home two nights early. Thought I'd surprise my loving fiancé . . ."

Tess took another sip of water, pleased to note that telling the story didn't make her stomach turn or her chest get tight the way it had for years. She really felt nothing for Brady anymore, nothing at all, and that was a blessing. Yet she could still recall, clear as day, walking into the penthouse that evening . . . seeing his wallet, keys, and phone on the marble counter . . . "I heard the shower running. So I went in to surprise him. Only I got the surprise."

"He had company," Logan surmised with a grimace.

"So cliché it's painful." Tess rolled her eyes. "I stood there for a few seconds, trying to process what I was seeing. Then the Harrison in me took over." Her slight grin was rueful, hollow. "First I went and grabbed my phone. I took a bunch of pictures. They were—excuse my word choice, but there's no polite way to say it. They were mid-fuck, they were all caught up in it, so they didn't know I was there. I got my evidence. Then I went all the way into the bathroom and started filling the sink with water. She saw me first, and she screamed. By the time they got out of the shower and he started trying his pathetic excuses, I'd gone back to the living room and gotten his phone." Her brows arched with a hint of satisfaction. "While he watched, I dropped it into the sink."

"Filled with water!" Logan barked out a stunned laugh. "Man, that's hardcore."

"He deserved that and more."

"Damn right he did."

"Needless to say, I found out later he had been cheating on me with three different women, all on a regular basis. I found that out because when I had Brady thrown out of the apartment and barred from any access to the building, he tried to sue me. My brother Charles had his personal private investigator do a full check." Tess shrugged. "As for what he insinuated about my father messing with his career? Truth is, I always suspected the same thing. But I never asked him outright. We had *one* conversation . . . I tried to find out if he'd done something. Because I'd heard through the grapevine about Brady's troubles and wondered at the coincidence in timing. You know: We broke up, then he was fired, no one would hire him in the upper circles . . ."

Her eyes grew distant, but a hint of a smile lifted her lips. "My father just took my face in his hands and said *no one messes with the Harrisons and gets away with it. And no one messes with my little girl and gets away with it, that's for damn sure*. His little girl . . . I was thirty-one, for Pete's sake."

Tess smiled absently and reached for her water glass. "I dropped it after that. I know he did something. But the fewer details I knew, the better off we all were."

Logan let out a low whistle. He knew the Harrisons

were rich and connected, but that was a kind of power he couldn't begin to grasp. That was another world.

She shrugged. "The whole thing was a disaster, and I'm glad it's behind me. What can I say? Brady broke my heart. I was crazy in love with him. I thought we were going to get married, have a bunch of beautiful kids . . . now, I just thank God I found out before it was too late."

"He's a goddamn fool." Logan leaned in and covered her hand with his. It was big and warm and made her feel good. "I know it must not have felt like it at the time, but you were lucky. Good riddance."

"I know. Agreed, one hundred percent." She took a deep, cleansing breath, then removed her red shell jacket and placed it over the back of her chair. She'd finally warmed up enough to start shedding layers. "It's easy to talk about it now, because I don't feel a thing. But it wasn't for a long time. Took me a long time to heal."

She smoothed out her fleece pullover, soft swirls of red and magenta. Her black ski pants made a crinkly noise as she shifted in her seat. She looked back up at Logan, who was staring thoughtfully at her. Ugh, she'd been talking too much, and probably making herself look like a sad sack. "I'm fine, Logan. Really. It's all in the past, and I'm nothing but grateful for the way it worked out. You saw him for yourself, he's a total jackass."

"That he is," Logan agreed. "I can't even picture you with him."

"It was a past life. A past me."

"I get that. We all have a past life and different versions of ourselves, don't we." He leaned back and stroked his beard as he added, "I'm still sorry you were hurt so bad. You deserved better."

"Again, agreed, a hundred percent. A hundred and ten!"

They smiled at each other.

"You know . . ." She hesitated, deciding whether to continue, then forged ahead. "My brothers and I, we used to think we were cursed. If you asked any of us about finding love about five years ago? We would have scoffed at you. The Harrisons had a disastrous track record."

"What do you mean?"

"Well, to begin with, our parents had a doomed, dreadful marriage, then an epically ugly divorce. My brother Charles, his first marriage was a train wreck. Then me and Brady . . . It was like the Harrison destiny to not have love in our lives." Her voice trailed off as the waitress appeared with their appetizers. She set down a caprese salad in front of Tess and a platter of loaded potato skins before Logan.

"You really thought you were cursed?" Logan asked with a dry chuckle. "I know your brothers. You all seem too pragmatic and savvy to believe in bullshit like that."

"Well, thanks, and you're right. But come on, all four of us? That was a hell of a coincidence, none of us ever having relationships that worked out . . ." She reached for the salt shaker and added a dash to her plate. "Now, of course, we know it's not the case. Over the past few years, all three of my brothers found the loves of their lives. Their true soul mates. They're all very lucky. And very happy."

"But not you, though," Logan murmured.

"Nope. Guess third time, for the third brother, was the charm. Lady Luck ran out of turns for me." Tess straightened in her chair and picked up her fork and knife. "I'm fine with that. I'm so glad they're all happy, and I'm going to make my own happy ending when I have my baby."

They ate quietly for a minute. Logan's head was filled with new questions, and also new insight. He'd had enough heartbreak of his own to understand her desire to remain alone after a betrayal like that.

"Did you date at all after you and Brady split up?" he asked. "I mean, if that was years ago . . ."

"Yes. I mean, I didn't at first, not for a while. Had to nurse that broken heart and heal. I didn't trust. At all." Tess took a bite of her food and moaned with pleasure. "Oh my God, this is good. I was so hungry."

"Me too," he admitted, grinning as he dug into his own food. "Enjoy."

They ate in silence for another minute before Tess said, "It took me two years to start dating again, but I did. I wasn't going to let a loser like Brady ruin the rest of my life, give him that power over my future. So yes, I dated. And I met some very nice men. And some very blah men. But none of them . . . It was nothing special. No fireworks, no real connections. And, as I'd learned the hard way, there were also men who were only interested in my last name and what it could get them. At least, after Brady, I could spot those bloodsuckers in ten seconds."

"That's a situation I can't imagine having to deal with," Logan admitted. "I don't envy you that. Dating is hard enough. To have to wonder if anyone's genuine, or after your money . . . That just sucks."

"Yup." Tess shrugged. "So . . . here I am. I tried, but the fairy tale hasn't happened for me. And, as Brady so kindly pointed out, I've always wanted children. More than anything. Well, I have money, resources . . . So I'm going to make that happen on my own."

"I almost punched him in the face when he brought that up," Logan growled. "I wanted to, so bad."

"I appreciate it, but he's not worth the possible jail time." Tess grinned wickedly. "I bet your fists could be registered as lethal weapons, from the looks of you. You hit him once, you might have killed him. Then I would've had to visit you in jail. And while you're a very attractive man, I don't think an orange jumpsuit would suit you."

He laughed, but then said, "I could tell from one short meeting that Brady Hillman is a waste of air, a total douche-bag. You were probably the best thing that ever happened to him. His loss."

Tess merely smiled and took another bite. "I can't believe I ran into him here of all places . . ." She shrugged again. "Whatever. Hopefully, I'll never see him again."

"Did you see that friggin' Barbie doll he married?" Logan said with a disapproving scowl. "Ugh. She was a serious bitch, and so fake."

Tess giggled. "You mean you don't like overly prominent plastic curves?"

"I like curves fine, when they're real. None of hers were."

"You could tell, huh?"

"Couldn't you?"

Tess shrugged, her brows lifting as she said, "Well, he always liked busty women. God knows that's not me. I remember wondering why he liked me so much when all his exes were these hourglass-shaped women . . . I hadn't realized at that point he was into me for my money, not for me." She dabbed at the side of her mouth with her napkin. "The thing is, it used to make me feel so insecure when I was younger. Being a beanpole. I hadn't embraced my body yet."

"And now?" Logan asked quietly, eyes locked on her.

"Now, I totally, gladly accept myself for who I am. But it was so hard as a teen, and even in my early twenties," she admitted. "It was *really* hard, actually."

He was fascinated. "What do you mean? Why?"

"I was too tall, too skinny, and flat chested," she said plainly. "My mother was . . . I don't want to say a *movie star*, because that gives her more credit than she's due. But she was a B-level actress, she was in a handful of movies back in the seventies. We all look just like her, my brothers and I—it's practically the same face. But she was a real bombshell, sex goddess type. Hourglass curves, and only five-foot-five. Whereas I, however, inherited the Harrison DNA: tall and lean. Apparently, my father's grandmother was six feet tall." She fidgeted with the napkin, folding it in her lap. "My father offered to get me a boob job for my sixteenth birthday."

"Are you serious?" Logan sputtered. "Please be kidding. Jesus."

"Dead serious. I was mortified. Ah, the teen years . . ." Tess shot him a wry smirk. "My mother had abandoned us, my father was . . . my father. My brothers were great when they were around, but I just wanted to either go out with my friends, or hide in my art studio and paint. To be normal. But I wasn't. I was a flat-chested giant." She grinned ruefully, her tone weary as she said, "Do you have any idea how hard it can be for a very tall girl? I hit five-ten by the time I was fifteen. I was taller than my own brothers for a few years, much less some of my teachers. And forget about the boys."

"Well, I was five-ten at thirteen," Logan said. "You wouldn't have scared me."

"Where were you when I needed you?" she joked, throwing her hands in the air in mock frustration.

"Well, I'm here now! Better late than never."

They laughed together.

"It wasn't until my early twenties that I started to love

being tall. 'Til I started getting off on towering over people, embracing the power of it." She eyed him and added, "Come on. You're huge. You know that being tall can grant some unspoken power. That people treat you a bit differently."

"I never really thought about it," he said earnestly. "But I'm a guy. I didn't have to. I mean . . . yeah, I knew deep down people would think twice before messing with me just because I'm big. So . . . I guess I just proved your point after all."

Her voice lowered as she leaned across the table and murmured conspiratorially, "Now, I love wearing high heels. At the Holiday Ball, in my stilettos? I was six-foot-two." Her smile was radiant. "Even my two older brothers were an inch or two shorter than me. Pierce is six-two; he looked me in the eye. Heh."

"I bet you stood there like a goddamn Amazon warrior princess," Logan said reverently. "I bet you do every time."

"Goddamn right." Her smile brightened before she took another sip of water.

He could only stare at her. Respect, appreciation, lust, bemusement, and genuine like all flowed through him at the same time. She was something special. Other women, given what she'd had since birth, could very easily coast through life. But Tess was as down-to-earth as they came, with a good and still-open heart, despite her past heartaches. Tess Harrison was a rare woman. He could almost *feel* his crush on her deepen, which was both a rush and a curse.

"Your entrées are ready!" the waitress said with a smile as she brought a tray to their table. She cleared their appetizer plates, set down their steaks, and refilled their water glasses before leaving them again.

"That was a hell of a story," he said once they were alone again. "Thanks for sharing all that with me."

"Thanks for having my back in the lobby," she said. "You jumped right in! You were great."

"My pleasure." He readjusted his napkin over his lap, his mind buzzing with thoughts that all of a sudden came pouring out of his mouth. "I just have to say . . . you're a stunningly beautiful woman, from head to toe, inside and out. Jesus, Tess, your legs alone . . ." Heat rose in his face as he realized she was gazing intently, hanging on his words. The words he probably shouldn't have said out loud. He cleared his suddenly dry throat and tried to switch gears a bit.

"And, being a tall man myself? I like when I don't get a crick in my neck from talking to a woman and having to look doooown. So I love that you're tall." Noting her smile at that, he cut into his Black Angus. "I had no idea you'd ever been insecure, because you're one of the most grounded, self-assured women I've known in a long time. You carry yourself like a queen, and you should. You're insanely beautiful." Jesus, he was rambling now. He shoved another bite of steak into his mouth to have a reason to stop talking.

"I don't know what to say," she murmured. Her eyes were bright. "Those are some high-level compliments. I'm incredibly flattered. Thank you."

He only murmured back, "I meant every word."

"But for the record, I'm no queen. I'm just a lady from Long Island." Obviously touched, she smiled warmly. He basked in the pleased look on her face as she lifted her utensils to slice into her filet mignon. They ate quietly for a few minutes, letting the music and chatter around them fill the silence comfortably.

He was surprised at how at ease he was with her. How they didn't have awkward silences, spurred by the need to fill the gaps. Maybe it was because they were both pretty self-confident people, but maybe it was because they were really in sync. And when they did talk, he was finding it easier and easier. For a worldly, incredibly wealthy woman from a different world, Tess was approachable and open. He liked her more every time they spent time together.

"So, mister, I spilled my guts," she said when half their meals were gone. Her eyes sparkled with curiosity and a hint of mischief. "Your turn. Tell me some more about you."

He sighed inwardly. Had to know that would come, didn't he. "Really?"

"Really. Come onnnnnn, Carter." Her tone was light and playful. "Tell me something. I'd like to think you know you can, and that you know it'll stay with me."

"I do know that," he said quietly, only admitting that to himself as he said the words aloud. He took a gulp of water before saying, "Okay, yeah, reciprocation is fair play. I'll tell you some of mine too. But . . . Tess, some of it is ugly. That's just the truth."

"Logan . . ." Her voice sobered. "We've all had ugly. And no matter what happened before, now you're a strong, good man."

"Well . . . yeah, *now* I'd like to think I am, and I was when I was younger. But in between . . ." He winced. "There's a block of time there I'm not proud of. I fucked up big-time. Took me years to forgive myself. Some days, I still wrestle with the things I did. Or things that happened . . ."

Tess reached across the table and took his hand. Her

skin felt warm and unbelievably soft. "Hey. You don't have to tell me anything you don't want to. Ever."

"I know that." He squeezed her hand and gazed at her. Then he took one more bite of his steak, savoring the taste before he said, "Well, how about to start with, I know a little something about betrayal too. I was married. To my college sweetheart. We were together for six years, married for the last three of them. I loved her more than anything in the world. And when I needed her the most, when I hit the lowest point of my entire life, she left me."

Chapter Ten

"I'm listening," Tess said gently as she laid down her utensils. "Go on, please."

"Okay." He set down his fork and knife too. "Warning you again though . . . some of it's ugly."

"I can handle ugly, Logan. You don't scare me."

"I bet very little scares you, actually."

"You'd be dead wrong. But go ahead."

He nodded, trying to figure out where to start. He took a long sip of water, feeling the cool relief of it slide down his suddenly tight throat. Then he said, "Rachel and I met in our junior year at Tulane, in a psych class. Love at first sight, immediate connection, the whole nine. Within two weeks, we were inseparable. I proposed the week after we graduated, and we got married the next spring."

"So young," Tess murmured. "How old were you both, twenty-three?"

"Barely." He picked up his fork again and started pushing around the brussels sprouts on his plate. "Her degree was in psychology, mine was in social work. We both wanted to help people. It seemed like a perfect match. Maybe at first, before I blew it sky-high, it was." He shrugged, not lifting his gaze from the plate. "We had an apartment in downtown New Orleans. She got a job in a medical center that catered to higher-end clientele, working there while she started her master's. Me, I was working down in the poorest areas of the city, also while getting my master's." He felt the wry twist of his lips. "But it pumped me up. The work, I mean. I was so idealistic, thought I was making a difference."

"I'm sure you were," Tess said. "Sounds like admirable work to me."

"I don't know. Maybe I did. I was young and naïve. Rach and I didn't have any money, but we had each other. She was going to eventually make lots of money, and I was going to change the world. Our future looked bright." He noticed how still Tess had grown. When she listened, she really listened.

"We both got our master's degrees, she started working with a private practice, and I was down in the ditches. Soup kitchens, homeless shelters, community centers, all of that. I felt like I had a purpose. I was crazy in love with my gorgeous, brilliant wife. Life was good for a while." He stopped, drumming his fingers on the table. He hadn't thought of the good times in a long time, and doing so now didn't bring any warm fuzzies . . . more like a hollow feeling. Like it'd all happened to someone else.

"So what happened?" Tess's voice brought him back to the present.

He blinked as new memories crashed into his head. With a tight sigh, he said simply, "Katrina happened."

"As in . . . Hurricane Katrina?" she asked tentatively.

"Yup." Again, as it had a thousand times before, the image of little Rodney Parsons's body floating in the murky, filthy water assaulted him. Logan briefly squeezed his eyes shut, willing it away. "I was right in the thick of it. Where I was working . . . those people had nothing, or close to nothing. So when the storm hit . . . in a nutshell, we had no idea what hit us. And I tried to help people, I was frantic, but I couldn't do anything for them. Not enough, anyway. And people I knew died." His eyes met hers. He saw the empathy there, but she sat quietly, listening raptly. "Whatever you saw on TV? It was worse. It was a true circle of hell, what we lived through down there."

"I can't imagine," she murmured. "I won't insult you with platitudes. It sounds horrific."

He raked his hands through his hair. His chest tightened and his blood pulsed in his head, the familiar signs of his demons trying to rear their vicious heads. "I'm not going to go into details now, all right?"

"Sure. Whatever you want."

"Good. So . . . um . . ." He edited in his head, trying to decide what to share and what he wanted to keep to himself. There was so much . . . and he didn't want to talk about any of it. But Tess had trusted him with some of her secrets, and he wanted to do the same. He wanted to place some trust in her, and he wasn't even sure why.

"I can tell you still carry it with you," she said quietly.

He nodded at that. "Yeah. But not every day. It's not as bad as it used to be."

"It sounds traumatic. If you don't want to tell me any more, that's fine."

"It was traumatic. I was devastated, angry, shaking my fist at the universe . . . and I had survivor's guilt for years. PTSD lingers, crops up once in a while. Something like that is hard to shake." He reached for his water and took a few gulps, draining the glass. "Back then, the devastation, the deaths of people I'd come to know and care about . . . I took it personally. So many things I believed in, I just . . . I lost faith in the system, because it failed us. And how was I supposed to do social work in a system that was clearly broken? I didn't want to. I couldn't cope, and I spiraled."

He let his eyes drift away, then made himself look at Tess directly. "Within a few weeks, I started drinking to numb the pain. I drank every night . . . then it started during the day too. Then, after a few months, I stopped going to work. Rachel kept trying to help me, but at that point, I couldn't be helped, because I didn't care about anything anymore. I trashed my life, basically. Threw it all away."

"You were drowning in grief and guilt," Tess said softly. "You needed help."

"I didn't ask for any. Too proud. Too broken at that point. I was lost." He rubbed the back of his neck. This was his history, the truth. He wasn't uncomfortable telling the story, but had to admit he didn't want this beautiful, smart, totally together woman to think less of him. He hoped she wouldn't, but if she did, there wasn't much he could do about it. At least he was being honest. "By six months after Katrina, I was unemployed and in an alcoholic stupor. And my wife gave up and left. Rock bottom."

Tess didn't say anything. She just willed him to keep talking by the absorbed, intent look on her face, the kindness in her eyes that shone without pity or judgment.

So he did. "I hated her for that. I felt so betrayed. So much for those vows, huh? *For better or worse, in sickness and in health* . . . For a psychologist who wanted to help people, she felt I was beyond help. But the thing is, she wasn't totally wrong. You can't help someone who doesn't want to help themselves."

"But you were her husband," Tess said. "I . . . I wasn't there. I don't know what went on. But she should've stayed."

"Thanks. But. In the short run, she saved herself, and in the long run, she did me a favor." Logan put down the fork and shoved back a bit from the table. He leaned his forearms on it and looked Tess right in the eye. "Because that's what it took for me to look around and see how bad things had gotten. That I'd lost everything that mattered to me. My career, my wife . . . myself." He cleared his throat.

"So. My mother flew down to New Orleans and kicked my ass into gear. Said she refused to stand by anymore and let me kill myself. She'd hoped Rachel would pull me out of it, but she didn't. So my mom literally threw me into the shower, smacked me sober. And said she'd pay for rehab if I'd go, and really work at it, not half-ass it. If I didn't do that, I would've probably ended up dead, and I knew it. So that's what I did."

"How old were you then?"

"Got out of rehab a week before I turned twenty-seven."

"Thank God," Tess said on an exhale. "You still had your whole life ahead of you. I'm glad you got the help you needed."

"Me too."

"I hate to think of what kind of pain you were in," she said gently. "That you went down that road, and that far."

"Thanks. I'm okay now. Really." He sat up straighter in his chair. "So what you said before, about a past life, a past you? Same here. Yes, once in a while something reminds me of it all, and things crop up in my head. But I've got a handle on it, it doesn't handle me. I'm a different person now. With a different life." He offered a contented grin. "It's quiet and pretty simple. I do honest work, and no one's welfare depends on me or my help. No drama. That works for me."

She cocked her head to the side, apparently considering his words. "Wait a second." Tess leaned in, her eyes narrowing. "People *do* depend on you. You still help people, you just—"

"I don't have their *lives* in my hands, Tess," he said firmly. "Yes, I still help people. But it's nothing like what I was doing before. At the end of the day, I leave my work at work. No one's hungry, sick, homeless, desperate . . . and I don't take the work home with me. In here." He tapped his temple, then scratched at his beard and shifted in his seat.

"What about your ex-wife?" Tess asked.

"What about her?"

"Do you know where she is now?"

"Yeah. She moved to California. Has her own private practice. Remarried a few years after she left me. Has two kids. A good life. She deserves that. Why not." He fiddled with the fork beside his plate. "About a year after I got out of rehab, I wrote her a long email. Wanted her to know I'd gotten sober, moved back to Colorado, and took my life back. Also, I owed her an apology. I also needed to rail at her a little, but mostly, I needed to own what I'd done. And to get some closure. She answered me . . . we went back and forth for a few weeks. But that was it. That was years ago already."

"Did you get that closure?" Tess wondered aloud.

"I did. We addressed a lot of things that needed to be addressed. But . . . I'll never get married again. I don't, uh . . . I don't do relationships." He tried for a wry grin and a lighter tone. "I prefer to be alone now. Surely you, of all people, can understand that."

She blinked at the parallel he drew. "I do, but . . . wow, it's different. I want a family so much, but I never found the right person to do that with. You had the person. You were married, you . . . Did you want all that before the bottom fell out? A family, that kind of life?"

"Before? Yeah." His voice was gruff. "After? No. Too much loss."

They sat in heavy silence for a minute. Then he sighed and said, "See? Warned you. That's some dark stuff." He shook his head raggedly. "I shouldn't have told you."

"Stop that," Tess commanded. "I asked because I wanted to know. I'm glad I know." She reached across the table for his hand and squeezed it, sending a streak of electricity up his arm. "You're still my friend. I don't think any less of you. If anything, I think even more of you."

He gazed at her in muted awe, this beautiful, amazingly empathetic woman. "*Are* we friends now?"

Her shapely brow lifted. "Yes. I'd like to think we are. Aren't we?"

He couldn't hold back the smile that spread on his face. "Yeah. We are."

"Good." She rubbed the top of his hand with her thumb, so soft, before she pulled her hand back. "And the truth is, knowing some of that? There are things about you that make more sense now."

His brows shot up. "You say that like . . . you were trying to figure me out."

"Maybe I have been." Tess changed the subject with a hint of a grin. "So I gather your mother—who sounds like a badass, by the way—doesn't like your loner mentality and thinks she's going to get you to change your mind somehow?"

His eyes caressed Tess's features. Damn, she was clever. Pulling him out before he fell too far down the hole. Grateful, he nodded. "Something like that. I just think she wants more grandchildren. My brother has kids, but he's too far away." Logan smirked. "I hate to burst her bubble, but I don't want kids. After what I've seen . . . I can't bear it. The idea of something happening, or the potential of more loss . . . It's too much. No family for me. End of story."

Tess gaped at him. Finally, he saw a lick of something like pity in her eyes as she murmured, "Wow."

"Wow nothing. Fewer ties, fewer chances for me to fuck up again, or to lose something so big that the next time, I won't get back up again. It's pretty simple, really." Logan suddenly ached for a beer and grabbed his glass. It was almost empty. He sucked an ice cube into his mouth and chewed on it, anything for distraction.

Tess just folded her hands in her lap. "Whatever works for you."

"That's what works for me."

"It sounds lonely," she said quietly.

He shrugged. "On occasion. But so what."

She pressed her lips together and nodded.

"Tess, I didn't mean to sound harsh."

"You didn't. Not to me, anyway. But you sound pretty harsh on yourself."

"I have to be. Gotta keep myself in line."

Sounds more like you're still punishing yourself, she thought. But that wasn't her business.

"Look," he added, his voice softer. "I came back from hell. I worked hard to do it, and I'm happy now. I'm good. It could've gone the other way. I'm grateful for what I have."

"That's a good way to be."

"I think so. Give me the simple life."

The waitress hovered nearby and Tess waved her over.

"Would you like to see the dessert menu?" she asked.

"Hell yes," Logan said enthusiastically.

Tess arched a brow at him.

"Hey, gotta let me have one vice. Mine's sugar. I admit it."

"So the way to your heart is with sweets, huh?" she teased.

"You got it. What about you?" He locked his pale green eyes on her, searching, a sly grin on his face. "What are your hidden vices? How does Tess Harrison indulge herself?"

"Umm . . ." She thought it over, grinning back. "I'm no sugar junkie, but I'm a sucker for flowers."

His brow furrowed. "Flowers? You eat flowers?"

She burst out laughing, "No! I love fresh cut flowers," she said. "I always have them. I have them both at my office in the city, and in my home, in several rooms. I need that burst of color, that hint of life, especially in the winter. I spend quite a bit of money on that, so I'd say that counts as my indulgence."

"That's a damn nice one," he said with appreciation.

"And when I got here, you'd filled the house with poinsettia plants," she said. "That, um . . . went a long way. I loved that."

"Without even knowing," he said, his smile growing. "Gold star for me."

"Absolutely."

By the time Logan pulled up in front of Tess's house, she was warm, full, tired, and happy. "I had a great time today."

"I did too," he said with a smile. "Thanks again for inviting me."

"Any chance you'd like to do it again sometime soon?" she asked. "You're a worthy ski partner, and I had fun with you."

"Yeah, I'd like that," he said. "But next time, I pay for my lift ticket."

"Deal. Sometime next week?"

"Sure. Give me a call, we'll work out a time."

"Well, *you* have a job with a real schedule. Right now, I don't. I'm free as a bird. So you give me a call."

His eyes held hers as he said, "Okay. I'll do that. You're on. Got yourself a ski buddy."

God, she wanted to kiss him. Sitting so close in the warmth of his truck, he smelled good and his eyes were intense and his mouth was inviting and she wanted to kiss him so bad. But this new friendship—all the things they'd revealed to each other that day—she didn't want to cross any lines or mess it up. For now, she'd hold back.

But still couldn't resist flirting a little bit. "So," she said boldly. "Are you coming in to soak in my tub or what? The offer stands."

His gaze turned hot, a full-out smolder that made her belly do a wobbly flip. "The offer is more tempting than you know." His voice had dropped low and dead sexy, making her shiver. "But I think I'd better head home for tonight."

They stared at each other for a moment, pure electricity crackling between them. She could feel her blood in her veins, racing now, hot and needing, as his eyes lowered to her mouth for a few seconds before lifting to meet her gaze again.

"You sure?" she asked. Her heart thumped in heavy beats.

"Only so much temptation a man can take," he murmured. "And you're testing my limits as it is, Tess. You have to know that."

"I didn't know that."

"Well . . ."

She leaned in, her face so close to his that she could feel his hot breath feather against her lips.

"Tess." He whispered it as a protest, but his eyes gave him away. He wanted her too, she could see it all over his face.

She closed the distance between them, pressing her mouth to his. It was a brush of her lips against his, just the slightest touch. But his hand lifted to cup the back of her neck and hold her there. He took control of the kiss, gently but surely, slanting his mouth over hers to take more of what he wanted. Her mouth opened with a little sigh as their tongues met and swirled slowly. As they leaned into each other, his fingers threaded through her hair and his other hand came up, cradling her head in his hands as his mouth consumed hers.

Her senses reeled. His full beard tickled her face, surprisingly soft against her skin. The feel of his mouth on hers, his hands in her hair, his big, warm body so close . . . her head swam with it all. He deepened the kiss and groaned softly into her mouth, and she was lost. She surrendered willingly, kissing him back with the same slow, sensual pace he'd set, her fingers clutched in his ski jacket. She could have kissed him for days.

He broke away slowly, leaning his forehead against hers, eyes still closed. "Jesus," he whispered. When his eyes opened to focus on her, they were heavy lidded with lust. "You . . . you better go inside now."

Still catching her breath, she touched his cheek. "You sure you don't want to come in?"

"I do want to," he said, his voice thick. "Too much. So I'm not going to."

She pulled back, trying to hide her disappointment. "Okay."

"Tess . . ." He stared at her, his mouth opening and closing as he fought with what he wanted to say. "You're an amazing woman. I like that we're . . . kind of friends now. Let's try to stick with that for now, okay?"

The disappointment sharpened in her gut, but she pasted on a smile. "Fine."

"Ah crap. No, no, don't say *fine*," Logan demanded gently. "When a woman says *fine*, it's never fine. Even a loner lumberjack like me knows that."

She couldn't help but giggle.

"Tess, you're the most beautiful woman I've ever seen," he said earnestly. "Don't think for a second that I wouldn't love to go inside with you right now, because I would. But you have an agenda, you're gearing up to go through some medical . . . stuff . . . and I don't want to get in the way of that."

She gaped at him in shock. "I . . . I don't know what one thing has to do with the other."

"You have big plans," he murmured, trailing the backs of his fingers along her cheek, eyes locked with hers. "I'd be a distraction. You said it yourself, you don't want any distractions right now." His gaze turned wicked and hot as he added, "I promise you, it'd be a fantastic distraction. A sexy, fun, passionate distraction . . . but this friendship we've started? Means more."

"We're attracted to each other," she said flatly.

"Can't deny that." He touched his mouth to hers again, a light brush of his lips, and her whole body shuddered. "But I shouldn't go inside with you. Not tonight."

Her nerves jangled, every nerve ending alight and aware of him. Her heart beat hard and fast as she nuzzled into his palm, stared right into his eyes, and whispered, "If you insist."

"I do," he said, not breaking their gaze. "C'mon, you know I'm right. Last thing you need right now is us starting something up like this. Didn't you tell me your first doctor appointment is tomorrow?"

She didn't like it, and wasn't sure she fully agreed with

it, but had to admit she'd thought along those lines herself before his kisses had turned her brain to mush and her insides to jelly. With a heavy sigh, she nodded and pulled back from him. "Pretty early, in fact. I should go inside and get into bed."

Logan growled, his head falling back against the leather seat. "Had to put an image like that in my head right before you leave. You, climbing into bed . . . not nice, Tess. Not nice."

She laughed lightly, and he grinned back at her. Their eyes held for a long beat and she took a slow, deep breath, exhaling it before she said, "Good night, Logan. Thanks again for a great day."

"Back at you," he said. "Good night, Tess. Sleep well. Good luck tomorrow."

With a sweet smile, she climbed out of his truck and into the cold night.

Chapter Eleven

Tess got home from her morning yoga class at noon. She poured some food into Bubbles's bowl, then showered, all the while absently humming the last song she'd heard in the car. When she emerged from the bathroom in her fluffy wine-colored robe, her long hair wrapped up turban style on top of her head, she sank onto her bed. Yesterday, she'd spent most of the afternoon painting, but she wasn't in the mood today. She had to check her work email, have some lunch, maybe make a few work calls. She also wanted to text Logan and thank him again for the day before.

They'd gone skiing again, and like the first time, followed an afternoon on the slopes with a long meal and easy conversation. They told each other stories about their siblings, chatted about work, and he talked a bit about his mother's condition, which apparently was declining. When he confessed that he was worried his mom would start campaigning in town to find him a girlfriend so she could quickly marry him off before she died, Tess had teased him mercilessly, anything to take the sad look out of his eyes. And it had worked.

Since the ten days since their first skiing excursion,

he'd started texting her on the days he didn't come by her house to take out the trash. Only once a day, just a short and sweet Checking on you. Everything okay? which she would answer, and they'd end up texting for a few minutes. Getting to know each other, kind of friends, even though the attraction between them simmered at a low boil whenever they were together. She liked him. She trusted him.

She picked up the phone to text him and noticed that the light was blinking. She checked the message; Dr. Fuller from the fertility clinic had called while she was in the shower. Excitement and nervousness rocketed through her.

Her initial visit to the fertility clinic ten days ago had been interesting. She'd had a brief physical exam and filled out a million forms. She'd had a lengthy interview with the doctor, who'd fielded her many questions and filled in some blanks. Dr. Fuller was a warm, clearly knowledgeable person; Tess felt like she was in good hands. Her gut told her she'd found the right place and the right people to help make her dreams come true.

Since then, she'd pored over donor profiles. The clinic was at the top of their game when it came to both medical and psychosocial profiles, one of the main reasons she'd picked them. Their screening process was extensive, which further inspired her confidence. Hell, the cost didn't matter to her. The basics of the procedure could be done anywhere. She wanted to ensure quality, across the board, and this clinic had that going on. She was in.

Sitting back on her bed, she tucked her legs beneath her as she returned Dr. Fuller's call. She was on the line in under two minutes. "Hi, Tess, how are you?"

"I'm fine, thank you." Tess's heart rate picked up a

notch, a new rush of anticipation whooshing through her. "Why'd you call?"

"I wanted to share your test results with you," Dr. Fuller said. She sounded calm and at ease, which put Tess more at ease. "Just the basics, which are, you're in top shape. You're very healthy, and I think you won't have any problems conceiving."

Tess's heart soared. "Really? That's wonderful!"

"Now, understand," Dr. Fuller cautioned, "that doesn't necessarily mean you'll get pregnant on your first try. It's absolutely possible, but you are in your late thirties, so that's the only risk factor here. Your blood work is great, your hormone levels are right where they need to be . . . I'd bet once we start, you'll be pregnant within six months. Hopefully less, but the point is, you don't have anything to show you'll have a real problem getting pregnant. Okay?"

"That's great," Tess said, practically bouncing where she sat. "So how soon can we start?"

"Well, have you been monitoring your ovulation?"

"Of course. And I actually just started ovulating yesterday. I'm at peak week."

Dr. Fuller chuckled. "That's good, but have you chosen a donor from the database yet? We need to go over that part . . . kind of important."

Now it was Tess who laughed. "I know. That's the hard part. I've narrowed it down to a few candidates, but . . ."

"That's not something you want to rush, Tess."

"I know. I agree. I just . . ." She sighed and conceded, "I might need a little more time, and I feel like I'm going to lose this month, and I don't want to lose any more time."

"It's more important to be sure about your choice than

to be fast." The doctor's voice softened kindly as she added, "Tess . . . you'll be fine. You have time. Honestly."

After the call ended, Tess released her hair from the towel turban, shook out the long, damp curls, and lay back on her bed to stare at the view beyond. The entire back wall was made of glass, showcasing the majesty of the snow-capped mountains and pine trees outside. Clear blue skies and bright sunshine made the scene as picturesque as a postcard.

A donor. She had to choose one. She needed a sperm donor who was fabulous, who'd pass on amazing traits and attributes to her child. She wanted a Superman . . .

An idea had taken hold this week and she couldn't shake it. Now, after Dr. Fuller's phone call giving her the green light to start, the idea grew claws and dug into her, a deep gut reaction. She had a sperm donor in mind, a "known donor," as it were. From what she knew of him, he was a truly good person, with high intelligence, great compassion, and strong morals. He loved to help others and had a dry sense of humor. He was self-sufficient, capable, hardworking, and kind. He also happened to be drop-dead gorgeous and physically strong. Yup, all the traits he possessed were ones she'd love to have in a son or daughter of her own. And bonus, he was unmarried, totally unattached. So all week, the more she thought about it, the more it made sense.

Logan Carter was a dream sperm donor.

But would he ever agree to it? It was a hell of a thing to ask someone.

He'd made it clear he wanted no ties in his life . . . but the fact was, that made him only a more perfect donor. If he would give up all claims to her child, leaving her to raise her child on her own, that was ideal. Tess *wanted* to be a single parent; she had those bases covered. Maybe that would appeal to him? Or would he run like hell and never even talk to her again?

She drew a long, deep breath and expelled it with determination. No time to waste. The green light from the doctor spurred Tess into action. If Logan said no, she'd deal with it and go back to the donor database provided by the clinic. The only thing to do was ask. She had nothing to lose and so much to gain.

She texted Logan. Hi Thor ☺ Please call me when you can? Need to ask you something.

To her surprise, her phone rang thirty seconds later.

"You know I don't like it when people call me Thor." His deep, sexy voice, a playful rumble in her ear, sent a current of electricity skittering through her.

"I do know that," she said, smiling. "That's what makes it fun."

"Great," he grunted, clearly joking. "What's up? Everything okay?"

"Yes, everything's fine. I, um . . ." She took a deep breath, trying to calm her suddenly pounding heart. "I want to talk with you about something. Any chance you're free for dinner tonight?"

"Tonight?" he repeated. "Uh . . . yeah, I can do that. How's seven o'clock? Is that too late?"

"No, that's perfect." She wanted to invite him over, order in dinner, and have the privacy of her home for such an important conversation, but she knew he'd been purposely staying out of her house unless necessary. The attraction bubbling between them was easier to put off when they were out in public places. She quickly tried to think of the quieter restaurants she knew. Somewhere they could really talk. "How about Sophie's Bistro? Do you know it? It's on Montdale, near the yoga studio . . ."

"Yeah, I know it. Should I pick you up, or meet you there?"

"Meet me there." Tess had a feeling if it didn't go well, he'd need that escape. "I'll make a reservation."

"Okay. Um . . ." Logan paused. "What are we talking about? Anything serious?"

"I have a proposition for you," she said. "And I guarantee it's not what you think. In fact, you couldn't guess if you tried."

"Really. Now I'm intrigued."

"Good, that means you'll show up."

He laughed. "Like I'd ever stand you up. See you at seven."

She flopped back onto the bed, her heart racing and body wired with adrenaline. Asking Logan to be her sperm donor was kind of crazy. He'd probably say no. And, when he turned her down, there was a chance he'd stop talking to her altogether. Anything was possible. *But* . . . she bit down on her lip, a smile spreading on her face. But what if he said yes? It would be the answer to all her prayers. She could almost imagine what their baby would look like. Hope and nervous elation filled her.

Tess had managed not only to get a reservation at Sophie's, but for her favorite table, half hidden in a back corner, away from the main sea of tables. Its location added an air of intimacy to the already cozy atmosphere. They were as private as a couple could be when dining out in public. But when their entrées arrived, she fidgeted with her fork, pushing around the food on her plate. Although the sesame/ginger tuna at Sophie's Bistro was one of her favorite dishes in all of Aspen, she had no appetite.

She'd made it through small talk with Logan, asking

him about his day, and answered his as well . . . but she wasn't able to think about anything except her ovulation cycle, the whole process, and how the hell she could ask him to be her donor.

A few bites into his flatiron steak, he frowned slightly as he looked at her and asked, "You okay?"

"Me?" she asked, her voice lifting an octave. "Yeah. Great. Why?"

"You're not eating. And all night you've seemed . . . nervous. Not like yourself." Logan's eyes narrowed on her. "What's going on, Tess?" He reached for his club soda and drank.

Busted, she put her fork down. "You're right. I'm not quite myself tonight. Sorry about that."

"No need to be sorry, but just tell me what's going on." His shrewd, pale green eyes now locked on her, no mercy. "You said you had a proposition for me. Whatever it is obviously has you off your game. Talk to me. I'm listening."

She nodded and took a long, cleansing breath, trying to stay cool even as her heart fluttered and took off like a racehorse. "I don't know where to start."

"Should I be worried?" he asked.

"No. God, no. *I* should." A hint of a nervous smile flicked across her features.

He put down his fork and knife, sat very still, and gazed at her, waiting patiently. "Just blurt it out if you have to," he finally coaxed.

"Okay." She cleared her dry throat, stole a quick sip of water, and took another deep breath. "You know I want to have a baby."

"Yes, I do."

"You know I went to the clinic and met with the doctor, had an exam, all of that."

"Yes, I do." His steady gaze softened with concern. "Did something happen? Are you okay?"

Her heart did a fluttery thing at the look on his face. He was so kind. He *cared*. Genuinely cared. She wasn't sure how or when that happened, but he did, she could tell, and it moved her. "I'm more than okay," she assured him when she found her voice again. "I'm great. Perfect health. And my doctor thinks I shouldn't have much trouble conceiving."

"That's fantastic." Logan's warm smile made her skin heat up. "I'm glad for you, Tess, really."

"But there's one major factor I don't have in place yet," she barreled on, making herself talk before she lost her nerve, which was a possibility. "I still need a sperm donor. I haven't been able to decide on one yet."

"How does that work?" Logan asked. "They have, like, what, a database or something? Is that where you choose?" He picked up his utensils again and cut into his steak, taking a bite.

"Yes, exactly. And I've been going over them, and there are a few decent candidates based on the bios, but . . ." Her heart thudded so hard she wondered if he could hear it. "This is my child we're talking about. I want to find someone who will bring a lot to the table, so to speak. It's a tall order."

"Well, sure it is," Logan said. Now that she was talking, she supposed he'd relaxed some, because his eyes weren't searing through her anymore and he was eating. Casual again, no problems here. "I don't envy you that. Must be hard, and nerve-racking. Plus, you just hope these guys— the potential donors—are telling the truth, right? You don't really know, since you don't know them."

"Yes!" she enthused, leaning in. "Exactly that! I know the clinic has a stringent screening process, but sure, those men can lie about some things, how do I know? So . . ."

A new wave of determination zipped through her, and she folded her hands on the table as she leveled her gaze on Logan. "There's a thing called a *known donor*. A lot of women go that route. They're able to go into the process fully confident, because the donor is someone they know. Could be a boyfriend, or just a friend . . . someone they already know and trust."

"Makes sense," Logan said, and took another bite.

"I'm glad you think so." Tess swallowed hard. "The thing is, I have someone in mind to ask. I know it's a monumental thing to ask of someone, but I have gotten to know this man. And I think most of his attributes—both physical and emotional—are ones that I'd be proud to have in my own son or daughter. I just don't know how to get the words out."

Logan half smiled, still chewing . . . then stopped chewing. He swallowed hard, meeting her eyes. "Tess . . . this proposition of yours. It wouldn't be . . ."

"Yes, Logan." Her heart nearly thumped its way out of her chest, but she said, "I'm asking you if you'd consider being my sperm donor."

Chapter Twelve

Logan's heart nearly stopped in his damn chest. "You've got to be kidding me."

"Not at all." Tess met his stare, a confident gleam in her eyes that unnerved him. "There would be conditions, of course. And legal documents and the like I'd need you to agree to and sign. But yes, I want you to be my donor. The more I've thought about it, the more I know you're a fantastic choice."

"The more you—you've *thought* about this?" he stammered. "About me?"

"A lot."

"This is nuts." He practically flung down his knife and fork. "You've been here for what, two weeks?"

"Tomorrow will be three, actually. But I know what I know."

"And what's that, Tess?" He felt his blood race and start a low simmer. "What do you know?"

"That you're a smart, caring, seriously decent man," she said fervently. "That you possess quiet strength and deep compassion for others. You also have a sense of humor, dry as it is, and you're clever and friendly. Those traits alone made me unable to knock you off the top of my wish list." She fidgeted with the edge of her plate, rubbing at something that wasn't there. "Add to all that your physical attributes, of which there are many, and it made so much sense. You're . . . you're the package deal I've been looking for. You bring so much . . . I'm convinced it's the right choice." She sat up a little straighter, took a quick breath, and met his stare directly. "So, that's my proposition. I'm not asking for an immediate answer, but for you to think about it. Would you consider being my donor?"

He gaped at her, stunned speechless. His head was spinning.

"I'd need you to have a full screening, of course," she continued. "Both medical and psychosocial. But we know each other. We've become friends. So we can actually talk about things, which is such an amazing advantage! I can ask you any questions directly, and I trust you'll be truthful with me in answering them." She drew a quick breath and licked her lips. "It just makes so much sense to me."

He stared at her, this beautiful, commanding woman, as a million thoughts raced through his head. Finally he said, "You're out of your damn mind."

She blinked but said simply, "I disagree."

He swore under his breath. "Tess, I'm . . . flattered. Really. I had no idea you thought . . . so highly of me."

"I do."

"Thank you. But no way can I help you on this." His chest was tight, and he had to push out air to speak. "It's a terrible idea. You haven't totally thought it through."

"On the contrary," she said with such composed sureness that it threw him. "I've thought of little else the past few days."

Jesus. How could he make her see he was the worst candidate on earth for something like this? "I'm a recovering alcoholic," he said staunchly.

"Stress on *recovering*. Which speaks volumes about your character, willpower, and strength."

"Thank you, but that doesn't mean it's gone forever. I could relapse at any time."

"I suppose you could," she conceded. "But if you haven't relapsed even once in eleven years, the chances get lower as more time passes. My money's on you."

"And that's okay with you? That risk factor?" He glared at her, trying to get her to understand. "It's in my genes, Tess. It's a disease."

"I'm fully aware of that. I'm not downplaying it."

"But you are, enough so that it passes the tests? Both medical and psychosocial?"

Her lips pressed together as she formulated her thoughts. He was about to forge ahead when she said, "Yes, it warrants notice. But not enough to knock you out of contention." Her voice and expression turned wry as she added, "My own father is a borderline alcoholic, who just won't ever admit to it. He certainly didn't have traumatic circumstances like you did. You've worked hard to overcome that part of your life, and you have. Admirably. That strength of mind and character outweighs the potential risk. At least, for me." She smiled softly. "Besides. You won't be raising the child. I will. Even if you do fall off the wagon . . . it won't be around my child. So. Next rebuttal. Hit me."

Logan's jaw went slack. "You're serious. You're fucking serious about this."

"Dead serious," she said.

"My mother has cancer," he said. "What about that? That's in my medical history."

"My aunt had breast cancer," she said. "Thankfully, she beat it, but she had it. That's a direct link too. Unfortunately, most people have a relative who's had cancer. I can't take any potential donor off the list for that. What else?"

He raked his hands through his hair and sat back. This woman was insane. She was out of her goddamn mind if she thought he was the answer to her prayers. But she seemed so fiercely convinced, it was mind-blowing. And made him want to shake her. He pulled at the neck of his sweater, which suddenly felt too tight around his throat. "I'm not a good candidate."

"I think you are. For many reasons."

"Why, because we have some chemistry? You're attracted to me, you think I'm good-looking?" he said, knowing he was losing control but unable to stop the slide. "You want to make sure your child is tall and pretty? That's super flattering, but not enough of a reason to—"

"Of course you're good-looking," she said flatly. "Yes, I'm attracted to you. Come on, you're gorgeous. That's just a fact. Do your physical traits help keep you on the yes list? Absolutely, I won't deny that. You will make strong, beautiful children. But that's not enough of a reason for me to ask you to be my donor, to make up half the DNA of my child." Her elegant brows arched as she added sharply, "Give me a little more credit than that. I can find a good-looking man anywhere. It's what's inside that counts. Do I really have to say that?"

He scratched at his beard. She kept throwing him for loops, and her single-minded focus on what she wanted was scary as hell. He had to get real with her. Remind her he was so far from perfect, it was laughable that she'd even consider him a prospect. "There's something you seem to have forgotten about me." His voice hardened, and every muscle in his body went taut with tension. "I don't want kids."

He thought it'd be the thing that stopped her cold. But

her big blue eyes took on an almost victorious gleam, and she practically purred, "That, Logan, is what makes you absolutely *ideal* as my donor." She smiled, and he imagined that must be what she looked like at work when she was about to close in for a killer deal in the boardroom. It was both glorious and intimidating. "I don't want you to be my baby's father. I want you to be the sperm donor. There's a world of difference in there. Can I explain further? Are you willing to listen?"

Too mixed up to say much, he nodded, figuring the least he could do was hear her out. Plus, hell yes, he was curious to know what was going on in that sharp mind of hers.

"I want to have a baby and raise it on my own. I don't want a partner, and I don't need a father figure." A long, wayward curl bounced into her eyes, and she brushed it back impatiently. "You know I have the resources to ensure I can raise a child well. I have the money, I'll make the time, and I have so much love to give . . . my child will want for nothing."

"Except a father." Logan couldn't believe that'd burst from his mouth, but it had.

She didn't even blink. "I have three amazing brothers," she said. "My child will never lack for male role models or fatherlike affection. If anything, I can say with full confidence that my child's three uncles will make sure he or she never feels unloved, or feels a lack of that kind of attention."

Logan found himself nodding. "Well . . . I've never met Pierce, but from what I know of Charles and Dane, you're probably right."

"I know I'm right. We're all very close. My child will have three doting uncles, three lovely aunts, and a ton of cousins. He or she will have a big, loving family." That hurdle cleared, Tess barreled on. "I hate to say it, but the fact that you've told me in no uncertain terms that you don't want kids is so ideal for me, it's ridiculous. The fact that you don't want to be a father is *perfect*, because I don't want you to be its father."

She paused for a moment to let that sink in. "In fact, I'll be drawing up legal documents for my donor—you, hopefully, but if not, whoever I choose—stating that the donor agrees to relinquish any and all parental rights. All parental rights, all financial rights, *everything*. This child is going to be mine, and mine alone. I take full responsibility. I *want* it that way. I'm not asking you to be a father. I'm not asking anything of you . . . except for your badass DNA."

Logan wanted to be affronted, offended, and outraged. But seeing it from her side, it all made a lot of sense. Did that make her controlling? Maybe. It also showed just how much thought she'd put into this. She was clear on her wants and decisions, wasn't hiding that, was going to cover her ass legally . . . He had to give her credit for covering every angle.

"Does that make you feel any better about it?" she asked, her voice softer and eyes shining with . . . ah hell, hope. She was really hoping he'd say yes to this craziness. "You'd still have your freedom, your own life. I'm just . . . well, to be blunt, I'm just asking for your sperm. That may sound callous, I know that. But also completely open and honest." Her tongue darted out to lick her lips. "I think you possess so many qualities I'd love to have in my child, Logan. I can sit here for a while and list all your good qualities . . ." She tried to grin, probably to offset the hesitance he caught in her voice.

Then those brilliant blue eyes of hers got glassy, and his heart nearly stopped in his chest. "Will you help me, Logan? I know it may sound a little wild, and I know it's a lot to ask. I do know that. I'm not taking this lightly, and neither should you. But would you at least think it over?"

He couldn't breathe. He couldn't think. Something rose up in his chest and cut off his air. He shoved away from the table and shot to his feet. "I'm sorry, Tess." His voice felt rough in his throat. "I can't. No. Just no."

She looked up at him, the hope in her eyes dissolving into disappointment. Goddammit, that sent a lance through his gut. But she blinked it away, put on her best game face, and murmured, "All right. I understand." She sat up a little straighter, recomposing herself as her gaze dropped to the table. He was glad for that, because that stark look in her eyes had been almost too much to take. Then she reached for her water glass . . . and he noticed her hand was trembling.

His entire core clenched miserably.

"I have to go." He pulled his wallet from his pocket and threw a few bills on the table. He couldn't look at her. He knew it was wrong, but he had to get out of there. "I'm sorry." Grabbing his coat from the back of his chair, he headed for the door and stormed out into the night.

For three days, Logan stewed over Tess's unbelievable request. The first day, he was upset and a little angry, but by that night he admitted to himself there was no good reason to be angry. How could he be anything other than flattered, really? The anger was misdirected. He was angry at *himself*, for being a damn coward. Running out on her like that . . . Jesus, what a dick move. He was better than that . . . or at least he thought he was, but he'd high-tailed it out of that bistro like he was racing Usain Bolt.

He'd let her down, in more ways than one. He should

have handled it so much better. He was ashamed of his knee-jerk reaction. Tess Harrison might be a formidable woman, but he knew it couldn't have been easy for her to ask him what she had. She made a good case, he had to give her that. But despite her confident voice, level gaze, and regal bearing throughout most of it, her sad eyes and shaking hand at the end were what he couldn't get out of his mind. Every time he replayed that moment in his mind, he cringed. He hated that he'd hurt her in any way. It'd been fight or flight in its purest, caveman form.

On the second day, he moved to indignation as he reminded himself he owed her nothing. They barely knew each other, right? If she was disappointed, that wasn't his fault. He'd told her flat out, several times, that he didn't want a family of his own. He did *not* want kids. He hadn't even gone into the depths of his reasons for this, but he'd given her enough background that she'd had to know he'd likely turn her down. Yet there she sat, strikingly beautiful and brave as she listed reasons—many reasons—why she'd chosen *him* as the man she wanted to help her make a baby. The gravity of that decision humbled him when he thought about it, and by the second night, when he lay in bed unable to sleep, it really hit him. He was honored that any woman, much less a woman like Tess, would think highly enough of him to make such an important, life-changing request. It was astonishing and terrifying at the same time.

By the third day, he thought mainly of Tess herself. What a unique woman she was. He was unbelievably flattered that of all the men she could choose to father her child, she'd thought about it at length and chosen him. *Him*. She must've known men with more money and power, higher educations, equally attractive . . . and, not blinded by love or need, had decided he was the one she wanted to father her child. If that wasn't the most mind-bendingly flattering, touching thing anyone could ever think of someone, he didn't know what could top it.

And how had he repaid her lovely desire and bravery in asking? By blowing her off in every way. He hadn't spoken to her, texted her, not a word to her since he'd walked out on their dinner. If he'd wanted to prove to her he was a total fucking asshole, he was doing a fine job of it, wasn't he.

She hadn't tried to contact him either. He didn't blame her.

But no matter what he did, he couldn't get her out of his head. He worked every day, he hit the gym, worked some more, watched movies at night . . . but nope, there she was, in his mind. Her presence had infiltrated him, and he couldn't get away from it . . . from himself.

She even permeated his dreams. Not the occasional steamy, erotic dreams that had him waking up hard and needy. No, these dreams all featured that crushed look that had flickered in her marine-blue eyes before she'd managed to cover. Some dreams, she was at his house, trying to talk to him, with him rebuffing her, trying to get away from her, feeling like shit about it even as he did so. In one dream, she rocked in the rocking chair at his mother's house, holding a little pink bundle in her arms. When he went over to take a peek at the baby, she glared at him, stood up, and stalked away from him, slamming the door behind her. That one woke him with a start, bathed in sweat. What the hell had that woman done to him?

At the end of the third day, he knew he couldn't just avoid her forever, and he didn't want to. He wanted to talk to her, to reach out . . . He just had no idea what the hell to say beyond *I'm sorry*. And he had to go over there that evening to take out her garbage . . . Maybe when he did, he'd try to talk to her. If she even wanted to.

But he had dinner plans. He'd go do her trash run afterwards. By the time he pulled into his mother's driveway at six, the stars overhead had been twinkling for a while already. His breath came in white puffs against the clear, frigid night air.

Annmarie looked up at him from the couch as he let himself into the house. Her smile faded into a frown of confusion. "What happened to you?"

"What do you mean?" Logan shrugged out of his coat and dropped it onto the armchair. "I'm fine."

"You're a rotten liar."

"Good to know."

"You look down. Or pissed off. Or both." She grabbed his shirtsleeve as he sat down beside her, and demanded, "Talk to me."

He shook his head, then mumbled, "I hurt someone's feelings. Someone I like and respect. I've been a total jackass. So I'm just . . ."

"Mad at yourself. Stewing over it." She sighed and patted his knee. "So fix it."

"I know. I have to. I'm just not sure if I can."

"Only one way to find out."

"Yup." He scrubbed his hands over his face. "So, lady? Ready for dinner?"

"I'm not too hungry," she said. "Just something simple would be fine. I was going to make a can of soup and tell you not to come, but I knew you wouldn't listen."

"Got that right." He got back up and headed for the kitchen. "I'll make you something simple, and you're going to eat it."

162   *Jennifer Gracen*

"Yes, sir, Mister Bossman, sir," she joked, and lay down again.

He found two cans of split-pea-and-ham soup in her cupboard and heated them, and sliced some of the thick sourdough bread she had. They enjoyed a quiet dinner.

"Tell me something," Annmarie ventured. "Any chance the person you're beating yourself up over is a woman?"

He looked at his mother. The hope in her eyes . . . He couldn't stand to disappoint another woman he cared about. Not this week, anyway. "Yeah. But it's not—"

"You seeing someone?"

"No, Mom. We've . . . just spent a little time together. We talk. Went skiing a few times."

"Ah! I miss skiing. Wish I still had the energy." She ripped off a piece of bread and dunked it lightly into her soup. "Where've you been skiing?"

"Ajax."

"Great runs. She any good?"

"Yeah, she is, which is nice."

"Of course it is." Annmarie chewed her bread slowly, then asked, "Any chance you'll tell me who this is?"

Why not? Let his mom have her thrills. "Tess Harrison. The one who—"

"I know who that is. You went out with her on New Year's Eve. Pretty girl?"

"Stunning," he admitted. "In fact, she might be the most beautiful woman I've ever seen. Not kidding."

Annmarie's eyes flew wide. "I wanna see a picture then, dammit!"

Logan laughed for the first time all day. It felt good. And the spark of excitement in his mother's eyes made him feel even better. He pulled his phone from his jeans pocket. "Here, I'll show you, all right? Sate your curiosity before it gets out of control." He typed in the Harrison

Foundation website on the search engine. "But Mom, she's just a friend. Don't get too nuts, okay?"

"Yeah, yeah." She waved her hand impatiently. "Gimme!"

He chuckled again and scrolled until he found the picture of Tess from the Harrison Foundation Holiday Ball a few weeks ago. In that knockout red dress, silk and sparkles draped over her long, willowy frame, her long dark curls everywhere. The one that had made him lose his breath the first time he saw it. "Here." He handed the phone to his mother.

And watched her eyes bug out of her head, making him chuckle again. She gaped at the photo, then looked up at him. "She's gorgeous! You weren't exaggerating."

"I rarely do, Mom."

"Is she a model? An actress?"

"No. Her mother was, but she's a businesswoman. She comes from a very wealthy family in New York. Long Island. She runs their charity foundation, and she's damn good at it, from what I can tell. And she's a painter on the sly, though most people don't know that. That's her real passion, art. She loves to paint." Logan found himself running off at the mouth and swallowed a spoonful of soup.

Annmarie handed him back the phone, staring hard. "And you're just friends."

"Kind of. I mean . . . we're starting to be. Or, were." Recollection slammed him in the gut, the lick of shame washing through him. He shoveled more soup into his mouth.

"So what happened?" Annmarie folded her hands on the table and stared him down. "Come on, honey, talk to me. Maybe I can help."

"She . . ." He sighed and put his spoon down. He couldn't tell her everything. It occurred to him with a jolt that she'd probably be all for his being Tess's donor, and holy hell to that. "She's a good woman. A really good one. And she asked me to do something for her that I just can't do."

"Can't? Or won't?"

"Both."

"And would that be something like becoming her boyfriend?"

"No," he said with a wry grin. "I wish it were that simple."

"You like her," Annmarie almost purred, her eyes narrowing on her son.

"Yeah, I do. She's really . . ." He huffed out a breath and admitted out loud, "If I were going to date someone, she'd be the kind of woman I'd want. She's got it all."

"So what's the problem? She's rich and you're not?"

"Nah. I thought so at first, but no. She's not like the others. She's genuine. Down-to-earth. Kind and unpretentious."

"So what's holding you back?" she asked. "I don't see a problem, other than you're a grumpy stubborn jackass."

He laughed and conceded, "You're not totally wrong on that."

"You haven't had a woman in your life for such a long time. When are you going to take another chance?"

"I'm not looking to do that."

"Why on earth not?"

He sighed again, frustration building in his chest. Telling her only parts of it wasn't helping after all. "It's complicated, Mom."

"I bet you're making it complicated. Just stop over-thinking for once. Get out of your head and back into life."

"I have done that," he asserted curtly.

"Not enough," she retorted. "You live a loner's life.

When I'm gone, you're going to be completely alone, and that saddens me."

"Well, don't die, then." He picked up his glass of ginger ale and chugged.

"Logan . . ." Her gaze turned somber.

His stomach lurched. "No. No, Mom. The doctor said if you keep up with the protocol, you have a shot at beating this."

"A shot. Odds aren't in my favor. It's not going my way."

"So what." He pinned her with his gaze now, both glad to turn the topic away from him and needing to talk sense into his bullheaded mother. "You have to keep fighting. I'd do it for you if I could, but I can't."

"I know you would," she said with a soft smile. She reached across and patted his arm, gave his hand a squeeze that he returned. Then she pushed back from the table. "Couch time for me."

He moved to rise and she held up a hand. "I'm fine. I'm tired, but I'm fine. If I need your help, I'll ask."

"No, you won't, you stubborn mule," he grumbled.

She fixed him with a look and drawled sarcastically, "Gee, sounds like someone I know."

"Hey, tree, I'm just the apple."

She laughed and walked away from the table. "Okay if you clean up?"

"Like I'd let you help."

"You're the best, darlin'." She turned back to look at him, leaning against the door frame that separated the tiny dining area from the living room. "You really are the best, Logan. The best son a woman could ask for, and the best man I know. I hope you know how much I appreciate you, and everything you do for me. I love you."

He swallowed hard to dislodge the lump in his throat and managed roughly, "I do know. And I love you too."

"I don't mean to nag." Her smile twisted, turning a little wicked. "Well, that's not totally true. You need me to nag you sometimes."

He barked out a laugh. "I wouldn't know who you were if you didn't, lady."

"Damn right. But when I nag you about dating . . ." She sagged a little against the door frame. "I just want you to find someone, to know you won't be alone. It's a big world to be alone in. And . . . I saw what happened to you before when you isolated yourself. I desperately don't want that to happen again."

His stomach churned anew. A flash of a memory seared through his brain: When his mom came down to New Orleans, after he'd finally confessed to her he'd lost everything, she'd found him lying drunk as hell on his living room floor. And sprang into action, grabbing him from under his arms and tugging until she got him to his couch. She'd grunted and pushed; he was a big guy, and it took strength she barely had, but she'd picked him up off the ground, literally. God, how scared and sad she must've been, finding him in squalor like that . . .

"It won't happen again," he managed, his voice gruff. "I swear that to you. I was a different person then."

"I know you were. You've come so far, that guy's in the rearview." She reached up to rub her shoulder as she spoke. "But you've got a big warm heart in there that you've tamped down for a long time. You're a giver. I want you to find someone to give all that good in you to, you know? And someone who can give it back to you. You deserve that. We all do." Annmarie's moss-green eyes clouded over. "I had that with your father . . ." She smiled briefly, a mixture of sadness and pride in her features. "You would've been a great father. You're so much like him. It's such a shame you never had any kids. They'd have been lucky to have you for a dad."

Her words hit his chest like she'd kicked him with steel-tipped boots.

"Maybe I'll stick around long enough to at least make sure you find a solid woman to share your life with. That's all I want for you, honey. I don't want . . ." She paused, cleared her throat, and said so quietly he almost couldn't hear, "I don't want you to be lonely like I've been since I lost your father. After he was gone, at least I had you and your brother. Having you boys . . . that saved me. Gave me purpose, and light, a reason to live on and to live well." Her eyes locked on him. "When I'm gone? You'll have no one. You understand now? Why I worry about you? I don't care how old you are. You never stop worrying about or wanting for your children." She lifted her chin in a defiant gesture and added, "I'm not sorry for that."

He stood slowly, his throat too tight to speak, and went to her. Drawing her into his arms for a hug, he could feel the loss of weight on her, feel the bones in her back . . . She'd never felt so fragile in his arms before. "I love you, Mom." He closed his eyes and kissed the top of her head. Her short blond hair, which had always been silky, felt coarse beneath his mouth. When it had grown back after the first round of chemo, it'd come back different. It still startled him on occasion. "I'll be okay, no matter what. I swear it. Don't you worry about that."

"I know. I know." She withdrew from his embrace, patted his cheek. "That beard is so thick. Again, so much like your father . . ." With a smile, she made her way to the couch.

Logan watched her as she went. Her pace was slow but steady. She didn't need his help. So why did he have to rein in, with everything he had, the urge to help her? She was proud and still okay; he had to stop hovering. When she needed him, he had to trust she'd ask.

"So you never did say what Tess asked you for," Annmarie said, once she was settled into her usual spot on the sofa. "But whatever it was, I say do it. Because life is short, and you like her, and why the hell not."

"I want her to have what she wants," he blurted. "She deserves it more than anyone. I just . . . don't think I should be the person to give this particular thing to her."

"Damn, you're cryptic tonight."

"I don't want to betray her trust."

Annmarie nodded. "I can understand that. You're always honorable. One of the things I'm proudest of. So I'll just ask you one thing." Her tired eyes held his intently. "If you give her this . . . thing. Do you have anything to lose?"

That made him pause. "Truthfully? No, if I give her what she asked for, even on her terms, I have nothing to lose."

"Well, then." Annmarie grasped the woven blanket and spread it over her legs. "I'd say it warrants further consideration, don't you?"

Something hummed in his core. "Maybe it does," he murmured.

Chapter Thirteen

Tess stroked Bubbles's soft fur as they curled together on the couch. With her other hand, she held her e-reader as she read. The fire crackled in the hearth . . . and her stomach growled. She glanced at the clock, then out the window. It was dark outside; she'd missed dinner altogether. Getting lost in a good book had helped make a few hours fly by. And even though she was hungry, she felt serene too. For the first time in three days.

It was nice to have had those few sweet hours without thinking of the ovulation cycle she was wasting, or the profiles of the potential donors she'd combed through again, or most of all, Logan Carter.

While their talk had gone pretty much how she'd suspected it would, she hadn't been prepared for his total abandonment. Three days now, and not so much as a word. She'd gone through the gamut of emotions: upset, sad, angry, disappointed, offended, heartsick. She was starting to wonder if he'd ever speak to her again, or if he was just going to completely avoid her from now on.

Didn't he have any idea how hard it'd been for her to

even ask that of him in the first place? She hadn't been that nervous in a long time. She grunted as she thought of the look on his face as he'd bolted from the restaurant. Sheer panic. And nothing since. Well, if that was his stance, he may as well stay away, for a hundred reasons.

Today, she'd called the clinic and made an appointment for the following afternoon. Time to forge ahead. Narrowing it down to three possible donor choices based on their bios, she intended to have a choice made and the process started by the time she left Dr. Fuller's office. Being proactive in the face of resistance or a setback always made her feel better. There was no more time to waste. She wanted her baby, dammit, more and more with each passing day.

She put the e-reader down and sat up. As soon as she did, Bubbles jumped off the couch and barked as her tail wagged faster.

"You need to go out?" Tess asked.

Bubbles ran for the side door and barked again.

"I'll take that as a *hell yes, Mama, I need to go.*" Tess smiled and rose from the couch. She pulled on her coat, shoved her feet into her Uggs, and grabbed the leash from its hook on the wall. It was freezing out, so Tess didn't linger—and thankfully, Bubbles didn't want to either. She did her thing and they were back inside within three minutes. As soon as Tess was out of her coat and boots, she went to the kitchen to make a cup of tea. She filled the silver kettle with water and put it on to boil. Her cell phone dinged with a text. She glanced at the screen to see Pierce had written: Hey, big sis. How's it going? Miss you.

"Awww," she cooed aloud before typing back, Hi! Miss you too. I'm fine. Enjoying the mountain air, and the peace and quiet.

Good, glad to hear it. Do any skiing?

Yup. Went several times. It was great.

Atta girl.

How's Abby feeling? Tess couldn't help but smile, thinking of Abby being pregnant . . . and that Pierce would be a father. That still amazed her.

Sick as a dog, he answered. Every damn morning. It's awful. She throws her guts up here, then again when she gets to school. I feel so bad for her.

Ugh! Tess wrote, wincing for her sweet sister-in-law. Me too. I'm sure it'll pass in a few more weeks. Give her a big hug for me.

I will. I'll call soon, we'll talk and catch up more. Just wanted to check in.

He always had. Even when Pierce had lived in England, he'd always checked in with her regularly. Tess was so glad that even though he was married now, his life full in different ways, they were still close. Glad you did, she wrote. Yes, let's talk soon. Love you, Soccer Boy.

Love you too, Tessie. Be good.

Tess smiled as she put down the phone. The kettle whistled and she moved it to a different burner, then crossed to the far cupboard and rummaged through the many tins and boxes of tea. There had to be close to twenty different kinds. She couldn't help it—she loved hot tea on a cold winter's day or night, so every time she saw a kind of tea that she thought she might like, she got it. Another one of her indulgences, she supposed, recalling that chat with Logan . . .

Logan. Ugh. She pushed him out of her mind. She didn't want to be upset with him. She knew what she'd asked of him was huge, and didn't blame him for declining. It was the total silence afterwards that had her so damn disappointed in him.

Deciding to go with the hot cinnamon spice, she dunked the tea bag into her mug once, twice—and the doorbell rang, making her startle. Bubbles barked like mad from the other room and came racing by, a blur of white fur and sound, flying right for the door.

Tess wasn't expecting anyone. Her heart skipped a beat; could it actually be Logan? Nah, he was staying away from her like she had the plague. Her long legs had her across the house in a few seconds. "Who's there?" she asked loudly over Bubbles's barking, through the door.

"It's me, Tess."

Wow, it *was* Logan. Interesting. A wave of something whooshed through her, a mixture of trepidation, annoyance, and a little thrill. But the annoyance took over. She straightened to her full height, her chin held high as she opened the door . . . and didn't say a word. She just looked at him. Frigid mountain air rushed in.

Bubbles barked and yipped and leapt up to Logan for attention.

"Hey there, little miss." He bent briefly to pet the dog and give her some love. After a few seconds, appeased, Bubbles took off, headed back to the warmth of her doggie bed by the fireplace. He straightened up again and offered Tess an awkward grin that was more like a grimace. "Hey." His voice was soft, tentative.

He stood there in his usual outfit: blue ski jacket over a navy fleece hoodie, jeans, work boots, navy wool hat pulled down over his mop of blond hair . . . and hints of frost in his beard that glinted as the light hit. Did he have to be so damned handsome?

"Hello." She kept her tone and gaze cool, affable but not welcoming.

He shifted his stance as his eyes traveled over her in brief appraisal. She didn't know what he was assessing; she wore a red and black striped sweater over black leggings. Nothing glamorous. She grew more irritated by the second. Her limbs felt taut from holding back the tension. She swept her long hair back and lifted her chin another notch.

Then he said, "Your body language is screaming *fuck you, Logan, go away*. I don't blame you. I've been an asshole. I handled all this horribly."

Astonishment sucker-punched her. But all she said was, "Yup."

He nodded, and she could see the remorse in his eyes. It was genuine. At least that was one thing she knew for sure about Logan Carter. He was a lot of things, but he wasn't a liar. He was as true as they came. He cleared his throat and said, "I'm here because I'd like to talk. To apologize, and . . . some other things. If you'll hear me out. Can I come in?"

Her heart melted a little, but she'd be damned if she'd let him see that. "Sure." She moved aside to let him pass. He entered the foyer and looked to her for cues; she turned and walked farther into the house. "I was just making some tea. Would you like some?"

"No, thank you," he said as she went back to the kitchen, and he followed. "So . . . how are you?"

"Fine, thanks." She removed the tea bag from her mug and placed it on a nearby saucer. She lifted the steaming cup to her face and inhaled the delicious scent of the tea, her eyes closing for a second from the pleasure. Then she turned away, saying over her shoulder, "Let's talk in the dining room." It was more formal there. The thought of curling up beside him on the couch was more than she wanted right then. "And take off your coat if you're staying."

"I'd like to stay." His deep voice was so earnest, it made her stop and turn back to look at him. He was behind her, his eyes tight with ambivalence, making the corners crinkle appealingly. "We have a lot to discuss."

That made her stomach do a little flip. But she was Tess Harrison, and dammit, she knew how to cover her emotions when necessary. That was Life As a Harrison 101. "Really," she said. "Then let's do that." She went to the dining area, gesturing with a sweep of her hand for him to sit where he wanted. She sat at the head of the polished wooden table as he shrugged out of his coat and hoodie.

"You took the power position," he noted as he placed his things on a chair. "You're pretty pissed at me." He yanked off his hat and dropped it onto the same chair, quickly raked his fingers through his golden hair to brush it out of his eyes, and took the seat closest to her, at her right, watching her with intent.

She sipped her tea as he settled his big frame into the ornate, high-backed cherrywood chair. In his blue and gray flannel, her rugged, sexy guest looked slightly out of place at the long, elegant table. She kind of liked that. Finally she said, "Yes, I'm pissed at you. But probably not for why you think."

"Do I get to guess?"

"You don't have to. I'll tell you outright, if you really want to know."

His pale green eyes met hers. "C'mon, Tess, I know

why. And you *should* be mad. I would be too, if someone I'd come to think of as a friend disappeared on me without a word for days. Much less after I asked something enormous and made myself vulnerable."

Impressed with his insight, she only nodded and sipped again.

"I'm very sorry for how I've behaved," he said. "It's inexcusable."

"Well . . . it's not *totally* inexcusable," she said. "Not the first few hours of it, anyway. I took you off guard, I shocked you with something major."

"Damn right you did. But the two days since? No excuse."

Respect sparked in her core. But hurt and disappointment still reigned. "There I have to agree as well. And before you proceed any further, you should know I'm not interested in excuses."

His eyes rounded for a second. "You get formal when you're furious. Like . . . haughty. Even your word choices . . . Interesting. I have to remember that. The more regal and frosty you get, the more trouble the other person's in."

He kept impressing her with how clearly he understood her, but she wasn't ready to take her icy wall down just yet. "You're not in trouble, Logan. Things are just . . . different now."

"I deserve that. But . . ." He leaned in a drop and asked softly, "Any chance you'd be willing to let me back in? I'd like to try."

Her heart skipped a beat and she swallowed hard. Damn. Damn him and his magnetism and natural charisma and sharp perceptiveness and his beautiful eyes staring into hers. "Don't know yet. But I do appreciate your coming here and trying to make amends. Better late than not at all, I suppose." Her hands circled her mug, hot beneath her skin. "What did you want to discuss?"

"I hate the formal Tess." He rubbed the back of his neck and sighed. "Makes me want to shake you and get the real Tess to come out. The sweet one, the warm one."

She just stared at him, even as her breath caught.

"And I hate that guarded look in your eyes," he said. "I know I'm the one who put it there. Yes, I let you down. I'm so sorry. I just needed time to think. To process your . . . request."

Her heart squeezed. She sipped some more tea, welcoming its warmth as it helped stretch out the silence. If he wanted to get back into her good graces, she still needed more.

He sighed again, heavily. "Mostly, I wanted to apologize for bailing on you like I did. I'm really sorry I acted like such a dick. You deserved better. I'm very sorry."

"Thank you." She set the cup down. "I appreciate that."

"And"—his eyes met and held hers—"I've missed you. That surprised me."

She didn't move, transfixed. The waves of intensity and longing that came off him were so strong and raw, they were palpable.

"Somehow, my little texts with you became a bright spot in my day. I . . ." His voice softened, but his gaze didn't waver as he admitted, "I missed that. And you. I've enjoyed the growing friendship. I only hope I haven't wrecked it permanently."

Her stomach filled with butterflies. She drew a long, deep breath, then said, "Your coming here to talk like this . . . goes a long way. It's not wrecked permanently. I've . . . I enjoy you too. We can try to move on from this."

His stare intensified. "Do you still trust me?"

She blinked at that. His direct question deserved an

honest answer. "Not like I did before, but yes, mostly I still trust you. What you did doesn't change who you are."

His nod came slowly, processing. "Fair enough. All I can do is try to earn your full trust back."

She just stared. That was something he wanted? Did she mean something to him, then? The way he'd started meaning something to her? Her heart did a little fluttery thing that made her draw another deep breath.

"Well. Okay, so . . . there's the other thing I want to talk about." He scratched his beard, his eyes flickering away and back again before it seemed like he was ready to forge ahead. "If you still want me to be your donor, even after what a jackass I've been . . . I'm willing. Actually, I'd be honored. I want to help you. I'll do it."

Her jaw dropped and her heart rate skyrocketed as she stared at him. He . . . he was saying yes? He wanted to help her? *He'll do it?*

"Wow. Your whole face just . . ." His sensual lips twisted in a grin. "Who's the shocked one now?"

She huffed out a breath, stammering, "I . . . I, yes, I'm in shock. That was the last thing in the world I expected you to say."

"I'm sure." He grinned, but it faded as he asked, "Is it too late? Did you scratch me off the list for being an asshole?"

"I took you off the list because I thought your response was a loud and clear *hell no*," she said. "But . . . Logan. Seriously?" She edged a tiny bit closer, questions filling her mind even as her heart thudded away. "What changed your mind?"

"I've been thinking about it." He snorted and added wryly, "Haven't been able to think of much else, really."

She gaped at him, stunned speechless.

He reached forward, cautious, tentative, and took her

hand in his. His skin felt a little rough, and so warm, as his huge hand wrapped around hers. "I can't tell you how flattered I am that you want me to . . . well, I was going to say be the father of your child, but that's not it, really. That you want any of my DNA in your child. That you think that highly of anything I have to offer."

"I do," she whispered.

"Still?"

"Still."

He squeezed her hand and she squeezed back as they looked into each other's eyes. "You'll be an amazing mother, Tess," he said. "I have no doubt of that. You deserve to have the baby you want so much . . . and any child will be so incredibly lucky to have you for his or her mom."

Tears sprang to her eyes. "Oh, Logan. Thank you for saying that."

"I mean it. I really do, or I wouldn't be here. Also . . ." He caressed the back of her hand with the calloused pad of his thumb. The gentle intimacy of the gesture fired sparks in her as he continued. "I have to admit that the more I thought about everything you presented, the more it made sense. I mean . . . you think my physical and mental traits are ones you'd like in your child? That's amazing to me." Something like awe lit his eyes.

"But then there's the other part: I don't want kids." His voice was firmer now. "I made that pretty clear. And you know what? That *does* work to your advantage. Because you don't want a partner, or a guy who wants to be an active part of your child's life. You're not asking me to be a father, you're not asking anything of me except to just . . . contribute, and then leave you and the child alone. Which is pretty much the only way I'd agree to it, because I don't want that responsibility. So all that makes me a dream candidate, doesn't it? I'm the right guy to ask."

Her breath caught and tears slid down her cheeks. "Yes. Yes, all of those things were considerations in my decision."

"Okay." He reached up and brushed her tears away with gentle fingers, gazing at her with kindness and acceptance. Something inside her melted and overflowed with warmth. "So. What do you need from me? Testing, I guess?"

Still stunned, she stared for a few more seconds, then blinked, sniffed hard, and nodded. "Umm, yeah. Yes. I have an appointment at the clinic tomorrow at one o'clock. Any chance you'd be free to come with me? I guess they could tell us what we need to do, test you there, start everything . . ." Her voice trailed off as her eyes locked on his face. "Are you sure about this, Logan? Really sure?"

"Yes." He took both of her hands in his and met her gaze without flinching, without hesitation. Something passed between them, electric and warm and pure. "I want you to have the child you want. I'll do . . . well, my part." He grinned. "Awkward."

They laughed together. Her heart felt light, her soul free. She couldn't believe it. Her whole world had just changed . . . She was going to have her baby. He was going to help make her biggest, most important dream come true. Overwhelmed, she jumped up from her chair and flung herself at him, hugging tight. He rose as he hugged her back, bringing them both to standing. They held each other as she whispered against his ear, "Thank you. Thank you so much. Thank you."

Logan held Tess close. The moment was so powerful, so charged with emotion, it made his heart beat harder and his head spin. Her gratitude, joy, and relief were tangible, moving him more than he could grasp.

He ran a hand over the long curtain of her hair, down her back and up again as she whispered fervent thanks against his ear. The catch in her voice, the raw feeling . . . so many feelings. God, she made him feel, both emotionally and physically. He savored the feel of holding her. The feel of her body against his had his blood pulsing, skin heating. She was softness and warmth and beauty, intoxicating . . . He could drown in her. But all he said was, "You're welcome."

After a minute, he pulled back to look into her face. Her beautiful features seemed imbued with light. Had he done that? Before it went further, he said, "There's a few things I need to go over, though. I, uh . . . have a few questions. And, actually, a request of my own."

She blinked, then snapped right into action mode. He so admired her focus, her sharp edge. Must've been partly the awesomeness that was her, and partly having to keep up with an overbearing father and three powerful brothers. "Let's go into the living room and get comfortable, then. Sounds like this talk is about to get even more interesting."

Chapter Fourteen

Logan's heart started pounding in thick, heavy beats as he trailed behind her. The fire blazed in the fireplace, Bubbles seemed to be asleep in the corner, and he sat with Tess on the long, rust-colored couch. She sat on one end, facing him, tucking her long legs beneath her as she pushed her wild mane of curls back from her face.

"So," she said. "Talk to me. I'm sure you have questions."

"Yeah . . ." He cleared his throat. "Couple of things."

"The legal stuff?"

"Well, sure, we can start with that. I assume you're going to have papers drawn up by your top-notch New York lawyers. What exactly am I signing?"

"You'll be waiving all rights to any claim of paternity. I'll put your name on the birth certificate, for my child's sake. Every child needs to have that; a blank space would be mean. But as far as legal or financial rights or responsibilities, custody, anything of that nature, you'll have to agree to give up *all* of that. To be blunt, this won't be your child, Logan. Only mine." Tess paused, searching his face. "You sure you're all right with that?"

"One hundred percent," he said firmly. "I'd like to look the papers over, just to see what I'm signing, but yes, I'll agree to all that. C'mon, Tess. You can give a child everything in the world. Me . . . not so much. But . . ." He hesitated, not wanting to offend her, but he had to ask. "That goes both ways. You won't change your mind at some future point? Come after me and demand that I be a dad, start asking things of me? Sue me over it?"

She blinked and her jaw dropped. It was crystal clear to him those things had never even crossed her mind, which reassured him. "No," she said. "I won't. But if you want me to sign something swearing to that, I will. Reciprocation is fair play."

He only nodded. He trusted her. Then he said, "Reciprocation . . . Funny you bring up that word. Because I have a request of my own. Separate from this." Shit. What he'd thought of made sense on the drive over here, but now, saying it out loud filled him with apprehension. He'd sound like an idiot. Well . . . too bad. "I'm not saying my agreeing to be your donor is dependent on what I'm about to ask of you—it's not. Okay? I agree to do this, and on your terms. No worries there. But . . . yeah, some reciprocation of goodwill would be appreciated. I need a favor."

She smiled and said, "Okay, I'm listening."

"This might sound crazy," he admitted. "Yeah, it probably is. But I'm going to ask you anyway. Because I realized tonight, you're in a position to help me out with something too."

"Go on. How can I help you?"

He sighed. Was he really going to do this? Yup. Yup, he was. It was worth it. "My mom's dying. There, I said it."

Tess's gorgeous eyes filled with sadness. "I'm so sorry to hear that."

"Thanks." He swallowed hard and barreled on. "I realized that she's focused on me so intensely these past few months because she's afraid after she passes, I'm going to be alone . . . and maybe go back to drinking." He held up a hand before Tess could say a word. "I know I won't. I know I'll be wrecked with grief, but I'd like to think I can get through that without the bottle."

"I'm sure you will." Her voice was gentle, kind but not pitying. He loved that.

"Thank you. Anyway . . . so the thing is . . ." He shifted in his seat, raked his hands through his hair. "I thought, maybe if she sees I'm not alone, it'll help her relax . . . make her happy. So would you be willing to pretend to be my girlfriend for a while?" He watched her eyes widen. "Yes, I know it'd be a lie. I don't mean to deceive her, I don't want to play with her emotions, you understand? I just . . ." His chest tightened. "I want her to have whatever peace she can while she's still on this earth. If she doesn't have to worry about something dumb like this . . ."

"I'll do it," Tess said. "I can do that. You're doing me a tremendous service. I'd be very happy to return a favor, and for a good reason."

Now it was his turn to be slack jawed. "You don't think I'm crazy?"

"No. I think you're a son who loves his mother and wants her to be happy in her final days." Her mouth curved softly. "I can't think of anything more decent than that."

"Even though we'd be lying to her."

"For a really good reason."

He wanted to laugh. He was shocked that he'd even thought of something like this in the first place, and she was ready and willing to go along with it? Either she was amazing, or as crazy as he was. Possibly both. "It's insane. I know that. I just . . ."

"I said yes." Her grin and tone were playful. "But we'll

have to construct a story. Basic things, in case there are questions."

"Yeah, you're right. Okay."

"Also, right off the top of my head? What about the fact that I'll be going back to New York in a few months? How do we address that when she asks?"

"Oh. Good point. Uh . . ." *Damn*. He thought quickly. "We'll just say at that point, we're having a long-distance relationship. Your life is in New York, mine is here. You're rich and more flexible, you have the house here, so you can come visit me and all that. It'll work. But . . ." His chest constricted again. "I'd love to say she'll still be here by the spring, so we'll have to come up with a more elaborate story then. But I don't know if she will. This could be a few months, or more than a few months. I don't know. I really don't. You still okay with that?"

"Yes. It's okay. I'm in for as long as you need me to be, Logan."

"Thank you." He gazed at her with wonder. "You're pretty awesome."

"Back at you." She smiled.

Something in his chest flared with warmth, a sweet blast of feeling. "I appreciate this. I really do. And hey, since it's not a real relationship, feel free to kick my ass anytime I do something you don't like."

"I'd do that even if we were in a real relationship." Her eyes sparkled with more mischief. "But now that I have your blessing? Game on, Carter."

He laughed. "Great. So, listen . . . You're out here all by yourself. I know what a strong woman you are. But during the, uh . . . process, you can lean on me. And on this thing, I'm your cheerleader. I want you to have your baby." He reached out and took her hand. "I know I bailed on you before. It won't happen again. I'm here for you, Tess, however you need me. You'll see."

Her mouth dropped a little, those pretty lips forming an O of surprise.

"You need a ride to or from the clinic, you want someone to go with you, you want someone to be here to hold your hand when you get home . . . I can do that." He rubbed his thumb along the top of her soft skin. "All you have to do is ask. Okay?"

"I'd really like that." Her voice dropped, was a little thick. Light pink dusted her cheeks. "That's . . . that's comforting to know. Thank you."

"You'll see that you can trust me again."

She shook her head. "You don't have to prove—"

"I want to." He cut her off firmly, leaving no room for debate. "So. Your appointment's at one? What time should I be here? We'll go together; I'll pick you up."

"Noon, if you could. Twelve fifteen at the latest. The clinic's just outside city limits, and I always like to be five minutes early wherever I go."

"Okay then. Noon tomorrow, done deal." He kept rubbing her hand. It felt good, and she wasn't pulling it away, so maybe she liked it too. "I don't know what the testing involves. I can tell you I'm clean as far as STDs and all that fun stuff."

She grinned. "Good to know. I'm not sure either. I guess to see how high your sperm count is, if they're healthy swimmers, all of that."

"Well, I'm not twenty-eight, I'm thirty-eight. Don't know how age affects it, but I'm sure it does . . ." He frowned. "I'll be thirty-nine in May. Think it's a problem?"

"Easy, old man. I'm sure it's fine." She tipped her head

to the side, assessing him. "Did you and your ex-wife try to have children?"

"No, we tried *not* to. She was on the pill. We had too much going on, we weren't ready yet. We weren't going to try for kids until we were thirty. We had a plan . . ." Memories crept in. They didn't cause a kick of pain; he didn't feel anything, which was good. He shrugged. "So I don't know if my boys are good swimmers. I use condoms."

She blinked at that. "Use? Present tense? Are you seeing someone?" Her hand slowly but surely slipped out of his.

"No, I'm not seeing anyone now. But I've dated. Had some . . . encounters." He shrugged again. "I don't do relationships, but I'm not a very good monk." He grinned, but peered harder at her. "Does that bother you?"

"Not at all. Your dating life is none of my business," she said. Her tone held no malice, no edge. "I was just surprised. I thought, from your use of present tense, that you were seeing someone."

"There was someone I was seeing last year, kind of on and off," he said. "Casual, not serious. But after a while, I knew she wanted it to become more, and I didn't. So I thought it was fair to her to end it. That was about five months ago. End of the summer. Haven't had any sex since then, by the way. Guess you should know that too?"

Tess bit down on her lip, trying to hide a grin. "That's honest. But you know, you didn't have to tell me that if you didn't want to."

"Hey, if we're going into something like we're about to go into? It's a big deal. We need to be open and honest. Have each other's back. That's how I see it, anyway."

She looked at him with bright eyes, nodding in agreement. "I like that. A lot, actually. You mean, like a team?"

"Yeah, sure. I mean . . ." He shifted in his seat, scooted

a bit closer. "You're trusting me with the biggest thing you could. I'm trusting you with lying to my mom to make her happy, which is a big deal to me. We've both got a lot to lose if it went sideways. So yeah, we need to be a team." He wasn't sure, but the look on her face seemed like she was kind of in awe, and delighted, and even excited. She took his hand in hers, and he welcomed the return of her soft skin, the warmth of it. A swell of something strong washed through him.

She slid along the cushions, edging closer. "We better come up with a story together. Because the thing is, if we're going to sell this to her, you'll have to sell it to the other people in your life too. You realize that, right? If I'm your girlfriend . . ."

He swore under his breath. "Hadn't thought that far ahead."

She caressed his hand, echoing the tenderness of his earlier gesture. "We're a team now, right? We can do this. It might even be fun."

He stilled. Her words sank in . . . What he'd asked her to do sank in. "Why are you so willing to do this, to lie for me?" he asked.

"Because I know you," she said. "Besides, the bottom line is, if you can do something so huge for me, this is the least I can do for you."

He gazed at her, reached out with his free hand to brush a stray curl back from her eyes. "You're one of the most generous people I've ever met," he murmured.

"I could say the same for you right now," she replied. "And you're making me feel so assured about all this . . . You're an honorable man."

"I don't know about that. Some of the thoughts I'm having this second aren't very honorable." Lust zipped through him as he stared at her. Her beautiful face, her alluring presence . . . Christ almighty, she cast spells on him, he was convinced of it.

Her eyes, so blue, took on a new light. She looked at him from beneath her long lashes, the look of a siren. "You know . . . this arrangement . . . if I'm going to be your fake girlfriend, we'll have to kiss and stuff." Her thin brow lifted, a sassy look if he ever saw one. It made his skin heat. "Maybe we should practice."

His blood seared through him, racing south. "Jesus," he half growled.

"Haven't you thought about that?" She scooted another inch closer, tempting him, enticing him.

"Truth? Yeah, it crossed my mind. More than once."

"We do have chemistry," she murmured as he moved closer. "Don't we?"

"Yeah, we do. Maybe we should start that practicing . . ." His heart was close to bursting out of his damn chest, but he managed to look right into her eyes. His blood pulsed through his body. God, he wanted her right there, right then. She was so close, he could smell her light scent, some musky perfume, vanilla maybe? Something that drugged him. She was staring at his mouth now . . . The air was thick with sexual tension.

Yet they both hesitated. "Kissing on demand is a little different than getting lost in the moment, huh."

She breathed out a tiny huff of a laugh, her disbelief pretty clear, at how things had turned. She licked her lips and said, "I was just thinking that. Suddenly we both got shy. What's up with that?"

Grinning, her fingers inched forward to touch his knee, and his cock throbbed. Jesus, he was so turned on already, and all she'd done was move in close and lightly touch his knee.

"I mean," she continued, "if we're going to be a fake couple . . . we'll need to spend a little time together. And the more we get to know each other, the more real it's going to seem. Right?"

"Right." He intertwined his fingers with hers. "Well. This just got even more interesting, huh?" They laughed together, breaking the tension a little. But his body was on fire, and he had to calm it down. "Or, maybe I should go now," he said.

Her eyes flew wide. "What? Why?"

"Because I'm raging inside," he admitted gruffly, noting the way her high color deepened. "I don't know if I'll be able to stop at two or three kisses."

"Who said you have to?" Her voice was low and a little wicked. "I'm not going to count . . ." Her eyes had gone dark with desire. In her gaze, he clearly saw the same lust he was battling. She closed the distance between them, practically putting herself in his lap. Her warm breath fanned against his lips as she whispered, "Practice time. Kiss me."

He didn't need to be asked twice. He pressed his mouth to hers, taking slow, sumptuous sips from her lips as his hands gently cradled her head. She responded slowly at first, but he held her, kissing her until her muscles relaxed under his hands and she eased against him. Within a minute, their mutual attraction took over like wildfire. Her mouth opened to him and he deepened the kisses, his tongue sweeping inside, wanting to taste her, desperate for more. She arched against him, pressing herself close as her arms snaked around his neck. His fingers tangled in her hair, such a thick mass of curls, so soft . . .

"Just friends," he whispered against her lips between kisses, assuring her as much as himself. "Friends with an agenda . . . that happens to include sexy time."

She smiled, melting into his arms. "I like the sound of that."

He kissed her again and again. "Me too."

She tipped her head back to offer better access to her throat. He kissed, licked, nipped his way along her chin and down her neck. Her fingers twisted in his hair, her sighs of pleasure making his blood race. "Best deal I've ever made," she said on a hitched breath. "Both sides, nothing but win."

He chuckled lightly. "I don't know how we got here."

"I don't either," she said, arching against him as his hands ran up her sides. He kissed her neck as his hands covered her small, perfect breasts, bringing a sweet moan from her. "Friends with an agenda is going to be really fun, I think . . ."

He caressed her breasts with one hand while tangling the other in her hair, and looked into her eyes. "Hmm . . . this is more than kissing." His thumb feathered over her nipple, which pebbled beneath his touch. Even as her breath caught, he asked, "Is this okay?"

She arched forward, pressing her breast harder against his hand. "Hell yes, that's okay . . ," With a soft moan, her eyes slipped closed as she let him explore her. Watching her face, he fondled one breast, than the other, mesmerized by her. He was rock hard already, and his jeans felt way too tight. Her delicate features flushed with color as her willowy body undulated beneath him . . . she was breathtaking.

"God, you're beautiful." His hungry mouth consumed hers, taking her under with commanding kisses. He eased her down to lie back against the cushions, positioning himself over her as his demanding mouth took and gave. "I want you right now. So much."

"I want you too," she admitted in a whisper. Her fingertips ran along his beard as they drowned in each other. "But . . . I think . . ."

"If you can still think while I'm kissing you," he said, "I'm not doing a very good job of it."

She laughed. "Believe me, you're doing a good job of it. Too good . . ." He ravaged her neck again and her head fell to the side to give him better access. "It's been a while since I had sex too, you know."

"How long?" he asked as his lips trailed down her throat.

"Labor Day weekend."

"About as long as me." He lifted his head and stared into her eyes. "Maybe we should fix that."

"That's kind of what I was thinking about," she confessed in a whisper.

He crushed his mouth to hers, kissing her deep and hard and hot. She wrapped her arms around his neck and pulled him closer as their tongues tangled, bringing a lusty groan from deep in his throat.

"Tess . . ." He aligned his body with hers. She fit him perfectly. "This is getting dangerous now."

"I know." Her hands moved over his broad shoulders, down his back. "But I can't seem to stop."

He growled against her mouth. "Christ, woman." They kissed urgently, the heat level rising, their hands roaming . . . "If we don't stop," he rasped, "I'm gonna get you pregnant right here, right now."

Her eyes flew wide and she froze.

"That was a joke," he said quickly, even as his erection throbbed against her belly.

"Well, wait." Her hands went to hold his face. As he looked into her eyes, he could see something working behind them as she said, "What if we . . . I mean, you *have* agreed to be my donor . . . There's more than one way to get me pregnant. And one way is a *lot* more fun than the other."

Now it was his turn to go wide-eyed. He stopped cold and stared down at her, all flushed and gorgeous beneath him. "Can we do that?"

"Why not?" She shifted her hips only a drop, but the friction against him made him want to moan. "I mean . . ."

"I have to take tests, you said." His brain was foggy with lust, and his body aligned with hers made it even harder to think. But he held her gaze. "What *are* you saying?"

"Well, if we do things at the clinic, it's a limited number of attempts," she said. "But if we do it the old-fashioned way . . . more attempts would mean a better chance of success, right?" She brought his head down to press his mouth to hers for another kiss. "Not to mention that we're like a house on fire here . . . We're both unattached, we're clearly attracted to each other . . ."

"Ya think?" He ground his erection against her, making them both groan.

She kissed him, her hands on his face, stroking his beard as their tongues swirled and he pressed into her. "Is that weird?" she asked. "Would you be okay with that?"

"Would *you* be okay with that?" he countered. "Because I have no problem sleeping with you, lady. Right now, I want you so bad I can't think straight, because what you're suggesting makes total sense to me."

She wrapped herself around him, her long legs and graceful arms, and kissed him passionately. He responded in a heartbeat, gladly sinking into her, holding her close and tight as they kissed. Her hips rocked against his erection and he groaned into her mouth.

But she pulled away. They were both panting, as breathless as if they'd run a sprint. "Wait. I guess we should talk to the doctor first. About doing it that way. The natural way. I guess?"

His whole body pulsed with want and need, but he nodded. "Probably."

"Okay. Tomorrow. But tonight, you don't have to stop kissing me yet . . ." She grinned, a mixture of adorable and seduction, and his insides flooded with fresh desire.

"Actually, I do," he said when he found his voice. "Because I don't want to stop, and if we need to talk to your doctor, make a plan . . . we should stop now."

"Okay. Yes, all right." Her fingers traced over his cheeks, along his beard. "But I really don't want to, for the record."

"Neither do I, for the record." He smiled down at her in wonder. Her eyes were bright with desire, her cheeks flushed, her lips a bit swollen from their kissing. "You're so damn beautiful, you know that?"

She smiled back and whispered, "So are you."

He couldn't help it, he lowered his head to kiss her again. He had to, he needed to. But he worked to bring down the heat, to kiss her slowly, until it was a sweet, tender exchange instead of an urgent blast of fiery need. "When we have sex for the first time," he finally said, his voice low and deliberate, "it's not going to be on the couch. I'm taking you in that big, fantastic bed of yours, you're going to wrap those insanely gorgeous legs around me, and we'll go all night."

She gave a tiny shiver. "That sounds wonderful." Her eyes locked on his. They were still wrapped in an embrace, and his hard-on hadn't gone down, but they were breathing calmer. "Really, the more I think about it, it makes sense."

"What does?"

"Your being my donor the old-fashioned way. If it's here at home, instead of a clinical setting, I'll be more relaxed. And the more times we try . . ."

"I hear you."

"I'm talking about sleeping together regularly, Logan. We're both clear on that?"

"Yeah." He brushed her curls back from her face. "Are you *sure* about this?"

"If you're okay with it, yes."

"Tess." He ground his hips against hers, his rock-hard erection pressing against her warm heat, making their breath catch. "I want you. I'm more than okay with it. I just don't want to cross any . . . inappropriate lines, you know?"

"I know. And I appreciate that so much. Like I said, you're an honorable man." Her blue eyes danced as she reminded him, "I'm the one who suggested it. And it's my show, right?"

"Absolutely, Miss Harrison. You're the boss."

"Well, I guess I am, but . . . yes, it's agreeing to regular sex, but not a relationship. We wouldn't be actually dating, more like friends with benefits. But it's a team effort."

"There's that word again," he cajoled. "Team." He tweaked her nose and grinned. "We'll be a good team. It's nice to think of us helping each other. And come on, this kind of help? Can be a hell of a lot of fun. Just know that . . . the lusty stuff aside . . ." He looked into her eyes and promised, "I'm here for you. As a friend."

She caressed his face, ran her hand through his hair, and said, "Right back at you." Her tone, filled with emotion, made his insides squeeze. "And I'm a good friend to have. I promise."

He kissed her once more, long and deliberate, as if silently sealing the deal. They looked into each other's eyes and smiled. Then he lifted himself off of her. It wasn't without difficulty; his jeans felt downright constrictive. When he got home, he'd have to either take the coldest shower ever or just take care of himself; he'd never get to sleep this fired up. They untangled themselves from the embrace and separated.

"I'll leave in a minute," he said. "Little hard to walk with a raging hard-on."

She laughed, a warm, full sound that shimmered over his skin. "Stay as long as you want." She licked her lips, definitely swollen from his kisses, and swept her hair back with both hands. "And I'll try not to think about how much I want to see and touch that raging hard-on of yours."

He groaned in agony. "Not helping!"

They laughed together this time.

She grasped his hands, looked into his eyes, and said. "Dream Team. That's us. You're making my dream come true." She lifted his hands to her mouth and kissed his knuckles. "Thank you again, Logan. So much. I really don't know how to thank you."

"You already did. So stop thanking me now," he said. "Giving me a complex."

"Too bad."

He grinned. "Come on, seriously, you don't have to thank me anymore. Please. I know you're grateful, I promise."

"Fiiiiine." She grinned back. "How's that hard-on doing?"

The thought of her thinking about it made it throb anew. "It does better when you don't talk about it."

She barked out a laugh and released his hands. "Oh, Logan. We can really . . . We can have fun with this."

"Yeah. Maybe we can." He took a deep breath, trying to shake the lust from his system. "Friends," he said, scrubbing his hands over his face in an effort to break her spell. "Friends who can trust each other."

"And who maybe can enjoy some sexy time too," she whispered.

He reached up to cup her chin and said somberly, "It'd be an honor."

Her eyes rounded, a look of astonishment sweeping her features. "I . . . wow."

He smiled, dropped a light kiss on her mouth, and released her. "Don't forget, along with the promise of fantastic and frequent sex, I'll have legal papers to sign. That's all on you, right?"

"Yes." She smoothed out her sweater, working to re-compose herself. "I'll call my attorney in the morning. You sure you're okay with all that, right? And I'll add in the part that I'll never come back to try to make you do anything down the line."

"I'll sign all the papers," he said. "I don't want a baby, you do. He or she is all yours. You don't have to worry."

"And when we're with your mom, or out in public, I'll be the best damn girlfriend you could ever ask for," she said. "For as long as you need me to be."

Unaccustomed to the intense emotions that were knocking him around, he moved in and lightly pressed his mouth to hers. Her hands lifted to hold his jaw as she returned the kiss, caressing his beard as she did. The gentle, almost tender kiss ignited something fresh, deep inside him. Something like a renewal. He was looking forward to seeing what came next. Life had just gotten a hell of a lot more interesting.

This situation would benefit them both. They could be friends, helping each other achieve their goals. They were both being open about their wants. No pressure on him about a relationship or expectations, which was how he liked it. There'd be papers to sign, keeping it all legal from her end. And the most important part: Tess would have the baby she so deserved to have. If he passed all the tests, and the doctor gave them the green light, it was all good.

As for her being his fake girlfriend, that could actually be fun—he could see that now. He knew his mother would adore her. Tess would get what she wanted, and he'd get what he wanted. And there could possibly be hot sex thrown in there between friends, a game-changing bonus he hadn't seen coming. Game on.

They were being honest with each other, had a clear agreement, carefully planning everything together, with everything out in the open. What could possibly go wrong?

"So, Mr. Carter?" Those wide blue eyes of hers absolutely sparkled as she smiled gently. God, she was so damn pretty. What a bonus. "We have a deal?"

He cupped her chin again and smiled as he looked at her. She was a fascinating woman. This Long Island lady had blown into his life like a force of nature. She was smart as hell, kind and funny, knew how to separate business from pleasure . . . and also was open to mixing the two. The spots of color on her high cheekbones deepened as he gazed at her. Holy hell, this strikingly gorgeous woman wanted him as much as he wanted her.

Well, he couldn't think of a more worthy teammate. Or a friend. Or a sexier potential lover. All he knew was he was a lucky man, having fallen somehow into an ideal situation. He could help make this incredible woman's biggest dream come true. That was paramount, and made him feel better than anything he'd done in a very, very long time. He could help someone . . . make a lasting difference. Do something deeply good, just for the sake of it, and then be able to walk away.

"Miss Harrison," he murmured, "we have a deal."

Chapter Fifteen

Logan sat quietly during lunch; hell, he didn't have to say much. Tess and his mother were chattering away like old friends. They'd hit it off immediately, as he'd thought they would. How could anyone not like Tess? She was open, friendly, down-to-earth. And really smart. Annmarie liked that, he knew that as well as he knew her. Having been a middle school math teacher for twenty-five years, Annmarie was sharp as a tack, with a keen barometer for bullshit. Tess passed the bar with flying colors before she'd ever stepped foot in the house.

As Annmarie peppered Tess with questions about her job and New York, Logan ate and mused about the past six days. Two visits to the fertility clinic; the first one, he'd filled out a bunch of forms, had a quick basic physical exam, then been discreetly ushered into a cushy, private room to give up his sperm sample. He'd felt awkward and sat there for two minutes, mildly embarrassed at why he was there. Then he brushed it away, took a deep breath, and got down to business, looking at it as a job that had to be done, a simple task. All he had to do was think about Tess . . . how she'd felt beneath him, the taste of her mouth, the softness of her skin . . . and he'd been able to deliver the goods in record time.

The day after that, he'd gone to tell his mother about the new relationship he'd started, and how soon did she want to meet his new girlfriend? Even now, he couldn't help but smile at the delighted, shocked look on Annmarie's face. That alone had been worth the barrage of questions that followed. He hadn't seen his mom that energized in months.

The next evening, he, Tess, and his mom had gone out to dinner at one of Annmarie's favorite restaurants. Tess had just been herself, and Annmarie loved her immediately. The little things Tess had thrown in—touching his arm or hand here, dropping a quick kiss on his cheek there—had helped sell the premise. By the end of dinner, Annmarie was convinced they were a happy new couple, and her obvious joy filled him with relief. Yes, it was a lie. And he hated lying to anyone about anything, most of all his mother. But was it harming her, or anyone else? Dammit, she was happy. His dying mother was happy. Some white lies were worth it.

Now, as Tess answered questions about the Holiday Ball, he gazed at her. God, she was great. She was cool as could be, not overselling them as a couple, just being her fantastic self with the right additional amount of random gestures of affection. And she was so goddamn gorgeous, just looking at her made his blood heat. Dressed simply in an emerald green sweater, jeans, and knee-high tan riding boots, she was relaxed and chatty and exuded light. She didn't seem like a haughty head of a huge New York City company or the precious sweetheart of a powerful billionaire family. She was just . . . normal. Both pleasant and enchanting in every way.

Playing the smitten boyfriend to her was easy as could be, because the fact was, he was crushing on her, he could admit that. But that was it. A little crush, a lot of lust, but mostly easy camaraderie. There was no pressure here; she was his friend now. It was amazing, all the way around.

She glanced over at him from beneath her lashes and smiled. "You're staring," she said flirtatiously.

"Can't help it," he replied. "You're gorgeous." Being able to say things like that was more fun than he'd ever cop to.

"Awww." Tess's smile bloomed as she said, "Back at you, Thor."

He rolled his eyes and laughed. "Remind me to kick Ford's ass for telling you that stupid nickname."

"If the huge Norse-god shoe fits . . ." Tess let her voice trail off and winked.

Annmarie sighed a little. "You two are adorable. I love it."

"Well," Tess said to her, "thanks for making such an incredibly handsome son. I do enjoy looking at him. It's a nice bonus, since he's such a great guy."

Damn, she was good at this. Logan warmed inside at her words; yeah, they were fake, but they were perfect, exactly the kind of thing his mom would like to hear. Flirting with her was fun. He reached for her hand and gave it a quick squeeze of approval. She winked at him again, then pulled her hand free to take another bite of her pasta salad.

Earlier that day, they'd had their second visit to the clinic. The test results were all in. His sperm were totally viable, passing all the markers. The whole package combined, apparently, made him a good candidate. It was a go, if they both agreed to it. The look of pure elation that washed over Tess's face . . . her face flushed and her eyes shone with tears of joy. He'd been so happy for her happiness, he'd reached out and hugged her.

Then Tess and Dr. Fuller had an extensive conversation, which Logan sat and listened to without a word. It was Tess's decision. However she wanted this to play out, he'd abide by it without question. Tess asked Dr. Fuller about their getting her pregnant the old-fashioned way, and the doctor was fine with it. She explained to both of them about the timeline; how having sex a few times before, during, and after the ovulation period would certainly tip the odds of conceiving in Tess's favor. They could try it that way for a few months, and if Tess still wasn't pregnant, they could embark on more direct, clinical methods. By the end of the appointment, Tess had made her decision. Logan would be her known donor, and they'd go about conceiving the natural way.

Then they'd gone back to his house to have lunch with his mom. And all he could think about was getting started. He knew that was a little weird; it's not like they were dating and he couldn't wait to get his new lover into bed for a romp. They'd be having sex for one reason only, a very set agenda and goal. But . . . yeah, getting to take this lovely woman to bed, and all the fun, erotic ways he could try to get her pregnant . . . it was mind-boggling to think about, actually. He was a little scattered . . . and eager, excited, nervous, all of that.

"Hey." His mother's voice cut into his thoughts, jostling him from his reverie. "Where are you?"

"Sorry." He flashed a grin. "Just have some things on my mind, got lost in there."

"You okay?" Tess asked.

"Great," he assured her. He grasped her hand and lifted

it to his lips, lightly kissing her knuckles. Her eyes held his for a long beat. An unspoken message passed between them, and a rush of color went to her face. Yeah, she was thinking about it too. A burst of liquid heat swept through him as he contemplated what lay ahead for them . . . the thought of having her . . . maybe even that very night, if she wanted to get started. God, he hoped she wanted to. He supposed he'd find out soon enough.

That evening, Tess had hoped a long soak in the tub would relax her, but it hadn't worked. Her mind and body were all hyped up, anticipation holding her in its merciless grip. After a nice lunch at his mother's house, Logan had driven her home.

"Will you come back tonight?" she'd asked, her voice feeling small in her throat.

"You want me to?"

"Yes, I want you to. I think . . . we can get started on our other secret project. If you want," she added hastily. "If you don't want to—"

"I want to." His voice was low and deliberate as he admitted, "I've barely been able to think about anything else since we left the clinic."

"Me too," she confessed in a whisper. Her heart rate skyrocketed and her stomach did a wobbly flip. "So . . . what time is good for you?"

"Well, I put off work this morning to go to the clinic. I need to do some things now; they'll take all afternoon, into dinnertime maybe . . ." He gently scratched at his beard as he thought, a gesture that was becoming endearingly familiar to her. "You have dinner without me, do your thing. I'll come over at eight. Is that good for you?"

"Yup. I'll see you then."

All afternoon and evening, Tess's mind had churned without stopping. So much to think about, so much to absorb. She was going to have her baby. It was so overwhelming and wonderful . . . and now, the icing on the cake, a pseudo-date with Logan. Entering into the process of trying to get pregnant by actually having sex, that was a fringe benefit she hadn't counted on. To say it was thrilling was an understatement. Simply put, Logan was hot as hell.

She was excited, exhilarated, turned on, and a little giddy. But the nervousness overrode all that, and she wondered why. There was no reason to be nervous; she trusted Logan completely. He was a good man, and he'd be good to her in bed, she just knew that. She supposed it was just basic, anticipatory pre-sex jitters.

She wanted to get pregnant, yes. But she also wanted to please him. If he was going to be doing her the tremendous favor of having sex with her regularly, she wanted him to enjoy it. That was normal, wasn't it?

She laughed at herself. Nothing about this situation was normal.

Standing in her bedroom in her warm, fluffy robe and slippers, she tried to decide on what to wear. Did she bother to get dressed, knowing why he was coming over? Did she wear lingerie, or was that overkill? Did she just stay naked under her robe, the easy access way? She huffed out a sigh of frustration. Why was this difficult to figure out? It wasn't like she was going out with him first. They were just staying here, at her house . . . spending the night in bed and having sex.

Her face flamed as she thought about their short but sexy tumble last week on her couch . . . the way Logan's hands and mouth had felt on her body. A little shiver went through her and she couldn't help but smile. She turned back to her dresser with determination. Lingerie. Men liked lingerie. He was doing her the biggest favor ever. The least she could do was wrap up the package in pretty and make him smile.

At eight o'clock sharp, the doorbell rang. Bubbles barked and did her thing, racing to the door, as a new rush of excitement flooded Tess's body. Oh God, oh God . . .

She opened the door and a whoosh of frigid air hit her. "Oh!" she gasped. "Whoa, it got cold out there!"

"It did." Logan's green eyes glittered beneath his wool cap, pulled low. His words came out on a white cloud. "Luckily, I finished up by seven."

She grabbed his arm to pull him inside. "Jesus, even your coat is freezing!"

"Yeah, well," he said, "it's about five degrees out right now."

"And you were working outside today?"

"Yeah. But then I went home, took a hot shower, ate. I'm fine, Tess."

She looked him over. He wore a royal-blue parka over his regular outfit of fleece-lined hoodie, jeans, work boots, wool hat, and heavy gloves. His cheeks were ruddy from the cold, and the look on his face showed he was amused and a little confounded by her concern. So she grinned and said, "Okay, tough guy. Glad you're here and inside now. Let's get you warmed up."

"Sounds good." His eyes took on a playful sparkle. "Funny thing is . . . I can think of a few ways to do that."

Her heart started beating a little faster. "Mmm. Me too."

They stood there and grinned at each other, the air around them crackling.

"But how about we start with some hot tea?" she said.

"That'd be great, actually." He pulled off his hat and gloves. Bubbles nuzzled his leg and let out loud, staccato barks. As he unzipped his parka, he crouched to pet her. "Hello there, little miss." His large hand stroked across her fur and she licked his skin. "Kisses hello? Well, don't I feel special."

Tess smiled. The man was adorable with her dog. Total gold star for him. "Take off your coat, go sit by the fire and warm up. I'll make you some tea."

Ten minutes later, they sat together on the couch as he sipped some black chai tea. She noticed how his gray and green sweater set off his eyes, that pale mossy color she'd never seen on anyone else. The ends of his hair were still a little damp from his shower. His large, powerful frame took up space . . . actually, just his presence did. She liked that about him; her Viking hottie, big and commanding even when just sitting quietly. With a soft smile, she curled up into the arm of the plush couch, tucking her soft robe under her legs.

"So . . ." He cleared his throat. "How are you tonight?"

"Fine. Nervous, but fine."

The corner of his mouth curved up. "Really? Well then, I'll tell you the truth . . . I'm a little nervous too. I thought it was silly to be, but . . ."

She smiled. "Same here. Why are we nervous? It's not like we've never done anything before. We're friends, we like each other, we trust each other . . ."

"All that's true. So I don't know." He sipped his tea. "Maybe because it's not . . . I don't know, an organic thing, how we planned this tonight? It's not a natural progression, a spontaneous thing, like the other times we got carried away?"

"I guess."

They sat in awkward silence for a minute. The fire crackled and popped in the fireplace. Bubbles crossed the floor and went to her doggie bed, circling around in it three times before flopping down.

"I trust you, Logan," she said softly. She offered him a little grin. "It'll be fine."

His eyes warmed at that. "I'm glad. You *can* trust me, Tess." He set the mug down on the glass coffee table, then turned to face her. He reached out his hand, open palm up, and she slipped her hand into his. "We'll get this done. You'll have your baby. One way or another. Just have faith."

Her throat thickened from his gentle, supportive words. "Thank you."

He smiled, then said, "Know what? Come here, but turn around. Sit with your back to me."

Her brows furrowed as she looked at him, not knowing what he wanted. But she did as he asked. His large hands swept her long hair away, then settled on her shoulders and began to gently knead them. A moan of pleasure fluttered out of her.

"I'm scheduled for a massage next week," she said, "but the hell with that. You're so hired."

He laughed, a deep rumble from his chest. "Trying to help you relax a bit, that's all."

"You can tell I'm that tense?"

"Yup." His fingers made tiny circles along her neck and her eyes slipped closed. "So," he said casually. "Top five favorite Beatles songs. Go."

She snorted out a laugh. "Oh please. Like I could pick only five."

"I knew I liked you." His hands smoothed back down to her shoulders, working magic. "This robe is so soft . . . it's nice. But it's kind of in the way. So, um . . . you wearing anything underneath? I'm thinking it'd be easier to just massage your skin."

Without a word, she undid the knot of the robe and let it slide off her shoulders. She heard his breath catch as her dusky purple negligee was revealed to him. Wanting to see his reaction, she turned her head to peek over her shoulder. The mesmerized look on his face made it worth it. "For you," she whispered.

"Jesus," he murmured, his eyes locked on her body encased in silk. He fingered one spaghetti strap over her shoulder. "My God . . ." He licked his lips as his eyes traveled over her body. "I have a confession to make." His hand ran slowly down her bare arm, then up again. His eyes met hers and held. "You're the most beautiful woman I've ever seen in my life. And I've always thought that. From the moment I first saw you. That's the God's honest truth."

"Wow." She turned a little more to better meet his now hungry gaze. "Thank you. I'm very, very flattered."

"You're very, very beautiful." His hands skimmed up her arms, then turned her away from him to resume his massage. As he rubbed her shoulders, he cleared his throat. "That nightie is stunning on you. I can't wait to peel you out of it."

She smiled brightly, mentally congratulating herself. "Glad you like it."

"Like it? Full disclosure: I'm totally turned on right now. You take my breath away, Tess."

Her breath hitched, but she managed to say, "Good to know."

"Yeah, well . . . all we have to do now is get you a little more relaxed . . ." His warm, powerful hands were so gentle on her skin, Tess couldn't believe it. "So. You can't pick only five, fair enough. I don't think I can either. So just tell me some of your favorites."

Her mind was cloudy with growing desire; it took her

a few seconds to figure out what he was talking about. Oh, Beatles songs. Right. Okay. "'Blackbird,'" she started. His fingers kneaded the muscles in her neck. "Um . . . 'I Will.' 'Julia.' 'She Came In Through the Bathroom Window.' 'Across the Universe.' 'Paperback Writer.' 'Taxman.' 'She's Leaving Home.' 'Two of Us.'"

"Ohh, 'Two of Us' is an all-time fave song of mine, period. Excellent choice." Logan's hands never ceased or strayed from her neck and shoulders. She was turning to putty. "Those are all good ones, ma'am. You're a true fan. I approve."

"Are the Beatles your favorite group?" she asked.

"One of them," he said. His fingers stroked her skin without demand, giving nothing but tenderness. She felt like she was slowly melting into a big, pleasured pile of goo. "I like classic rock best. Mainly from the sixties and seventies, some eighties. Not much after, say, Pearl Jam and Soundgarden. Guess I'm a bit of a throwback."

"Thor is an old-school rock god," she teased. "I can see that being your style."

"What do you listen to?"

"A little of everything . . ."

They talked about music for a while, her back to him, his hands comforting on her skin and his deep voice soothing in her ear. She gazed at the fire and felt herself loosen up; he successfully calmed her body and distracted and quieted her mind. By the time he gently eased her back against his chest, she was totally comfortable.

"How do you feel?" he asked.

"Like a warm puddle of mush," she replied. "You're good at this. You're a genius, actually. I'm completely relaxed now."

"Mission accomplished."

"And then some."

"Great. But you're not going to fall asleep on me, are you?" His voice, low and playful, vibrated from his chest against her back as his arms slipped slowly around her.

"No way." She tipped up her chin to look at him. He was already gazing down at her, an interesting mixture of calm assurance and growing desire clear in his eyes. His hand slid up her side, skimming her ribs, the side of her breast, over her shoulder. Their gazes locked. She reached up to touch his face, running her fingertips along his beard until she pulled his head down. Their mouths met in a sweet kiss.

She felt the flames of desire flicker and spark inside her as they kissed, the delicious heat building at a slow and steady pace. He shifted her in his arms for better access, his big hands sliding along the silk as they settled into a full embrace. Her mouth opened and his tongue swept inside, tasting her, consuming her bit by bit. The kisses deepened, a slow, sensual burn. He lifted her up to sit on his lap, facing him, pressed against him, so he could wrap his arms around her and hold her close. Her fingers sifted through his hair as the kisses burned hotter. Fire seared through her body, want and need rising in her core. She rolled her hips against his erection and he groaned into her mouth, his fingers digging into her hips.

"Are you ready?" he asked in a thick whisper against her lips.

She nodded even as her heart rate took off like a shot.

"Then let's go to your room," he said, kissing her jaw, her chin, then back to her lips. "You deserve a bed, to have this done right. Not here on the couch."

She only nodded again. The air felt stuck in her lungs.

Without missing a beat he stood, lifting her with him, holding her against him in his strong arms.

"What are you doing?" she asked in surprise as he cradled her.

"Carrying you." He kissed her, long and deep, holding her securely. "Wrap your legs around my waist."

She did as she was told. Breathless from his gesture, swept away, she dipped her head into the crook of his neck. "My room's at the end of the hall," she whispered against his skin.

"I know where the master bedroom is," he assured her.

Seemingly without effort, he crossed the length of the living room, went up the stairs, and down the hall to her bedroom. The only light in her room was the dim softness of one small lamp on the dresser. He set her down carefully on the king-size sleigh bed and smiled down at her, sweeping her hair back from her face.

"I can't believe you just did that," she whispered.

He silenced her with a deep, commanding kiss, aligning his large, warm body with hers. With a whimper of submission, she let herself drown in sensation. They held each other and kissed, letting the passion build. Any traces of her initial nervousness or awkwardness were fading away. She wanted him more with each minute.

"You're wearing too many clothes," she finally said.

He grinned, then sat up and pulled his sweater off over his head, tossing it aside. Then he stood up and pushed off his jeans. Standing before her in only tight navy boxer briefs, Tess sucked in a breath at the sight of him. She'd known he had a great body because it was obvious, but seeing him unclothed for the first time . . . He was magnificent. That six-foot-four frame had muscles everywhere. His arms, his chest, his abs, his thighs . . . good Lord. The Thor nickname was perfect, really, whether he liked it or not. She got up onto her knees and reached up to let her fingertips drift through the light dusting of hair on his broad chest, over the Celtic tattoo on one strong shoulder . . .

"Damn," she murmured in appreciation. Her fingers ran eagerly over his skin, warm and firm. His eyes blazed as he watched her explore his body. "And you think *I'm* gorgeous? Look at you . . ." She moved in to press her lips to his chest, her mouth trailing along his skin, kissing, licking, nipping at him everywhere.

His breathing now staggered, his voice dropped low as he said, "Glad you like what you see. That must help . . ." His hands threaded through her hair.

"I like what I see, what I feel . . ." Her teeth scraped his nipple and he hissed, his fingers tightening in her curls. "Mmmm."

"Holy hell," he breathed, letting her take control for a moment, obviously enjoying her touch. Then he asked, "Tess, before we . . . is there anything I need to do?"

She pulled back to look at him and joked, "I can only think of one thing."

He snorted out a laugh. "Well, yeah, that. But I meant, like . . . I don't know, anything else? To help you. I don't know, during, after . . . ?"

She blinked as she realized he was serious. "Oh." God, he was such a good guy. "Well . . . it's going to be a little awkward, but as soon as we're done, I need to raise my hips. That helps, supposedly." She flicked her chin toward the curved wood headboard of the sleigh bed. "I figure I'll just swing my legs up over that. Maybe you could shove a pillow under my hips. That's about it, I think."

"Easy enough." He leaned over her, slowly easing her back to lie down again. He hovered over her, leaning up on his elbows as his body settled on top of hers. With a playful grin, trailing his fingertips along her face, he murmured, "All right then, Long Island Lady. Let's get you pregnant."

Chapter Sixteen

Tenderly, Logan lowered his head and consumed her mouth with his in a deep, sumptuous kiss. Talk about pressure to perform. If they could just get this first time out of the way, get past the awkward fumbling as they learned each other . . . the chemistry was there. The trust was there. They just had to get past the first round.

She needed him to be a calm, assuring presence. He sensed that as soon as he'd walked through the door. The look in her eyes . . . He'd seen such vulnerability there. It wasn't what he'd come to expect from her, and made him immediately want to comfort her and put her at ease. And yes, he'd done that, but now he had to seal the deal.

He wasn't in bed with her just because he was a lucky guy and this gorgeous woman was attracted to him. He was there for a very specific purpose, and that was the most important thing.

It helped that they liked each other. It helped that they were friends now. It helped that they'd spent some time together, getting to know each other more and getting more comfortable around each other. It helped that she'd worn that unbelievably gorgeous nightie, the soft color so beautiful against her delicate skin, the satin and lace enticing him. But he had a job to do.

"Tess . . ." he whispered against her skin. Biting down softly on her earlobe, drawing a gasp from her, he trailed his lips and tongue along her neck. "Close your eyes. Stop thinking. Just feel. It's going to be okay." He reached up to caress her body over the smooth silk, marveling at how perfectly her small breast fit in his large hand, like she was made for him. He covered her in kisses. "It's going to be better than okay. If you let yourself go a little, I'll make sure it's going to be *great*." He fondled one breast, then the other. She undulated under his touch, her nipples pebbling through the silk. His heart beat harder, lust flooding him, making his cock swell. "We're going to make this happen. If not tonight, then another night. As many tries as it takes. But we got this. So relax, Tess. Okay?"

He pulled up to look at her, and her eyes seemed to glow with appreciation. Finally she smiled and whispered, "You're a really good friend." She sifted her fingers through his hair, gripping his head to bring his mouth back to hers.

He kissed her deep and hot, letting the growing hunger inside him take over. She responded instantly, kissing him back with matching passion, their tongues tangling. They kissed, caressed, pressed their bodies together, letting their hands roam and their mouths devour.

He kissed his way down her body over the soft silk, down between her breasts, down her belly . . . He nudged the hem of the negligee up with his face until he could kiss the skin of her belly.

"Your beard is tickling me," she whispered. "I love it."

He smiled against her skin and circled his tongue around her navel, then trailed it lower. With a gasp, her fingers twisted in his hair as her breathing got choppy and soft sighs turned into needy moans.

He ran his fingers over her satiny panties and felt the heat there. The thin material was already damp. A surge of something like victory rushed through him; she was with him, as aroused as he was. He peeled the panties off of her, trailing his fingers down her thighs and following the motion with hot, openmouthed kisses. He'd been dying to let his hands run up and down her mile-long legs from the first day he'd seen her, and this was a dream come true. He savored it, letting his mouth follow wherever his hands traveled.

She moaned louder now, nudging his head back to where she wanted him. He wanted it too; he was dying to taste her. He sealed his mouth to her warm folds, spreading her legs wider with commanding hands. She cried out, her fingers in his hair, and her hips rose to meet him. He devoured her, feasting on her without stopping, her passionate response making his own desire burn hotter in his veins.

"Wait," she panted. "Logan . . . let me touch you. You're the one who needs to come, not me."

He almost lost it right then. He groaned against her swollen flesh, the vibrations making her cry out loudly; her back arched off the bed. "Oh God, wait . . . I . . ." She panted hard, writhing against him. "I can't hold back much longer."

In answer, he flicked her clit with his tongue, sucking hard on it as he slid two fingers inside her. Roused by her wet heat, he moved them in and out, fast and sure. She came with a throaty shout, breaking apart beneath him. Her thighs clamped around his head and her hips rocked against his face as she cried out again and again, her hands in his hair as the orgasm made her limbs shake. He didn't stop his efforts and held her tight, driving her to another level, not letting up as another orgasm hit and she moaned low, holding on to him as if for her life. Loving her erotic response, his whole body hummed with lust, with every nerve ending lit up with desire.

After her last raspy moan, when her grip on his head lessened and her legs fell open, he pulled back and shifted up. He was so hard, the pleasure of it bordered on pain. She was still trying to catch her breath as he aligned his body with hers and pushed into her with one fast, hard thrust.

His mind spun out from the astonishing feeling; he hadn't been inside a woman like this, without a condom, since he'd been married. The incredible feel of being inside Tess without barriers made him shudder and groan, his eyes slipping closed in ecstasy. Thank God he didn't have to worry about coming too fast, because he was going to and he knew it. He gripped her hips and swiveled his, going deep, thrusting hard.

She looked up at him as her legs, those long, beautiful legs, lifted to lock around his waist. She held on to his shoulders, her warm breath against his skin, nipping and kissing him as her hips rose to meet his. The sensations overwhelmed him . . . She felt so damn good . . . too good. He was lost. Moving faster, it only took a few more thrusts before his body tensed and he went flying over the edge. He came hard, groaning into her neck, fingers digging into her hips as his body emptied deep inside her. They held each other tight, both of them breathless as he shuddered, then stilled.

She kissed his shoulder and he lifted his head to look at her, still feeling dazed. Her skin was flushed and her blue eyes sparkled with carnal satisfaction. "That was fantastic," she whispered. Then a tiny grin lifted the corners of her mouth. "I'm sorry, but could you let me up?"

Still panting, he could only nod as he withdrew and lifted himself off of her. She immediately swiveled her body around the opposite way and swung her legs up over the massive headboard. Blinking away the haze that still fogged his brain, Logan grabbed one of the four pillows. As he slid the pillow beneath her, raising her hips on an angle, Tess smiled at him gratefully.

"Is that good?" he asked.

"That's perfect." She reached out to stroke his beard. "Goddamn, Logan. You are *good* at your job. Lucky, lucky me."

He laughed and couldn't help himself, he leaned over to kiss her. "And here I was thinking I was the lucky one." He brushed a stray curl away from her eyes. "You're okay?"

"Are you kidding? You didn't hear me when I came? *Both* times? I must've scared away the deer outside."

He laughed even harder. "Made me feel like a super-hero. I admit it."

"You are, Thor." With a wink and a smile, she took a deep breath and brushed all of her hair back with both hands, then let her arms flop to her sides. Her eyes closed and she took a few deep, cleansing breaths.

When he felt clear again, he leaned up on an elbow and watched her. "How long do you have to stay like this?"

Her eyes opened to look at him. "Dr. Fuller said ten to fifteen minutes is fine, not more than that."

"Huh. Okay." He eased himself down to lie beside her. They both relaxed; her eyes slipped closed again, and he let his gaze wander over her. In the dimly lit room, she looked serene, sexy, and sated. Like an absolute goddess, as far as he was concerned. "You are so damn beautiful, Tess. And passionate. That got a little . . . *whoa*."

"It did." Eyes still closed, she grinned. "Yay us."

He chuckled warmly. "This is going to be the best job I've ever had."

"I'm glad to hear it." She smiled wider. "You liked the lingerie?"

"Jesus. I almost fell off the couch when I saw you in it. Hell yes, I liked it."

"I can get more . . . Wear something different every time, if you want." She turned her head to look at him and reached out to gently stroke his beard. He liked when she did that, and that she seemed to like doing it. "I want to make you happy when you're . . . working with me. You like the lingerie? It's the least I can do."

Something warm flowed through him. He was doing this for her, and she was thinking of how to please him? "I appreciate that. And sure, you can if *you* want to. But you can wear a damn burlap sack and I'd still want to get into bed with you." He trailed the backs of his fingers down the middle of her body. Her pale skin was like velvet. "Besides, you look best like this. Naked. There's nothing more stunning than that."

Her eyes rounded and she smiled again, pure delight. "You're a flatterer."

"Nah, I tell the truth."

"Either way, thank you for the compliments."

He dropped a light kiss on her lips, then shifted to sit up. "I'm getting some water. I'll bring you back some. You stay put."

"That'd be fantastic, actually. Thank you."

He rose from the bed and padded out into the hallway. As he walked through the quiet house, it hit him that he was walking around naked, like he belonged there. He didn't. He'd do well to remember that. He was their house manager, and just a friend. They were having sex, but they weren't lovers. Shit. The lines were a little blurred right then . . .

As he grabbed two small bottles of water from the fridge, it occurred to him he wasn't sure what to do now. Probably time to leave. Surely she didn't expect him to stay the night? Or did she? Shit, this part was weird. Now what?

By the time he got back upstairs, he'd made up his mind. He'd go home. But in the door frame, he stopped cold at the sight of her. Her graceful, naked body stretched out sinuously on the huge bed, her long legs still curved up over the headboard. Her long mane of curls fanned out beneath her, the dark brown of her hair an appealing contrast to the caramel-colored sheets.

Damn, damn, damn. She was beautiful in every way. And she'd chosen *him* for this. Would he ever get over the wonder of that? He didn't know.

When he cleared his throat, she turned her head to smile at him.

"Here you go." He crossed the room to sit on the edge of the bed, handing her a bottle as she sat up. Turning to position herself beside him, she thanked him as she took it and gulped half of it down. He grinned at her thirst, then worked to make his voice light as he said, "I'm gonna get going in a few minutes. Let you get some sleep."

She blinked, and he caught a split second of surprise in her eyes. Had she wanted him to stay longer? Then she covered quickly like the pro she was and said brightly, "Okay. That's fine." She flashed him a grin as she drank down more water.

He drank his too as his mind worked. "That's okay, right? I mean . . ."

"Yeah, it's fine. Logan. We're friends. That's it. I want you to be comfortable. You want to stay or go, it's up to you. Whatever you want to do, it's fine with me."

"I just figured . . ." He shrugged. Lovers spend the night wrapped in each other's arms. They weren't lovers. They were just friends, with a specific agenda that they'd successfully completed. "Seems like the right way. I'll come over every night if you want . . . but then I'll go home. Okay?"

"Okay. I told you, whatever you want," she said, no hint of ire or hurt in her tone. "Besides, I know you get up very early for work in the morning. It makes sense."

She smiled again and he relaxed a bit. She wasn't clingy, had no expectations . . . Goddamn, she was great. He leaned in and kissed her forehead. "How are you feeling?"

"Amazing, thanks. How about you?"

"Same," he assured her. "This was fantastic." He grinned again before rising to his feet. "So . . . how do you want to do this? Every night this week? Every other night? What's the plan? Your call."

"Well, I actually was at peak ovulation *last* week," she said. "Truth is, I don't know how effective this cycle is going to be. I'm already at day nineteen in my cycle; we might have missed the window. So . . . maybe the next three or four nights, and then we can start again in a few weeks, closer to my next ovulation start, like maybe day ten? That way, your sperm count will really build up again, and the timing is just right." She peered up at him. "Is that okay with you? Sounds so clinical, I know. Sorry."

The thought of not sleeping with her for a few weeks was disappointing. But this was a job, not a pleasure run. "Don't be sorry. Having to plan like this, of course there are elements that sound clinical. That's fine. It's whatever you need, Tess. You call the shots, tell me when to come over, and I'm on board. Okay?"

"Okay. Thank you." She raised her water bottle in a toast, and he clinked his to hers. "To the Dream Team," she said.

He raised his bottle in salute to her and drank down the rest of the water. "You stay here, stay warm. I'll get dressed and let myself out."

"You sure?"

"Yeah, of course. Um . . ." He winked and reminded her, "I *do* have the key. I can lock up."

She chuckled. "That's true . . ." She finished off her water, set the empty bottle down on the nightstand, and lay down. She grabbed a different pillow and pushed it beneath her head. As her curls spilled everywhere—over the pillow, her shoulders—he pulled the soft, thick comforter up over her, tucking her in beneath the swirls of rust, caramel, and brown.

"You're good to me," she murmured with a smile.

"You make it easy to be. And you? You just got tired, I can see it." Her eyes had grown hooded and heavy. "Get some sleep now. With dreams of that baby dancing in your head."

She smiled broadly. "That sounds perfect."

He dropped a kiss on her forehead as she snuggled into the pillows. She looked radiant, sexy, adorable, and just plain sweet. Something in his chest pinged as he touched her cheek. "Sleep well. I'll text you tomorrow."

"Sounds good. Good night, Logan. And um . . ." She bit down on her bottom lip. "Thanks again."

"Okay, that's the last time you thank me for this, got it?" He went to where he'd dropped his briefs and jeans. Pulling on the briefs, he demanded, "You are *not* going to thank me every time. In fact, you're not going to thank me again in the bedroom, ever."

"Jeez. I didn't mean to irk you," she said. "I believe in

expressing my gratitude and appreciation whenever it's warranted."

"And I think that's great. A very admirable trait, really. But about this? No more." He zipped up his jeans and pinned her with a look. "I know how you feel about my help. I promise I do. So that's that."

"Yes sir, Mr. Carter." She yawned. "So, the plan is, we'll do it again tomorrow night. And the night after that, too. Then we'll leave this cycle and wait for the next one, starting up again on day ten. Okay?"

"Okay." He pulled on his sweater, then located his socks.

"And," she added, her voice softer as she grew more drowsy, "let me know which night this week you'd like me to come have dinner with you and your mother."

"That'd be great. Will do." He gazed down at her. She looked so warm and cozy, he was tempted to climb back into bed with her. But no. They weren't like that. "All right, I'm going. Good night, Long Island Lady."

"Good night, Thor." She grinned and her eyes slid closed.

He gazed at her for a few seconds longer, then went to turn off the lamp on the dresser. The room went dark and he quietly left the room, closing the door behind him.

Chapter Seventeen

Tess rolled up her yoga mat slowly, frowning. The class hadn't helped; she still felt a little crampy. Deep in her heart, she knew she wasn't pregnant, that her period was coming. Dammit.

"Hey, Tess. You okay?"

She looked up, blinking. It was Carrie, the yoga instructor. "Yeah, I'm fine."

"You just don't seem like yourself today. You're always smiling . . . today, not so much." Carrie's pale blue eyes peered harder. "You sure you're all right?"

Tess nodded and edged closer. "Just getting my period. So I'm a little off. That's all."

"Ahh. Say no more. I hate those days." Carrie gave her arm a little squeeze. "Feel better. See you next time."

"You bet." Tess took her things and left the room. Ten minutes later, she was sitting in her SUV. Snow had started to lightly fall; the flakes floated in the air, drifting like tiny bits of icy magic. She stared at the beauty outside her windshield . . . and a harder cramp hit, making her suck in her breath. Her eyes filled with tears. She sniffed them back willfully and started the engine, wanting to get home before the snow got heavier.

When she got home, she took a quick shower, then got into her favorite fleece pajamas, the red ones with the baby penguins. She pulled back the curtains so she could watch the snow fall outside the wide windows, then turned on the gas fireplace. It was one o'clock, when she usually ate lunch, but she wasn't hungry. She got into her bed, curled up under the blankets, and let herself have a little pity party.

Very few women got pregnant with the first attempt. She and Logan had only had sex three times last week, then she'd let it go, knowing it was too late in her cycle. The odds had been slim and she knew it. In her head, she knew all of that. But her heart . . . the disappointment welled inside her, merciless. Tears slipped free and rolled down her cheeks. She swiped them away and burrowed deeper beneath the covers.

Her cell phone buzzed with a text. Logan. How goes it, Long Island Lady? I texted this morning and you didn't answer . . . ?

She sighed. He'd texted a few minutes before she'd gone into her yoga class, so she hadn't been able to respond then. But she hadn't responded after it, and she could have. What should she say? *Hi, I'm here, in a fetal position, crampy as hell and feeling sorry for myself*? No. He was her friend, not her boyfriend. She couldn't lean on him like that, even though he'd told her she could. Yes, they texted or talked daily, and had spent time together over the last few weeks. But it felt like whining for her to tell him the truth. So she didn't answer the text. She pushed the phone away, closed her eyes, and decided on a nap instead. Exhaustion overcame her fast and hard, and she gladly let it drag her under.

* * *

Bubbles was licking her face. As Tess opened her eyes, she was foggy and disoriented. The light outside had changed; the sky was a darker gray and the snow was still falling. She reached for her phone to check the time and her eyes widened. She'd been asleep for almost two hours. She had texts and emails waiting, the many icons across the top letting her know people were looking for her. And she could feel it . . . She'd gotten her period. With a sigh, she got out of bed and went to the bathroom. After that, she took Bubbles out for a quick potty break and filled her bowls with fresh water and food. She made herself a quick cup of chai spice tea, grabbed a bag of white cheddar popcorn, and went back to bed.

When she was settled under the covers again, she checked her voice mails first. There were two messages: one from Logan, one from Dane.

"Hey, Tess." Logan's deep, sexy voice in her ear sent a shiver over her skin. "Not like you to not answer texts. Hope you're okay? Let me know. Call me, text me, something. I'll come and check on you by dinner if I don't hear from you. Bye."

She couldn't help but smile. He was sweet to be concerned. And yes, she hadn't answered for just a few hours, but she couldn't accuse him of being overbearing. He was right, she always answered right away. If it were the other way around, she might be concerned too. She'd text him back after listening to the second voice mail.

"Tesstastic! How are ya, girl?" Dane's jovial voice boomed over the line. "It's me. Julia and I got back from Cancun yesterday, we're home. New York is fucking cold and gray and I'm ready to leave again. Going back to work sucks. And you're not around, and that sucks too. I miss you. Call me, let's catch up. When are you coming home? Hope all is well. Love you."

She smiled, feeling his warmth. Her brothers adored her, and she adored them. She was very lucky to have such close siblings, and friends. Why was she still keeping her plans from them? She wasn't sure. She'd have to think about that some more.

Burrowing into her pillows, she texted Logan. Hi, I'm sorry I worried you. I'm alive.

His text came back almost immediately. There you are. Hi. Glad you answered, I was starting to worry. Just wasn't like you.

I know, sorry. Not feeling great today, she wrote. Had yoga, fell asleep after, took an unplanned two hour nap. And got my period. So . . . yeah. That.

Ah. Sorry you're not feeling well.

I'm fine. Just tired, crampy, and in a bit of a funk.

Ahhh. I get it. Well, don't be. We'll just try again. Don't worry, Tess. It'll happen.

His kind words made tears spring to her eyes. Stupid hormones. Thanks, she wrote. I know. I'm fine.

Okay. Need anything?

Nope. Having popcorn in bed. Maybe wine for dessert.

He didn't answer right away. Then his text came in: Thought you weren't drinking these days?

She winced. I was joking, she wrote back. No worries.

You're upset, aren't you. Tell the truth.

She blinked back the tears. A little. But I'm okay. She sniffled, astounded at how well he knew her already. Are you at work?

No. Hospital with Mom. Radiation. Then I'll take her home, settle her in, etc.

Gotcha. Send her my best. Hope she's okay.

I'll tell her you said hi. Better go. I'll call you later. Enjoy your popcorn.

Thanks. Bye.

She put the phone down and shoved her hand into the popcorn bag. As she ate and misery welled, she decided popcorn alone wasn't going to cut it. Ordering dinner in was required tonight. Something delicious, with a decadent, chocolatey dessert.

The doorbell rang at seven thirty, startling Tess. She was curled up on the couch with her e-reader. After self-medicating with lobster bisque and pasta primavera with shrimp, then a slice of chocolate mousse pie, she'd fallen into a food coma, content to read on the couch all night and ignore the world. Now she slipped her feet into her slippers and went to answer the door.

Logan stood before her, snow falling around him, looking ruggedly handsome. Her heart soared a tiny bit. "Hi," he said.

"Hi," she said with surprise. "What are you doing here?"

"You just didn't sound right, even in texts." He lifted his hand, holding a white bag. "I brought cookies. With chocolate in them. Thought maybe you needed some."

Her eyes welled with tears. "You're so sweet," she whispered. "Come on in."

He did, closed the door behind him, and brushed the snow from his coat. Then, with his free hand, he tipped up her chin to study her face. Without a word, he pulled her into his chest and hugged her.

She broke down, sobbing into him. He dropped the bag lightly to the floor to wrap both arms around her. The feel of his solid embrace made her go molten. "I knew it wouldn't happen right away," she mumbled between sobs. "I knew we started after I'd ovulated, and we only did it a few times, so I knew the chances were small. Why am I so damn disappointed?"

"Hope's funny that way." He rubbed her back, caressed her hair. "Shhh. It's okay. You're allowed to be disappointed."

She cried, so grateful for his understanding and tenderness it flooded her completely. Clinging to him like a lifeline in a storm, she cried. And he held her close.

"So you were staying for February anyway," he said. "And March too, if need be. And maybe even April. We'll have sex every night if you want. You'll have your baby, Tess. It just might take time. The doctor told us that." His large hands gently ran up and down her back. "It'll happen. I'm not going anywhere. Okay?"

She looked up at him, floored by his words. "You'll really do that? Keep at this for months, if need be?"

"Like sleeping with you is such a hardship," he said warmly. He quirked a grin, making her return it. "As long as it takes. I made you a promise. I keep my promises." He wiped her tears from her cheeks.

She stared up at him. The gentleness of his touch never ceased to amaze her. That such big, powerful hands were capable of such tenderness . . .

He searched her face. "You okay now?"

"I'm a hot mess today," she grumbled. "The hormones own me. I'll be back to normal tomorrow."

"Okay." He pressed a kiss to her forehead, then leaned down to pick up the cookies. "Well, look. These are damn good cookies. From Pistelli's bakery, you know them?"

She nodded. "Best pastries in Aspen, some say."

"Those 'some' are right. So you don't wanna waste 'em." He grinned softly, making the corners of his eyes crinkle, appealing as hell to her. "Why don't you make some tea, and we can just hang out and watch a movie or something. Or, if you'd rather just be alone, that's fine. Don't be shy, tell me to go, I'll leave if you want. I just wanted to check on you and bring these by."

She sniffed hard and swept her hair back from her face. He was such a good man. A good friend. Affection welled inside her. "Please stay. Cookies, tea, and a movie sound wonderful, actually. I'd like that."

"Cool." He smiled and unzipped his coat. "What movie do you want to watch?"

Logan went through the next few weeks feeling lighter. It was the only word he could think of to describe it. Work was fine, his mother was happy for him, and his evenings were either spent at the gym or with Tess. For a fake girl-friend, it was the best relationship he'd ever enjoyed. The lack of pressure was ideal. He'd tried to do that with other women, but it hadn't worked. With Tess . . . everything worked. It was so easy, felt so natural. Knowing there were no expectations, and none down the road, enabled him to be himself. He hadn't let himself do that with anyone since Rachel. He'd made a connection with Tess that was real, and the truth was, it felt really good. He could admit that to himself.

January turned into February. They went skiing three times, since Tess wanted to get her time in on the slopes before the next cycle. Once they started again, she didn't want to go skiing, possibly jostle anything, and he understood. He loved skiing with her, it was always a rush. Some nights, they went out. To dinner, or to Ford's Coffee House. It amused Logan that Ford was a little jealous of his new "girlfriend"; Logan knew that, given the opportunity, Ford would've pursued her himself.

Some nights, they stayed in. They had dinners with his mother, or watched movies together at Tess's place. He hated to admit that Annmarie was getting weaker; he saw it little by little. But his fake relationship made her happy. She wasn't just happy for him, she really liked Tess. And Tess was great with her, always bringing flowers or pastries when she visited, being attentive and sweet when they talked. Her kindness toward his mother made his genuine affection for her grow. He adored her. She was a great friend, and held up her end of their bargain beautifully. He couldn't ask for more.

By early February, among his small social circles and her larger ones in Aspen, he and Tess were thought of as a couple. And Logan was oddly proud of that association. If he had to be thought of as tied to someone, who in the world was better than her? She was an incredible woman. He found himself thinking of her often . . . okay, almost all the time.

Their friendship had put a spark back into his quiet life. He loved their chats, the playful banter and texts that made him smile. And their chemistry was so compelling, that the time they spent together almost always ended up in hot and heavy make-out sessions. Yes, they were just friends, but they couldn't seem to keep their hands off each other. But always, they had to stop before it got too intense. She'd explained that the dry weeks meant no action for him. The longer he went without sex, the better his sperm count would be when they started up again. It made him ache, but he understood and was fine with it. They had an agenda to stick to, and the rules made it easier to stay clearheaded.

Then it was the second week of February, and back to Game On for the Dream Team. When day ten of her cycle arrived, he woke up hard, ready to go. He'd missed her body. Now that he knew what to look forward to, he couldn't wait to get back to it.

That afternoon and evening, however, he had a job to finish at the McLellan property, goddammit. The timing sucked. All day, as he worked on fixing the damaged portion of the outside wall of their house, all he could think of was getting in bed with Tess. Knowing they could go at it again, knowing he didn't have to go home and take another cold shower, knowing she was waiting for him . . . it was torture. Finally, at six o'clock, he texted her he'd be on his way over, he just was going home to take a quick shower.

Don't bother going home, she texted back. Come shower here. I'd love to watch . . .

Holy shit. His cock throbbed in his jeans. The hell with getting dinner first, he'd eat a protein bar he had stashed in his truck. He texted back immediately: Yes ma'am. Be there in fifteen minutes.

When she opened the door to him, wearing that soft, plush red robe of hers, he immediately wondered what was beneath it. She pulled him into the house and hugged him hello, as she always did, but his whole body roared to life. He took her face in his hands and kissed her, plundering her mouth, pressing her tightly against him.

"Someone's all fired up," she murmured when he set her mouth free.

"It's been a long almost-three weeks," he said, taking his coat off between kisses. "I'm eager to get to work . . ." He yanked off his wool cap. "Gotta admit, I love this job."

She laughed and took his hat and coat. "Your shower can't be too hot. Raising your body temperature isn't ideal for sperm count or mobility. But a quick lukewarm shower . . . I'd *love* to watch that. You game?"

"You like to watch, huh?" His voice pitched low as he stared at her. The thought of her eyes on him had his whole body pulsing with desire.

"If it's you? Yes. Yes, I believe I do."

They went up to the master bathroom, one of the most magnificent bathrooms he'd seen in all his Red Mountain houses. Skylights above, warm wooden walls, a window that showcased the mountains. There was a huge shower, all chrome and elegance, encased in glass; and a deep tub with jets, which was wide enough for two adults to share, even when the two in question were as tall and big as they were. The bathroom was bigger than his living room, for Christ's sake. But it was nice and warm.

Sitting in her red robe, Tess perched herself on the edge of the tub to watch, crossing her long, bare legs. Her hair tumbled over her shoulders, down her back, and her bright blue eyes sparkled as they locked on him. "This is going to be delicious," she purred. "Strip for me."

"Holy crap." His brows shot up and a short, shocked laugh flew out of him. "You're in total voyeur mode."

"It seems so." She bit down on her lip, unable to hold back a wicked grin. "Do you mind?"

"Mind? It's turning me on like crazy."

"Oh good. I need you turned on."

"You don't have to work at it, Tess." He pulled his white

wool sweater over his head, then the T-shirt beneath, and let them drop to the floor. Her eyes traveled over his body, taking in what she saw and apparently liking the view. Hot pink bloomed on her cheeks and chest as she watched him leisurely unbutton and unzip his jeans, as he pushed them off and toed off his heavy socks. His erection raged in his boxer briefs as he kicked the pile of clothes aside.

"My sexy friend," she said, her voice thick with growing desire, "you are exquisite to look at. Hot damn."

He grinned, even as lust made his blood roar in his ears and race through his veins. "Could you take these off for me?" he asked, low and deliberate as he stepped closer. He stared down at her as his cock strained against the cotton. "Friends help each other, right?"

"Of course they do," she murmured playfully. She reached out to slip her fingers into the waistband. Her touch made his heart hammer in his chest. As she pushed down the briefs, his hard cock sprung free. She grasped it and ran her thumb over the head, diluting the drop of pre-come there, making him suck in his breath and groan.

"I'm not going to get through a shower if you touch me like that," he said, his voice strangled.

She let him go. "Hurry up, then, handsome. I want that inside me."

He gripped her shoulders and lifted her to her feet, kissing her hard, consuming her mouth, possessing her. She whimpered into his mouth as she kissed him back, arching against him. Then she pulled back and gasped out, "Shower. Go."

It took all his willpower to turn away from her. He made sure the water was warm, not hot, per her instructions. Through the glass, his eyes met hers. Sure enough, she was watching him. Arousal coursed through him as he soaped up his body, as her intent gaze never left him. Her eyes followed his hands, lingered on his raging erection, hungrily tracking his every movement. He was done in two minutes, unable to believe how wildly turned on he was just from her watching him. Her eyes on him had the same stimulating effect as if she'd actually touched him. He toweled off as quickly as possible, then grabbed her hand and yanked her to her feet.

They kissed passionately, grabbing at each other, groping and panting as they fell to her bed together. He rolled her onto her back, undid her robe and pushed it open, then stopped breathing for a second. She wore red and black lace, a matching bra and panties set. "Jesus Christ," he whispered, then ran his hands over the lingerie, over her body. "You're so damn beautiful." He wanted her so bad, his hands were shaking. "I'm too far gone," he warned her. "First time's going to be quick." He hooked his thumbs into the lace at her narrow hips and dragged the panties down her legs. "Second time will be longer. But I can't wait, and you don't need me to, so . . ."

"Do it," she said, her face flushed and heavy-lidded eyes dark with desire. "Take me quick and hard."

His mind reeled. Almost frantic, he positioned himself over her and drove into her, slamming hard. They groaned together, limbs intertwining. She was so wet, ready for him. He leaned up on his elbows and pumped hard and fast, no holding back. She held on, meeting him thrust for thrust, both of them lost to mindless animal lust. Panting, clawing at each other, his demanding hips rocked as he possessed her. Her nails dragged down his back, grabbing his ass and pushing him deeper inside . . . He came with a loud groan, his whole body stiffening as he felt himself empty inside her. Eyes squeezed shut, mind gone, the waves of intense sensation crashed over him and dragged him under.

His climax spurred hers on; her legs tightened around his waist as she cried out, holding on, her nails biting into his back. He opened his eyes to look at her, her head thrown back and mouth open as she shattered beneath him, and he crushed his lips to hers to swallow her moans.

Their bodies trembled as they kissed and rode out the aftershocks. They worked to catch their breath. A light sheen of sweat covered their flushed, naked bodies. The kisses slowed, their breathing evened out, and he sank down on top of her.

"Oh my God," she finally gasped out. Her eyes held his. "That was . . . What the hell was that?"

"The quickest but hottest sex I've ever had?" he offered.

"Me too. Holy God . . ." She stared at him in wonder. "I've never been so turned on in my life."

"Same here." He kissed her, then looked at her lips. "Your mouth's a little swollen. I got a little rough at the end. I'm sorry."

"Don't be," she said. "I think I left marks of my own, though."

He grinned down at her. "Fine with me, tigress."

She snorted at that. "You were horny when you got here."

"Yes, ma'am. Thought of this all day."

"Me too," she admitted. Then she shifted beneath him. "Gotta raise my hips."

He pulled out and rolled off of her so she could swing her legs up over the headboard. He helped position a pillow under her hips, then kissed her mouth and smoothed her hair back. She was still wearing the bra; in his crazed state, ravaging her desperately, he'd never even gotten that off of her. He reached out to touch the lace. "This is hot as hell." He ran his fingers over her breasts and she sucked in a breath. "Still sensitive?"

"Yes."

"Good. We're going another round tonight. I want more."

"Fine by me." She smiled and reached up to play with his beard, the way she often liked to. "Could you please bring me some water?"

They lay side by side in bed for almost half an hour, quiet and relaxed. He loved that they didn't always have to talk. She wasn't one of those people who felt the need to fill a silence with chatter; she was comfortable enough in her own skin to not have to do that. It was one of the things he liked most about her, actually. Her being so at ease with herself made it so easy to be with her.

But as always, he couldn't keep his hands off her for long. He ran his fingers over her soft skin, paying particular attention to her red and black lace-encased breasts. "You're stunning."

"Thank you. You like the set?"

"I almost came right when I saw it, almost blew it like a horny teenager."

"You were really fired up." She grinned. "I have to watch you shower more often. That was a major turn-on for both of us."

"My naughty little voyeur," he murmured, taking her mouth in a sumptuous kiss. "Who knew?"

"I didn't know!" she said with a laugh, eyes bright. "That was new for me. I just thought about watching you shower . . . and I wanted it." Her fingers sifted through his hair as she blushed. The light in her eyes made something spark and kindle inside him. "But something about this whole scenario . . . It's different. It's kind of been . . . freeing for me. Even in bed. Is that weird? Does that make any sense?"

"It makes total sense. It's been like that for me too." He

kissed her again, letting himself drown in the feel of her. "I want you again. Ready?"

"Yes."

It was a slow and leisurely exploration this time. His hands, lips, teeth, and tongue canvassed every gorgeous inch of her, a sweet and sexy discovery, and she reveled in his body the same way. When they were ready, she sat up and nudged him to lie on his back, then straddled his hips. He guided himself inside as she slid down slowly onto his hard shaft, both of them moaning softly at the amazing feel of joining.

She rode him slowly at first, taking her time, clearly reveling in every sensation. He gazed up at her, watching her grind into him, as her long curls tumbled over her shoulders, her breasts, all around her. Her eyes closed, her head fell back, her pelvis ground into him sinuously . . . He felt drugged by passion and her beauty.

They moved together in perfect sync as he drove up into her. He felt himself getting closer; trailing his hand from her breasts down her body, he found her clit and rubbed it with his thumb, making her cry out and grind harder. He picked up the pace, thrusting up into her faster, with more power, until she cried out his name and shuddered. Her orgasm brought on his roaring, mind-bending release as he panted and held on to her hips.

She sank down to collapse onto his chest and he held her close, then rolled her onto her back. Still breathing heavily, her eyes stayed closed as she murmured, "I'm like jelly. I can't move. Ohhh my God."

With a satisfied grin, he reached for a pillow and lifted her hips for her, sliding it beneath her in the necessary position. She whispered thanks. He pressed a kiss to her mouth, then flopped down beside her. They lay side by side for a few minutes as their bodies quieted. When he started to almost doze off, he made himself push up onto his elbows. "I better get going, or I'm going to pass out here."

"You can if you want," she said. Her eyes half opened to look at him, tired and sated. He felt a spark of pride that he'd made her look that way. She was captivating.

But he said, "I think it's best that I go home."

She looked at him for a long beat, then said, "All right," and let her eyes slide closed again. "Is it okay if I don't walk you to the door?" she whispered.

"Of course. Go to sleep." He dropped a kiss on her forehead, then reached to pull the comforter up over her. "I'll text you tomorrow."

"Okay . . ."

He watched her for a minute. Her breathing turned slow and deep, and her features relaxed completely. He envied her sleep; he was ready to sleep for a week. He thought about just lying back down and doing that. It was tempting . . . She was tempting . . .

Nope. They weren't lovers. Lovers stayed the night. Friends with benefits didn't cuddle or sleep over, no matter how mind-blowing the sex had been or how much they genuinely liked each other's company. He gazed at her beautiful face for a few seconds longer, then got out of bed and went to get dressed.

Chapter Eighteen

Tess put down her brush and stepped back to better survey the canvas. Painting was both her love and her infinite frustration. She could never quite get onto the canvas the exact vision she had in her head, no matter how hard she tried. It seemed elusive. But she loved the process, the actual painting itself . . . She always lost herself in it.

She went to add some more cobalt blue to her palette when her cell phone rang behind her. She didn't answer it; she never answered it when she was painting, letting the call go to voice mail. Her head tipped to the side as she studied her work, trying to decide what to do next. She was so close to being finished with this painting, and it meant a lot to her. It wasn't often she gave away her artwork as a gift, but she had a feeling—hoped—this one would be appreciated. Her heart was in it.

The phone rang again two minutes later. And again two minutes after that. Annoyed, she finally stomped over to look at the screen. It was her father. "Hello?"

"Finally!" Charles II bellowed. "Why aren't you answering your phone?"

"Why aren't you leaving me a message when I don't?" she shot back.

He paused. "Well. Having a good morning, are we?"

"I was, until this." She so wasn't in the mood for him today.

"My, my. You sound a bit testy."

"I'm painting. You're interrupting. You know how I get."

"I do. So I apologize for interrupting." Her father almost sounded earnest. "But I'm tired of leaving voice mails and not getting a return phone call. I deserve better. I don't like being ignored."

"Sorry," she said. With a sigh, she sank into the armchair in the corner. She wouldn't be able to paint now, her concentration had been broken. "But what if I was on the slopes? Would you have kept calling for hours? Just leave me a voice mail, Dad."

"I told you, I'm tired of your not answering them." His tone gained a steely edge. "You've been away for six weeks. This is ludicrous already. It's time for you to come home, don't you think?" Ah, *that* was the Charles Harrison II they all knew. Demanding, surly, arrogant, expecting the world to stop on a dime at his command.

"No, I don't think," she said. "In fact, I'll definitely be staying here through March, possibly April too."

"*What?*" he shouted. "Why?"

"Because I have some things going on here," she said mildly, unfazed by his anger. "And until I see them through to completion, I'm staying here. I can do my work for the foundation from here, I'm not slacking. I'm just not physically in New York."

"What the hell's so important there that you're staying?"

"That's . . . my business. Sorry."

Blistering silence from him. She could almost feel him thinking, trying to work out an angle, trying to figure out how to find out what she was doing in Aspen. God knew he had the connections and wherewithal; if he dug hard enough, he could probably find out. He certainly had in the past. Her personal life was rarely her own; he'd dug into her business more times than she could count. Being his only daughter hadn't been easy, ever. The sense of ownership and entitlement where she was concerned hadn't been clear to her until her college years, but once she'd realized it, it'd been an eye-opening game changer.

"A secret lover? Good for you."

"It's no one's business but mine."

"Aha! Struck a nerve. Must be a yes."

"Stop," Tess snapped. "Now."

"I'll come out there myself if I have to," he finally warned in a low voice.

"Oh my God. Seriously? I'm turning thirty-eight in a few weeks," she said, fighting not to lose her cool. "What are you going to do, force me onto your private jet and take me home? Been there, done that. It'll never happen again."

He hissed out a stream of air in frustration. "You were what, twenty-one then? And still bringing that up? Come on."

"Twenty-two," she corrected him. "And being literally dragged onto a plane in Milan by your goons is something I'll never forget." *Or forgive you for*, she added silently. "So why are you coming out here? For what purpose? To bully me into coming home, aka doing what you want? That ship sailed long ago."

"Listen to you. My goodness. Is that really what you think of me?" he asked.

"Yup. Based on *your* track record." A burst of anger shot through her veins. "I'll never forget what you did. You're lucky I ever spoke to you again after that stunt."

"Let's not go off the rails, here. The past is the past," he said dismissively.

"Really? Past events affect the present."

"We're fine in the present."

"I am," Tess said. "But how about you? How's your family, Dad?"

He grunted in response.

"You lost Pierce," Tess said. "Dane and Charles barely talk to you. You ready to put me on that list too? The past matters. As for the present, don't you threaten me that you're going to come out here, because I have my own life. Don't threaten me, ever."

"I'm not threatening you!" he yelled.

"Wish I could replay the tape," she said. "Sure sounded like it to me."

"Excuse me for missing you," he spat. "For being concerned for you."

"Oh, stop it. You're not. You know I'm fine, or you would've heard otherwise. You just don't like that you don't know why I'm choosing to stay in Aspen, what I'm doing." She sighed. "You still want to control my life, even now. Nothing's changed."

"That's not true," he proclaimed.

"Sorry, Dad, but it sure sounds and feels like it." She rose and started pacing the studio. Stress wasn't good for her. She drew long, deep breaths in through her nose and out through her mouth. "If you simply missed me, you would've left me a voice mail saying so. Not called me a bunch of times, been obnoxious about it, then made demands when you reached me."

"I'd say you sound like your brothers," Charles II said, "but apparently you haven't been in contact with them very much either. You're not talking to any of us."

"Yes, I am," she said, but felt a pang. The truth was, she

hadn't been good about returning texts and calls. It wasn't like her. Why was she shutting them all out this way? It was something she needed to examine more closely. "Dad, I'm fine. I didn't want to argue with you. Let me get back to painting, okay?"

"You haven't even asked how I'm doing."

"You sound fine to me. Same as always."

He snorted. "Sorry to bother you. Excuse me for caring." He hung up.

She growled as she set the phone down. Pierce didn't understand why she still talked to their father, why she stayed loyal and tried to keep communication open. Days like this, she didn't understand it either.

She went to the low table for her water bottle. As she sipped, she stared out at the scenic view outside the glass wall. Acres of evergreen forest stretched before snow-capped mountaintops in the not-too-far distance . . . The majesty of it never failed to move her. She gazed at it all as she calmed herself. She *had* been testy, and went straight into combat mode. But her father was capable of things . . . She knew him all too well.

Of course her mind went back to Milan. She'd gone to Italy the summer after graduating NYU, to travel and paint and find herself a little more. She spent a week in Venice, two weeks in Rome, then went on to Milan. There she'd met Paolo, on her second night in the city. She couldn't help but smile now as she recalled him. Handsome, sweet, sexy as hell, and nine years older than her, they'd hurled themselves into a passionate fling. She was only supposed to stay in Milan for a week. She ended up staying for three.

It would have been longer, perhaps. But her father somehow caught wind of why she'd changed her plans, and didn't like it. He'd sent his people—security goons—to Milan to bring her home. The memory of those three men, standing in her small flat, watching her pack her things, still made her blood boil. She'd had no say in the matter. She'd barely even been able to wish Paolo a tender but tearful goodbye, but at least she'd been allowed that much. She'd never forget the way he caressed her face and whispered sweet nothings in Italian against her ear as he hugged her that last time.

They'd lost touch soon after she returned home. It hadn't been a great love, but it had been an intense connection, and Tess had hoped it wouldn't die out so fast. She figured he'd been turned off by her father's interference and couldn't really blame him. It wasn't until years later, after she got engaged to Brady, that she'd found out the truth. Glad that she'd found someone suitable to marry, her father told her how he'd threatened Paolo to make him stay away from her. Paolo had been indignant, but Charles II had won. Their relationship had healed and gotten past the whole debacle, but she'd never fully forgiven her father for it.

There had been other incidents over the years, big and small. There had been the way he treated her brothers as well, Pierce in particular. He claimed everything he did was for the good of the family, out of love. But the years of limitless power had warped his mind. She remembered him being a loving father when she was very small . . . but that had been before her parents' marriage had blown sky-high. Now, the bottom line was: Charles Harrison II was controlling, egomaniacal, and ruthless. His children, though grown, were like trophies as much as people. The heart attack had softened him some. She'd seen that. But not enough. A seventy-year-old leopard couldn't change his spots.

Now she wondered what he'd do if he found out her current plans and didn't like them. Would he somehow shut down the clinic? Put Dr. Fuller's career in jeopardy? Find Logan and threaten him within an inch of his life? She took a long sip of water. Yeah, she had damn good reason to keep her dreams and plans to herself.

She knew her brothers would never tell their father her plans if she asked them not to. They were loyal to her above him, without question. But . . . what if they didn't approve either? They all had their own wives now, their own families. If they started with the *maybe you just haven't found the right person yet, give it more time* crap, she'd pull her hair out. Maybe she wasn't giving them enough credit. But she just didn't want to argue or defend her position to anyone. She'd made this decision on her own, and was handling it on her own. It was how it had to be.

Because she knew what her brothers already knew, though none of them had said it aloud. The Harrison money and power was as much of a curse as it was a blessing. All the money in the world couldn't buy happiness, or the love of your family. Their own parents were both walking proof of that. Biggest cautionary tale ever.

The four siblings always stuck together, understanding one another in a way outsiders simply couldn't. And all four of them had fought through the murky parts to blaze their own paths to happiness—finding love, creating family. Her three brothers had somehow found their happy endings. It was her turn, dammit.

Logan had signed the initial papers waiving paternity rights. There'd be more to sign once she was actually pregnant, but he'd been completely agreeable every step of the way. And, if all went well, he was even willing to freeze a few samples so later on, a year or two down the road, she could give her child a sibling or two.

She'd given up on finding romantic love, but she could

create a family and have that joy, that bond, on her own. That was all she wanted now. And she wasn't ready to share that with her brothers, or her father, or anyone. For now, anyway.

Aspen had been a welcome retreat so far. Everything about it, from its quiet natural beauty, to spending time with Logan, to painting and reading and just . . . being on her own. The exhilaration and thrill of leading her own life away from the watchful eyes of her family was astonishing. The freedom . . . she'd never known how much she needed to break away from the Harrison clan until she'd done it. Being a dutiful daughter, a constant source of support as a sister, the face and responsibility behind the Harrison Foundation . . . being away from it all was revitalizing. A powerful renewal.

Movement outside caught her eye and she focused on it. A large, dark bird soared above the trees, cutting through the bright blue sky. A hawk? She narrowed her eyes and watched . . . No, it was an eagle. A bald eagle. Her breath caught as she watched the magnificent bird sail on the wind. Free to soar. She smiled as she watched him fly.

Tomorrow was Valentine's Day. Fuck. Again Logan raked his hands through his hair as he thought about it. Tess hadn't mentioned anything . . . He wasn't sure if he should do anything; they weren't a real couple. But an agreed-to bargain or not, they were sleeping together. A lot. And mutually enjoying it. And enjoying each other as friends. Not to mention if he didn't do anything, his mom would be suspicious.

Doing a little something for Tess couldn't hurt, right? He was surprised to find that he wanted to. Best of all, since she hadn't brought it up, she likely wasn't expecting anything. So that would be fun too, to surprise her.

He was out on a work call, on the other side of Red Mountain. He had wood to chop up for the Andersons, but texted her before he could rethink it. Hey there, Long Island Lady. Hoping you don't have dinner plans for tomorrow night? Then he picked up his axe, swinging with precise movements. He savored the burn in his shoulders, his arms, and the muscles in his back as he took in lungfuls of cold, fresh air and chopped at the logs in the snow.

It was a good workout. He'd just started to break a sweat when his phone buzzed in his pocket. But he set down the axe, curious to see Tess's answer. She'd responded: I have no plans for tomorrow night, Thor. I was thinking you were just going to come over and try to get me knocked up.

He burst out laughing, then texted back: Can I do that after a nice dinner? It IS Valentine's Day. If I don't take my best fake girlfriend out, Mom will be suspicious.

Good point. Yes, dinner would be lovely. She sent a wink emoji, then added, I'll dress up pretty for you, valentine style. One sexy red dress, coming up.

Oh man, he wrote, his blood racing at the thought. Well then, while you're at it, consider this my official request for lingerie underneath. If not on Valentine's, then when?

Request granted. I'm on it.

Best news I've heard all day. ☺

You know, we'll probably have a better Valentine's Day than most real couples have. No stilted silences, guaranteed sex at the end of the night . . . We win!

He laughed again. Her sense of humor never failed to delight him, and her vibrant personality . . . It had put some light into his life. She brought light to his dark. He was grateful for that. Smiling, he texted back, We SO win.

When he got to her door the next evening, he realized he was more than relaxed, he was almost . . . chipper. Maybe a bounce in his step. He was looking forward to a nice night ahead. It was great to be able to spend Valentine's Day with a woman who wasn't expecting anything from him but companionship, a good meal, and hot sex. Not just any woman, but a genuinely amazing woman, one he liked more with each day. Tess was . . . special. A rare gem. He wanted the night to be nice for her. She deserved that.

So when she opened the door and her eyes lit up at his offering, he felt like he'd scored a slam dunk. "Oh, Logan . . ." She smiled brightly as she looked over the enormous bouquet of two dozen red roses. "These are gorgeous."

"Just like you." He hadn't wanted to go the dozen-red-roses route; it seemed too cliché for a woman as classy as Tess. At first, he'd asked the florist to mix together different types of red flowers, but it looked a little odd. So, *two* dozen roses, then.

He followed her inside as she said over her shoulder, "Let me just put these in water, and then we can go."

His eyes greedily traveled over the tight red wrap dress that clung to her body. Long sleeves, low V-neck, it accentuated every graceful angle and curve. Falling above the knee, it also showcased her knockout legs down to her red stilettos. He let out a long, low whistle of appreciation. "You . . . that dress. *Wow.*"

She tossed him a flirty glance and grin. "Glad you like it," she said before disappearing into the kitchen.

"I love it," he said, following her, unable to take his eyes off her. "I'll love it even more later, when I peel you out of it." His mouth actually watered at the thought. His dress slacks felt too tight.

"Sounds fun to me," she said with a sensuous grin.

His cock throbbed and he shifted his stance. As she set the bouquet down on the marble-topped kitchen island, he opened his coat and noticed her gaze sweep over him.

"You dressed up for me," she remarked with surprise and delighted approval.

"Yeah, a little. You said you were, so . . ."

She went to him, running her hand over his crisp white button-down shirt. He hadn't worn a tie, just the shirt and navy dress slacks, but she seemed to revel in his outfit. Her eyes lit as she looked back up at him with a smile. "You look very handsome." She leaned in and dropped a quick kiss on his mouth, then went across the room to the cabinets. She bent over to pull out a tremendous crystal vase and he almost groaned from the view. Blood rushed south.

While she wrestled the roses into the vase, he crouched down to say hello to Bubbles and play with her for a bit, needing a distraction. He was too turned on; he wouldn't be able to go to dinner with this raging hard-on and burning need.

"When you suggested getting together for Valentine's yesterday"—Tess fussed with the roses, positioning them to her satisfaction—"well, I got you a little something. Now that I'm staring at these gorgeous flowers, I'm doubly glad I did."

Logan straightened to his full height. "You didn't have to get me anything."

"I know. That's what made it fun."

He had to smile. He'd thought the exact same thing about her, hadn't he? "Then thank you in advance." He moved around the kitchen island, the outsized bouquet of flowers between them. "Is it edible?"

Chuckling, she went to one of the many drawers, polished wood beneath marble countertops, and pulled out an envelope. She held it out to him with a smile. "Only if you like to eat paper."

He opened it to find a season pass for skiing at Ajax Mountain—for the *following* year, all bells and whistles included. It was a great gift. And too expensive. And showed real forethought. His eyes flicked up to hers. "I . . . I don't know what to say."

"You love skiing," she said. Her long, graceful fingers reached out to push around some of the flowers in the vase. "This will assure me that next year . . . Well, forgive me, but if your mother's gone"—she glanced at him, and he nodded to show it was okay—"and I'm not going to be around to drag you to the slopes on a regular basis, since I'll hopefully be home in New York with a newborn—I thought if you have this, you'll be motivated to get out and do something fun once in a while." Smiling gently, her voice dropped as she added, "And maybe you'll think of me with a smile when you do."

A slow wave of heavy emotion rolled through him . . . something that made his heart squeeze and his insides warm at the same time. Jesus, she'd cut him off at the knees with this. He tried to swallow back the lump in his throat. His voice was rough as he managed to say, "I'll always think of you with a smile, no matter what I'm doing."

Her smile deepened. "I'd love to think so."

Damn. He adored her. Only that second did he realize that he did, much less the depth of feeling. He cleared his throat. "This is an incredibly considerate gift. Thank you." He moved around the island to gently pull her into his arms. She melted into him, wrapping her arms around his waist and letting her head fall onto his shoulder. His eyes slipped closed as he savored the feel of her against him.

And it hit him like a sledgehammer to the gut: This time next year, he'd be completely alone. More so than ever before.

His mother *would* likely be gone, which was devastating. He couldn't bear to think of it, though he knew full well it was reality. And Tess would be living her life in New York with her baby, thousands of miles away. She'd become such a presence in his daily life . . . someone to chat with, laugh with, and yes, make love with. She'd be gone, their bargain completed, her need for his presence and services fulfilled. So she'd go on with her life, he'd be here, alone . . . and he'd miss her. He'd miss her like hell. The thought of that left him reeling, like a hole had been blown right through him.

He drew a long, deep breath as it all crested over him, trying to hold his ground. His hands ran over her long hair, up and down her slender back, sliding along the soft fabric of the dress as he breathed her in. She smelled so good, a musky vanilla scent that always made his senses fire to life. "You won't visit once in a while?" His voice felt thick in his throat.

"Of course I will," she said. "But it won't be for a few months at a time, like this winter. A week here, a week there . . . and, well . . ." She drew back to look at him as she said quietly, "Have you thought about that it might be hard for you to see the baby once he or she is born? I know you're giving up your rights gladly; right now it's just an idea. But . . . it may hit harder when you actually *see* the baby. And if so, I don't want to do that to you. I might stay away more than not."

He hadn't considered that. Suddenly he could barely

breathe. But he looked her right in the eye as he said, "That's kind. But I'll be fine with it." His voice was husky, his chest tight as he stared at her. "Don't worry about me. And definitely don't stay away from Aspen because of me. Okay? Everything will be fine. I promise."

She only smiled, tender warmth in her gaze. "Let's go to dinner."

They went to Sophie's Bistro. He knew it was one of her favorite restaurants and he liked the warm, cozy atmosphere, but he'd also chosen it for another specific reason. As they walked inside, he confessed he wanted to wipe away the memory of their last meal together there, when he'd bolted and left her there. "This time," he said, "we'll replace that debacle with a nice memory."

She smiled, clearly touched. Her hand lifted to give his beard a quick, affectionate rub. "That's very thoughtful. Thank you."

Something like affection unfurled in his chest. "I even asked for your favorite table, that one in the back that's hidden away."

"How very Valentine's Day of you, Mr. Carter."

"I've done romantic in my time, you know," he said, quirking a grin. "I'm rusty as hell at it, but for you tonight, I'm trying."

"Nice work, fake boyfriend." Tess winked as they were shown to their table. "It's very appreciated. Everything you've done tonight. I haven't been romanced in any way in a long time."

"That's criminal," he murmured as he sat.

Dinner was lovely, the food delicious, the vibe between them genial and relaxed, as it usually was. They talked about random things, from movies and TV to their college coursework two decades ago to the work he'd done at the Andersons' property and the work she'd done long distance the day before. The dim lighting, warm earthy colors of the restaurant, and tea light candles flickering in a bowl on the tabletop, all served to reinforce Logan's opinion that Tess was the most beautiful woman he'd ever laid eyes on.

Her hair sometimes reminded him of a mermaid's storied mane. Tess's thick, dark curls fell over her shoulders, way past her breasts, the ends spilling onto the table. No matter how often she swept them away, they always seemed to reclaim their position around her face, as if they had a life of their own. Her high cheekbones, generous mouth, and wide blue eyes were so strikingly shaped . . . Her lithe body always called to him, making his blood stir. But all that, as incredible a package as it was, wasn't what made her so out-of-this-world stunning.

It was the light inside her. She was so easy to be with, while at the same time, he felt like she was way, way out of his league—and he couldn't believe she continually chose to hang out with *him*. Tonight, he couldn't stop gazing at her, filled with appreciation and warmth, drawn to her with an almost magnetic, unearthly pull.

He supposed it was because their friendship had become so solid, so genuine. They had each other's backs in a way that he . . . Truth was, he hadn't felt so supported, understood, or appreciated by anyone in a really long time. She'd filled a void in his life he'd refused to acknowledge existed. What would he do when she went back to New York?

As it had been earlier, the thought was a kick to the stomach, and his fingers actually flexed at the unwelcome idea. It'd only been a short time, but he liked having her in his life and had grown comfortable with it. With her. Jesus, how had that happened, much less so quickly?

"Dessert?" the waitress asked.

"No, thanks," Tess murmured with a smile. "We'll have that at home."

Logan's insides flooded with aching desire, both his body and his heart. Suddenly he wanted nothing more in the world than to take her home and make love to her. He wanted her all to himself. He wanted to bury himself deep inside her, hold her close . . . somehow shut down all his raging thoughts. "Check, please."

As they shrugged into their coats, his whole body started to hum with searing heat, the familiar rush of primal lust that gripped him whenever he thought about being with Tess. He was growing edgy with it. But as they got to the door and he opened it wide, they were blocked by a woman who was walking in.

"Sorry," the woman apologized. Then his eyes met hers, hers locked on his, and his heart skipped a beat. *Holy shit. Ugh, no.*

"Carrie!" Tess smiled brightly, lifting a hand to squeeze the other woman's arm. "Hi, how are you?"

Carrie's icy blue eyes blinked off the shock as she looked from Tess to Logan and back again. "Tess. Wow. Hi." She swept back her long blond hair, and as her stare settled on Logan, her jaw tightened a little bit.

He cursed up a blue streak in his head. Yeah, this was going to get awkward.

Clueless, Tess tipped her smile up to Logan. "This is Carrie. She's the fantastic instructor of my yoga class. Carrie, this is—"

"We know each other," he murmured, unwilling to play dumb or lie. He nodded in deference to Carrie, who was staring at him hard now. "How've you been, Carrie? You look good."

"Thanks. Well. Small world." The corners of her mouth twitched, something like a grimace. She crossed her arms over her chest and let her gaze lock on Logan. "I didn't know you two knew each other."

"Tess is my girlfriend," he said softly. Carrie's eyes got wider. *Shit, double shit.*

"Girlfriend," Carrie echoed. "Interesting. I thought you didn't do relationships. In fact, I believe I'm quoting you directly when I say that."

"I don't," he said. "Or, I didn't." He sighed. He couldn't tell her the truth about his and Tess's deal, but he hated the hurt he caught in her expression. Then he met Tess's questioning gaze with a solemn one of his own . . . and watched her smile fade as understanding quickly dawned in her eyes. That was Tess: astute, intuitive, and sharp as hell. "Carrie, look—"

"No, that's fine. That's great. At least now I finally understand." Her eyes narrowed on him, like heated lasers. "I get it. Maybe if I'd been an heiress, you'd have wanted a relationship with me, instead of my just being your regular booty call. Money like hers helps you swallow your reluctance, I'm sure."

Tess stiffened at his side.

"Don't do that," he said to Carrie, low and tight. "Don't insult her when you're pissed at me. You're better than that."

"Go to hell, Logan. I'm better than *you*." She shoved past both of them and stormed into the restaurant.

He stared after her, jaw clenched tight, heart pounding. Tess's hand on his arm brought him back.

"Let's go," she murmured.

He glanced down at her, saw the utter calm and regal cool of her expression . . . ah shit. This wasn't good. She was in Ice Queen mode. This wasn't good at all.

Nodding and placing a hand on her back, he escorted her out into the cold night.

* * *

Tess sat very still in Logan's truck, her hands in her lap. She was grateful for the warm air heating her, but something inside her had gone stone cold.

He was embarrassed and upset, she knew that. It was radiating off him in waves. But she sensed he wasn't ready to discuss it. His jaw was clenched tight, his posture stiff.

She was a little upset too. That surprised her. Because really, truthfully, she had no right to be upset with him or the situation . . . but she was. She went into her own head to try to figure out exactly why as they drove in heavy silence back to her house.

By the time they got home, the tension was still thick as could be, and both of them had gone quietly rigid. She opened the door and Bubbles came running, barking her happy hellos. Logan crouched down to pet her as Tess removed her long coat and hung it in the closet. They moved into the living room and she turned on some lights.

"Would you like some tea?" she asked as he pulled off his coat and set it on one of the armchairs.

"No," he said gruffly. "I want to talk about what happened."

"Okay." She stood there, intertwining her fingers in front of her.

He shook his head in displeasure. "You're mad. I don't blame you. I'm sorry."

"I'm not mad. And you have nothing to apologize for," she said. "First of all, you have a life of your own, and who you slept with before me is none of my business. Second, you didn't insult me, she did."

"I hated that," he bit out. "She was just lashing out."

"You think I don't know that?" She crossed her arms

over her chest and sighed. "Guess I'll be switching into a new yoga class. It's a shame. She's great at it. I liked her."

He sighed and raked his hands through his hair, then over his face. "Okay. So, she was the one I was seeing last year, obviously. It started as a casual fling, but she . . . started having feelings for me. After a few months, she wanted us to date exclusively, turn it into a real relationship. I didn't." He started pacing the living room. "So yeah, when she saw us together, that's one thing. But for her to hear you're my girlfriend, when I told her in no uncertain terms that I didn't do relationships? Of course she's surprised, and probably hurt, and I feel bad about that. I do." He scratched at his beard as he added, "But she had no right to sling an arrow your way. That was uncalled-for."

Tess shrugged. "Don't worry about that. I'm fine."

"No, you're not. It's all over you. You're back in 'untouchable princess' mode, and I hate it." He stopped and looked at her mournfully. "I'm sorry, Tess."

"Stop apologizing," she demanded. "You did nothing wrong."

He pinned her with a sad look. "Then why do I feel like you're a million miles away when you're standing right here?"

She stopped cold at that. He was right, and that wasn't fair. They were friends. She could tell him anything. She trusted him enough, and respected him enough, to do that. "All the way home, I tried to figure out why I'm at all bothered by this. It's got nothing to do with me, and I have no right to be put off. But here's the truth . . ." She lifted her chin a bit, twisting her hands as she admitted, "It's been easy to get lost in this. Especially tonight, with the romance of Valentine's Day and all that . . . It was really lovely. I was really enjoying it all. But the lines got blurred tonight, and I'm mad at myself for forgetting that."

He shook his head in frustration. "I was enjoying it too. We were having a great night. But—"

"Logan . . ." She took a deep breath. "The truth is you're sleeping with me because we made a deal. Because you *have* to. But you slept with her simply because you *wanted* to. And I'm . . . a little jealous about that." She pushed her hair back over her shoulders. It was hard to admit it out loud, but she would. "I wish you wanted me for the sake of just wanting me, like you did her at one point. I envy the fact that she attracted you on her own, without strings or a pact. I have no right to, but I'm human. So . . . yeah, it stings a bit." She tried to shrug as she added, "That's on me. I'll get over it."

He stared at her so forcefully, she felt her skin heat. Closing the space between them in two long strides, he gripped her shoulders and said in a low, intense tone, "We're telling the truth? Okay, truth. Yes, we made a deal. I'm sleeping with you because of it. Lucky, lucky me. But if you think I don't want you, you're not as smart as I thought you were."

She swallowed hard as her heartbeat upped its pace. His hands ran up and down her arms as he stared into her eyes, compelling her to not look away. "I love sleeping with you, Tess. I think about it all the time, and I shouldn't. You're my *fake* girlfriend. Friends with benefits, and that's it. But being in this thing with you . . . It's *fun*. Because you're amazing." A grin bloomed on his face. "You're easy to talk to and goddammit, woman, I'm sorry, but I *love* getting in bed with you. That's the truth. Legal papers and all, deal or not . . ." He trailed his fingers along her cheek, her silky jawline. "I've never been so attracted to a woman in my entire life." He peered harder, brows furrowing as he whispered, "Jesus, Tess, do you really not feel that from me? Have I ever made you feel like making love to you is a chore?"

"No," she whispered. "No, never." Her heart pounded against her ribs. The things he was saying, along with how jealous she'd become at the thought of him wanting Carrie enough to sleep with her over and over, and the way he was looking at her now, all hot and intense and drop-dead sexy . . . Oh God, she had feelings for him that went way beyond friendship. She'd fallen for him, and it'd been so seamless she hadn't even been aware of it. Until right now.

The realization hit her hard as she stared back up at him. This big, gorgeous Viking, this sweet and sensitive man who asked nothing of her and gave so much . . . she was crazy about him. She looked forward to seeing him every day, loved talking to him, loved being with him. Ohhh, she was in big trouble. He was only so at ease with her because they were just friends. He'd just said so himself. So any sticky feelings beyond that? That was *not* part of the deal.

"Tess," he continued, blissfully unaware of the turmoil raging inside her. "Yes, we started this as a plan, each of us giving the other something we needed. But we've bonded. We're real friends now. And our friendship means a lot to me. *You* mean a lot to me." He sighed as he admitted, "Carrie never did. She was really nice, and we had fun in bed, but I never felt *anything* for her, which is why I thought it fair to her to end it when I did. I was trying to spare her feelings. You understand?"

Tess only nodded.

"Sure, I wanted her then. But my Long Island Lady . . ." He quirked a grin. "I want you now. All the time. Deal or not, friends or not, you're the most beautiful, desirable, sexy and sweet woman I've ever met. So don't be jealous of her. I *want* you." He lowered his head and took her mouth in a commanding kiss.

She swayed as she let herself fall into it. His hands slid up her back and into her hair, holding her to him as he plundered her mouth with deep, hot kisses. She couldn't think straight, and she didn't want to deal with what she was feeling. A piece of her wanted to run away from him, right there and then. But it was the end of her ovulation cycle. She needed to do what they were there to do. So she reached out and unbuttoned his shirt as they kissed, pulling the shirttails out of his pants with demand.

He pulled back to look at her, brows lifted, his gaze a silent question.

"No more talking," she whispered. "Let's go upstairs and get to work."

That stopped him. He frowned, cradling her face in his hands. "Wow. Wait. We need to—"

"No. I don't want to talk anymore." She pulled away and headed for the stairs. It was easier to lie to him when she wasn't looking at him, so she said as she walked, "You and your friendship mean a lot to me too, Logan. We're good. So let's go."

She was halfway up the stairs when she realized he wasn't behind her. She turned to look; he stood where she'd left him, in the middle of the living room, staring after her with a stormy, confused look on his handsome face.

"We're fine," she said firmly, even as her heart hammered inside her chest, making it hard to breathe. "Please join me upstairs?"

His eyes narrowed on her, pale green lasers scouring into her. Then he scrubbed his hands over his face, drew a deep breath, and started walking to join her.

Their sex wasn't playful or fun. Intense and red-hot, the atmosphere in her dark bedroom was similar to the charged tension of makeup sex after a fight. They grabbed at each other without mercy, reckless and demanding. She dug her nails deep as they trailed over his back; he bit her and possessed her and made her scream for more. When he went to position himself over her, she brusquely turned her body, offering her back. She couldn't do missionary position tonight. She couldn't look into his eyes as he moved inside her . . . not with the emotions pinballing through her now. He'd be able to see how she felt about him if he looked deeply into her eyes, and she couldn't bear the thought of it.

She glanced at him over her shoulder, signaling without words that she wanted something rougher and darker than she usually did. So intuitive, so in sync when they were in bed together, his eyes held hers for a long beat. Then, gripping her hips, he took her from behind, slamming into her hard as he went deep. She moaned loud and low, her fingers twisting into the sheets.

He took over and she gladly let him, giving herself up. Pounding into her, the sounds of their bodies slapping together and lusty groans and labored breathing took them quickly to another level they'd never hit before. He grunted over her, driving into her with mindless animal lust. She urged him on with her moans and motions . . . then she cried out his name, her head dropping down as the shouts tore from her throat. The erotic sounds sent him flying over the cliff. He dug his fingers into her hips as he groaned and bucked and shuddered and emptied himself deep inside her.

They fell to the mattress together in a tangled, sweaty heap, her hair everywhere, both of them breathing as hard as if they'd run a race. He held her close, spooning her, her back to his front as they worked to calm down.

Finally, he dropped a tender kiss on her shoulder. "There's

no way in hell you can think I don't really want you after that." He moved her hair aside to better expose her skin and kissed her shoulder again. His sexy voice rumbled in her ear, sending tiny shivers over her. "What Carrie said? She's dead wrong. I don't give a fuck about your money, and you know that. And yes, our deal is our deal, but I'm insanely attracted to you." His hand ran down the length of her side, stopping at her hip. "Please tell me you know that?"

God, what he was doing to her. And he had no idea. She nodded and let her eyes slip closed. "I know that, Logan."

"Okay. Good." He kissed her neck and pulled her even tighter against him, closing one hand around her breast and one on her waist as he cradled her.

She let herself glory in how it felt to be held by him, the smell and feel of him . . . then she tried to pull away. "Gotta raise them up," she murmured.

He let her go more slowly than usual. She swung her body around into position, lifting her legs up over the smooth curved headboard. He pushed a pillow under her hips. They lay together in silence.

She waited for him to do what he always did: go to get them both water, talk for a few minutes, then leave for the night. And it took a minute, but then he did get up from the bed and pad out quietly, and he did bring back a bottle of water for her, sitting on the bed beside her as usual.

"I'm glad we're friends," he said softly, gazing down at her.

"I am too," she said. "I'm glad we can talk openly like we did tonight."

"Same here. And I feel like . . . you *heard* me. You know. So that's the end of that." He paused, as if he were going to say more, then drank more water instead. "I better get going. I'm tired."

"I'm exhausted. You destroyed me here. That was . . ." Her voice trailed off.

"I'm not sure what that was," he admitted in a whisper. "But holy hell, it was intense. You're more than a tigress, you're a damn lion." The corner of his mouth lifted, and he leaned down to kiss her lips. "I hope I didn't leave bite marks. Or bruises on your hips . . . oh man. You're gonna be marked up tomorrow. You have such pale skin . . . I'm sorry."

"Don't be," she said firmly. "I loved it. Besides, you don't get away with nothing. You'll be feeling those scratches when you shower." She couldn't help but grin back.

"Ah shit," he laughed. "Probably true." He stared into her eyes. "We're cool?"

"Totally." Her heart squeezed as a voice whispered in her head. *Liar. You're a hot mess. Get him out before you beg him to stay.* "Get home safely, okay?"

"I will, don't worry. Always do."

"Thanks for the flowers, and dinner."

"My pleasure. Thanks for the ski pass. And wearing that incredible dress, and . . . everything. Tonight was . . ." He paused, seeming to search for the right words. Finally he said, "It was certainly memorable."

She snorted out a laugh. "It was that."

"Seriously, most of it was great. Think of the good parts." He stroked her hair with tender fingers, making her heart ache and want more. "I'll text you tomorrow."

"Sounds good."

He gave her a small smile and rose from the bed. She watched him get dressed, her mind racing and her heart in turmoil. She didn't want him to leave. She wanted him to hold her all night as she dealt with these astonishing new realizations, these intense feelings she'd been clobbered by tonight. She wanted him, period. But she couldn't act on it, or tell him. Ever. It was a dealbreaker and she knew it.

If she told him the whole truth, he'd leave. Because what he'd told Carrie, and Tess herself, was his truth: He didn't do relationships. He'd been hurt too much by his ex-wife, and lost too much after Katrina. So they could be friends as long as he didn't feel pressured for more, as long as it was the initial deal he'd agreed to.

The last thing she could do is tell him what she'd realized tonight . . . that she was falling in love with him. And as much as his prime directive was not to be tied to anyone, hers was equally clear: She wanted a baby more than anything in the world. More than her own romantic happiness. So she wasn't willing to jeopardize whatever this was between them. If she told him what she was feeling now, he'd run for the hills like he had when she'd first asked him to be her donor—only this time, he wouldn't look back. Her own heart, her own feelings and desires, would have to stay on lockdown. Logan felt a bond with her, and that was great. She believed him when he said that she and their friendship were important to him. But he didn't want to be loved, and he didn't want anything lasting, and that wouldn't change.

When he said good night, she pressed her lips together and said nothing, only lifting her hand to give a jaunty little wave as he left her bedroom and closed the door behind him.

Chapter Nineteen

Tess went for a long walk the next morning, trudging up the hiking path along Red Mountain. She had too much swirling inside her head and heart; clear fresh air would be a good balm for that. The sky was crystalline blue and the air frigid. Snow covered the ground, but someone had cleared the narrow hiking path. Probably Logan, she realized. He managed over half of the houses on Red Mountain. A solid, capable, steady man like him was in high demand among the high-end clients.

Logan . . . God help her, she wasn't just falling in love with him, she was already in love with him. She'd have to call on every trick she'd ever learned about masking her emotions in the boardroom to get through being with him in the bedroom. The easy affection and camaraderie they shared would help; she could still be playful, touch him, tease him . . . but she'd have to be careful about anything more than that seeping through. If he sensed she wanted more, he'd likely end the deal . . . like he had with Carrie.

Tess focused on visualization as she walked. She put her mental energy into thinking of her future baby. She visualized sitting on her couch back at home, cradling her baby in her arms . . . and Logan, sitting with them, smiling. *Damn.* Even in her mindful fantasies, he made his way into her thoughts.

When she got back to the house, her cell phone light blinked like crazy. She picked it up to see several texts waiting for her. Grabbing a bottle of water from the fridge first, she drank some down before settling into the sofa. Bubbles leapt up to snuggle her feet as she scrolled through the texts.

One from Carrie. Wow. Hi Tess. I wanted to apologize for last night. I was mad at him, not you. I shouldn't have sniped at you, and I'm really sorry.

Tess answered immediately. Hi Carrie. I understand completely. Apology accepted. Thanks for reaching out.

To Tess's surprise, Carrie responded right away. Thank you for being gracious. When I got to work this morning, I saw you already dropped my class. I feel awful. I thought you enjoyed it.

Tess pursed her lips as she thought about it. Then she typed: Yes, I enjoyed it very much And yes, I dropped it first thing this morning. I thought, for obvious reasons, it was the right thing to do.

Carrie didn't answer for a minute. Then her text came in. I hope you'll reconsider, but I understand if you don't. Either way, I'm sorry about the rude comment. Not my best moment.

I'll think about it, Tess responded. And again, I do appreciate your apology. We're good.

Tess sat back, settling deeper into the plush cushions of the couch. Carrie was a good person, and she was glad they'd talked. But was it fair to rejoin her class, and maybe have either of them feel uncomfortable? Probably not. She could take another class with a different instructor.

Next text was from Logan. Good morning. Just thought

I'd let you know that my back looks like I got in a fight with a wildcat and lost. Ouch. And hot damn.

Warmth unfurled low in her belly as she smiled. Raaaawwwr, she typed back.

He didn't answer right away. Probably working.

Next text was the group text thread she had with her three brothers. Her brows lifted as she saw all three of them had piped in.

Hi Tess, Charles had started. Got an angry call from Dad. Seems you put him in his place, so hooray for you. But he said you told him you might not come home until April. That's not true, is it?

Don't ever believe anything the old man says, Pierce had written next. Don't you know that yet? He's a shit stirrer. Tess would've told us if she was going to stay away that long.

I don't know, Charles said. Yes, he's a shit stirrer, as you say. But he sounded pretty adamant about it. I had no answer for him.

Because maybe it's true, Dane had piped in. We've discussed how our darling Tesstastic hasn't been as communicative as she used to be. Maybe he wrangled that bit of news out of her when he pissed her off . . . Um, Tess? Honey? Feel free to clue us all in. Don't make us wonder, just set us straight.

Shit, Pierce had written. You've got a point, big brother. Tess? What he said. Get in touch, okay?

Yes, please do, Charles wrote. So the next time Dad calls to rage about you, which will likely be every day now that he's focused on this, I can tell him to STFU and leave you alone.

You should tell him that anyway, Pierce wrote at the end of the thread. Tess can do whatever she wants, she doesn't have to answer to him, FFS.

"Oh my God," Tess breathed. She quickly texted them all: I'm here, I'm here. Went for a hike on the mountain and came back to this. You sound like a pack of hens.

Cluck cluck, Dane wrote back immediately. Tell us what's going on, please. You're staying there until the spring? Is that actually true?

Yes, she wrote. As of now, staying until March for sure, possibly April. Don't know yet. She held her breath, waiting for the avalanche.

Jesus Christ, Dane wrote. Why?

Aw man, Pierce wrote.

Fuck, Charles texted. I hate it when Dad's right & I was in the dark. Goddammit.

Sorry, Tess wrote. It wasn't planned initially . . . I'm playing it by ear. I've got a situation here that's turned into . . . How could she tell them without telling them? She paused, then wrote, It's on a month-to-month basis now. So I'm rolling with it as it goes.

WTF??? Dane texted. What does that even mean?

Could you be a bit less vague? Charles asked.

So, Pierce wrote. What's his name? ;)

Tess barked out a laugh at that. Not only because he'd kind of guessed correctly, but she knew if she told him both of their parents had asked the same thing, he'd be so ticked off. I'm fine. I'm working remotely, I'm exercising every day, I'm painting and skiing and enjoying myself. That's all anyone needs to know right now. Please respect my privacy.

None of her brothers responded to that for a full minute. She sighed.

I love you guys, she wrote. I promise, I swear, that I'm fine. And I'll be better about answering calls or texts from now on. Okay?

Okay, Pierce said. It's your life, Tess. Do your thing. We're here.

Oh, fuck that! Dane wrote. I'm the only one with a million questions here?

No, Charles answered. But if she wanted to tell us what's

going on, she would. Clearly, we're not to be privy to such information.

Stop being surly babies, Pierce wrote. It's not about us. Leave her be. Respect her wishes.

I am! Dane shot back. But I don't have to like it. I'm worried. And I miss my sister, and I don't like not knowing what the hell's going on that's keeping her away for months at a time. There, I said it, and I'm not sorry, but I'll stop now.

Ditto, Charles wrote.

She couldn't help but smile, even as she rolled her eyes. I love you all, she texted. I'm a lucky girl to have such protective brothers. Thank you.

Just don't disappear, okay? Dane wrote.

That'll never happen, Tess answered. Besides . . . by the time I get home, I have a feeling I'll need you all more than ever. Just taking a break from the world right now.

I get that, Pierce wrote. Been there. Take it easy, okay Tessie?

I am, she wrote. She smiled to herself as she tucked her legs beneath her. It's been wonderful.

The kids miss you, Charles responded. Give them a call soon, if you would?

I will, she wrote back. I promise. Which night is good?

Friday, Charles wrote. After 8:00.

Will do, Tess wrote. All of you send your wives my love, okay?

I miss my buddy, Dane wrote. That's all. Love you, Tesstastic.

Her heart gave a squeeze as she wrote. Awww. I miss you and love you too. All of you. Talk to you soon. Xoxo

With an exhausted exhale, she dropped the phone onto the coffee table. Then she scooped Bubbles up and hugged her close as her brothers' words pinged around in her head. She appreciated that they missed her and were concerned . . . but she wasn't going to tell them or anyone what was going on until she was already pregnant. This was for her. This whole situation was hers and hers alone.

Another text dinged in. She picked up the phone to look. From Logan: You okay today, tigress? No bruises or anything, I hope? Was wondering. Concerned.

He was sweet. She kept her response light. Not much. Come over tomorrow night and see for yourself. Last night of this ovulation.

Yes ma'am, he wrote back. Busy at work today. Just wanted to check in. Text you tonight.

Have a good day, she wrote, adding a smiley emoji.

You too.

Logan's ruggedly handsome face appeared in her head. She sighed. Well . . . the situation was *almost* hers alone. There was also this wonderful man who was doing her the favor of a lifetime, whom she'd just realized she was in love with, and couldn't ever tell him that or he'd probably shut her out of his life. That . . . complicated things a bit.

Logan held his mother's arm as they walked slowly into the hospital. She was having one of her bad days, drained and no appetite. He'd tried to get her to eat some lunch, but she'd shooed him away. He'd managed to beg and bully her into drinking a cup of chicken broth before they'd left her house. Now, they sat side by side in the doctor's office, waiting for him and her latest results. Logan had a bad feeling deep in his gut.

He was on edge and he knew it. His leg bounced as they sat.

"Stop with the leg," Annmarie chided. "You're making me jittery."

"Sorry." With effort, he stilled his movement. "I'm nervous. Can't lie."

"Don't be," she said. Her face looked pale and drawn. "Whatever it is, it is. Worrying won't change that."

She was right and he hated it. He tried to think of good things . . . skiing with Tess, or being in bed with her. That only put him a bit more over the edge. Her ovulation cycle past, they were in the No Sex Zone now. It'd been two weeks since he'd been inside her, and every muscle in his body was tense with craving. They still spent time together, continuing the ruse for his mom. But being close to her only amplified his longing and need . . . He wanted her all the time. When he'd told her that on Valentine's Day, he hadn't been kidding. And he'd surprised himself with the fervor of his words . . . his feelings.

The doctor came in, greeting them as he closed the door behind him, file folders in his hands. Logan took one look at his face and his heart plummeted to his stomach.

The words came in something of a blur as he listened. The latest scans showed . . . efforts were no longer effective . . . two new tumors in her lymph nodes . . . could go at them aggressively . . . Logan felt dazed. His blood rushed through his body, roaring in his ears and pulsing behind his eyes. His stomach twisted nauseously.

"That's it then," Annmarie said quietly. "No more. No more treatment."

"Mom," Logan choked out.

She shook her head and held up a hand. "My body. My life. My call." Her eyes were clear as she looked at her son, then the doctor. "I'm going to die anyway. Time to stop poisoning myself and prolonging it. I go out on my terms."

Logan swallowed back a rush of bile. His mind raced as he looked frantically from one to the other, but he knew. He knew nothing he said would sway her or change her mind; he'd gotten his stubborn streak from her, after all.

He knew this was the real beginning of the end. The doctor looked a little sad but accepting, as if he'd known this was coming. As they talked, discussing it all, Logan felt sick. Desperate, enraged, and lost. But he held it together. For her. Anything for her. He gazed at her, fists clenched in his lap. She needed his strength and support, now more than ever. He could fall apart at home, in private.

Tess startled when her doorbell rang at seven in the evening. Sitting in the small room designated as an office, she'd been catching up on work emails at the cherrywood desk. Her hair was pulled back in a ponytail, and she wore her most comfortable black sweater and multicolored leggings. She wasn't expecting anyone. Maybe Logan had dropped by? She hurried to answer the door and opened it wide.

Logan stood there, looking . . . like something was very, very wrong.

"Hey," she said softly. All her inner sirens wailed at the look on his face. "What happened? Something happened, I can see it."

"Can I come in?" His voice was a low, tight rasp.

She grabbed his arm and pulled him inside, closing the door behind him. He stood there silently.

"Is your mother all right?" Tess asked, fearing the answer.

"No," he said. He shook his head, lifted his eyes to meet hers . . . The pain there took Tess's breath away. "I . . . I just . . ."

"Shhhh." She pulled him close, wrapping her arms around him. His arms lifted to return the embrace, his hold tight, clinging to her.

"I need you tonight," he whispered in her ear. "I just needed to see you."

"I'm here," she whispered. She pulled back to look into his eyes and touched his face. "I'm here, honey."

His eyes filled with tears and it was a kick to her stomach. "I can't talk."

"You don't have to." She peeled him out of his coat, got him to kick off his boots, and took him by the hand. She led him up to her bedroom and nudged him to sit down on her bed. He watched without a word as she flicked the switch to start the gas fireplace, then turned off the lights. "Come here, you."

She lay down on the bed, pulling him down with her, then curled herself around his large, solid body. Dropping a kiss on his cheek, she burrowed into him as his arms banded around her. Her head on his chest, she heard the thick pounding of his heart, felt the way his fingers held tight, and her heart ached for him. She caressed his arm, his beard, his chest as they lay there for a long time, holding each other in the near dark.

"Thanks for this," he finally whispered after an hour.

"You don't have to thank me," she said. "Feel any better yet?"

"A little, actually." His hand ran up and down her back. "You soothe me."

"Good, I'm glad. Can you tell me what happened?"

He gave her the short version, his voice low and ragged. Her eyes squeezed shut at the horrible news. His fingers sifted through her hair as he talked, but she now understood the coiled tension in his muscles. When he finished, she whispered kindness and leaned up to press her lips to his.

They kissed languidly, sweetly, a joining of mouths with affection, not lust or duty. But soon the kisses deepened, tongues swirling and hands roaming, sparking heat that burned with a hint of urgency.

"I need you," he whispered, husky and a bit desperate.

"I'm right here," she whispered back with warm assurance.

They made slow, tender love by the flickering light of the fire. She held him close as their bodies rocked together, as he lost himself in the sweet escape of her body. He kissed her, stroked her, looked deep into her eyes as he moved inside her. And she met his searching gaze, his languorous thrusts, his every need at every point. She was a goddess, a savior, a lifeline. When she came, she held him so close it was if they were one. His orgasm rolled through him and he sailed over the precipice in relief, holding her tight as he found release, saying her name over and over like a prayer.

Covered in a light sheen of sweat, they stared into each other's eyes and kissed, a million sweet and tiny sips as their bodies calmed.

"You need to raise your hips," he murmured.

"Not tonight," she said. "I need to hold you and not let go."

His mind reeled. In his angry grief, he'd come to her. After settling his mother in at her house, he'd driven straight to Tess's house without conscious thought. And Tess had welcomed him without a moment's pause, giving him the support, comfort, and affection he needed so desperately. Her. He needed *her* desperately. She was all he wanted.

He hovered over her, pushed back her hair from her face, and stared into her beautiful blue eyes. Emotions rolled through him, waves of warmth and connection. He pressed his lips to hers. "You're amazing."

She only smiled and kissed him back.

He rolled, pulling her with him until they settled side by side, still locked in an embrace. "I'm wiped out," he murmured. "What a day . . ."

"So go to sleep," she said, stroking his beard.

He glanced down at her. "Yeah?"

"Yeah. Do you want to leave this bed right now?"

"Not for all the money in the world."

"So give in. Go to sleep." She kissed his cheek and added in a whisper, "It's okay."

Suddenly overcome by exhaustion, he kissed her once more and closed his eyes.

He woke with a start in a dark room. Disoriented, he tried to piece together where he was . . . Hair tickled his chest. Tess's warm body was aligned with his. He had no idea what time it was. She slept soundly, curled into his side. He listened to her slow, deep breathing, letting it hypnotize him back to sleep.

When he opened his eyes again, there was light. Dark gray light poured in from the floor-to-ceiling glass wall of Tess's bedroom. The forest and mountains were barely visible outside, but still a stunning view. He lifted his head to look over Tess's sleeping body to the alarm clock on the nightstand. It was just past six in the morning. This was usually when he woke for the day, but he felt tired deep in his bones. He let himself give in and closed his eyes once more.

Movement on his arm jostled him out of sleep . . . a tiny wet tongue on his face. Sputtering, he raised up on his elbows, then laughed. Tess wasn't licking him awake, Bubbles was.

"Naughty girl," Tess reprimanded the dog. "Let him sleep!" She gave Bubbles a gentle push away from Logan.

"It's fine," he said, flopping back down. Sunlight peeked from between thick clouds over the mountains. Again, he gazed at the view, enjoying it. Then he realized he was waking up in that big cozy bed beside Tess for the first time, and he wanted to savor it. The bed felt as amazing as he'd always suspected it would, but waking up with her was even more amazing. Warmth stole through him. He pulled her in close and lightly kissed her lips. "Good morning, beautiful."

"Good morning." She smiled, a lazy, sweet curve of her mouth. "How'd you sleep?"

"Both like a rock, and restlessly," he said. "It was weird. When I was asleep, it was so deep, I didn't even dream. But I woke up a few times . . . Guess my brain wouldn't let me be."

"I'm not surprised." She gripped his chin and pressed kisses to his mouth. "Glad you slept at all. You needed it."

"Yeah, I did." He trailed a fingertip along her cheek. "Thanks for letting me stay over."

"Thanks for not arguing with me. I could see you needed to pass out."

"I did. I . . . I needed to be here with you." He only realized just how much as he said the words. His throat got a little thick. "You gave me the comfort I needed last night. Thank you. You're an incredible friend."

"I'm glad I could give you what you needed," she murmured. She kissed him once more, then sat up. "How about coffee? Can I make you some breakfast?"

"Yes to the coffee," he said. "But I'm making *you* breakfast. Time to treat you with my culinary skills."

"On top of your already incredible bedroom skills? You're a man of many talents." She got out of bed and he relished the view of her lithe naked body. He tried to ignore his morning wood as she crossed the room to grab her soft red robe. But as she pushed her feet into the matching slippers, she eyed his growing erection. "How about after breakfast, we take care of that . . . ?"

His cock twitched at the thought. "I like how you think, lady."

He pulled on his jeans, didn't bother with the sweater, then made himself comfortable in her kitchen. Enjoying the space and high-end appliances, it was a pleasure to make omelets with onions, mushrooms, and Swiss cheese. She toasted some whole wheat bread and made coffee. They sat at the kitchen table and ate together in quiet comfort.

"This is really nice," he said.

"It is." She smiled. "And you're a great cook. Thanks for this."

"That's nothing," he asserted. "I really can cook, you know. I need to cook for you more often."

"Then do it. Stay over more often and cook for me." Her eyes sparkled.

The words were playful, but they set off something inside him.

Being with her felt so natural, so right, because it *was*. Yesterday, when his world teetered off its axis, he'd gone running to her. She'd been like a beacon in the storm . . . and she'd given him exactly what he needed, and so much more.

Somehow, she'd become the best, brightest part of his life. She understood him, was there for him without hesitation, and appreciated him. She made him laugh. She made him burn with desire. She was a supportive friend, a sensual lover, a smart and insightful woman he had utmost respect for. She brought out the best in him, things in him he'd buried so deep, so long ago, he'd forgotten they existed. He gazed at her now, realizing the quiet but unavoidable truth: He loved her.

How the hell had that happened? It was supposed to be a deal, plain and simple. A carefully planned arrangement. Friends with benefits, not deep true love. He didn't do relationships, dammit. He kept himself isolated on purpose; he wanted no ties to people . . . so he'd never get hurt again like he had before. This was shattering.

"You just disappeared into your head," she said gently. "Want to share?"

He cleared his throat, suddenly dry. No, he didn't want to share. He needed time to wrap his head around this. He needed to stomp it down where it belonged, into the ground. She was counting on him to be only her friend, no strings attached. To get her pregnant, with a baby he'd already signed away his rights to, so she could go back to New York and live her life, with him in the rearview mirror, an appreciated footnote in the long story of her life.

She touched his hand, a feather's touch, leaning in to peer harder. It made his heart skip a beat. This beautiful woman . . . God, she owned his heart. Holy fuck, his head was spinning.

"Hey. Logan." She frowned, eyes searching. "You okay?"

He had to say something. To at least tell her she meant the world to him. If he started now, maybe one day she could look back and know how much he'd cared, and he'd have that much. Because loving her, having anything more with her than what they had now, wasn't an option. "Tess, I—"

There were voices, the jangling of keys, and the front door closed. Both of their heads swiveled toward it in alarm. Tess's hand tightened on his. "Someone's here."

"What the hell—?" Logan began, but his question died in the air.

"Hello?" a familiar male voice called out. "Tess?"

"Oh my God," she breathed, eyes round with horror. Her eyes flickered over Logan's shirtless torso, her own robe-clad body. But there was no time. A few seconds later, her three brothers stood in the kitchen doorway. Tall, strong men, frozen in their tracks, three pairs of bright blue eyes wide with shock.

Logan drew a long sigh.

"Thought I smelled something cooking," Pierce quipped.

Chapter Twenty

"What are you guys doing here?" Tess asked. Her heart pounded in her ribs. This was *not* how she'd wanted them to find out about her plans. Oh God, this was going to be something.

"We thought we'd surprise you," Dane said.

"Feels more like an ambush," she said flatly.

"Not at all!" Dane exclaimed. "But yeah . . . this is awkward. Fuck."

"Hello, Logan," Charles said. His voice was calm, but sharp. "So . . . you've been keeping Tess company. Interesting."

Logan nodded to all three of them in greeting, then turned to Tess and murmured, "I'll stay if you want, but I think you need to talk to them without me here."

"That's probably best," she agreed. "Thanks."

He rose from his seat. He was a few inches taller than any of her brothers, and twice as built, a solid wall of muscle. Looking especially strong without any shirt on, his jeans slung low on his narrow hips, she marveled at him for the thousandth time.

"Take it easy on her, okay?" he said to them. "Let her talk."

A muscle twitched under Charles's eye as he said curtly, "Don't tell us how to handle our sister."

"She doesn't need handling," Logan said, a little terse. "That's the point."

"Thanks for the tip," Pierce said. "But we know that."

"I love getting advice on how to deal with my sister," Dane said, "from someone who barely knows her."

"I don't know what I love more," Tess said from her seat. "When people talk about me like I'm not right here, or when my clueless brothers are rude to my friends."

"Looks like more than friends," Dane noted.

She bristled, and opened her mouth to speak. But Logan spoke first.

"Whatever we are," he asserted, "it's none of your business. Last time I checked, Tess was a grown woman with her own life."

"You're starting to get on my nerves," Dane growled.

"I've always liked you, Logan," Charles rumbled. "But you're on thin ice at the moment."

"Really." Logan didn't move a muscle, but the vibe emanating off him was raw power. "How so? Enlighten me."

"Push me and find out," Charles replied, his stare and voice like steel. "Maybe I don't like the shock of walking into my house to find the house manager half-naked with my sister."

"Maybe it's not our business," Pierce pointed out, "and everyone should calm down."

But Logan glared at Charles. "And there we go," he said. "It's down to that, huh? *The* house manager." His chiseled arms crossed over his broad chest, making his biceps bulge a little. "Tell me, how's your wife doing? The one who started out as your nanny. Or should I say, *the* nanny? Must be a nice view from that high horse of yours."

Charles's face flushed with rage and he opened his mouth to speak.

"All of you shut up!" Tess shot to her feet, shoving her chair back with a scrape against the tile floor. "Jesus, this is just . . ." She looked to Logan. "I don't need defending, but thank you for wanting to. I'll call you later, okay?"

His jaw set tight, he simply nodded and walked out of the kitchen.

"What the hell, Tess?" Dane asked. "This is your big secret? Why you're staying away from home, not returning calls? You could've—"

"This is *my* life!" she yelled. All three men stilled, eyes again widening with shock. She hadn't shouted at them in anger in years. Blood pumping through her veins, she pulled the sash on her robe tighter before advancing on them.

"I don't have to tell you anything if I don't want to! I don't have to answer to anyone on this goddamn earth!" She felt the blood pulse in her head, her skin heat as her heart rate skyrocketed. "How *dare* you. How dare you all walk in here and condescend to Logan. He's become an amazing friend to me, and has been hardworking and loyal to our family for several years." She glared at Charles. "You owe him more respect than that." She looked to Dane. "You both owe him an apology." She looked between them and snapped, "Considering you both ended up marrying your employees, from lower income brackets than you were in, you have a hell of a nerve walking in here and trying to dismiss him like that when you know nothing about our situation." Her eyes narrowed at Charles as she added, "He was right to call you on your hypocrisy. I'm horrified."

Charles's jaw dropped open. Dane's pink face matched Charles's, and he stepped back as if she'd pushed him.

"Tess." Pierce spoke softly. "Honey. Calm down. This isn't an ambush. Yes, we were out of line just now. We've just been really worried about you. We thought we'd come here, surprise you, visit with you for a day or two . . . We didn't expect to walk in to find you and Logan like that. It was a shock, that's all."

"No. She's right," Charles said, still red-faced, his voice clipped as he looked Tess in the eye. "Logan was too. We're fucking hypocrites. I hate that. But we were just . . . really surprised. Can we start over here?"

Dane stared at her. She recognized that look . . . He was deeply upset. He could never stand for her to be mad at him. Not when they were kids, or teens, or young adults, and apparently still not now. He said nothing, just stared at her with rounded eyes and flushed cheeks. She could never stay mad when he looked that way, like a lost little boy . . . It made her temper simmer down.

The sound of the front door opening and closing made her shudder. Logan . . . God, the look on his face. After a night like last night, why'd this have to happen? He'd come to her for her comfort, she'd tried to give him what he'd needed, and then to have to leave like this . . . Damn, what horrible timing.

She huffed out a sigh. "I'm going to tell you all what's going on," she finally said. "I haven't told anyone. But I'll tell you. And you'll listen until I'm done talking, and you won't give me an ounce of grief, or I'll lose my shit like you've never seen. Okay?"

"Okay," Pierce said. He glanced toward the refrigerator. "Can I get a snack first?"

She breathed out a weary laugh, her tense shoulders relaxing some. "Go for it."

As Pierce went to the fridge, she went to Dane and hugged him. He immediately hugged her back. "I'm sorry," he said against her hair.

"Me too," she said. "I shouldn't have yelled at you."

"We deserved it." He rubbed her back. "If someone came bursting into my kitchen, unexpectedly breaking up a happy morning after, I'd be pissed off too." He pulled back to look down at her. "Sooo . . . Logan Carter? Really?"

"The guy's like a mountain," Pierce said as he opened a bottle of water. "His muscles have muscles. At least you found a guy tall enough for you." He leaned a hip against the center island and winked.

"Just didn't think he was your type," Dane said.

"Good for you," Pierce said. "Why not?"

She rolled her eyes and said, "It's not what you guys think."

"He's a good man, from what I know of him." Charles went to the cupboard to pull out a mug. "I was rude. I'm not proud of it I'll find him and apologize, today. I'll make it right." He crossed to the Keurig. "Coffee, anyone?"

"I'm going to get dressed," Tess said. "Meet you all in the living room." She left the kitchen, heart still beating fast, mind spinning out. She hoped Logan wasn't too upset. Or that her brothers wouldn't be when she told them what'd been going on.

Logan glanced at the phone as it rang yet again. All three of the Harrison brothers had tried to call over the course of the day, leaving apologetic voice mails that sounded sincere. He was sure they were; the Harrison brothers were decent men, and he did appreciate their attempts at a cease-fire. But the run-in had only served to undermine his growing restless agitation. He wasn't part of Tess's world. He wasn't even her boyfriend or her real lover. He was her fake boyfriend, her friend, and her damn sperm donor. That was it, and he'd be way better off to remember that.

He'd gone to the gym straight from Tess's house that morning, needing to get out some aggression on the punching bag and the treadmill. A hot shower after that, then he went to work. He'd been too busy to answer calls or texts. And there had been several texts from Tess, trying to reach him throughout the day. He'd ignored them.

By after dinner, her new text lanced his heart and made him feel guilty as hell. Please talk to me. I'm concerned about you. I care. Don't shut me out. Please.

He sighed. This was a mess. This whole thing was a mess, and his mother was dying. But Tess . . . She deserved better than what he was giving her at the moment. Lying on his couch in the darkened living room, with only the flickering light from the TV, he muted the volume of the hockey game and called her.

"Hi. At last, there you are." Her voice was filled with relief, obviously glad to hear from him. It made him feel even worse for not getting back to her sooner. "Are you okay?"

"I'm fine," he said. He stretched out his long legs and crossed them at the ankles. "Are *you* okay?"

"Yes. Got a few minutes to talk?" she asked.

"Absolutely."

She told him everything. How at first she'd yelled at her brothers, then sat them down and told them about her plans and how Logan fit into them. Her brothers had taken it all in stride. They weren't opposed to the idea like she'd thought they might be, and of course had a million questions, which she'd answered. Then they'd offered her unconditional support—both now, during the process, and later, when she was raising her baby on her own. She felt awful for ever doubting them, in the face of their warmth and unity. All in all, it had gone well, and the four of them were fine.

"I'm really glad for you," Logan said. "Really. That's great. You'll need their support in the future."

"Yes, I will. But there's another thing . . ." Tess sighed. "They all tried to call you to apologize. They all said you hadn't responded at all. Would you please consider it?"

"You mean I'm not fired?" He tried to keep the edge off his voice, but failed.

"Of course not," she murmured. "Logan . . . they were so out of line, I was furious. But they're protective of me and always have been. Too protective at times. It doesn't excuse their behavior this morning. I'm just trying to explain it, not justify it."

"Tess." Logan sighed. "I get all that. I do. But the reality is, I'm not a part of your world. Never will be. This morning was . . . well, a good reminder."

She was quiet for a long time.

"I'm not saying that to hurt you," he said gently, his own stomach twisting. "But I *am* just the house manager. And your sperm donor, not your lover. So . . . maybe it was just a good reminder for both of us."

"I thought you were also my friend," she said dejectedly.

He winced. "I am. That's also true, Tess, don't doubt that."

"I thought we'd gotten past this a while ago," she finally said. "When we got to really know each other and became friends. The money thing, the different worlds thing . . . I guess I was wrong. I hate that I was wrong."

"You weren't wrong. It's just . . ." His stomach churned now.

"They really got to you today," she murmured. "How sad."

His eyes squeezed shut. "It wasn't just them," he said raggedly. "It's . . . everything right now. Too much going on. My mom . . . Tess, my head's a little messed up. That's on me."

"I'm here for you," she said. "You know that, right?"

"I know. Thank you." His jaw clenched. He needed to keep her at arm's length. He couldn't want or need her the way he had last night. He couldn't let himself give in again to how amazing it'd felt to be cared for that way. It would only lead to disaster.

She was quiet again, then ventured, "How's your mom doing today?"

"Same. Drained, not eating. Waiting to die. It's wonderful."

"Logan."

"I don't know what to say. How to sugarcoat that."

"You don't have to sugarcoat anything with me," Tess said. "Ever. Don't you know that too?"

His heart went wobbly. "Yeah. I do. Look, I'm sorry. I'm feeling too raw right now. I think I just need to be alone for a while. Process all this."

"I understand," she said, gentle, not pushing or demanding or needy.

He was the needy one. She had no idea.

"It's the no-sex weeks of your cycle anyway," he pointed out. "I mean, we broke that rule last night, but—"

"You needed me," she said softly. "That was about comfort and friendship. Pure and simple. So we sent the rules to hell for one time. No worries."

God, he loved her. He loved her so much. She was tearing him apart. The more supportive and caring she was, the more it cut off his air. He swallowed hard, his heart rate rising.

"So. Changing the subject. My brothers are staying for another two days," she said. "The three of them are going skiing tomorrow. I'm so jealous. I can't go, in case I'm pregnant and don't know it yet, blah blah blah. You know the drill."

He grunted in response, unable to speak. Emotion had his throat closed up.

"So . . . I guess it's a good time to give you the space you need," she said. "I'll talk to you after they've gone. How's that?"

"That works," he said. The light from the TV flickered, suddenly annoying him. He reached for the remote and turned it off. Darkness settled over him, and it was like a salve. "Enjoy their visit."

"Logan." Her voice was soft, tentative. "I feel like you're . . . you're not okay, and that's not okay with me," she said.

"I'll be okay," he said, even though he felt bone weary as he said it. "Just need to be alone for a bit. It's my way."

"All right. But if you change your mind, text or call me, all right?"

"Yeah. Talk to you soon."

She hesitated. He could feel the desperation across the line, she wanted to help him somehow . . . and he wasn't giving her an inch. She finally sighed. "Be good to yourself, honey. Talk to you soon." And she ended the call.

He lay in the dark for a long time, trying to make sense of the chaos in his head and heart. There wasn't any way, really. He just had to deal with what life had dealt.

He thought of his mother . . . his childhood with her,

how she'd basically rescued him as a young adult, and her recent years of battling cancer. She'd been the one constant in his life, his rock. He thought himself to be a strong, self-sufficient man, but the thought of losing her had him down on his knees.

He thought of New Orleans . . . of Rachel, of school, of his time in the homeless shelters, of the kind, sad people he'd come across in his work, of the horrors of Katrina. His years there had so altered and shaped him and his life . . . he'd tried to be his best self, and ended up his worst self. Fighting for his soul, for his life. He'd had to leave it all behind in order to survive.

And he had. He thought of his return to Aspen, his quiet life here, how he'd modeled it into a safe existence. And it had been. He'd been doing fine. Or, he'd thought he was, not realizing he'd been mostly going through the motions. Until Tess, and their deal, had infused his life with color, music, and light.

He thought of Tess . . . of her warmth, beauty, and kindness, of how her body felt aligned with his, of the baby he was trying to give her. He wanted that for her.

But when he gave her that gift, when she had it, she would leave. And his mother was dying. And in the past, other people he'd cared about had died under his watch. He had no control over any of it, over anything.

He thought he'd gotten to a place of acceptance with that. It had taken years of hard work, but he truly had. Now, he felt like he'd been thrown back into the raging sea with barely a life jacket to keep him afloat as the waves kept knocking him around.

Tess was a lifeline. She sure had been last night, when he'd felt like he was drowning. It was an illusion. Because he'd fallen in love with her, and that . . . wasn't going to work out, even if he wanted it to.

He knew she cared about him. He could feel it in every fiber of her being last night. But would she want him as anything beyond a friend? As a *real* partner, a lover? No. She'd made that very clear from the start. She wanted a baby, but not a husband. She wanted autonomy. He couldn't change the rules now, she wouldn't want that. And did he really want to change the rules? Living on his own was more than a code, it was his survival tactic. He couldn't bear to risk putting himself out there and losing anyone again. What if the next time, he couldn't get himself up off the ground again? His mom had saved him last time . . . She wouldn't be around if it happened again, and right now he wasn't sure if he had it in him to get back up on his own if his heart got shredded.

So he had to accept that this was how it was going to play out: Tess would be alone in New York, he'd be alone in Aspen. She'd have her baby. He'd have memories. She'd come to Aspen once in a while, they'd see each other, it'd be awkward . . . Fuck, he loved her. How could he ever settle for a glimpse of her a few days a year for the rest of their lives? Maybe he'd have to quit working for the Harrisons once she had her baby. It might be too much for him to see her after all.

He sighed deeply. He'd built his life in such a way that he'd have to experience as little loss as possible. Now it loomed like a tsunami, threatening to take him under.

The thought of losing his mother was devastating. There were no words for that. He couldn't begin to fathom how hard that would hit. But add to that the thought of living his life after that without Tess . . . It made him ache so hard, it hurt.

Soon the two most important people in his life would both be gone—one by the cruelty of illness, and one by planned choice. He'd have plenty of time to miss them as he spent his days alone. For a decade now, he'd wanted nothing more than to be alone, hadn't he? *Careful what you wish for*, he lamented ruefully. There was nothing he could do about his mom. It made him sick to think of it. And Tess . . . He had to be her friend, and accept that this is how it would be, like what he signed up for. She didn't ever need to know his heart belonged to her. It would complicate things . . . it was safer that way.

He lay there for hours before sleep finally took him.

Chapter Twenty-One

Tess's cell phone was ringing. Well, singing at her, about how he used to rule the world . . . She quickly finished typing the last words of her email to a client before she answered the call. "Hi, Dad."

"Hello. How are you?"

"Fine, thanks. And you?"

"Fine. I heard all three of your brothers paid you a visit to check on you." Charles II sounded mild, but she waited for the rest. "It's okay if they pop in to surprise you, but not me, eh?"

"Actually, at first, I wasn't at all happy to see them," she said firmly. "I don't like surprise visits of any kind. But yes, they were here, and we had a nice, short visit."

"So I heard. Charles said you're fine, doing well, relaxing. Didn't have much to say beyond that."

"Because there's nothing much else to report," she said. "I'm fine. I told you all I was." She breathed a tiny sigh of relief. Her brothers had sworn they wouldn't clue Dad in to her plans, but this confirmed it. "Is that why you called?"

"Yes, and to just . . . say hello." Charles II paused. "I didn't like how we left things last time. You know, Tess . . .

I'm far from perfect. But I love you. Always have. You're my only daughter, which makes you special. I'm sorry I upset you."

She drew a long, deep breath and exhaled it slowly. "I know you love me, Dad. You've just had a really messed-up way of showing it sometimes. I thought we'd gotten past that by now. I'm in my late thirties, for God's sake."

"I'm aware of that."

"You just . . . need to loosen the reins some, you know?" she suggested. "You make me so damn mad when you pull that controlling, manipulative shit. I won't stand for it. You should know that by now. None of us will stand for it. So just . . . stop."

He didn't say anything.

She sighed and said wearily, "I love you too, Dad. No matter what, that'll never change. I love you. You hear me?"

"I hear you. And it's good to hear."

They talked pleasantly for a few more minutes, and Tess was glad they'd cleared things up a bit. At least, for the time being. But when she turned back to her computer to finish her work for the day, she glanced for the hundredth time at the date in the bottom right corner. She bit down on her bottom lip, unable to hold back a tiny grin of excitement.

She should have gotten her period that day. She hadn't.

A fresh surge of hope whooshed through her. But she willed herself to focus and get back to work. She could get her period the next day. It didn't mean anything yet.

But she couldn't help but hope.

"Hi!" Tess smiled brightly.

Logan smiled back, and it hit him how much he'd missed her. It had only been five days since he'd seen

her, but it felt like five weeks. When he'd texted her that
morning to invite her to dinner, it was the first time he'd
contacted her since the day he'd left her to deal with her
brothers. Now, his insides warmed at the sight of her,
going molten. Man, he had it bad. "Hi yourself. Come
on in."

She stepped into his mother's place and opened her red
parka with one hand, balancing the paper bag she held. He
took her coat for her, setting it aside on an armchair as she
clutched the bag and went into the living room. The condo
was small, but warm and welcoming. Annmarie sat on the
couch, looking the same as the last time Tess had seen her,
which was a relief. "Hi, Annmarie. How are you?"

"Fine, thanks." Annmarie smiled. Her eyes ran over
Tess's tight black top, leggings, and knee-high black
leather boots. "That's a great outfit. Shows off your figure.
Kind of makes you look like Catwoman, or a ninja spy."

Tess laughed as she sat beside her, still holding the bag.
"Thanks. I don't have a whip or a sword or anything. No
Chinese stars in here, I'm afraid."

"Pity," Annmarie joked.

"Ha!" Tess looked herself over as if she'd only just remembered what she was wearing. "Maybe the boots are a
little sexy, but the rest is just comfortable."

"Pffft." Annmarie dismissed that. "Yes, the boots are
hot, but so's the rest of you. I wish I had legs like yours.
You're a sexy woman, go on and flaunt it."

"Well, thanks." Tess grinned and shot a glance over at
Logan, who winked in amusement.

But his insides heated a little as his eyes quickly traveled over her. He wanted to peel her out of her clothes and
let his fingertips claim every sultry inch of her. "She's the
sexiest woman on earth," he said.

"Awww," Tess said. She put down the bag, rose up to go

to him, and said, "Give me a hug for that one, my hottie boyfriend."

He snorted out a laugh, but was glad for an excuse to touch her. When she pressed herself against him and wrapped her arms around his waist, something inside him melted all over again. God, she felt so good. He held her close and stole a quick kiss, just like a real boyfriend would. After all, his mother was right there.

Tess looked into his eyes and whispered lightly, "Hey there. I missed you."

It made his heart stutter in his chest. She had no idea how she possessed him, now had free reign over his heart. "I missed you too," he said, his voice feeling thick in his throat. "Sorry about that, but . . . thanks for giving me the space I needed. I'm better now. And it's great to see you." He kissed her again, because he could, and whispered, "She's right, you know. You look amazing."

"Thanks." She lifted her hand to give his beard an affectionate scratch, her blue eyes twinkling. "I'm glad you're feeling better."

Annmarie cleared her throat. "Should I leave you two lovebirds alone? It's no problem, just let me know."

"No, of course not." Tess pulled herself out of his embrace and returned to sit beside her on the couch. She reached for the bag she'd brought and placed it in Annmarie's lap. "We have to have lunch, so we can have these."

"What are they?" Annmarie asked.

"Cookies from Pistelli's bakery," Tess said. "Your son got me addicted."

He laughed and said, "Easy to get addicted to those."

"I love their cookies," Annmarie cooed. Her obvious delight warmed Logan's heart.

"Well, I thought you might like some once we got some lunch in you," Tess said.

Annmarie gave her a long look. "A ploy to get me to eat? What am I, a five-year-old? I get the reward of dessert if I eat lunch? Ha!" She chuckled and tsked as she added, "You're transparent, my sweet girl."

Tess merely shrugged and said, "Not sorry."

Logan's already mushy heart expanded. Tess clearly cared about his mother . . . he loved her even more for that. He rose from his chair and said, "I'll get lunch to the table, then. You can entertain my mom with stories about your brothers while I set up."

"Are your brothers entertaining?" Annmarie asked.

"Sometimes. They sure think they are." Tess laughed wryly.

"How many brothers do you have?" he heard Annmarie ask just as he walked out of the room.

He'd made a hearty but simple lunch, a Crock-Pot full of beef and vegetable stew he'd let start cooking the night before. Full of iron, protein, and some fats, it would give his mom some strength if she'd eat even a tiny bit of it. He knew she had no appetite, but still held out hope.

As the three of them ate, Logan hung back as he usually did, letting the women talk. Tess always cheered his mom up and drew her out of herself; she got her engaged in animated conversation, made her forget her troubles for a short while. He shook his head wryly as he suddenly realized she had the same effect on him.

For days, he'd wrestled with his feelings . . . about dealing with his mother's mortality, and about his unexpected, unwanted love for Tess. But finally, last night, he'd come to a place of quiet acceptance, and even an uneasy peace. Because it all reminded him of something he'd forgotten when Katrina had hit: Life is short. You have to grab life's gifts with both hands while you have them.

All this was temporary, a situation that would end. But at least Tess wouldn't be dead at the end of it, unlike his mother. She'd be thousands of miles away, living her own life, but still. He'd steeled himself into a decision: With both of these women who meant the world to him, he'd make the most of his time with them, limited though it was, as much as he could.

He'd have plenty of time to miss them and hurt over it after they were gone. So while they were still here, he'd embrace it and let himself enjoy being with them, and not get too tied up in the wrenching, bittersweet notion of how finite things were. He had to live in the present moment. It was all any of them had, anyway, really.

Whatever his mom needed or wanted, he'd make sure she had it. Same went for Tess. And he'd be there for them with a smile on his face and love in his heart. He'd deal with the massive crash afterwards . . . and try his best not to dwell on the *afterwards* part when in their company.

He looked at his mother across the table. This amazing woman had given him everything she had, his entire life. He hoped to return the favor up to her last breath. His brother wasn't around, and likely wouldn't come until she was literally on her deathbed to say goodbye. She needed Logan's strength now. She didn't need his anguish or fear, she needed his rock-solid support, and she'd get it.

Tess threw back her gorgeous head and laughed at something Annmarie said. She didn't need to know he loved her. She had very specific needs where he was concerned. The lines had blurred in that he'd never counted on their becoming such good friends. Some moments, it felt like a true partnership in every sense of the word. He knew she cared about him, and he thought she know he cared about her. But he had to remember her ultimate goal was independence, standing on her own once she had her baby . . . and to love and respect her enough to give her that.

He could do this. He could make his time with both of them meaningful. He could have that much. It would wreck him on the other end, but at least he'd have good memories to hold on to, and with the knowledge that he'd made the days with them count.

Tess threw him a sideways glance, asking without words if he was okay. He grinned softly and winked at her in response. He could do this. He had to.

Later that afternoon, after a few rounds of poker and Annmarie had dozed off on the couch, Logan helped Tess on with her coat. "Thanks again for coming over," he said. "She really enjoys spending time with you. And the cookies were a nice touch."

"Hey, she ate half a bowl of stew," Tess said as they walked to the door. "She wanted those cookies."

"Nah, she did that for *you*."

"I don't care why she did it, I'm just glad she did." She touched his face and dropped her voice to a whisper. "She still seems okay, honey. She's . . . she's not dying tomorrow, you know? You still have some time with her."

"Yes, I do." He couldn't help himself, he leaned in to brush his lips against hers. "Thanks for caring."

"Of course I care." She stared up at him. "I care very much."

He couldn't bear it. So he took her mouth with some slow,

sumptuous kisses. "I missed kissing you," he confessed in a whisper.

"Definitely my favorite perk of the deal," she said with a grin.

That made something squeeze in his chest. *The deal.* They were together only because of the deal. Scary how often he forgot that. He pulled back.

"I wanted to tell you something this whole time, but not in front of Annmarie." She pulled him farther away, almost right up to the door. Her eyes lit up with excitement. "Um . . . my period was due two days ago. And I haven't gotten it."

His eyes flew wide as they locked on her. "Whoa. That's . . . do you think . . . ?"

"I don't know," she said, "but fingers crossed." She practically bounced on her toes as she added, "I'm giving it another couple of days, and when I'm a full week late, I'll take a test."

"I . . . wow. You really think it could've happened that fast?"

"Why not?" she said with a dazzling smile. "We certainly had enough sex at the right times, all month. See? This is why the home method is so much better than a clinical setting." She slid her arms around his waist and held. "I can't lie, I'm really, really hopeful. I'm never late, so . . ."

"That'd be wonderful," he murmured against her hair. He hugged her tight, even as the searing feeling in his chest spread to his limbs. "My fingers are crossed for you too." Jesus. She could be pregnant. A flare of primal masculine pride burst deep inside him. He'd gotten her pregnant, she might be already carrying his baby . . . *no.*

No, *her* baby. This was her baby and hers alone. He had to rein it in.

"I was wondering . . ." Tess pulled back to look up into his face. "Eventually, I'll start showing . . . Once I'm pregnant, are you going to tell your mother about the baby?"

He huffed out a heavy sigh and scrubbed his hand over his face, then dropped his voice to a whisper. "Yeah, but . . . I'll have to figure out how. I don't ever want her to know we were lying to her. It'd do much more harm than good. I'll . . . I'll figure it out."

"It's totally your call, of course," Tess said. "Whatever you want to do. I just was thinking . . . that maybe it'd be great for her to have some happy news. She always wanted this for you, right? Well, what if it made her want to start fighting again?" She gnawed on her lip, a heart-wrenching gesture of sudden and unusual uncertainty. "I don't mean to sound insensitive. You always hear stories like that, how people hold on . . . I just thought . . ."

"I appreciate the thought," he said. "I know what you're trying to say. But yes, *when*"—he made sure to emphasize with sureness—"not *if*, but *when* you get pregnant, because if you're not now, we'll try again in March, and as long as it takes . . . When you are, I will tell her. She'll be over the moon about it." Even though his mother was sleeping in the next room, he still kept his voice at a low murmur to add, "She never needs to know about the deal, or the papers I signed, any of that."

"Right, of course not. As for our 'relationship' . . . we'll just keep it going as long as she's . . . As long as we need to." Tess's gaze sobered a bit. "I keep my promises, Logan. I'll be your girlfriend and play this out as long as necessary. I . . . I want her happy too. She's come to mean a lot to me. I also don't ever want her to find out about our arrangement. We'll work out the my-being-in-New-York part and the baby part as they come. Okay?"

He stared down at her. She had no idea what her words meant to him. She had no idea he was already crazy in love with her. So much so, in fact, that for the first time ever, the thought of having a baby didn't feel like a noose around his neck. It didn't feel like something he could possibly lose, and another loss that would destroy him. His and Tess's baby . . . It felt like sweetness and love, and even something like hope for the future instead.

Oh God, he was so supremely fucked. He really was.

He caressed her soft cheek, pressed a kiss to her forehead, and managed to whisper gruffly, "Sounds good to me."

Chapter Twenty-Two

A week later, Tess walked into her house in an idyllic daze. The appointment with Dr. Fuller had confirmed it: She was indeed pregnant. It was very early, but her biggest dream had come true. She'd have a baby of her own to love. She wouldn't be alone anymore. She'd have her own family.

Overcome with another burst of elation, she spun around in a little pirouette in the middle of her living room, arms open wide, and whooped with pure joy. Bubbles came running, barking and prancing in little circles at Tess's feet. Laughing, she bent over to scoop up her dog and hug her. After, she wrapped her arms around her middle and stared down at her still flat belly. Her breath caught and her eyes stung with happy tears. *A baby.*

God, she had so much to do. People to call, plans to make . . . Well, she couldn't really do some of that until she was safely out of the first trimester, and this baby wouldn't arrive until sometime around Thanksgiving, which seemed both light-years away and too soon when there was so much to do to get ready.

But she knew who had to be the very first to know. And she wanted to see the look on his face when she shared the news. Hey Thor, she texted. Can you come over as soon as possible? Need to see you. I'm fine, don't worry.

Logan's text came back immediately. Sure you're okay?

Swear it. But come over ASAP.

Finishing up here. Just on the other side of the mountain. Give me half an hour.

Great, she texted back. See you soon.

Bubbles barked and jumped at her feet, the familiar dance of need.

"You gotta go, Bubs? Come on, sweetie." Tess took her outside for a few minutes, then went to the kitchen to change the water in Bubbles's bowl. She sat on the couch as she made a call to her ob-gyn's office back in New York and stared out the enormous glass wall at the picturesque scenery beyond, her beloved mountaintop view. Damn, she'd miss that view when she went home.

And it hit her: She'd be leaving sooner than planned now . . . and she didn't want to. The thought of not seeing Logan regularly made her heart twist in her chest. She wanted to tell him how she felt. She wanted to proclaim her love for him, shout it from the rooftop . . . but he'd pull away from her. He wanted to be alone; he'd made that clear from the start.

The doorbell rang and she swallowed those thoughts. She flung the door open wide and beamed at him. "Hi!"

He stood there, the sun shining down on his golden hair, and studied her for all of two seconds before he said with a grin, "You're pregnant, aren't you."

"I *am*!" she cried, and flung herself at him. "I just got back from the clinic. We did it, Logan. I'm going to have a baby!" His arms came up to band around her . . . and as a new wave of emotions battered her—gratitude, relief, and joy, mixed with the sadness of knowing she'd be leaving him soon—she started to cry.

"Hey now . . ." He held her as he edged her back into the house, closing the door behind them with his foot, never letting her go. "You okay? Are these happy tears?"

"Yes," she whispered. *Mostly.* "I'm overwhelmed. I just . . ." She sobbed into his shoulder.

"Shhhh." He held her for a few minutes, rubbing her back, whispering sweet nothings into her ear. She lapped up his affection, bathed in it.

Finally she sniffled and pulled back enough to look at him. "Sorry," she croaked.

"Don't be ridiculous." He reached up and wiped her wet cheeks with both big thumbs. "It's huge, life-changing news. That's got to be a lot to take in. You hoped, you went after your dream, you planned . . . and your plan worked. It's everything you've ever wanted."

No, it's not, a voice whispered in her head. *I want you too. I want it all. I want the baby and I want to be with you. We could be a family together.* A startled gasp flew out of her at her own thoughts, and her face heated.

"What?" he asked, brows furrowing with concern as he stared down at her.

She shook her head, her mind racing for a cover. "Just overwhelmed."

"Okay," he said, but his searching gaze still lingered, as if he sensed she wasn't telling him the whole truth. "I think a celebration dinner is in order too."

Tess reached up and cupped his face, letting her fingers play in his thick, soft beard. God, she loved his beard. "That's very sweet. Thank you."

"It'll be nice. You okay now?"

"Yup. I'm fine."

His gaze turned from one of concern to one of wonder. "I can't believe you're really pregnant. It's so soon."

"Your boys must be great swimmers," she said. With a mischievous grin, she added, "Michael Phelps–level swimmers, baby. You should get a gold medal."

He choked out a laugh. But then his face changed and he said quietly, "So . . . here's a question." His expression grew somber. "How much longer are you staying in Aspen? Are you going to stick with the doctors here, at the clinic for a while? Or is their job done, and you'll be going back to New York?"

A lump thickened Tess's throat. She swallowed hard and said, "Funny you bring that up. While I was waiting for you to get here, that was the only other call I made. I have an appointment with my OB in three weeks. So . . . I'll be here for another two weeks or so, but then yes, I'll be heading back to New York. I'll need to start preparing."

Logan's moss-colored eyes flashed and his fingers squeezed her arms, so quickly she guessed it was involuntary. But he nodded and said, "I figured as much."

She leaned in, pressing her chest against his, and stared into his eyes. "I know you've now fulfilled your end of the deal. I'll never be able to thank you enough. But Logan . . ." *I love you. I don't want to leave you. I wish we could be together somehow.* "We've become such good friends. I really enjoy spending time with you. You . . . You've been the best part of my time here. I mean that. And I hope you'll still . . . well, just want to spend some time with me before I leave. Beyond the appearances for your mother. I know you're not really obligated to, now that I'm pregnant, but . . . I mean . . ."

He peered deep into her eyes, slowly sliding his hand along her jaw to cup her chin. His voice was gruff as he murmured, "Of course I will. I want that too." He trailed his fingers along her cheek, then played lightly in her hair. "I told you a while ago, your friendship means a lot to me too. I don't text you every day, call you, hang out with you, solely because of obligation. That changed a while back." His gaze was so intense, it made her shiver. "I enjoy spending time with you too. It's very mutual, Tess. If nothing else, I hope you know that. That I . . . really care about you."

She drew a long, shuddery breath and let her head drop onto his shoulder. *I love you, you big lug*, she wanted to shout. *I wish you'd let me love you, and I wish you could love me back*. But she fought to make other conversation. "So, we'll, um . . . we'll tell your mom that I'm going back to New York soon, but that I'll be visiting you here once a month, for a few days each time." She looked at him again. "Which I will, Logan. I won't disappear. I'll hold up my end of the deal, don't worry."

He only nodded. She saw so much in his eyes . . . There was a lot going on, but she couldn't read him. She wished she knew what the hell he was thinking. She could *feel* that he wanted to say something, in almost palpable waves radiating off him . . . but instead, he lowered his head and brushed his lips against hers, a tentative gesture. She leaned into it and turned it into a full, deep kiss. The spark ignited quickly; they stood there kissing, caressing, holding tight . . . It had been weeks since they'd slept together.

"Is it wrong to say I want you right now?" he asked gruffly, breathing hard.

"I was thinking the same thing," she said, grasping his face to kiss him again.

He grabbed her ass and pressed her tightly against him. She felt his cock getting harder by the second. Unable to help herself, she wiggled a little against him and he groaned. "The benefits part of this friendship . . ." he said between kisses as he made his way along her jaw, her neck, trailing his hot open mouth along her skin. "We've always been totally in sync there."

"Indeed. So maybe it's the perfect way to celebrate the good news," she suggested, her head falling back as he nibbled the sweet spot behind her ear. Her body arched, pressing against him. The feel of his erection already insistent against her belly made her feel powerful, sensual. She ran her hand along the ridge in his jeans.

He lifted her up in a swift motion, bringing a surprised gasp from her even as her legs locked around his waist. His wide, amused smile was so free and gorgeous, it took her breath away. Oh God, she loved him so much. She'd take him any way she could, as much as she could, for her short time left there.

With one hand on her back, the other in her hair, he kissed her and said, "Let's celebrate upstairs. For the rest of the afternoon."

Chapter Twenty-Three

Logan woke up in the dim light of sunrise. He was in Tess's big, cozy sleigh bed, with her against his side. A peek at her nightstand clock showed it was just past six a.m. Tess slept soundly; naked, warm, endlessly tempting. But he sighed as he drew her even closer, careful not to wake her. Today was the day. He'd been dreading this for two and half weeks.

It was the damnedest thing, though. They'd acted as much like a real couple in these past weeks as he'd ever been with his ex-wife. They'd gone out and stayed in, shared meals and laughs, made love every night . . . And yeah, they said all the time how they were just friends. Like a disclaimer. Every time he felt that intense pull that sometimes had them staring into each other's eyes, one of them would remark on how amazing their friendship was.

He never told her, never even hinted at it, but she owned him, heart and soul. And today, she was going back to New York to live her life with their baby . . . no. For the hundredth time, he reminded himself it was *her* baby. He wouldn't get to see this child grow up. He'd rarely, if ever, see the child at all. To think when he'd started this, he'd been fine with that . . .

God, he'd been so fucking stupid. Thinking he'd do her this favor, that it wouldn't really tie him to her, that he'd get to do a good deed but stay on his own, that he wouldn't get emotionally attached. He'd been blindsided. Tess Harrison was the most incredible person he'd ever known, and this deal had become everything.

She'd become one of his closest friends . . . maybe his best friend, really. She knew him in ways no one else did. No one since Rachel. He hadn't let anyone. But when he wasn't looking, without even realizing it, he'd let his walls down and let Tess in. And she seemed to understand him, appreciate him, just for who he was. And she . . . She was a marvel. She radiated light, kindness, intelligence, strength. Add to that how damned beautiful and sexy she was. He loved everything about her.

Now he had to let her go, and it would come just short of killing him to do so.

He wanted to ask her to stay. He wanted to tell her he loved her. He wanted . . . He wanted lots of things, but none of them would be fair. He'd signed papers. He'd made promises. He'd sworn to honor her and her decisions. If he tried to change that now, she'd leave him in the dust.

He very clearly remembered what she'd said the night she'd asked him to be her sperm donor: *I want to have a baby and raise it as my own. I don't want a partner, and I don't need a father figure . . . The fact that you don't want to be a father is perfect, because I don't want you to be its father . . . This child is going to be mine, and mine alone . . . I want it that way.*

She wanted independence. He loved her enough to let her go. But first, he had to get through driving her to the damn airport . . . He actually had to help her leave.

She curled closer into him in her sleep with a tiny sigh,

tossing her long, perfect leg over his thigh. He moved his hand down to caress her skin as he thought about the night before. It'd been a goodbye dinner at his mom's house. When it was time for him to take Tess home, Annmarie had clutched Tess in a tight hug.

"I'll be back soon," Tess told her, returning the hug. She'd looked over Annmarie's head to Logan, the bittersweet look of surprise on her face wringing his heart out. Tess patted Annmarie on the back. "This isn't goodbye. It's just goodbye for now. I'll be back in two months for a visit. I won't be able to stay away from your son for longer than that."

As Logan thought, *Nice touch, sweetheart*, Annmarie had pulled back to look up into Tess's face and say tremulously, "It's been such a pleasure getting to know you, Tess. Truly. You're a wonderful woman."

"Oh my goodness," Tess murmured, obviously touched. "I feel the same way about you."

"Thank you for making my son smile again," Annmarie said, her voice catching. "Thank you for making him happy."

Logan felt his heart drop to his stomach. He almost swayed where he stood.

"If I've done that, that's wonderful," Tess said quietly. "He's an incredible man, your son. I adore him. Thank you for sharing him with me."

At that, Logan's breath caught, emotions ravaging him.

And as he recalled it again now, he felt his eyes prick with tears. Jesus, what had he done? He'd perpetuated a lie to make his mom happy, and justified it as granting a dying woman her wish. But now . . . Annmarie had grown to care deeply about Tess, and vice versa. Was that fair, to either of them? He didn't know anymore. He didn't know anything anymore. There were no lines, much less blurred ones . . . only chaos. In such a short time, everything had changed. *He* had changed.

But he held all that inside. He made sweet, tender love to Tess to wake her up. They showered together, they ate breakfast together, and he helped her pack up the last of her things. He carried her suitcases to the car and helped her with Bubbles. They drove to the airport in silence. She held his hand the whole way there, and he savored the feel of her soft, warm fingers intertwined with his.

At the airport, he unloaded her stuff and took it to curbside check-in, then offered to wait with her . . . but Tess shook her head. When he saw tears in her eyes, his heart stuttered and his stomach started to churn.

"My God," she whispered huskily, "I'm going to miss you so much."

He tried to swallow back the lump in his throat. "I'm going to miss you too. More than you know."

She flung her arms around him, holding tight as if her life depended on it. He held her close, breathing her in, memorizing her scent and the lines of her body and the thick softness of her curls between his fingers . . . and trying not to let her tears pierce his heart. He failed. Every moment ripped his heart out a little bit more.

"This isn't goodbye," he whispered, echoing her words to his mother the night before. "It's just goodbye for now."

"I know," she said, sniffling and trying to compose herself. "I know. I've just gotten so used to seeing you, being with you . . ." She pulled back to look up at him, and the tears streaked down her face. "Thank you for everything. *Everything*, Logan. This winter with you . . . I'll cherish it for the rest of my life. I need you to know that." She grabbed his face and kissed him hard.

He yanked her in tight, kissing her back with all the passion and love in his heart. "I will too," he choked out between kisses. "You're my Long Island Lady. You're amazing. So don't disappear, okay?"

"Not a chance." She pulled back, leaning her forehead against his, stroking his beard, her eyes closed as the tears rolled down her face. "I have to go," she finally whispered raggedly.

He watched her go to the truck and lift Bubbles out of the backseat. Ah man, he'd even miss that cute little dog. He scratched her behind the ears and said, "You take good care of your mama, okay?"

Tess gasped out a sob. He cupped the back of her neck and pulled her in for one long, last kiss. "Take good care of yourself," he commanded in a rough murmur. "Let me know how you're doing. I know it won't be every day like it's been here, and that really, I have no right."

"We're close now," she said staunchly. "Of course you have a right."

"Well, then. Just let me know once in a while that you're okay." He stepped back before he lost it and asked her not to go. "If you need anything, you let me know. I mean it."

"I know you do." She smiled sadly, wiping away her tears with her free hand. "You too, please. If your mom takes a bad turn, if you need to talk, if you need anything . . . please call me. Text me. Anything."

He nodded, staring back. "Goodbye, sweetness. Safe flight."

Her eyes welled again, but she smiled through it one last time. Clutching Bubbles close, she turned away to walk into the terminal.

Logan watched her go until he couldn't see her anymore. Then he got back in the truck and pulled slowly away from the curb to drive back into town . . . back into the way it'd been before a whirlwind named Tess Harrison had blown into his lonely life. The difference now was, he hadn't cared before that he'd been lonely. Hadn't even realized it, really. Now he knew it, and it was a sharp, throbbing misery.

He scrubbed a hand over his face at a red light, chastising himself. This emotional goodbye had knocked him sideways. For fuck's sake, it wasn't like he'd never see her again. It was the second week of March, and she'd promised to come back in mid-May. But things wouldn't be the same again, and he knew it. The daily banter and contact, the night after night of passionate lovemaking . . . Hell, they might not even be lovers ever again, since the fact was he'd fulfilled his end of the bargain. And she was too amazing a woman to stay alone forever. Someday, surely she'd meet someone else . . . He scowled and shifted uncomfortably in his seat. The thought tore him apart.

He pulled into his driveway, cut the engine, and sat there for a long time, aching.

They'd talk. They'd stay in touch. But he had to work on letting go of her. Because even though he'd see her again, she'd never come back to *him*. Distance would remind her of who she was and where she belonged. That this had been a deal. She was pregnant now; she didn't need him anymore.

Chapter Twenty-Four

A sharp buzzing sound woke Tess with a start. She opened her eyes, looked around, and realized that, yet again, she'd fallen asleep on the couch in her office. Thank God it was there; she'd napped every day since she'd been back in New York. The way pregnancy slammed her with exhaustion, napping every day, sometimes twice a day, was the only way she was getting through. But compared to puking every morning, she'd gladly take the fatigue.

She'd kept herself busy for the past five weeks. Poring over websites for ideas on decorating the baby's room and all things baby; spending time with her brothers and their families; getting a plan in motion for how she would handle her job once she became a single mother; reading articles daily on pregnancy, childbirth, newborns, infancy . . . All of which were necessary, but also a way to think less about Logan. She missed him so much it hurt. And she felt him slipping away a little more each week.

The intercom on her phone buzzed again. The phone was on her desk . . . all the way across the room. She was so tired; it felt like it was miles away. With a weary moan, she closed her eyes again. Whoever it was would have to wait . . .

A gentle hand patted her shoulder. "Tess. Hey, sleepyhead. C'mon now."

"Huh?" She opened her eyes and focused on her brother, who was crouching down to look into her face. "Hey, Dane."

"Hey, Tesstastic. You okay?"

She yawned. "Fine. Just tired."

"You're out cold at twelve thirty in the afternoon. Is that normal?" he asked, brow furrowing with concern.

She laughed lightly. "Yes. I'm fine. Ask your brothers' wives if you don't believe me."

"Well, from what I heard, both Abby and Lisette spent a good part of their early pregnancies with their heads in the toilet, so no thanks." Dane grinned and shifted from his crouch to sit in the armchair adjacent to the couch.

"Yeah, I've been spared that much at least." Tess took a deep breath and sat up slowly. "No morning sickness at all, just tired most of the time. I'll get past it soon. Almost done with the first trimester already, then supposedly I'll feel better, get my energy back." She stretched her arms over her head. "So why am I so lucky as to be blessed with your presence?"

"We were supposed to go to lunch," he reminded her.

Her eyes flew wide. "Oh no! You're right! Ah crap."

He laughed. "Jeez. You forgot all about me. Not like you."

"Blame it on pregnancy brain," she said.

"It kicks in this soon? Shit, you're in trouble then." He grinned wickedly, but his voice was gentle as he asked, "Do you want to cancel? Get back to your nap?"

"No, of course not." She rose slowly and stretched again. "Besides, I'm starving. Not working most of the morning has apparently made me famished."

"Are you carrying a baby, or an alien life form?" he joked. "Sucking the life force out of you, seeking nourishment . . ."

"You're a dork." She laughed as she crossed her office to her desk. "Let me just check the emails I haven't looked at to make sure there are no emergencies, and we'll get out of here. Give me five minutes?"

"No problem." He crossed one long leg over the other as he pulled his phone from his inside jacket pocket. "I'll tell Julia you say hi. She wants to see you soon, by the way. Dinner next week, maybe? Monday or Tuesday?"

"I'd love that," Tess said as she clicked into her inbox. "Tuesday works for me."

She scanned her work emails quickly; nothing there that couldn't wait. Then she checked her personal email, and there was one from Logan. Her breath caught. Since she'd returned to New York, he'd cut way down on contact, texting her every three or four days instead of daily, and no phone calls. She was hurt by the lessening contact, but supposed she shouldn't be surprised. Logan Carter went it alone. He'd made that clear from the start.

So what if she thought things had changed? So what if she thought she'd maybe seen his eyes get a little glassy during their emotional goodbye, or that he'd kissed her as fervently as she'd kissed him? He wasn't letting her stay close; that became more clear with each passing week. And it hurt. Truth was, thinking about him only made her miserable. She missed him like hell. Apparently, that wasn't mutual.

But he'd never sent her an email before. Usually, they talked via texts. So with curiosity building, she clicked on it. But when she opened it, she realized it wasn't just to her, but to her and her two older brothers. It had to be something about the house, then, since Pierce wasn't addressed;

Tess owned the ski house with only Dane and Charles, since Pierce had been living in England when they bought it.

> *Hello Charles, Dane, and Tess,*
>   *This is an official notice to inform you all that I'm cutting back on my work. My mother's health has started to seriously decline and I'm needed there. Effective today, I'll be turning over regular care of your Red Mountain house to Richie Wood, one of my most reliable colleagues. I've worked with him for years, and I can personally vouch for his trustworthiness, his dependability, and his just being a great guy. His cell number is . . .*

Tess felt her blood pressure start to rise. Annmarie was worse? Why hadn't he said so? Why hadn't he told her anything? She could feel her blood race through her veins, leaving vague nausea in its wake.

Then another thought hit, like a kick to the chest. Was this really solely about his mother, or did he just want to quit dealing with the Harrisons because of *Tess*? He'd been slipping away slowly. Was she being paranoid, or was this a real possibility? What the hell was going on? A million questions rushed through her on another wave of anxious adrenaline, leaving her breathless.

"Um . . . Tess?" Dane looked up from his phone, catching her eye from across the room. He looked ambivalent as he said, "I just saw an email from Logan."

"I'm just reading it now," she said tightly as her stomach roiled.

"You didn't know about this before now?"

"I'm as shocked as you are," she muttered.

"Huh." He peered harder. "Actually, you seem more so. Your face is all flushed."

She huffed out a hard breath. "I'm a little pissed off. I had no idea he was doing this."

"I thought you two were close."

"So did I," she bit out. Maybe it was the hormones, but she wanted to throw something. Instead she turned off her computer and shot to her feet. "I need lunch."

"Maybe you need to talk," Dane suggested in a soft voice, a tone one would use to talk to a child or wounded animal. "Are you okay? You look really upset."

"I am upset!" she cried. "I had no idea that . . . that he . . ." Her eyes filled with tears.

"Ah shit, honey. Come here." Dane stood and crossed to give her a hug. "Tell me something. If he's distancing himself, is that the worst thing in the world?"

She didn't say anything. Resting her head on her big brother's shoulder, she clamped her lips tightly, holding back her words as she willed her tears to stay in her eyes and not escape.

"I thought you two were just friends," Dane said.

"We are," she whispered. "That's the problem."

"Aha. You're in love with him," Dane guessed.

"Well, *duh*." Tess stepped back and sniffled hard. "It's complicated."

"Now there's an understatement." He smiled kindly as he added, "I've been waiting for you to fess up for weeks, you know."

"Oh really."

"Yup. I mean . . . you've been so excited and happy about the baby . . . but with this underlying sadness that's made no sense. Now it makes sense." He sighed. "You've been missing him."

The tears sprang up and rolled down her face. She sniffled and wiped them away with impatient flicks of her fingers. Her heart felt like it was lodged in her throat.

"My poor sweetheart. Shit." Dane let out another sigh. "Come on. Let's go get you and my growing niece or nephew fed, and you'll tell me all about it. Maybe I can help. If I can't, at least I'm here to listen." He tweaked her nose the way he always had when they were kids. "I love you, Tesstastic. I hate seeing you sad. I'm here for you."

His show of kindness left Tess wobbly with gratitude. She hugged him again and whispered, "Thank you."

When Tess got home that evening, she'd had an entire car ride through rush-hour traffic to think over her lunchtime chat with Dane. He thought she should tell Logan how she felt; she disagreed. But one thing she'd definitely agreed with: Call him, not text or email, and ask him directly what was going on.

As soon as she'd let Bubbles out to go potty, fed her, and sat down, she did something she hadn't done in over five weeks: She called Logan.

"Hey there," came his deep voice over the line, and it sent a shiver right through her. "How are you?"

God, she'd missed his voice. She knew hearing it would only make her miss him more, which was why she hadn't called all this time. Now, the sound of his low, sexy rumble made her want to crawl through the phone to get to him and wrap herself in his strong arms. But all she said was, "I got your email today."

"I figured," he said.

"Annmarie's worse? Why haven't you told me?"

"Umm . . . yes, she is, and because there's nothing you can do, so why upset you?"

"Because I care," Tess ground out. "Because I'd like to support you, and her, if I can. How about that?"

He paused. "You sound angry."

"I am," she admitted. "You've been contacting me less, which stings as it is. Now I find out she's worse and you're quitting my family through a formal group email?"

"I'm not quitting your family," he said. "I'm giving some of my houses to Richie because I'm not going to have the time to devote to them. Something's gotta give. I'm taking care of my professional obligations."

"Who are you talking to?" she exploded in a shout. She sprung up from the couch to pace wildly. "This is *me*, Logan. You're talking to me like I'm a fucking client."

"You *are* one of my clients."

"Not anymore. Right?" Her heart pounded, her blood raced. "And we've been a hell of a lot more to each other than that. So tell me the truth. Is this really about reassigning your jobs, or about getting away from *me*? Because I can't shake the feeling that in spite of everything we shared, all the wonderful things you said and did, you're doing your best to get away from me now, and this is just part of it."

Again he paused, then said in a low, deliberate tone, "Tess, my whole world doesn't revolve around you."

She stopped in her tracks, the air rushing out of her lungs. His rebuke felt like a slap. Embarrassment washed over her, but was quickly replaced by icy anger. She let it drape over her like a familiar cloak. "I never thought it did, thank you very much."

"Tess, look—"

"No, forgive me, Mr. Carter." She put on her coolest boardroom tone, even as it was hard to breathe. "Certainly your daily responsibilities have nothing to do with me. The assumption was my mistake, based on emotion and our history. I won't let that happen again."

"Stop it," he spat. "Don't go all Ice Queen on me. Clearly you're mad, but just hear—"

"Tell me about Annmarie," she said.

"Dammit, Tess—"

"Please tell me what's going on with her," Tess insisted. "That's all I want to know at this point."

He swore under his breath, then said tersely, "She's getting weak. She called me three days ago because she'd fallen and didn't have the strength to get up. I had to scoop her off her bedroom floor. Scans show the cancer's in her bones now. So yeah, it doesn't get better from here, only worse."

"I'm so sorry," she murmured, her eyes closing. *Damn. Damn it all to hell.* "I wish you'd told me."

"You're pregnant," he bit out. "I thought upsetting you needlessly wasn't good for you and the baby."

"I'm pregnant," she echoed, "but I'm not some delicate flower. I'm in perfect health. You don't have to spare me from things." She drew a shaky breath. "I thought . . . I thought we were a team. What happened to that?"

"You're gone," he said, and the seething anger she heard shook her to the core. "This isn't your problem, it's not your responsibility, it's not your anything."

She thought she might throw up. She swallowed back bile, then swallowed again to try to loosen the lump in her throat. Finally, she managed softly, "Again, forgive me. I thought we were close. I thought we meant a lot to each other."

"Tess—"

"Even though I'm not physically there, I wanted to continue to support you however possible. I see now you don't want that, and I was mistaken. My apologies. Please send Annmarie my best. I won't call you again." She ended the call and tossed the phone onto the couch.

She realized her hands were trembling. So were her insides. What the hell had happened? Why was he being

like this? Working so hard to push her away? She wrapped
her arms around her middle and started to cry. It didn't
matter. Clearly he felt nothing for her like she felt for him.
She'd misread him horribly and felt like a fool. Hurting,
angry, and upset about Annmarie, Tess sank onto the
couch, dropped her head into her hands, and cried.

"Jesus Christ, you're a hot mess."

Logan looked up from his untouched lunch. "What are
you talking about?"

"You. You're moping." Annmarie shook her head slowly.
"I mean, you've been a wreck since Tess left, but you're in
rare form today. What happened?"

"Don't wanna talk about it," he grumbled, looking back
down at his plate. He nudged the wild rice around aim-
lessly with his fork, pushing it into a pile beside the
roasted chicken he had no appetite for.

"It might help to talk about it," she said

He glanced up at her. "Nope."

"Oh boy. This is classic Logan. *Old* Logan, the one I
thought was gone. Pfffft." She tsked and reached for her
water glass with a slow hand. After she took a few sips,
she said, "So you want to hear what I was thinking?"

"Sure."

"I was thinking after I die, you should move to New
York and marry Tess."

He snorted and laughed ruefully. "Not gonna happen."

"Why not? You love her, she loves you. Why the hell
not?"

His eyes rested on her drawn face. "She loves me, huh?"

"Of course she does," Annmarie scoffed. "I've never
seen a woman so in love. And I'll tell you something else.

I never once saw Rachel look at you the way Tess does. Not once, in all those years."

Logan's eyes widened. He didn't say a word. He reached for his water glass and gulped before saying, "She's not in love with me, Mom."

Annmarie scoured his features, then her mouth made a little twist. "My God . . . You never said the words to her, did you?" she murmured. Her gaze locked on his like a hawk. "Tell me the truth. You've never said it to her, have you? Told her you love her."

"No."

"Jesus Christ, for a smart man, you're so damn stupid." She picked up her napkin off her lap and tossed it onto the table in disgust. "Why the hell not? What are you protecting yourself from? The incredible woman who's obviously in love with you? What is wrong with you?"

"I can't do this," he snarled, pushing away from the table. He got to his feet and drew a deep breath, trying to rein in his emotions. He placed his fists on the table and leaned on them. "There's a lot going on you don't . . . You don't understand, Mom."

"I understand *you*," she said. "I understand you're so afraid of losing someone you care about, you haven't let yourself get close to anyone since Katrina, since Rachel walked out on you, since all of that. Guess what?" Her stare was unflinching. "I'm dying. I'll be gone soon. You're going to lose me."

"Stop it," he snapped.

"You're going to lose me, my sweet boy," she said. "But you're going to survive it. Just like you survived everything else. Life goes on. So will you."

He stared back at her, his heart thumping so hard he thought it might explode out of his chest.

"So . . ." Annmarie rose slowly, eyes still locked on

him. "Do you want to live your life, or just survive it? There's a big difference."

He felt the blood rush to his face, heard it rush through his ears.

"Being alone isn't going to spare you heartache, Logan," she said. "It's just going to make you even more miserable. Don't you get that yet? You're not protecting yourself. You've been hiding."

"I have not," he said.

"Bullshit. Yes, you were. You were until you met Tess. And boom, you were alive again, for the first time in years." She shook her head at him. "You lose her, and you'll lose the best thing that's ever happened to you. And for what, self-protection? You're going to live a long, lonely life. Just like I did after your father died. Congratulations."

He couldn't move. He stood there and stared at her, heart pounding relentlessly, breath stuck in his lungs.

"Tess can live fine without you," his mother said. "She's strong as hell. Stronger than you, my dear boy. And she's incredible. Beautiful, smart, kind. So tell me something. You think she'll be alone for long? Because I'm here to tell you: no way. Someone will scoop her up."

He scowled and scrubbed his hands over his face. It was all true. Nothing he hadn't thought before, but to hear someone else say it made it sting worse.

Annmarie went to him, her hands lifting to cup his face, over his beard. She looked up into his eyes . . . She seemed smaller. Frail. His heart squeezed over that for the thousandth time. She commanded, "Don't let her go. You'll regret it for the rest of your life, Logan. I'm not kidding."

"She's already gone, Mom," he murmured raggedly.

"I've been pushing her away, and as of last night, I think it finally took."

Annmarie shook her head. "I'd bet this condo that if you went to her and poured your heart out for once in your stubborn life, you'd get her back." Her fingers dug into his shoulders, as if she could shake sense into him.

He sighed. There was so much she didn't understand. Which, of course, was his fault for lying to her in the first place. What a mess. "Don't worry about me, okay?"

"I'll worry about you 'til I stop breathing," she said. "I'm a mother. It's part of the job description."

His shoulders lifted in a lifeless shrug. "Sorry about that."

"Don't be sorry," she demanded. "Get your head out of your ass and get Tess back."

He breathed out a chuckle. "Got a way with words."

"Logan. Honey . . ." She grabbed his face again, made him look into her eyes. "You deserve to be happy. Do you hear me?"

He nodded, but his throat was too thick to speak.

"I thought you'd stopped punishing yourself for the past, but I see clearly now that you never did. Hear me." She shook him a little. "*You deserve to be happy.*"

His eyes stung. He didn't move, just met her intense stare.

"Does Tess make you happy?" she asked.

He nodded.

"Don't. Let. Her. Go." She stared harder. "Don't go through life like this. Yes, it's scary to think that you can lose the people who are important to you. That's why when someone great crosses your path, you've gotta hold on with everything you've got. It's what makes life meaningful. Our connections with others. It's a leap of faith, a risk . . . but it's a risk so worth taking."

Her hands slid down to his shoulders. "Logan . . . you can have happiness of your own. Fight for it. You have to try, or you'll never forgive yourself. I don't want that for you. You've wasted enough time beating yourself up, isolating yourself. Take a chance. She's wonderful, and she loves you. I know she does, even if you won't let yourself believe it." Suddenly she weaved where she stood.

Logan's hands shot out to grab her. "Whoa, I've got you. You okay?"

She felt wobbly to him. "Yeah. Just got a little light-headed. Looking up at you for too long made the blood rush back . . . Why do you have to be so damn tall?"

"Why do you have to exhaust yourself lecturing me?" he tried to joke back, even as he held her close to move her toward the living room couch.

"Because you're a frustrating moron," she grumbled, clinging to him as they walked slowly. "Good thing I love you more than life itself."

Chapter Twenty-Five

Logan moved through the next two days in something of a daze. His mother's words echoed through his mind over and over. She'd given him a lot to think about.

She'd been right. About everything.

He had spent the past decade-plus punishing himself. He'd come to a place of acceptance about the people who'd died and suffered during Katrina, but he hadn't fully forgiven himself. It was long past time to do that and let it go. It wasn't serving him, and dammit, it wasn't his fault the shelter had flooded. Every building in a four-block radius had been washed out; he wasn't God, it wasn't his fault, there wasn't anything more he could have done. There truly wasn't. Way past time to let that go.

As for Rachel . . . She hadn't been capable of giving him what he needed when he needed it most. He knew that. But it didn't mean he wasn't worthy of love and devotion. It meant she wasn't right for him, that was all. He had forgiven her for leaving, but . . . he'd never forgiven himself for choosing the wrong person. For being wrong about her, and feeling foolish for trusting and loving her. He had, and there was no shame in that. It didn't mean he couldn't, or shouldn't, love someone that way again.

And the Universe was laughing at him, because guess what? He already did.

And Tess cared about him too. He knew that. They'd connected, in a deep, true way that defied labels or explanation. If he didn't try to act on that, or at least tell her how he really felt, Annmarie was right. He'd regret it for the rest of his life.

But he'd hurt her deeply with his callous remarks in their last talk. He'd felt her anguish through the phone; it'd made him cringe. He had to fix it. He had to reach out . . .

First, however, was dinner with his mom. He got to her condo at five. Giving Richie some of his houses had been the right move, it freed up his schedule. He'd have plenty of time to work more hours after his mom was gone. For now, being able to see his mom every day was what he needed to do.

"Hi," he called out as he let himself into her place.

"Hi," she called back feebly. He could barely hear her.

He walked into the living room. She was on the couch, under three heavy quilts, her face pale. The TV blared the news; he grabbed the remote to mute it, then knelt beside her. She didn't look good. "Hey there." He put his hand against her cheek. She felt warm. "You okay?"

"I'm just cold," she said. "Couldn't get warm today." She shivered hard.

He swore under his breath, then said to her, "I think you have a fever, Mom. Let me make you some tea. We'll warm you up."

"Wait, before you do . . . look." She pointed across to the armchair and smiled. "I got a gift today."

"What?" Too worried to care about a gift, he glanced over at the chair in annoyance. Then stopped cold. It was a painting. "What is that?"

"Your lovely girlfriend sent it to me. It's wonderful, isn't it?" Annmarie's tired eyes crinkled at the corners as she smiled. "Look closer at it."

Logan went to the chair and picked up the canvas to study it. It was about a foot square. He knew Tess loved to paint, but she'd never let him watch her paint. He'd only seen pictures of her work on her phone, once he'd convinced her to show them to him. She'd been afraid to share them; too humble. Also, it was too intimate a thing to reveal that piece of herself to anyone. But she'd shown him.

"It's really good," he murmured as his eyes caressed the canvas. Greens, blues, browns, white . . . "You know what this is?" he asked, turning back to his mother. "It's the view outside her house. Up on Red Mountain."

"I thought so."

"That house is crazy gorgeous—the whole back wall, from the ground floor to the top, is glass. Like a big panoramic window instead of a wall. And this is the view. She really captured it beautifully . . ." Swirls of snow, a sea of forest pines, the majesty of the mountains under a bright blue sky. And her initials, modestly small black letters in the bottom right corner. His fingers caressed them. "She sent you this?"

"It came today," Annmarie said. "Awfully thoughtful of her."

"Yes, it was." He eyed a flowered card on the chair that must have been under the painting. He picked it up. "Mind if I look at this?" he asked.

"Go right ahead," Annmarie said.

He held the small painting in one hand to read the card with the other. Tess's handwriting was elegant and lovely, just like her.

Dearest Annmarie,

*I heard you're not feeling well, and hoped a
little gift might cheer you up a bit. Forgive me
for being presumptuous in assuming you'd want a
piece of my work, but you asked to see it several
times, so I hoped you weren't being merely
complimentary and meant what you said. (I think
you must have; you're a no-nonsense woman.)
So I hope you'll enjoy this painting. I worked on
it while I was there this winter . . . while I spent
time with your son. We used to sit on the couch
together and talk while staring out at this view.
While we did, I fell in love with him a little more
each day.*

*And bonus, I fell in love with you too. Hoping
you'll feel that love in this gift.*

xoxo
Tess

Logan felt light-headed. Like the air in the room had evaporated.

"She calls me once a week, you know," Annmarie said. "Has since she left."

"I didn't know," he managed.

"Yup. On Mondays. Just to say hi, and check on me. When I called her today to thank her for this, she sounded so sad. She hated that she didn't know I'd gotten worse. You and I keep shielding her from it. That's not fair. She cares about me."

"I know she does," he whispered roughly.

"I apologized for shielding her and promised I wouldn't again. She thanked me and told me, in as few dignified, tactful words as possible, that you two aren't speaking anymore. She sounded miserable." Annmarie shivered again. "I'm too tired to argue with you about it now. That tea sounds like a good idea. Could you please?"

Logan nodded, set down the card and painting, then willed his legs to get him into the kitchen.

Tess loved him. His mother had seen it clear as day, but he hadn't. Maybe he would have if he hadn't had his self-absorbed head up his own ass, as his mom had pointed out the other day. He hadn't seen anything. Nothing but his own fears and insecurities. If he hadn't been so wrapped up in his own crap and *looked* at her, he likely would've known. And not pushed her away, and not hurt her, and . . . *crap*.

He leaned against the counter for a minute, head spinning. Holy hell, she loved him. He was the luckiest man on earth if that was true. He had to ask her. Damn, he had to fix things. If he even could . . . he had to try.

But first, he had to take care of his mom. As much as his heart and soul were screaming for Tess at that moment, that came first. He put up the water to boil, then called his mother's doctor.

Tess woke up in darkness. Her insistent bladder wouldn't let her stay asleep. She lumbered out of bed, used the restroom, then got right back into bed. The message light on her cell phone blinked at her. She turned it over, glanced at the clock—2:32 in the morning—then burrowed into her pillows and closed her eyes. Probably one of her brothers checking on her; the three of them had hovered since learning she was pregnant. They could wait until morning. She quickly fell back to sleep.

When she opened her eyes again, it was because Bubbles had hopped onto her bed to nudge her as she snuggled. Tess smiled, affectionately stroking her dog's

soft white fur as she stretched her stiff limbs and yawned.
A glance at the windows showed a sunny day outside; early
spring had finally arrived. The buds on the trees were an
almost neon yellow-green, so bright against the blue of
the sky.

Bubbles yipped and nudged her again.

"Potty time, miss?" Tess singsonged. "You gotta go?"

Bubbles barked.

"Yeah, me too. I hear you." She glanced at the clock.
It was just past eight. She'd be working from home today,
so it was all right that she'd slept so late. She took herself
and Bubbles through their morning routine, then went
back up to her room to get her phone and check her messages. Sitting on her bed, she saw two voice mails had
come in the night before. She'd fallen asleep early, around
nine, so she'd missed them both. The first one was from
Lisette, inviting her over for dinner on Saturday. The
second one was from Logan. She felt her blood run cold
as soon as he started talking. He sounded . . . wrong.

"Hi Tess, it's me. Um . . . I've been . . . uh . . . shit. *Shit.*
I don't know what to say. There's so much. I just . . . Well,
I'll say the rest later, but for right now, I knew you'd want
to know that my mom's in the hospital. Went in a few
hours ago. She has a high fever, she's, um . . . It's not good.
I don't know . . ." He paused for a long moment, long
enough for Tess's heart to stutter in her chest. His voice
was raw as he said, "I wish you were here with me. I wish
I could just hold you. I'm scared. I'm sad. I'm upset. And
I miss you like hell."

Tess gasped and tears sprung to her eyes.

"I just needed to hear your voice. But I guess you're not
taking my calls. I don't blame you. I was an asshole the
last time we talked, and I'm really sorry for that. But . . .

man, you know what, that painting is amazing. My mom loves it. That was an incredible gift. Thank you for sending her that. Um . . ." He cleared his throat, but his voice was still gravelly as he went on. "So, yeah. She's not good. Neither one of us are, really. I, uh . . . I need you, Tess. I want you in my life. Please don't disappear. I'm sorry for being such a jackass. Call me soon, let's talk this out, okay? Okay. Hope you're feeling good. Bye."

Sniffing back her tears, Tess jumped off the bed and ran to her bathroom. She had to shower, and she had to pack. She had to get to Logan as fast as she could.

Chapter Twenty-Six

Logan stood in the cafeteria of the hospital, choking down one of the worst chocolate chip cookies he'd ever had. He hated this place. The antiseptic smell, the fluorescent lights, the air of despondency that seemed to pervade every corridor . . . He hated hospitals in general. Nothing good ever happened here.

His mom's fever hadn't lowered yet. The doctor said it was typical, but they hadn't found the exact cause yet. Her white blood cell count was high, she was on antibiotics . . . It was a waiting game. At least she hadn't had a seizure, and wasn't in pain or out of it. She was woozy, but clear of mind.

He'd taken her to the hospital the night before, gotten her admitted, and stayed with her for a few hours before they asked him to leave for the night. He'd gone home and called Tess, to no avail. Clearly, his attempts at pushing her away had finally stuck. Miserable about that, he'd barely slept, then gone back to the hospital first thing in the morning and stayed with his mom all day, watching those cooking shows she liked so much. Truth was, he liked them too.

He glanced at the clock on the wall. Half past one. This was the first time he'd left her room. She'd insisted he go take a walk, get some fresh air, which he'd begrudgingly done . . . It was spring outside. Hints of white and green in the trees, birdsong, flowers poking their heads out . . . signs of life. Signs of life while his mom was dying. Signs of life, like the baby growing inside Tess that he'd never get to know. He'd signed away all his rights, and she was hurt and angry, not talking to him. The world was cruel sometimes. He hated the world today.

He'd gone back to the cafeteria to grab something sweet. Sugar would help. But the cookies tasted like sawdust. He was spoiled; he wanted Pistelli's cookies, dammit.

So he left the hospital. They'd text him immediately if they needed him, and his mom seemed to be holding steady. Being away for less than an hour wouldn't be a problem. He drove into downtown, got a pound of mixed cookies from Pistelli's, then headed back to the hospital. Surely some decent cookies would not only cheer him up, but his mom too.

When he pushed open the door of his mom's room, he almost dropped the box. Tess was sitting at his mother's bedside. He blinked, gaping at her in disbelief.

Her big blue eyes locked with his. "Hi," she whispered as she got to her feet.

"Hey." She was there. Shock clobbered him. He didn't take his eyes off hers, but managed to put the box of cookies on the tiny table.

Annmarie looked from one to the other, then said to her son, "I was wondering where you went. Are those Pistelli's cookies?"

"Yes, ma'am." He still stared at Tess as if in a trance.

"Good boy. I'll enjoy those." Annmarie sighed. "Know what? I'm in the way here, but I can't go anywhere. Why don't you two go out in the hallway and talk?"

Logan tentatively held out a hand to Tess. She went to him without hesitation and slipped her hand into his. His heart expanded at the feel of her soft, warm skin as he closed his fingers around hers. They went out to the hallway, and as soon as the door closed behind them, she turned to hold him tight.

His arms banded around her, his eyes closed as his head dropped down to rest on top of hers, and his whole body relaxed for the first time in weeks.

"I'm so goddamn glad you're here," he whispered roughly against her ear.

Her fingers sorted through his hair, along his neck, his back. "I'm here, honey, I'm here," she whispered back. "I fell asleep early last night, I didn't get your voice mail until this morning. Once I heard it, I couldn't get here fast enough. I asked Charles to let me use the Harrison Enterprises jet . . . It was the quickest way."

His arms tightened around her, pressing her even closer. "Thank you for that."

"I love you," she said, her voice breaking. She pulled back to look into his eyes. He saw her tears, saw the raw emotions there . . . and it both broke him and saved him at the same time. "I love you, Logan. So much. I'm here for you, if you'll let me be."

"Oh, I'll let you. I love you too," he said. He reached up to hold her face with gentle hands, stroking her skin as if she were the most precious thing on earth. "I should've told you that a long time ago."

She stared at him, her mouth a little O of shock, apparently as surprised by his words as he'd been at seeing her.

"I have so much to tell you," he said. "We need to talk . . . There are so many things . . ."

"We will," she assured him. "Not right now. But we will. I'll be here for a few days. It's okay."

"No, this part can't wait. I'm sorry, sweetheart. I'm sorry I pushed you away. I'm sorry I hurt you. I was . . ." He sighed heavily. "I was messed up. But I'm clear now. I love you, I want you, I need you. You're the best thing that's ever happened to me, Tess." He brushed her hair back with both hands, then held her shoulders and looked right into her eyes. "I want us to be together. *Really* together. Not because of a deal, not because you're pregnant, but because you're my best friend and I'm crazy in love with you and I don't ever want to let you go again. I want to make this work somehow. Do you think we can do that?"

"Yes." Tears rolled down her face as she smiled at him. "Because I feel the same exact way about you, about all of that. Every wonderful word you said."

He sealed his lips to hers, kissing her passionately. She responded in a heartbeat, kissing him back with so much warmth and affection, it melted the last of the ice that had encased his heart for years.

"I love you so much, Tess," he said. "I'm completely, hopelessly in love with you. From the moment you got on that plane, I've missed you so much it actually hurt sometimes."

"Same here," she whispered, lifting her fingers to play in his beard. "I missed you every day. I've been lost without you."

"Christ, we've both been so dumb." He smiled. "It's so damn good to see you."

"You too." She caressed his skin, traced the lines of

his face with her fingertips, her eyes following every movement.

"How's the baby?" he asked, locking his arms around her waist as he gazed down at her. "You're not even show-ing yet. You feeling all right?"

"I'm fine, and the baby's fine," she said. She paused, swallowing hard. Then she looked right into his eyes and said cautiously, "*Our* baby is fine."

He stopped and stared. "*Your* baby. I signed my rights away. I respect your wishes, Tess. I'm not trying to—"

"Do you love me?" she asked.

"More than you can imagine," he said.

"Do you want to be with me?"

"More than I can express."

"Well . . . you got me pregnant. You *are* the father. So . . . if you do want us to be together . . . we would be a family." She looked directly into his eyes. "I've been thinking about it a lot. I've changed my mind, Logan. About raising the baby alone. That is . . . if I can raise this baby with you. As a couple. For us to be, like you said, *really* together."

"Jesus," he breathed. "Seriously? Are you sure?"

"It's the only way I'd change my mind on this. Because I want to be with you." She blinked a few times, and he re-alized she was nervous about putting it out there, that she thought he might still reject her.

"I want to be with you," he said. "I meant that."

"Well, the thing is . . . I'm pregnant. You didn't want kids. So . . . by any chance, has that changed? Because if not . . . I'd understand, but we'd need to come to some kind of understanding. I'm not asking you to be a father if you don't want to be one."

He stared at her, trying to formulate the right words. "I . . . Tess . . ."

"We've danced around too much," she said. "Both of us trying to do the right thing for the other, not saying what we really feel . . . Enough of that. Look where it got us. So just say it. Tell me exactly what you want. Right now. Please."

"I want it all," he blurted out. "I didn't want those things before—a relationship, kids—that's true. I was afraid, I admit it. But when I fell in love with you, it all changed. *I* changed. I want everything now, because I want it all with *you*." He took a shuddery breath, but didn't break their gaze. The light in her eyes and tremulous smile on her face encouraged him to go for it. "I want to be with you, I want to marry you, I want us to raise this baby together, I want to have a family with you . . . I want all of it. But you said you wanted to do this on your own, Tess. You don't want a partner, or a husband, or a father figure for the baby. I didn't tell you I'd changed my mind about everything because I was respecting what you said you wanted."

"Like you, I thought I knew what I wanted. And like you, when I fell in love with you, it changed my perspective. It changed everything." She wiped her tears away, sniffled, and kissed him. "I want all of that too, everything you said. *Everything*, with *you*."

They stared at each other for a long beat, smiles slowly blooming.

"We found each other," she whispered. "We're perfect together. We're the Dream Team, right?"

"I didn't have dreams anymore," he whispered back. "But you're my dream come true. In every way."

Again her eyes welled. "I did have dreams. But you surpassed them all, and then some." She smiled and kissed him softly. "Don't you ever let me go again."

"Not for anything in the world," he vowed, pulling her closer.

"Okay. Then let's do this." She kissed him again. "Together, we can have it all."

He gave her a gentle squeeze and murmured against her lips, "We already do."

Epilogue

Eighteen months later

Tess Harrison Carter laughed as she watched her husband crawl around on the living room floor beside their daughter. At eleven months old, Annabel was crawling like a pro.

"C'mon, cutie!" Logan cooed to the baby. He crawled backwards, encouraging her to chase him. The sight of her gentle giant on all fours with the baby made Tess's heart swell. "C'mon, peanut! You're fast as lightning, you got this. C'mon, sweetie, come and get me!"

Annabel screeched joyfully and headed for him. He stopped moving when she reached him, scooped her into his arms, and dropped little kisses all over her face. She squealed and giggled, loving it.

"I think your beard must tickle her face," Tess said from the couch.

"I'm trying not to give her beard-burn," Logan said, "but oh my God, I want to eat her up." He gazed lovingly into his daughter's eyes, the same brilliant blue as her mother's.

Tess enjoyed watching him play with Annabel, watching

him respond with such light and joy. This child had saved him from drowning in grief. Tess knew it was sheer will and her love that had kept Logan from going under after his mom passed away. Looking forward to the baby's arrival and basking in Tess's love had kept him afloat through the late summer. But when Annabel was born a week before Thanksgiving, Logan was reminded of how much he had to live for, how blessed he was, and he turned a corner in his healing.

His family was everything. He told Tess that all the time.

"We have to leave in an hour," Tess said, "if we're going to make it on time to Charles and Lisette's for his birthday dinner."

"Okay." Logan looked up at her. She was stretched out on the couch, wearing a plain red top and black yoga pants, her hair everywhere . . . She felt a bit worn. But he smiled a wolfish smile and said, "Hot damn, lady. You're gorgeous, you know that?"

"Well, thanks." Tess smiled, delighted. "So are you."

"That nap before must have helped. You look brighter now."

"I was tired," she admitted. She lowered her eyes to the baby squirming in his huge lap. "That little one does wear me out sometimes. And I love every moment."

"Me too," he said. He looked down to Annabel and started cooing at her.

Tess thought back on the past year and a half. She and Logan had split their time between Aspen and Long Island, and married in a small, private ceremony in Aspen in June, with only his mother and brother, her immediate family, and a few close friends in attendance. It had been a lovely, intimate wedding. Knowing a baby was on the way had made Annmarie happy beyond words; but sadly, she had passed away in late July.

After Annabel came, Logan had sold both his mother's condo and his place in Aspen. He'd insisted that he and Tess buy a new house together, his money matching hers, and they'd found a fabulous house on the water in Sandy Point, just a few blocks away from where Charles, Lisette, and their kids lived. Pierce, Abby, and their son lived nearby in Edgewater; baby Michael had been born only three months before Annabel. And Charlotte was only a year older than them. So all the baby cousins were growing up together, and there were Charles's three older children too. It all included Dane and Julia, of course, who lived their fast-paced life in the city at the hotel and took it slow during their downtime in the cottage they owned in Blue Harbor, which was in between Edgewater and Sandy Point. They were a doting aunt and uncle to all the kids.

Somehow, the Harrisons had finally gotten it together and had become a huge, happy extended family.

As for the patriarch, Charles Harrison II had the mammoth land of the Harrison estate all to himself now. Tess had given him back the guest cottage when she moved out, but he wasn't happy about it. He traveled a lot, worked a lot, and kept his distance from most of the family except for holidays. It made Tess sad that it was what he wanted, that he'd ultimately shut himself out of the family instead of finding a way to be more involved . . . but she wasn't going to fight with him about it.

Because at long last, she was completely content and happy. She had everything she'd ever longed for: She'd met an amazing, loving man to share her life with, her career was fulfilling and interesting, and she had the most wonderful, delightful child on the planet. She was so blessed.

She watched now as Logan set Annabel on her belly on the carpet. He gave her diapered tush a tiny pat and said, "Go to your mama. Go get her!"

Tess gazed at her handsome, sexy Viking. He'd adjusted well to life on Long Island. He liked New York, and once he'd let his walls down, he'd been embraced by the entire family. Most importantly, he'd found new purpose. He was finally putting his degrees in social work to use, working at the Harrison Foundation as a consultant in several capacities. He was damn good at it, too. Tess was proud of him, and knew he felt good about being in a position to help others.

They were deeply in love, and the best of friends. All was right with the world.

Annabel scooted forward, squealing and babbling as she crawled toward Tess.

Tess shifted, swinging her legs off the couch to hold her arms out to her daughter. "Come here, baby. Come on!"

When the baby reached her, Tess lifted her up and showered her with praise.

"Guess I better hit the shower," Logan said. "I'll be quick. And I'll be sure to take Bubbles out to go potty too."

"Okay. I'll get Annabel's things together, the baby bag, all of that."

"Teamwork!" He got to his feet and smiled down at his wife and daughter. "Love you."

"Love you too." Tess smiled back up at him. "By the way, I need to tell you something . . ."

"Sure, what is it?" Logan asked.

Still holding the baby, Tess patted the couch cushion beside her, and he sat. She let her eyes roam over his handsome face then leaned in, unable to keep herself from giving his beard a quick little affectionate scratch.

He grabbed her fingertips and kissed them. "What's up?"

"Um . . . I want to make an announcement tonight at dinner," Tess said. "Since *all* of the Harrisons will be there."

"Okaaaay . . . What are we announcing?" His pale green eyes studied her.

Tess smiled, took a deep breath, and said, "Remember when I said I had an errand to run this morning?"

"Yeah. So?" He reached out a finger to Annabel, who grasped it with a squeak.

"It wasn't an errand," Tess said. "I had a doctor's appointment. I wanted to confirm the test I took two days ago." Her smile deepened, the happiness bubbling inside her as she watched Logan's face light up with shock and delight.

"Get outta here!" he cried with a laugh. "Are you . . . ?"

"Yup. I'm pregnant," Tess affirmed. "Baby number two will be here in May."

"Oh my God!" Logan shifted to hug both Tess and Annabel at the same time. "That's amazing! I don't believe it. I mean, we just started trying. It's so soon!"

"I know. They won't even be two years apart," Tess said, looking down at Annabel, then back up to her husband. "Think we can handle it?"

Logan kissed her long and hard. Then, with a radiant smile, he said happily, "Together, we can handle anything. We're the Dream Team, remember? We got this."

Wonder what secrets still lurk
in the Harrisons' closet?
Keep reading for a sneak peek at more from
Jennifer Gracen.

IT MIGHT BE YOU

Coming soon from
Zebra Books!

Nick Martell pulled up in front of his parents' house. The engine on his sleek black Ford Mustang GT quieted as he cut the ignition, leaving him in silence to gather his thoughts. He had so much to tell his family, he didn't know where to start. A gentle breeze blew, making the long leaves of the palm trees overhead sway against the soft blue of the evening sky. He let his head fall back against the seat and drew a few long, deep breaths as he looked at the house.

It was the same as always. His mom had planted new flowers in the bigger pot by the front door, a bright hot pink. Nick grinned; it was her favorite color, and reminded him of her. He'd grown up in a modest three-bedroom home on a quiet street in a decent suburb, only five miles from the center of Miami. His father had been on the Miami police force for twenty-five years before retiring, devoted to the job and to his family. Nick had worshipped his dad as a kid, and aspired to be like him as a young adult, which was ultimately why he'd become a cop himself five years before. Five years of hard work . . . and now, some payoff. He figured his dad would be proud of him tonight, and the elation of that made Nick's grin widen.

Lew Martell met Maria Sanchez when Nick was three years old. Lew married Maria when Nick was four, and legally adopted Nick as his own when he was five. Though they didn't share blood, as far as Nick was concerned, Lew was his father in every way, and knew to the core of his soul that Lew felt the same way. Even a few years later, when Maria and Lew brought Nick two little sisters, he'd never been made to feel anything other than they were one hundred percent a family.

Yes, there was a blank space on Nick's birth certificate where the biological father's name should have been. Nick didn't care. When he was eleven, and a middle school project about genealogy raised questions, Maria had sat her son down and explained the truth: She had gotten pregnant via a one-night stand when she was twenty. Drunk at a party, she'd made a foolish choice—but she was adamant that Nick knew she never thought of it as a mistake. That she took responsibility for her choice, that Nick had been a gift from God to her, and most of all, that she never regretted her decision to keep her baby.

Maria told her young son that she never even knew the man's last name, which is why she hadn't put one on the birth certificate. All she could tell Nick was he was white, probably some basic Anglo-Saxon mix, and he'd never known she was pregnant. Ashamed of her situation, she hadn't tried to contact him. Maria had left her job and home in New York to live with relatives in Miami until Nick was born. When she met and fell in love with Lew, it had been another gift from God to her, and they built a family together, made a good life for their three kids.

Young Nick had been surprised, but didn't give the news much thought. It did explain why even though Nick was proud to be Puerto Rican, there was something there that always felt . . . off. He'd heard some of his aunts whispering once when he was six years old, something about his white father, and he'd assumed it was about Lew . . . maybe not. Maybe his gut instincts had been strong even then. Also, his nose was too narrow, his hair was a little straighter, different from his mom and his relatives; and though he got as deep a tan as most of his relatives in the summer months, his skin just wasn't quite the same rich dark gold as his mother's.

So even at the young age of eleven, Nick was glad to know the truth about his conception because it helped some things make sense, things he felt that before he just couldn't make sense of or verbalize. And knowing the truth . . . He'd pushed it into the recesses of his mind and went on with his life. It didn't alter who he was. He had a dad who loved him. That's all that mattered.

Now, as he walked up the front steps and unlocked the door to his parents' house, it was his father he couldn't wait to see the most. He knew his mom would be proud, but his dad would be bursting with it.

"Hello?" Nick called out as he stepped into the living room. The spicy aroma of his mother's cooking wafted in the air, enticing and comforting him at the same time.

"Ah!" His mother came in, rushing to hug him. She leaned back to look up into his face and held his cheeks. "You look good, *mijo*! You need a shave, but your eyes are smiling."

"I'm twenty-nine, Ma," he grumbled, teasing back. "You ever gonna stop telling me when I need to clean up?"

"No."

"I don't shave on my days off. I take a break. I've told you this."

She shrugged and made a disdainful face that clearly expressed her thoughts.

He just chuckled. Her dry sass was one of the things he loved most about her.

"So what's the big news?" she asked, her features brightening again. "I can't wait to hear whatever you're here to tell us. And I'm glad you asked for a family dinner to share it, so I get to see you."

Nick rolled his eyes. He faithfully came for a family dinner every other Sunday. "Like you don't see me. I come by!"

"Not enough."

He groaned and nudged her gently with his elbow. "Admit it, you're just happy to have an excuse to cook something special."

"You said you had really big news, so yeah . . . I *might've* made one of your very favorites."

Nick inhaled deeply, trying to figure out what she'd made by what he smelled. A slow smile spread on his face. "Ahhh. You made *carne frita con cebolla* for me, didn't you?"

"You got it." Maria smiled and it lit up her pretty face. "Anyway, it'd been a while since I made it, so why not?"

He was six feet tall, and she was a petite five-foot-two, so he bent to kiss her cheek. "You're too good to me."

"Don't you forget it." She was clearly pleased that she'd pleased him. "So c'mon in. Your dad's out in the yard and your sisters are in their rooms. I'll get them out."

"Actually . . ." Nick rubbed the back of his neck. "You know what? Maybe it'd be good to just talk to you and Dad first. Part of the news is great, but part is . . . a little . . . well, they might not fully understand. So maybe you'll help me figure out a way to tell them that won't . . . upset them. I dunno."

Maria stilled at that, scrutinizing her son for a few seconds before saying, "I'll get your father."

Five minutes later, Maria and Lew sat together on the couch as Nick pulled over the armchair to sit directly opposite them. He took a deep breath, then ran his hands through his thick hair and over his scruffy jaw before starting.

"The best news first," he said, unable to keep from smiling. "I got the promotion. I'm going to be an investigator."

Lew let out a loud whoop and jumped to his feet. Maria's eyes shone with tears of pride. Nick laughed as his father pulled him up for a tight hug. Lew clapped him on the back, grasped him by the shoulders, then pulled back to look into Nick's eyes as he said, "Goddamn, I'm so proud of you, son. I mean, I wanted this for you, but I know *you* wanted this for you. You worked hard, showed your mettle. You've been a damn good officer, but you're just too smart not to . . . Well, this is the right thing for you." He clapped his son's arms again, beaming with pride. "Good for you, Nick. Well done. Congratulations!"

"Thanks, Dad." Nick's throat felt thick, and he swallowed down the lump that had risen there. He'd known his dad would be proud, but this felt incredible.

"*Mijo* . . ." Maria stood and lifted her hands to cradle his face. "I'm so, so proud."

"Thanks, Ma." Nick knew she was happy, but also a little scared for him. That she knew being an investigator still meant dangerous work. That being the wife of a cop, and now the mother of a cop, meant she didn't sleep well every night. But he knew she was proud of him, and would continue to be. When her arms wrapped around his waist and squeezed tight, he hugged her back until she was the one to let go.

"When do you start?" Lew asked.

Nick took another deep breath as he released his mother. "Well . . . that's the other thing. Sit down. There's more. But it's totally different, not about work."

All three of them sat, and as soon as they did, Nick launched into it. "A few years ago, I wanna say three years ago? They had a bone-marrow donor drive at the station. Because Jim Connelly's nephew needed a donor."

Lew nodded. "Sure, I've heard of those. I've done one. It's easy as pie, just a swab in your cheek."

"Right," Nick said. "So I did it, and truthfully, I never thought about it again. But I guess they keep your name on the national and international bone marrow registry after that, because, well . . . I got a call two weeks ago. It seems I'm a match for a kid who needs a bone marrow transplant. He's got non-Hodgkin's lymphoma. Twelve years old."

Maria's eyes flew wide as Lew's brows furrowed.

"Really," Lew said.

"That's amazing," Maria murmured.

"Yeah. So . . ." Nick blew out a breath. "How do I nut-shell this . . . First the registry contacted me to tell me the news. I agreed to being tested further, went in, gave blood and all that. Earlier this week, they called to tell me that yes, I'm a strong, viable match. I agreed to go through with it right then." He saw the worry creeping into his mother's face as he talked. "Ma, I went in, talked for a while with a rep from the registry. I learned a lot. It's barely going to hurt, it's outpatient surgery. So please stop looking so worried, okay?"

"You're my son," she said. "And you're talking about a major medical procedure. I'm going to worry no matter what you say."

"That's your right," he said, tossing her a wink to try to lighten her up. "So here's where it gets a little unusual. Apparently, most donors and patients never meet or have contact, confidentiality rights and all. But the day after I confirmed I'd do it, the registry rep called me again. Said the father of the kid really wanted to talk to me, if I'd allow it. I figured sure, why not? I mean, I was going to do it no matter what. As soon as I heard I could help someone, there was no question in my mind I'd go through with it."

"Of course," Maria said. "That's who you are."

"So did you talk to the father?" Lew asked.

"Yeah. On Friday morning." Nick shifted in his seat, stretching out his legs to roll one ankle, then the other. "The guy couldn't be nicer, and I could hear the worry there and it really moved me. His son's just a kid. They're desperate, I get that. And long story short, I'm going."

"Where are you going?" Lew and Maria said at the same time, then looked at each other with a quick laugh at having said the same thing.

"New York. Turns out the kid's father is some mega-rich businessman—I'm talking billionaire, like *crazy* money. He wanted to talk to me to . . . well, offer incentive, I guess. He wanted me to understand that insurance should pay for everything that's medical, but beyond that, he wants to pay. He doesn't want me to spend a dime. He offered to pay for my flights, my hotel stay, rental car, everything I eat, do, touch. Even offered to cover whatever pay I lose at work for taking time off. Bottom line is, he didn't want me to be worried about the expenses if it would make me decide not to go there and do it. I assured him that I'm going to do it. And yeah, maybe take him up on the hotel part. Because if I have to go back and forth to New York a few times, or stay there? Might add up, I don't know."

"Nick . . ." Maria's voice sounded breathless all of a sudden. "You're going to New York?"

"Yeah, Ma. I leave the day after tomorrow." Nick watched her as he spoke; she seemed off. He hated for her to worry about him. "On Friday, when I got the promotion, it was amazing, but terrible timing. I'd just talked to the father that morning! So, at work, I explained what happened, and that I feel I need to do this. They were great about it. Better than I thought they'd be, actually." He ran his hands absently over his knees. "I'm taking an unpaid leave for two weeks. If I have to go a few more times, they're fine with it. And the time I need off for the surgery and recovery *will* be paid leave. They were fully supportive. After it's all done, and I'm back to one hundred percent, I'll start the new job."

"New York," Maria repeated. "Billionaires, you said?"

"Uh-huh. Why?" Nick stared harder now. She looked upset. No, it was different than that. She looked . . . spooked. "Ma, you used to live in New York, you know I'm not going to, like, a war zone or the middle of nowhere."

"Are they from Long Island?" she asked.

Lew flinched, his head swiveling to look at his wife as his eyes flew wide.

Nick's gut started humming and clenched, like right before something bad went down on the street. "What's going on?" he asked, looking from one to the other. "You're both acting weird."

"The boy," she said. "The billionaire father. What's his name, do you know?"

"Yeah, of course I know. I told you, I talked to him," Nick said. "The kid's name is Myles, his father's name is

Charles." Trying to joke to break the sudden heavy vibe in the room, he added in a mock snooty voice, "Get this for big money pretentious: His full name is Charles Roger Harrison *the third,* thank you very much."

Maria gasped sharply, her eyes rolled back in her head, and she fainted, slumping against her husband.

Connect with

Books by Bestselling Author
Fern Michaels

___The Jury	0-8217-7878-1	$6.99US/$9.99CAN
___Sweet Revenge	0-8217-7879-X	$6.99US/$9.99CAN
___Lethal Justice	0-8217-7880-3	$6.99US/$9.99CAN
___Free Fall	0-8217-7881-1	$6.99US/$9.99CAN
___Fool Me Once	0-8217-8071-9	$7.99US/$10.99CAN
___Vegas Rich	0-8217-8112-X	$7.99US/$10.99CAN
___Hide and Seek	1-4201-0184-6	$6.99US/$9.99CAN
___Hokus Pokus	1-4201-0185-4	$6.99US/$9.99CAN
___Fast Track	1-4201-0186-2	$6.99US/$9.99CAN
___Collateral Damage	1-4201-0187-0	$6.99US/$9.99CAN
___Final Justice	1-4201-0188-9	$6.99US/$9.99CAN
___Up Close and Personal	0-8217-7956-7	$7.99US/$9.99CAN
___Under the Radar	1-4201-0683-X	$6.99US/$9.99CAN
___Razor Sharp	1-4201-0684-8	$7.99US/$10.99CAN
___Yesterday	1-4201-1494-8	$5.99US/$6.99CAN
___Vanishing Act	1-4201-0685-6	$7.99US/$10.99CAN
___Sara's Song	1-4201-1493-X	$5.99US/$6.99CAN
___Deadly Deals	1-4201-0686-4	$7.99US/$10.99CAN
___Game Over	1-4201-0687-2	$7.99US/$10.99CAN
___Sins of Omission	1-4201-1153-1	$7.99US/$10.99CAN
___Sins of the Flesh	1-4201-1154-X	$7.99US/$10.99CAN
___Cross Roads	1-4201-1192-2	$7.99US/$10.99CAN

Available Wherever Books Are Sold!
Check out our website at **www.kensingtonbooks.com**